WHEN ALL THE WORLD SLEEPS

LISA HENRY & J.A. ROCK

RIPTIDE
PUBLISHING

Riptide Publishing
PO Box 1537
Burnsville, NC 28714
www.riptidepublishing.com

When All the World Sleeps
Copyright © 2014 by Lisa Henry and J.A. Rock

Cover art: Amber Shah, bookbeautiful.com
Editors: Sarah Lyons and Carole-ann Galloway
Layout: L.C. Chase, lcchase.com/design.htm

ISBN: 978-1-62649-079-6

First edition
March, 2014

Also available in ebook:
ISBN: 978-1-62649-078-9

WHEN ALL THE
WORLD SLEEPS

LISA HENRY & J.A. ROCK

RIPTIDE
PUBLISHING

For the real Kenny. Because we feel bad.

TABLE OF CONTENTS

Chapter 1 1

Chapter 2 15

Chapter 3 33

Chapter 4 47

Chapter 5 67

Chapter 6 83

Chapter 7 97

Chapter 8 113

Chapter 9 127

Chapter 10 141

Chapter 11 153

Chapter 12 167

Chapter 13 187

Chapter 14 199

Chapter 15 209

Chapter 16 231

Chapter 17 247

Chapter 18 257

Chapter 19 269

Chapter 20 289

Chapter 21 303

Chapter 22 319

Chapter 23 331

CHAPTER ONE

"Hey, Harnee's kid," Daniel Whitlock said, and the smile lit up his whole face.

Bel resisted the urge to plant his fist in it. "Officer Belman to you, Whitlock." He took his flashlight from his belt and shone the beam in Whitlock's eyes. The guy's pupils had almost swallowed his hazel irises entirely. "What'd you take?"

Whitlock turned from Bel and shoved his hands in his pockets, pulling his jeans tight across his ass. "I'm going home. You coming with me?"

They were in the parking lot of Greenducks, a rundown bar wedged between a former beauty salon and a mortgage firm. You had to go down a flight of half-rotted wooden stairs, and then you were in a basement full of cocksuckers. And not the kind you saw in gay bars in movies. No tanned and toned bodies, no goddamn angel wings or leather shorts. These guys stank, and they smoked, and they'd do anything for drugs. Bel only went into Greenducks when he was desperate enough to pretend not to notice the exchanges that went on.

"I ain't going nowhere with you," Bel told Whitlock.

Fucker. Goddamn filthy tweaker head case.

Liar.

Murderer.

Everyone in Logan, South Carolina, knew who Daniel Whitlock was—*what* he was. But what made Bel doubly uncomfortable right now was that unlike most everyone in Logan, Bel had noticed Daniel Whitlock long before he'd been in the papers.

Before he got his badge, Bel had worked a night shift twice a week at Harnee's Convenience Store, and Whitlock used to come in Thursdays around 1 or 2 a.m. to buy a Twix and a bottle of Mountain Dew. Always went through Bel's line.

"That stuff'll keep you up all night," Bel had said once, nodding at the Mountain Dew. Whitlock hadn't answered, and that was the first and last time Bel said anything to him beyond *"Have a good night."* But he'd noted the strong, easy slope of Whitlock's chest under his T-shirts. When it got colder, Whitlock had worn plaid flannel like all the other guys in Logan. But in the summer his T-shirts had been just a little too tight. Close-cropped hair the same linty brown as his faded sneakers. Beautifully defined features, almost too sharp.

"He don't want to join us, Danny," a voice said.

Bel hadn't noticed Jake Kebbler standing behind Daniel in the shadow of the bar. If Bel'd had to pick any of the Greenducks crowd for looks alone—besides Whitlock—he'd have picked Jake. Unfortunately, every queer in Logan had already picked Jake, over and over again. *"Looks like a gnat-bit curl of pork rind,"* Matt Lister had said once about Jake's dick.

Whitlock grinned. He pushed Jake against the side of the building. Kissed him. Risky—Greenducks gave queers a place to meet, but it sure as fuck didn't fly the rainbow flag. You came to Greenducks because it was the closest to safe you were gonna get if you liked restroom blowjobs—not because you were welcome there. And once you were outside, well, you were in hetero territory.

Jake tipped his head back then slowly collapsed. It was oddly graceful, like a dancer's swoon. Whitlock tried to catch him, failed, and lowered himself on top of Jake. Kissed him again, or maybe whispered something—Bel couldn't tell. Then he got up and walked over to his car, leaving Jake on the ground.

Nice, Bel thought. Your date passes out, so you're just gonna call it a night? Not that Jake seemed to care. Hell, he probably wouldn't even remember what had happened when the sun woke him in the morning with a face full of asphalt. Jake didn't have a brain cell left he wasn't bent on destroying with meth. And was that . . . yeah, Bel could just about make out the glow of a burning cigarette in Jake's hand. Stupid asshole.

Bel walked over to Jake. Wasn't like *he* could leave a man to burn to death. Which made him the only one. Whitlock was still standing by his sedan, staring at nothing.

"You stay right there," Bel called as he bent to check on Jake. Still breathing. Bel plucked the cigarette out from between Jake's skinny fingers and crushed it under his boot. When he turned around, Whitlock had taken a step closer. "I told you to stay there."

"Need something so bad." Whitlock sighed. He slid his fingers into the waistband of his jeans, like he was going to tug them down right there in the parking lot. "You wanna fuck me, Harnee's kid? Can use my car."

Bel had been a cop for three years now, and he'd been propositioned more times than he could remember. It was never like those letters in skin mags though. Usually it was some toothless skank old enough to be his grandma, giggling drunken high school girls, or narrow-eyed truckers who would nod to the side of the road in silent invitation like Bel was dumb enough or desperate enough for that. Might as well just roll around in the filthy bathrooms at the truck stop on US 601, pick up his diseases that way and take out the middleman.

And now, Daniel Whitlock. Who might have been *Dear readers, I never thought it would happen to me* material back when he was in high school—Bel, still in middle school, had noticed him right about the same time as he'd noticed those weird tingly feelings that made his dick hard—but doing it with a fucking murderer was never going to happen. And Bel was pretty damn insulted that Whitlock even thought he had a chance.

"Get your ass home," he said, curling his lip.

Whitlock reached for his car door.

"You ain't driving tonight," Bel told him. "Ain't you killed enough folk in this town?"

It didn't even register with Whitlock.

"You walk," Bel said. "You give me your keys, and you walk."

No argument. Whitlock dug around in the pocket of his jeans and held his keys out. "I'm going home now?"

"Yeah." Bel took the keys and crossed his arms over his chest. "You'd better start walking."

"Okay."

Bel shook his head. Goddamn drug-fucked nutjob.

He watched as Whitlock turned and squinted down the street, wobbling like a compass needle before it fixed its position. Then, his hands still in his pockets, Whitlock started to walk. Bel leaned against his cruiser and looked down at Whitlock's keys, thumbed through them and found a tarnished Saint Christopher medallion. Not so different from the one Bel's mama had given him when he'd become a deputy.

Bel sighed. Figured he couldn't let the guy get squashed like a possum on the side of the road. He didn't get to pick and choose who he looked out for.

He got in his cruiser, turned the engine over, and flicked the headlights on. Set off down the street at a crawl, keeping well behind Whitlock as he stumbled toward home. Bel wondered what it would be like living out there in the woods. Cold as hell in winter, probably, and mosquitoes as big as chicken hawks in the summer. Perfect for freaks like Whitlock and the Unabomber.

The twenty-four hour diner on Main was empty; Bel glanced in as he drove past at a snail's pace. Sue-Ellen was working, or at least she was leaning on the counter staring at the small TV beside the register. Across the street, Harnee's was open too, the H flashing intermittently again, so half the time it just read *arnee's*. Bel figured he'd stop in on the way back, just to show the flag. On weekends, the high school kids hung around in the parking lot, trying to get someone to buy beer for them. But tonight the lot was empty.

Bel remembered a long stretch five years ago where Whitlock hadn't come to Harnee's on Thursday nights. Recovering from what Kenny and his friends had done to him, Bel had figured, though he'd refused to join in his coworkers' gossip sessions about it. Long after Daniel must've healed up, he'd still been absent. People'd said his mama bought his groceries. Bel had almost missed him. The guy hadn't been friendly, but he'd been easy enough to look at. Then Whitlock had showed up the night of October sixteenth and had bought a lighter along with his candy and soda.

The next morning, the story had been everywhere.

Kenny Cooper's house had burned to the ground. Kenny inside.

Bel had followed Whitlock's trial with interest. Had even been called to give testimony about the lighter. And he'd been as pissed as anyone when the prosecution had opted to seek a conviction for manslaughter instead of first-degree murder. Wasn't like Bel gave two shits about losing Kenny Cooper—that asshole had been a waste of air. It was Whitlock's bullshit defense that had made Bel half-crazy.

Sleepwalking. Seriously. Like Whitlock was some kind of zombie lurching around eating people's brains, then waking up the next day not remembering any of it? Yeah, that was the shit you saw in movies. How about Whitlock was a crazy meth head who'd say anything to save his hide? The more Bel'd thought about it, the angrier he'd got, and the more convinced he'd become he'd seen signs Whitlock was off whenever he'd come into Harnee's. Something not right in his eyes. The way his body twitched while he was waiting for his total, like he was receiving small shocks.

And Bel wasn't the only one who, after the murder, suddenly remembered things they'd noticed about Whitlock. Sunday school teachers and guys he'd run track with and even the girl he'd gotten to second base with on prom night, all eager to chime in.

"Always knew there was something wrong with him."

"He had that look, you know?"

"I smacked him as soon as he put his hands on me. Knew he was no good."

And Bel had raged with the rest of the town when Whitlock had been released after eight months in jail. This wasn't about Kenny Cooper—it was about justice. You didn't burn someone alive and then walk free, no matter what some quack said on the stand about your sleep disorder. It was impossible to drive five miles *in your sleep*, shake kerosene around the base of a house like you were watering the goddamn plants, flip your lighter on, then go home and climb into bed.

Bel looked up the street again. Whitlock was still heading in the right direction. He was passing in front of the Shack now, where Bel drank most times. All the cops drank at the Shack. Hell, all the town did. It was closed at this hour, a few trucks parked out front still. Owners must have walked.

A battered red pickup swerved onto Main Street, going too fast. It overcorrected, swinging wildly toward the center line before it recovered. Bel recognized it: Clayton McAllister's truck, so it was probably Clayton at the wheel with a few of his buddies packed into the cab.

The truck headed toward him, slowing as it passed Whitlock, then braking and backing up. Too far away to hear what they yelled at Whitlock, apart from *faggot*. A beer can flew from the window and bounced on the road. The horn blared.

Whitlock stopped. He lifted his head to look at the truck.

Last thing Bel needed was Clayton and his drunk buddies figuring it was time for another gay bashing. Bel hit the lights, the red-and-blue strobes flashing. Just to let Clayton know he was there.

The truck didn't move, so Bel rolled his window down. Just in time to hear Whitlock yell, "Wanna suck my dick, cunt?"

The truck's door flew open, and Clayton jumped out. Bel was out of his cruiser in a second, moving automatically to stand between Clayton and Whitlock. "Fellas," he said, because Brock Tilmouth was getting out of the truck too. "I don't need any trouble here. Go on home."

"You hear what he said?" Clayton was a scrawny guy. Thin and rat faced. Had a few gingery hairs on his upper lip that were trying real hard to be a mustache. Pale blue eyes.

Bel glanced at Whitlock, who was standing slack-jawed, completely spaced out. "I heard, and you'll live. Get on home, Clayton."

"Wanna . . ." Whitlock slurred. "Hey, faggot."

Clayton shouted around Bel at Whitlock. "You're the faggot, freak! Didn't learn your lesson the first time?"

Bel's jaw tightened.

Hell, he thought as much as anyone that Whitlock deserved a beating. Not because he was gay, but because he'd gotten away with murder. Kenny Cooper had been Clayton's best friend. They'd bashed Whitlock first, which was what'd made him go all fire starter on Kenny, but everyone knew Whitlock had started it by offering to suck Kenny's dick.

And here Whitlock was making the same offer to Clayton. Goading him.

Bel could remind Clayton not to take the law into his own hands, but Whitlock had done just that—and gotten off almost scot-free. Less than eight months in prison, and what was it? Three years parole? That was a kick in the teeth to Kenny Cooper's family, his friends, and pretty much the whole town.

No justice in that.

What was it his gram used to say? Take an eye for an eye, and soon the whole world would be blind. You weren't supposed to go out and get your own revenge when you'd been wronged. You were supposed to trust the law to deal with it. But nobody said what to do if the law failed you.

Hurl beer cans and abuse, maybe. Couldn't blame Clayton for being angry.

But then, where was the justice in the law's reaction to Cooper bashing Whitlock? No arrests made, because Whitlock had sworn he hadn't seen the guys who'd done it. And yet everyone knew it'd been Kenny Cooper and his buddies. Just no one'd lifted a finger to look into the matter or prosecute Cooper.

So couldn't blame Whitlock for being angry either.

It scared Bel to catch himself thinking that way. He didn't blame Whitlock for his anger, but he sure as hell blamed him for killing Cooper.

"Enough, Clayton," Bel said, his voice hard. "You keep moving. I'm gonna get Whitlock home."

For a second, Bel thought Clayton was gonna fight. Was gonna lunge at Whitlock even though Bel was right there. At the very least, Bel expected Clayton to say something. But with a last glare at Whitlock, Clayton climbed back in the truck, put it in drive, and crept past Bel's cruiser.

When the truck was out of sight, Bel turned to Whitlock.

"Get in the car."

Whitlock didn't move. He gazed at the spot where Clayton had been and drew in a shuddering breath.

"Whitlock. I said get in the car." Bel stepped toward him, and Whitlock cringed back. Stared at Bel with eyes Bel remembered from nights at Harnee's—unfocused, bloodshot, the sockets bruised looking. He blinked in the glare from the headlights.

"You wanna walk all night, or you wanna ride home?"

Whitlock took a couple of steps toward the cruiser. Nodded at the back door. "In there?"

"Yeah. In the back, Whitlock." Bel climbed in behind the wheel. Whitlock hesitated.

"Get in the goddamn car. You're lucky I don't arrest you. What're you on, huh? If I searched you, what would I find?"

"You can search me," Whitlock said softly. He walked closer to Bel, who tried not to look at the front of his jeans. Whitlock leaned against the cruiser, one arm on the roof, his hip cocked, drawing the fabric of his T-shirt tight. "Want to?"

"Back of the car," Bel repeated. "You get in now, it's a ride home. You don't, it's cuffs and the station."

Whitlock gave a sharp inhale that made Bel's dick stir. Then he grinned, said, "Yes, *sir*," and stepped away from the window.

Bel couldn't see Whitlock's face as he slid into the backseat of the cruiser. Whitlock pulled the door shut and then sat staring straight ahead through the partition.

"Tell me how to get to your place," Bel said.

Whitlock didn't answer.

"You can do that much, can't you? Not so trashed you can't tell me where you live?"

No answer.

"I can get out to Kamchee, but you gotta tell me where your cabin is."

Whitlock glanced out the window.

Bel turned and slapped the partition. "Damn it, Whitlock!"

Whitlock jerked in the seat. He struck the partition right back, then fumbled for the door handle, but he was locked in. He planted his hands in a wide stance on either side of him, drew his legs up onto the seat, and stared down into the seat well as though it was full of alligators or something, shaking.

"Nutcase," Bel muttered, stepping on the gas. They headed toward Kamchee. Bel kept sneaking glances at his passenger. Whitlock's breathing gradually slowed, and Bel saw him looking around, confused but obviously trying to orient himself. He looked up finally and met Bel's eyes in the rearview mirror.

"I'm under arrest?" His voice sounded different—harder. Wary.

Bel shook his head. "I don't have time to screw around with that. Tell me how to get to your place."

"My car?"

Bel held his tongue. The guy was slower than a frozen creek, and Bel hated how much he liked looking at him. Only thing more fucked up than being a murderer was having a hard-on for one. "You can get it tomorrow."

Whitlock closed his eyes briefly and nodded. Told Bel how to get to his cabin.

"Not real smart, was it?" Bel asked. "Goading Clayton like that?"

"I don't know." The words were almost inaudible.

They drove in silence a while longer, until Whitlock pointed out the turn to his cabin.

When he let Whitlock out, Bel suggested, "Sober up."

But Whitlock seemed plenty sober now. Didn't sway or grin. His expression was focused, almost angry. "Thank you for the ride," he said stiffly.

He walked up the gravel drive and let himself into the cabin. A light went on. Bel got back into the cruiser and let out a sigh. He didn't want to think about the shit Dav had told him. She claimed there really were people who did things in their sleep and had no recollection later, and that Daniel Whitlock had been a model of good behavior since his release. Of course he had been—he didn't want to go back to fucking jail. Dav ought to know Whitlock was no saint.

Bel recalled Whitlock's reaction when he'd slapped the partition. The lashing out, the confusion, the fear. The change in Whitlock's voice, in his body. Was it possible . . .?

No. You had to be awake to drive yourself into town. To get down those stairs at Greenducks. To kiss Jake Kebbler out back by the dumpster.

You had to be awake.

The can was on the floor, on its side, tangled in the little string Daniel had set up so carefully on its pulley system before going to bed. Must have knocked it down there after getting the key. The straw was on his pillow. And strewn over his mattress were the open cuffs, wrist and ankle, and a tangle of chains.

Fuck.

He'd fucking drunk it.

He'd known as soon as he came to in the back of the cop's cruiser that drinking from the can had been the only way out, the only way to get the backup key to lower within reach. He should have known better than to set up the backup system in the first place, but in the last few days, he'd worried more than usual—what if something happened and he needed to get free? What if he couldn't wait until morning when enough light had crept around the blackout curtains to see the combination to the lock that he'd taped on the wall the night before, his eyes squeezed shut?

He'd thought the system would be complicated enough, *gross* enough, that his sleeping brain wouldn't be able to get around it. Drink the liquid to get the key for the left wrist cuff. Find the key for the right wrist cuff taped to the wall at the furthest extent of his reach. He'd practiced when he was awake, and he needed to be a fucking contortionist to do it. The effort to free himself had left him panting, exhausted. And that was before he'd filled the can with the most disgusting fluid he could think of.

Which meant he'd drunk his own piss to get to the first key.

The thought sent Daniel straight to the bathroom, where he went down on his knees in front of the toilet and vomited. Mostly beer. So great, drinking beer as well.

And fuck, he was tired. Whatever he'd been doing, he was tired.

He was *always* tired.

It was back to the ice locks, then. They only bought him a couple of hours of sleep, but at least he couldn't get out of them. No more emergency backups. Better to risk his own life than risk hurting someone else. Or worse.

He rubbed his face. God, he needed to sleep. But more than that, he needed to be able to trust that he'd stay put while he slept. He wished he knew why he was so hell-bent on getting free lately. Two nights ago, enough moonlight had apparently crept between the curtains to allow him to read the combination on the wall and make an escape. Tonight he'd drunk piss. And God knew what all he'd done once he was out.

When it first started happening, Daniel had thought his parents were playing some sort of elaborate joke on him.

"Daniel! What happened here?"

The living room wall had gone from beige to neon green overnight. The same neon green his sister Casey had bought to paint some banners for school.

He'd looked, astonished. *"It's green!"*

"What did you do?"

"I didn't . . ." But there was green paint all over his hands, his pajamas.

"Don't lie to me, Daniel!"

He'd stood there for a very long time in his paint-splattered pajamas, waiting for his mom's face to break into a smile. Waiting for the punch line that never came. Until, very gradually, it dawned on him that it wasn't a joke. That he'd done this thing. That saying over and over that he didn't remember sounded like the most pitiful lie in the world.

There were other incidents too; some small and some not so small. His parents had started locking his bedroom door at night. Daniel had gone out the window. Climbed onto the roof and down the gutter pipe, they figured. They'd started talking about mental illness then. No doctors, though. Couldn't afford it, and more importantly, they didn't want word getting out that their son wasn't right.

In college, it got worse for a while, until Daniel found Marcus, and Marcus beat him so hard that his body was too exhausted to move. All the other trappings of that—the bowing and scraping, the leather gear, the getting fucked—were inconsequential as long as Marcus beat him. Or he'd wanted them to be inconsequential, until he'd gotten used to sleeping beside someone. Started to think Marcus was more than a means of keeping himself under control. Shit, he'd *liked* the guy. But in the end, Marcus couldn't deal with a partner who didn't get off from the pain but needed it in a whole different way. Nothing sexual about Daniel's masochism.

After Marcus, Daniel hadn't gone looking for a relationship like that again or any kind of relationship. Too much work, trying to explain what he needed and why. Too hard to think about someone else walking out on him when he couldn't be what they wanted. But recently, he'd been drawn once more to the idea of what his and Marcus's arrangement was *supposed* to have been. He wanted someone who could keep him contained, keep his body exhausted—nothing more.

He looked at the marks on his wrists. Finding someone to control him would mean no more piss-can pulley systems. No more great escapes. No more late-night trips to Greenducks and waking in the morning with an ache in his ass and no memory of what had happened. He pushed his arms together to make the bruises match.

Gonna have to get tested again. Though maybe I didn't get up to any of that. He shifted experimentally. Nothing hurt. He could usually tell when he'd been fucked. No one in the Greenducks crowd went easy on him.

So what did I do?

Clayton McAllister. Officer Belman said he'd goaded him. Where the hell had he found Clayton?

Had he been *looking* for him?

"Dumbass," he whispered.

He rose from the bathroom floor and walked back into the main room. Ignored the bed and sat down at his desk instead. He turned the computer on and blinked in the glare from the screen.

In prison, they'd given him drugs to make him sleep. Dumb, because sleeping wasn't the problem. And the drugs only made it harder to wake up. Left him feeling sluggish and spaced out for days afterward. What he needed was something like he'd had with Marcus—but with someone who didn't mind beating him, even if he didn't get off. Someone who would keep him *contained.* There was a guy online he'd messaged yesterday who lived about thirty miles from Logan. Claimed to be a dom looking for a 24/7 slave. Promised he didn't care if Daniel never came. Said he preferred it that way.

Master Beau. His profile picture was a pair of high-shine leather boots. He'd said he wanted Daniel naked, on his knees with his arms bound behind his back, to lick those boots.

Need you to chain me up, Daniel had responded. *Keep me under lock and key.*

24/7, Master Beau had promised.

I got a job.

Don't need a job. Ur master will take care of u.

I got parole. Can't miss appointments.

U won't.

Master Beau hadn't even asked what the parole was for, which sent up a red flag. But Daniel was hardly the only one taking a risk here. Might have been stupid, agreeing to submit to the guy without having laid eyes on him. But no way in hell did Master Beau know what kind of crazy he was courting.

Daniel felt a little guilty for that, but it would be okay. As long as Master Beau locked him up, it would be okay. He couldn't hurt anyone.

Clayton. Might fucking hurt Clayton.

I want to hurt Clayton.

He clenched his fists. The strength of the desire was frightening, but it vanished quickly, leaving him gasping, choking.

He wasn't going to hurt anyone else.

Didn't want to.

But he needed someone to make sure he didn't. *Couldn't.*

He typed out a message: *When can we meet?*

Looked at it for a while, and then looked at the open cuffs on his mattress and the empty can of piss on the floor. His stomach churned.

He hit Send.

CHAPTER TWO

The floor polisher droned as Daniel ran it across the lobby of the Logan library. Vibrations ran up his arms and across his shoulders, where the muscles were pulled tight from the few hours' sleep he'd finally gotten. He'd woken with the sheets tangled around his throat from his efforts to get free again. The ice locks worked up to three hours, as long as he kept the cabin cold. But Daniel always took some time to fall asleep, afraid someone would walk in and find him chained to his bed. Which was dumb, because it wasn't like he got visitors.

His parents never stopped by, and Casey was away at college now. Daniel liked to think that was the reason she didn't contact him—too busy making friends and having fun—but he knew it wasn't. They had never been that close, not once she was old enough to realize what a freak he was. Must have felt like growing up in a lunatic asylum for her, the whole family acting as Daniel's unwilling wardens. Covering up his craziness until it all went to hell that night and there was no way anyone could hide it anymore. When the police came knocking and found him in his bed stinking of gasoline, his hands blistered. The look on Casey's face as she'd peered around her bedroom door: caught between horror and terror. Afraid of her own big brother.

After prison, he'd moved out to the cabin in Kamchee, where his family didn't have to look at him every day.

They were better off forgetting him.

Earlier in the afternoon he'd walked the five miles into town, because he didn't know where his car was. Didn't take long to find—the lot beside Greenducks. No sign of his keys though. Daniel had been checking the ground, hoping every glint of light would resolve itself into keys but finding only broken glass, when Mike had appeared from the bar.

"You have fun last night, Danny Boy?"

He hated being called that. He'd just shrugged and kept looking.

"Oh, man, you and Jake was tangled up like a pair of panty hose!" Mike had laughed, showing broken teeth. "Looked like you was gonna fuck right there in the bathroom before you took it outside."

Daniel hadn't said anything. Turned his burning face toward the ground and headed for work.

Now, with the doors of the library locked behind him and the polisher droning across the floor, Daniel let his eyes drift close.

He could write a fucking paper on sleep deprivation.

The way it slowed everything down, like he was swimming through molasses. The way he started to talk to himself, like a dumb, drunk kid with a hundred things to say. The way it made him dizzy. Drained every ounce of strength from his body and left him a shambling mess.

He blinked—saw fire, dripping like water down the walls. Jolted as the adrenaline rushed through him, and blinked again to clear his vision.

He stepped away from the polisher and leaned against the wall. Placed his palms flat against it, sucked in a breath, and held it until his lungs burned. Until he found his balance again.

He liked working in the library when it was closed. Liked the silence and the smell of the place: books, floor wax, and the slightly stale scent once the air-conditioning was turned off. Mostly he liked that he didn't have to talk to people. He saw the way they looked at him, knew what they thought. *There's the freak. Wonder if he's gonna snap.*

People hated him. They were afraid of him. He was afraid of himself.

He pulled his phone out of his pocket and checked his messages. Opened a new one from Master Beau: *Meet me at my place tonight. Gonna ride u so hard.*

So much for introductions, but Master Beau was desperate for a slave to ride hard, and Daniel was desperate for a lock he could trust. Beggars weren't choosers.

He sent back: *Got no car.*

Excruciating minutes passed until he got his reply: *I'll pick u up slave.*

Daniel stared at the message for a while, thinking of every single reason why this was the dumbest idea he'd ever had in his life, and then thinking of the look on Casey's face the morning after he'd burned Kenny's house down with Kenny inside.

He sent Master Beau the directions.

Bel was still thinking about Daniel Whitlock when he arrived at Dav and Jim's the next evening for the barbecue. Whitlock's cabin—too small for a guy to live in. Didn't he feel cramped, claustrophobic? And what business was it of Bel's?

He'd brought a package of ribs, but Dav and Jim already had plenty of meat, so he stuck the ribs in the freezer and nearly tripped on Stump as he stepped back. Dav whacked a bag of frozen hamburger buns against the counter to separate them and Stump skittered from the room.

"Dog's dumb as balls." Dav stuck the buns in the microwave.

"Jim having any luck training him?"

Dav shook her head. "Gun-shy. And we paid fifteen hundred for him."

"Well, maybe it was the name you stuck him with. He thinks you ain't got any confidence in him."

"I don't."

Stump's full name was Dummer'nastump. He was purebred lab, and Jim had bought him to duck hunt with, but so far the pup was a disappointment. For hunting, anyway. When it came to sitting on the couch staring adoringly at a guy, nobody could do better.

"Jim need a hand with the barbecue?" Bel asked, peering out into the backyard where his brother was firing the thing up.

"You know better than to ask that," Dav reminded him. "Grab yourself a beer and help me with the salads instead."

"Working tonight." Bel got a soda out of the fridge and leaned on the counter. "Hey, I saw Daniel Whitlock last night."

"Oh yeah?" Dav tore into a head of lettuce. "How's he doing?" Dav was Whitlock's parole officer. Only one in the town who believed

Whitlock's bullshit story. Made Bel feel awkward, bad-mouthing Whitlock in front of her, but it gave him some small satisfaction to be able to deliver evidence that Whitlock wasn't the upstanding parolee she thought he was.

"He came staggering out of Greenducks, high as a kite."

Dav put the lettuce down and wiped her hands on her shirt. "Daniel's never failed a drug test yet. He doesn't even drink beer."

"That's bullshit. Could smell it all over his breath last night."

"I know what you think," Dav said, fixing him with the same steely gaze that had hurried Jim to the altar—a man didn't say nothing except *yes, ma'am* when Dav got that look, for fear of losing his balls. "I know what this whole damn town thinks, and maybe it's because I didn't grow up here, but I don't buy the tweaker stuff. He's not using, and he's not crazy. Out of every offender who's walked into my office, Daniel is the only one who doesn't lie to me."

Bel shook his head, disappointed in Dav's reaction. "You believe him when he says he's gonna be a good law-abiding citizen from now on? Never gonna kill someone again?"

"He's trying, Bel. He deserves as much chance as the next man." Dav picked up a knife and began to slice the tomatoes.

If Dav were a bleeding heart, Bel would have dismissed her. But she wasn't. Couldn't afford to be, in her job. He thought again to that moment last night when he'd banged the partition and Whitlock had . . . had what? Jolted awake? Something had happened, but Bel wasn't sure what.

"Joe and Marcy are coming tonight, your parents too." Dav dumped the tomatoes on top of the lettuce in the bowl. "Maybe you should ask Joe what he's thinking, making you work when there's a game on."

"Uncle Joe doesn't play favorites," Bel said. "Anyway, I work a few game nights and miss a few barbecues and maybe I'll get Thanksgiving off. Billy coming?"

"He's gone hunting, Jim said." Dav frowned at the paltry mix of greens and tomatoes. "I hope your mama brings her potato salad."

Stump slunk back into the kitchen, peering hopefully at Bel.

"She always does," Bel said.

Dav had slotted right into the family. She'd been Bel's friend before she'd been Jim's girlfriend, now wife. She called him Bel, which was his nickname on the force. To the rest of the family he would always be Little Joe, all six foot two of him, to distinguish him from his Uncle Joe. Billy had been named after their dad, Jim after their grandpa, and Bel after their uncle. The Belmans had been recycling long before it was the done thing.

Plain unimaginative, in Bel's opinion.

Speaking of.

"You started thinking up any names?"

Dav's hand went unconsciously to her abdomen, even though she wasn't showing yet. "No. And keep that to yourself. You're the only one who knows apart from us. We're not telling people until after the first three months."

"My lips are sealed."

"They'd better be," Dav said. "Instead of standing there like a lump, pass me my drink, would you? Top shelf."

Bel opened the fridge and frowned at the beer bottle. "Dav?"

"It's cola. But I've got to throw your mom off the scent somehow. She's fixing on me like a bird dog."

"Yeah, Mama could teach Stump a thing or two." Bel bent down to scratch the pup's ears.

Dav rolled her eyes. "I'm pretty sure that animal's beyond teaching."

Stump gazed at them lovingly.

Master Beau was everything Daniel had expected, but it didn't matter. He'd said on his profile that he was in his forties, but he looked older thanks to his sun-damaged skin. He was big, his belly coming down past his belt, bearded, and he wore a trucker's cap low over his eyes. When he pulled up outside the library in his piece-of-shit truck, he looked Daniel over and said, "Your name Daniel?"

Like there was anyone else waiting on the sidewalk.

"Yeah, that's me," Daniel replied, wiping his sweaty palms on the back of his jeans.

"You ain't got a name now except Boy," Master Beau said. "Get in."

Daniel climbed into the truck, his heart racing.

The cab stank of cigarettes. Master Beau's fingers, tapping on the steering wheel, were stained brown and yellow. Daniel told himself it didn't matter, not if the man could give him what he needed.

"You gonna sit all the way over there?" Master Beau growled at him.

Daniel shifted closer, feeling the heat from Master Beau's body seep into him where their thighs touched. Swallowed down his revulsion.

Master Beau ground through the gears, turning onto Main. A police cruiser passed, and Daniel wondered if it was Officer Belman. He remembered when Belman used to work at Harnee's. And before that, when he was a skinny kid running around town. Never took too much notice of him though. Belman must have been four years younger, which was a lifetime when you were kids. The summer before Daniel graduated high school, the kid had hung around with Casey a bit. Had a brother her age and tagged along. Daniel couldn't remember if he'd ever spoken two words to him. Most of Casey's friends steered clear of her weird big brother.

A silver sedan followed the police cruiser, and Daniel looked the other way. His mom's car. What was she doing out at this hour? Heading home from her book club at Cherry Hanson's place, maybe, if they still had that on Wednesday nights. Which meant his dad would be at home, blustering and swearing as he tried to cook mac and cheese in the microwave.

"Don't lie to me, Daniel!"

God, he just wanted it to stop.

Master Beau reached down and fiddled with the radio. Found some shit song where a woman wailed about her cowboy leaving her.

"Yeah," Master Beau drawled, "this is a good one. Put your hand on my dick, Boy. Want to be nice and hard for when I get you home."

Daniel forced down the sudden spike of panic. He put his hand on the man's thigh, slid it up toward his groin. Long as Master Beau didn't ask Daniel to suck him, they'd be good.

Fuck.

What had Daniel been thinking? Master Beau was sure to want head at some point, and Daniel couldn't . . .

"That's it, Boy," Master Beau said, widening his legs. "Get on up in there."

Daniel rubbed his hand over the bulge in Master Beau's jeans. "I want to talk about our limits."

Master Beau looked sideways at him. "You got any, Boy?"

"I need to be locked up," Daniel said. Didn't mention he couldn't give head, in case it was a deal breaker. "Not—not always in bondage, but I need to be chained when I sleep."

Master Beau dropped his right hand from the wheel, and ground Daniel's hand harder against his crotch. "You and me are gonna get along just fine. I got a collar at home that will look real nice on you. You want me to chain you to the radiator and fuck you on the floor?"

"Yes," Daniel said dully.

"Yes, what?"

"Yes, Master Beau."

Daniel kept stroking Master Beau's dick the entire way to his place. Absently, trying to shut out Master Beau's groans. Wouldn't have thought the man could hold off coming for so long, but Master Beau did. Muttered at Daniel to ease off a few times, and grunted like a pig rooting around when he started again. Daniel had liked hearing Marcus make noises. It hadn't been any timeless romance he and Marcus had shared, but it had been a cut above this. Daniel had told himself he only needed Marcus for the pain, and yet he'd been secretly pleased when Marcus had refused to give him *only* that. Marcus had wanted to hurt Daniel, and Daniel had needed to be hurt. But Marcus hadn't liked that Daniel didn't like it. So he'd walked away rather than answer Daniel's demands for more.

Something kind of sweet about that.

"You like getting your ass beat?" Master Beau asked.

Do you want me to like it?

Probably not.

"No, sir. But it ain't a limit."

Master Beau grinned. "I like you." He wiped his nose with the back of his hand. "I'm gonna like you even better when you got my cock in your mouth. Gonna choke you till you puke, Boy. And you're gonna have to swallow it back down, 'cause I just got the carpets redone." He laughed, and Daniel couldn't tell if it was because he was joking or because he just liked the image. He sat rigid with panic as they pulled onto the interstate.

The one fucking thing I can't do.

If I don't have a choice, though . . .

Daniel lifted his hand from the cracked leather seat. Saw the patch of sweat he'd left.

Stupid piece of shit. Anything he does to you's gonna be just what you've earned.

Master Beau lived about thirty miles from Logan, at Watson's Landing. Wasn't much to the place except a bar, a junkyard, and a couple of houses. They turned onto a narrow street with ragged pavement, and into the driveway of the second house on the left. A light was on inside.

The house wasn't as shabby as Daniel would have imagined. The outside looked like it had been renovated recently. And it was . . . quainter, too. Like a country cottage. Daniel would have laughed if he hadn't been so worn out and so scared. He hated the exhaustion that came from sleep deprivation. He couldn't sink into it, could only let it jab him over and over. A repeated reminder—*Hey, you're tired. Hey, you can't do anything about it.* His eyes felt bald and blistered, his mouth dry.

He followed Master Beau up to the front porch. The big man fumbled with the keys, then opened the door and slapped Daniel's ass to move him inside.

A cloud of cigarette smoke hit Daniel as he stepped across the threshold. They weren't alone. There were two—no, three other guys in the dim room. They all stared at Daniel. Their faces were gray. Their hair was gray. Their smoke was gray. Actually, one of the guys had dark hair. His eyes were small and glinted, and he stood with his hand in his pocket. The other two were sitting. Daniel stared at them, half-hoping he was hallucinating.

Master Beau set a hand on the back of Daniel's neck. "Boys. Meet Boy." He shoved and Daniel staggered a few steps, caught himself, and tried to back up. He hadn't expected anyone else. He'd agreed to do the slave thing for Master Beau, but he wasn't gonna get gangbanged.

You wanna be locked up or not?
Not this much.

But he was thirty miles from Logan, and he had no way back except Master Beau. He'd have to wait this one out, see what happened. He nodded at the group. "Hello, sirs."

Master Beau cuffed him between the shoulder blades. "Don't speak unless I ask you a question. Shoes off. Get on your knees."

Daniel slipped his sneakers off and knelt, keeping his head bowed. The dark-haired guy kept shifting, and Daniel raised his head to watch him. He felt sluggish, like his heart was the only part of him that could move at a decent pace. Master Beau bummed a cigarette, muttered, "Be right back," and headed toward the back of the house. Daniel tried to breathe through the haze. Concentrated on the floor. The carpet did look new.

"You suck cock pretty good, Boy?" one of the older guys asked.

Daniel wasn't sure whether to answer or not. Master Beau had said *"unless I ask you a question."* But maybe that applied to all of them.

"I'm all right," Daniel said, his throat dry. He had been, once.

The group laughed.

"You're a lot prettier than anyone else Beau's brought around." The dark-haired guy.

Daniel glanced up and saw an outline in the pocket of the guy's stained khakis. A gun. The guy had a gun.

Daniel had to force himself not to rise and bolt.

No. Fuck no.

He took a deep breath, closed his eyes, and when he looked up again, he couldn't see anything in the guy's pocket.

Not real, you asshole. You're making things up.

But as he stared, he thought he could see the outline again. The guy had turned, and it was hard to tell . . .

Not a gun. Please not a gun. Please.

He was startled by a clanking behind him. A second later, a hand struck the back of his head. "Head down," Master Beau said.

Daniel swayed. Bowed his head, trying to forget the gun.

Master Beau sat in an armchair across the room. He held up two thick chains. Fear merged with a strange thrill—for a second, Daniel remembered Marcus. Remembered what it was like to fear what Marcus was going to do without fearing Marcus himself. Daniel hadn't liked the beatings, hadn't cared about the gear. But he'd liked what came after—drifting, too tired to move. Marcus's hand moving in slow circles on his back, skirting welts.

The thrill quickly turned to a queasy bitterness. Wasn't going to be any drifting with Master Beau.

You're gonna get just what you've earned.

Master Beau jingled the chains. "Crawl to me, Boy."

The chains scared him, but he needed them. Deserved them. He'd fucking killed someone. He was a murderer.

He hated himself for the times he forgot. The minutes or sometimes hours he went without reminding himself he was a murderer. It felt like the kind of thing you ought to keep close to you, ought to remember all the time, like being in love, or being the president, or having lost a child. It wasn't the sort of thing you forgot, and yet sometimes Daniel did, had to—just for a little while. But the few minutes of peace were seldom worth the guilt he felt afterward. For forgetting.

Almost as bad were the times he convinced himself Kenny Cooper had deserved it. When rage flared up in him big enough to make all the other angers Daniel had ever felt look like parodies. He'd never been as scared as he had been when Kenny had attacked him. Not even when he was younger and woke to accusations he didn't understand. *What have you done?* and *Of course you remember; don't give me that.* And *Daniel, what possessed you?* The fear of what he was doing in his sleep, that was psychological. His fear of Kenny had been visceral, no thought behind it, no slow build. Just a sudden, all-consuming terror. He'd been electric with adrenaline, spurred by an animal need to escape.

He could recall a few lucid thoughts, there and gone faster than puffs of breath on a cold night. When Kenny raised the butt of the revolver for the first time: *God, it's gonna hurt, it's gonna hurt, it's gonna hurt, might kill me, but maybe he'll miss, maybe I can make him miss. Please, God, please.*

Even amid the flood of fear, there'd been foolish hope—*maybe I can make him miss.* After the shock of the first blow, which had pushed Daniel under, created a pain so deep and full that Daniel's body processed it as cold first—just cold—even after that, the *Please God* remained. A second blow, quicker than the first, less buildup. The crack of his collarbone sounded like the crack of a belt against bare flesh. On the third blow, his mind finally went quiet. His body still struggled, jerking and flailing in grass wet with blood.

He wanted to hate Kenny, who'd left him with this fear that had lingered and transformed into something else—a fury Daniel wasn't sure he was entitled to.

You were allowed to hate him. Would've been all right even if you'd beat the shit out of him as payback. But you weren't allowed to kill him. What right you got to be mad now, when he's the one who's dead?

Daniel was breathing hard, looking at Master Beau's boots across the room, the mud on the cuffs of his jeans that darkened as Daniel stared, became bloodstains. Someone nudged him with their toe. "He said crawl, bitch."

A laugh. "Panting like a dog, ain't he?"

Master Beau held the chains and whistled.

"I'll help him." Someone moved. The man with the gun. He grabbed Daniel by the hair and shoved him onto his stomach, then started pulling him toward Master Beau. Daniel couldn't see the man anymore, couldn't see if he had the gun out or not, and pain tore through his scalp. He thrashed and kicked, and the man let go of him. Daniel was on his feet and running for the front door. Now the man would be angry. If he had a gun, he'd shoot.

Ignoring Master Beau's protest, Daniel threw open the door and ran out into the yard, barefoot. He'd have a better chance of staying out of sight if he cut through backyards, but he wanted to be able to get to town. So he followed the road. No headlights appeared behind him. He ran until he couldn't anymore, until he became aware of how torn up his feet were, and then he walked, his hands jammed into his pockets. The gravel on the shoulder hurt so much he had to walk in the street.

No cop to give you a lift this time.

He thought again about waking up in Belman's car. How freaked out he'd been. How Belman's *sober up* had been the nicest thing anyone had said to him in a while.

His breathing slowed eventually, and he started to berate himself. The guy probably hadn't had a gun at all. It had been Daniel's imagination.

Could've had one, though. Could've killed you. All of 'em, crazy fuckers. Animals.

Could've killed you.

Now that would really be getting just what you earned.

Daniel had believed in Hell when he was younger but had outgrown it in his late teens. In college there'd been plenty of atheists with whom Daniel had gladly allied himself. Religion was bullshit, they'd said. Fairy tales. Big Brother BS. But once he'd come back to Logan, Daniel had lost that certainty—the sureness that he was his own person, capable of doing the right thing without the fear of punishment or the promise of reward. When Kenny had broken his bones, he'd known there was a God, and that He hated Daniel. And when he'd murdered Kenny a year later, he'd known there was a Hell, and that he'd end up there.

Daniel, what possessed you?

When they asked him, Daniel wondered if they meant it. His dad would stare at him the morning after some minor crime Daniel had committed in his sleep, like he didn't recognize his son—or didn't want to. *"Come with me,"* he'd say, and lead Daniel to the next room, where he'd take off his belt. He wouldn't hit Daniel, just snap the belt a few times to satisfy Daniel's mother, and then he'd make Daniel do chores until he was exhausted. Those were actually the days Daniel slept best—right after a sleepwalking episode, when his punishment wore him out enough that he could sleep soundly.

What possessed him?

When he was a kid, he figured it was the devil. Easier to blame some outside force determined to rip their family apart than accept the alternative: it was his fault. Every crazy thing he did came from a subconscious that wanted to paint the living room neon green, or dig holes in the garden, or smash the china that had belonged to his mom's grandmother. Some part of him craved the destruction.

One Sunday when Daniel was twelve, Daniel's parents had him meet with Reverend Park after church. Reverend Park told Daniel about spiritual demerits. Daniel's behavior had earned him a great burden of demerits, and this made Daniel vulnerable to spiritual subsumption when he slept. Daniel had never figured out exactly what he was supposed to do about that. Didn't know how to unburden himself, or strengthen his vulnerable spirit.

"What'd you and Reverend Park talk about?" Daniel's father had asked as they drove home.

Daniel told him, stammering, and his father hadn't asked him to talk privately to Reverend Park again. They still made him go to church, and Daniel had prayed real hard to try to negate his spiritual demerits, but it didn't help. His parents mostly stopped yelling at Daniel for things he did in his sleep, but sometimes his mother cried, which was worse than yelling.

Casey was no help. She'd do things—one time she cut a lock of her own hair and told their parents Daniel had done it. She later admitted to Daniel she'd done it herself, then denied it when he tried to tell their parents. After a while, Daniel didn't know what was true—couldn't tell when people were just fucking with him. His college roommate had thought it was hilarious that Daniel sometimes got up in the night and wrote papers and had no recollection of it the next day. Jeff had once logged on to Daniel's computer while Daniel slept and deleted what Daniel had written of his lit paper, replacing the text with I LOVE HAIRY BALLS over and over again. Then he swore Daniel had done it while sleepwalking.

Then there were the drawings.

Those frightened him as well. Another unknowable power inside him. He couldn't reckon where that talent came from. Same place as the rest of the craziness, he supposed. He only knew that he couldn't draw when he was awake, but when he was asleep, he somehow could. Scared him as much as killing a man had, in some ways.

Jeff had taken to leaving charcoal and paper around their room in college, until Daniel had begged him not to.

"Dude, are you serious? Look at these!"

But Daniel didn't want to encourage it. Didn't want to let it out. Didn't want to see the evidence when he woke up in the morning. He'd caught his parents poring over one of his drawings when he was fourteen: a sketch of the Bridge of Sighs in Venice. Must have seen it on the TV or something. They didn't tape his drawings to the wall like Jeff did later. Daniel didn't know what they did with them.

He should never have come back to Logan after college. But it was over with Marcus, he couldn't hold down a job because he was always so exhausted, and he'd thought he would be more settled on familiar ground. So much for that.

He picked his way through the remains of a glass bottle on the road, mindful of his bare feet. Fuck. A faggot walking down the back roads in the middle of the night. Daniel was pretty sure he'd seen this horror movie. Might have been better off staying and getting gangbanged by Master Beau and his buddies.

Probably hadn't been a gun anyway.

Daniel shivered at the memory, real or not, and kept on toward Logan.

Took an hour before the first truck rumbled past, and Daniel flagged it down. Guy looked to be a stranger, thank God.

"Where you headed?" he asked.

"Logan," Daniel said, climbing into the cab.

He rode with the guy all the way back to Logan, counting down the miles on the odometer while the guy puzzled over things in his head. Because everybody knew someone who knew someone, and the guy had a cousin in Logan.

"Whitlock," he said when Daniel told him. "Used to know a fella of that name who ran the sawmill. Had some trouble, I heard, with one of his kids." He peered at Daniel curiously.

"Yeah." They were passing the turnoff to Daniel's cabin, just outside of town. "Here is fine, thanks."

"Killed a man," the guy said, looking narrowly at him as he pulled over. "The son was a fag and killed a man."

Daniel climbed down. "Thanks for the lift."

He was half-afraid the guy would come after him, run him down. The truck idled at the side of the road for a while, then roared off into town.

The dirt road was hell on his feet. He was limping by the time he reached his cabin. The mailbox had been knocked off its post again, a thick rope noose hanging in its place. Daniel was too tired to move it. Just limped past and pushed open the door of the cabin.

He stripped down to his underwear, washed his bleeding feet in the shower. He opened the freezer and checked the ice locks. They were ready. But the longer Daniel stared at them, the cloud of cold hitting him in the face, the less he wanted to take them out.

It was nearly 2 a.m. If he waited another hour, went to bed at three, he could set the alarm and get up at six just as the ice finished melting. Perfect time for a jog. He didn't work tomorrow, and that thought filled him with dread. Days when he had to figure out what to do with himself were the worst.

He could go to his parents', but visits there were always awkward. His father hardly spoke to him, and he could never tell if his mother wanted to see him or not. She said she did. Said he was still her son. But he saw the way she looked at him. Not afraid or angry or loathing like everyone else in Logan, but just . . . tired. Tired of looking at him and remembering the things people said about him, about her, about the whole family. Remembering what it had been like to have to show her face in town while Daniel was in prison.

And yet part of him didn't care. He'd been the one in jail.

Deserved it.

Whatever whispers and stares and hostility she'd faced had nothing on what Daniel'd gotten when he was released. What he *still* got.

Why shouldn't they stare? Why shouldn't they spit?

He could've done with some artificial sympathy.

Why shouldn't they despise you?

Because I'm doing the best I fucking can.

A familiar feeling rose in him. A perverse pride, a satisfaction in being a freak, an outcast, in *being* a nightmare after having so many of his own.

Yeah, I'm dangerous, and yeah, I'm a faggot; I burned a guy; lock up your kids, you fuckers, you hypocrites, you animals. You got any idea what it's like to feel your own brain slamming around in your head, to know the next minute might be the minute he breaks your skull, that your brain comes out?

He clenched his fists. Heard the echo of his heart deep in his unbroken skull.

They got no idea. Clayton stood there and watched, and he laughed, and nobody's got a mind to lock him up, spit on him. I'm the one they think they need to be scared of, and they're right. Let them think that. Let them fucking think that! The thought became repetition—the ferocious lashing out of a wounded animal backed against a boulder, bleeding into the dust.

Clayton had made a noise, too—a whoop, like the kind guys gave when their football team scored a touchdown. An encouragement, a celebration, a dare for Kenny to go further. That was after Kenny'd hit Daniel the first time, when Daniel was still aware enough to be afraid. When his senses were heightened by adrenaline, and he felt every shift in his body, every molecule of cold in the air. That whoop stayed with him. A victory. *Score.*

Now he started to shake. *Deep breath.* He left the locks in the freezer and did a few dishes. Left the pan on the stove so he could boil water again tomorrow night. Boiling water took the gasses out, made the molecules freeze tighter. Made the ice in the locks melt slower. Remembered that from school.

One hour to kill before he'd lock himself up. Just one hour.

He went ahead and turned down the temperature on the wall unit. He did that to keep the ice from melting too fast, and because right now the cold might help keep him awake. He tried to read, but that wasn't going to happen. So he sat in his ragged armchair and dug his fingernails into his forearms, watching the goose bumps rise on his skin as the room got colder. He forced his nails in as hard as he could, reminding himself of the pain he could have had with Master Beau. The pain that would have left him drained of any fight. He could have slept chained in Master Beau's house, knowing he was safe—at least from himself.

Strange how pain could work both ways—to keep him awake, and to make him sleep.

He must have nodded off, because he jerked his head up suddenly.

Fuck. He was gonna fall asleep before it was time. He tried to rise but couldn't. Closed his eyes again.

"It's all right to be afraid." His mother's voice, but he wasn't sure what she'd said it about. Daniel had been young.

"It's all right to be afraid."

His eyes flashed open. The AC unit read fifty-three degrees.

Not like this, Mom. It ain't all right to be afraid like this.

He closed his eyes. Almost laughed, because he'd tried to stop saying "ain't" in college, but it was a hard habit to break.

He was caught in that in-between state, not quite asleep but not awake. And he heard people talking, a murmur of voices like he was at a party. Someone laughed.

Casey. It was Casey's laugh, and for a second he swelled with happiness, because maybe she had come to see him, and maybe he could finally explain. Anything seemed possible in this in-between space. He might find Casey and tell her he hadn't meant to hurt anyone, and she'd understand. Even if she didn't, it was enough that she was here.

He jerked awake again. He was freezing, his nipples hard, the hair on his arms arching in an effort to keep him warm. This wasn't going to work. He got up and went to the tiny bathroom stall, opening the cabinet under the sink. He took out the black bag and unzipped it. It was full of things that had meant something back when he was with Marcus. That had meant safety, trust. Fear, yes, sometimes. But closeness too.

He took out a slim black plug. Unzipped a front compartment of the bag and got out the small bottle of cinnamon oil. He slicked the plug with it, took his underwear down, and pushed the plug up his ass until he felt it lodge. The initial wave of heat made him grit his teeth, made bile rise in his throat. Then the pain became manageable. He walked back out to the main room and sat in the chair. Couldn't sleep, not with his ass clenching and burning. Fuck, it itched even more than it burned. He shifted, glad for the discomfort.

"But you like it, right?" Marcus had asked him. *"What we do?"*

Shouldn't have told the truth, but Marcus had already guessed it. Puzzled around for about a month, his touch growing more cautious, more uncertain, until he came out and asked straight.

Maybe tomorrow Daniel wouldn't visit his mother. Maybe he'd go help Mr. Roan with the garden. Mr. Roan was his neighbor half a mile up the road. Eighty-two and too batshit to care who Daniel was. Mr. Roan loved to be outside, but was too far gone to do his chores efficiently. So Daniel walked over sometimes and raked or mowed or weeded. Next summer, Mr. Roan was going to have a vegetable garden, which Daniel had helped him fence and till. Now would be a good time to plant.

He let his mind go blank—sleeping while awake, nothing but the occasional spasm in his ass to remind him he was alive. How long had it been since he'd been fucked while he was awake? Best not to go there. Didn't want to be fucked. Hadn't wanted it—*really* wanted it—in years.

He checked his phone. It was time. He took the locks out of the freezer and put cozies on each one to insulate them. Set them down while he went to the bathroom and removed the plug. Rinsed it in the sink and set it on the counter. Tomorrow he'd give it a proper cleaning. He wiped himself off and returned to the main room, where he crawled into bed. Found a position that was more or less comfortable. *So fucking cold.* Set his alarm for six. Looped the cuffs through the iron rails on the bed and locked them closed around his wrists.

Told himself he couldn't move for three hours, so there was no point struggling even in his sleep.

Hoped his subconscious was listening.

When he'd first gotten these locks, it had been even harder to fall asleep, knowing the ice was already starting to melt, that he had to take advantage of what little time he had. Now he didn't feel the pressure so much. He closed his eyes and immediately began to drift despite the shivers that racked his body. He had a nice memory of Marcus kissing his shoulder, just above a welt from the flogger. Marcus's body warm against his. *"Good job,"* Marcus had whispered. You didn't get many people who were proud of you for lying there and taking it.

Same way you lay there and took it when Kenny beat you?

Tried to get loose, but he hit too hard.

What're you remembering that for anyway? Got nothing to do with Marcus. Remember Marcus.

But when he tried to remember Marcus, he remembered Joe Belman. The Harnee's kid. Remembered Belman's eyes in the rearview mirror. Belman driving him all the way home.

He finally slept.

CHAPTER THREE

Daniel thought it was a dream at first. The smell of gasoline and the smoke.

He stared into the darkness, pulling instinctively against the cuffs, his heart thumping wildly. Sometimes he dreamed of what had happened at Kenny Cooper's house, or at least what the police photographs told him had happened. He didn't know how much was a memory and how much he'd cobbled together the same way the police had. Certainly he had no memory of going to his dad's shed to get the gasoline, then heading to Harnee's to buy a lighter. Seeing himself on the grainy security footage, the Harnee's kid muttering a "Have a good night" when he left, was crazy. Just crazy. And then he'd gone to Kenny's place and burned it down.

No surprise that he dreamed about it, that it haunted him. He deserved every nightmare he ever got.

The sudden crunch of tires spinning on dirt woke him. Gasoline, smoke, and tires. Still took his brain a moment to put it all together. Then he saw the flicker of flames outside the window on the sagging porch of the cabin.

Panic flooded him. He pulled against the cuffs, harder this time, but they didn't give. Of course they didn't fucking give, no matter how much he thrashed around on the bed. He wondered what time it was, how much longer he had before the ice melted and he could reach the keys to the cuffs. God, maybe the fire would help him, would melt the ice faster.

"Help me," he rasped. Didn't shout it. He couldn't find the breath.

The cabin was filling with smoke, and Daniel was going to die here.

A sob broke out of him. He arched his back in one more abortive attempt to get free. Didn't want to die. This was worse than the fear of being shot; worse, because he was alone. Because he couldn't even run. Would it hurt? Fuck, he hoped it wouldn't hurt. Hoped the smoke would get him before the flames did. Had Kenny felt the same terror? This same gut-clenching god-awful panic? Had he seen the fire coming for him? Had he known it was hopeless?

"Help me!" This time it was a shout, a fear so great that he had to let it out even if he knew there was nobody to hear it. He shouted, struggled, and wondered how long it would take to die.

It didn't take long to patrol Logan. Forty-five minutes tops, and that included Bel driving through every row of the trailer park at a crawl. He saw a fox at the side of US 601, moving so fast that for a second he didn't know what the hell it was. He did a few traffic stops, wrote two tickets for speeding, and gave a guy a sobriety test just for the hell of it. The guy was an asshole, always writing smart letters to the paper about how the sheriff's department was wasting money, so Bel got great pleasure listening to him try to recite the alphabet backward. Not that he laughed about it then. No, he waited until the guy had driven off before he did that.

There was no chatter on the radio.

Bel stopped in at Harnee's to buy some gum, then walked across the street to the diner to say hello to Sue-Ellen and get a coffee. After that, he headed back to the station for a while and took care of some reports. He was heading out to patrol again when he saw the envelope he'd left on the front counter the night before: *Daniel Whitlock*. So the guy hadn't come in to collect his car keys after all. Bel picked up the envelope, figuring he might as well do a run out to the Kamchee Woods to stick them in the mailbox.

Nothing else to do.

Bel got in his car and drove to Kamchee. He glanced in his rearview mirror a couple of times as though he expected Whitlock to be there. Could picture Whitlock, quiet, staring straight ahead. Once he'd gotten into the car that night, once he'd stopped *leering*, Whitlock had looked gentle. Not crazy or strung out. A little lost, thoughtful.

Bel could remember some nights at Harnee's when Whitlock had looked like that. At peace, almost content. Like he was somewhere far away from Harnee's, far away from Logan. And Bel had thought he might like to be wherever Whitlock was. Bel's gram had gotten that look toward the end—like she had a secret that filled her with happiness. It had made it a little easier to say good-bye, knowing she was ready.

Bel didn't know if he believed in Heaven. When he was younger, sure, but now it was harder to buy into all that stuff. Sometimes he hoped there was one. Too hard, even for a practical man like Bel, to imagine the people he loved gone for good. And sometimes he was so angry at the shit people got away with that he found himself hoping there was a Hell. For the Kenny Coopers.

And the Daniel Whitlocks.

Bel turned off onto the dirt road that ran into the woods. Had to shield his eyes from the headlights of a truck heading back to the main road. Hunters, maybe. It was quiet out here. It was quiet in town too, considering what Bel knew of other towns from a few brief trips to Goose Creek and Easley. There ought to be traffic, people walking or on bikes. *People* period. Logan's downtown was dead. Half the shops were out of business, and parking signs had all been knocked down or shot full of holes. Could fire a gun down Main Street and hit nothing but a stray dog.

Bel stopped in front of Whitlock's mailbox. Or rather, the mailbox post. The mailbox was on the ground a few feet away. There was a rope looped around the post. No . . . *fuck*. Bel leaned out the window and picked it up.

A noose.

What the hell?

Bel dropped it. Whatever the fuck it was, he didn't want to know. Well, he'd deliver the keys in person. Or leave them on the porch or something. He continued down the drive. Smelled the smoke before he saw the flames licking at the front of the cabin.

Shit.

Bel leaped out of the cruiser, grabbing the radio on his shoulder. "Bob, you there?"

His radio crackled. "Yeah, Bel."

Bel opened the trunk of the cruiser, grabbing for the fire extinguisher. "I got a fire on Kamchee Road, at Whitlock's cabin. Can I get a fire truck out here?"

"On it, Bel."

Bel could feel the heat of the fire before he even stepped onto the porch. Could smell the gasoline as well. He aimed the extinguisher at the base of the flames. Not much it could do against the fire, except maybe slow it down.

A window shattered.

"Help me!"

"Whitlock, you in there?" Bel yelled back.

"Help me!" That voice was reed thin with panic.

Bel used the extinguisher up, tossed it, then shouldered the cabin door open. "Get the hell out of there, Whitlock!"

Because Bel would be fucked if he was gonna die trying to save the guy from a fire. The irony would probably kill him before the smoke.

Whitlock was lying in his bed, his hands cuffed to the headboard bars. He was wild-eyed, frantic.

"Please, please help me."

What the fuck?

You don't get to pick and choose who you help.

Bel hurried over to the bed, pulling his shirt up over his mouth and nose to shield from the smoke. He wrenched at Whitlock's arms, but the guy wasn't going anywhere. Bel remembered the bolt cutters in his trunk. "I'll be right back."

"Don't leave me!"

"I'll be right back," Bel repeated.

Back onto the porch, back through the heat of the flames, and back to the cruiser. Took too long to find the bolt cutters; by the time Bel pulled them out, the flames were climbing again. He raced to the cabin, through the smoke, and . . . *shit*, the hairs on his arms curled and burned away as the flames licked at him.

"You still there, Whitlock?" he called into the smoke.

Not like he was going anywhere, but it was better than asking if he was still alive.

"Yeah," Whitlock rasped.

Bel ducked, kept low, and headed for the bed. Found himself crouching on the floor, his face close to Whitlock's. No trace of confusion in those eyes tonight. Just fear. "Only gonna be a minute more, okay?"

Unless the roof came down or something. But cops weren't allowed to say things like that. Bel caught the first chain in the bolt cutters and snapped it. Leaned across Whitlock to cut the second one. "You got a back door?"

Whitlock nodded.

"Okay, get down on your knees and crawl. I'm right behind you."

Whitlock rolled off the bed and landed on the floor with a thump. He crawled, the ends of the chains still hanging from the cuffs on his wrists. Bel wondered who had chained him up like a dog and left him to die. Thought of the truck he'd passed on the way into the woods, and wished he'd gotten a look at it.

He followed Whitlock out the back, where he half rolled down the uneven steps and onto the ground. They both knelt there, coughing and hacking.

In the distance, Bel heard the sirens approaching.

Best sound in the world.

At the hospital in Goose Creek, Bel sucked in oxygen from a mask until the doc was satisfied he wasn't going to keel over. Whitlock, who'd gotten more than him, was admitted.

"Well, this is a fine mess," Uncle Joe muttered when he turned up unshaven, his uniform buttoned lopsided. "How you doing, Little Joe?"

"I'm okay," Bel said.

"I got Avery guarding the scene until the fire investigators arrive, and Ginny's gonna bring your car back to the station." Uncle Joe frowned, his forehead creasing with worry. "You see anything when you headed out there?"

"Saw a truck. Didn't get a look at it. And Whitlock was chained to the bed."

"Well, shit." Uncle Joe shook his head and sighed. "Guess I'd better go talk to him."

Bel followed him.

Whitlock was propped up on a bed in his room, a mask over his mouth and nose.

"How you feeling, son?" Uncle Joe asked. It was the same opening he used with anyone. Hell, Bel had heard him call men hardly any younger than him "son." Everyone older was "sir" but, like Uncle Joe said, that was a list that got shorter every year.

"I'm okay, Sheriff," Whitlock said, breathing mist against the clear mask.

"You wanna tell me what happened?"

Whitlock's fingers danced across the hospital blanket. "I don't know, sir. I was sleeping—"

Uncle Joe cocked a brow.

Whitlock flushed. "I mean, I woke up and the fire was already burning."

"That ain't right," Bel said. "Who chained you up, Whitlock?"

It had taken the firemen to get the cuffs off him. Thick, leather things. Bel had never seen anything like them before. You didn't forget someone putting those on you.

Whitlock dropped his gaze. "I did that."

"Excuse me?"

Whitlock's mouth thinned to a line. "I said, 'I did that.' I put them on me."

Bel exchanged a glance with Uncle Joe. *Freak.* Could be bullshit, though, like Daniel saying he hadn't seen who bashed him.

Uncle Joe nodded. "Okay, Whitlock. I'm gonna talk to you again, see if we can't get to the bottom of this. Where you gonna be staying?"

"Can I go back to my cabin?"

"I need you to steer clear until the fire investigator is done," Uncle Joe told him.

"How long will that be, sir?"

"Long as it takes." Uncle Joe hooked his thumbs in his belt. "You want me to call your folks?"

Whitlock jerked his head up. "No, sir. I'll, ah, I'll be fine."

"Okay then." Uncle Joe nodded at Whitlock, then he and Bel left the room.

"You gonna put a man on the door, Uncle Joe?"

Uncle Joe looked at his watch. "You got a few hours left on your shift. Might as well kill two birds with one stone. You stay and watch Whitlock, and the doc can watch you both. I'll send someone up to relieve you in the morning. Only if you're up for staying, mind."

"I'm fine," Bel said firmly. "Nothing but a bit of smoke. I've had sunburns that were worse."

Joe reached out and clasped his shoulder. "Glad to hear it, boy."

Bel watched him leave, then went and fetched a coffee and a chair, and sat down outside Whitlock's room. Nodded at the doc when he came to remove Whitlock's mask. Almost dozed off a few times, except that every time Whitlock moved his cot squeaked.

"Settle down!" he called through the door.

Five minutes later the cot squeaked again.

Bel sighed, stood, and opened the door. He leaned in the doorway. "Go to sleep, Whitlock."

"Can't," Whitlock said.

"Your eyes are hanging out of your head," Bel said. "'Course you can."

Whitlock shook his head.

"You want the doctor to give you something?" Maybe he'd had too many uppers and needed a downer to settle.

"No!" Whitlock's eyes widened. He lifted himself up briefly, and then slumped back down. The cot squeaked. "No drugs, please."

"Well, shut the hell up and go to sleep."

"I *can't*!" Whitlock's voice rose in pitch. "Please, I can't. Don't let me."

Bel watched him for a moment, unease gnawing at his gut. "You really chained yourself to that bed?"

Whitlock didn't answer, but his face colored.

"Why would you do that? You almost died tonight."

Whitlock wouldn't meet his gaze. "Bad shit happens when I sleep. Can't stop myself from doing it."

A day ago, Bel would have laughed if Whitlock had dared say that to his face. Kind of hard to find it funny now that he'd seen Whitlock chained to his bed. Even if it was bullshit, Whitlock believed it.

"Just . . . can't you just lay still?"

"Don't want to go under," Whitlock said in a low voice.

"Tell you what," Bel said. "You lay still, and I'll make sure no bad shit happens."

Something like hope flashed in Whitlock's pale face as he met Bel's gaze again. "You mean that?"

Bel shrugged. "Sure."

"Will you . . .?" Whitlock shook his head suddenly. "Sorry, no."

"Will I what?" Bel asked, wondering where the hell this was going. "Spit it out."

"Will you cuff me?"

Bel felt a jolt of something he couldn't put a name to. Wasn't sure he wanted to name it. "That what it's gonna take?"

"Yeah," Whitlock whispered. "Please."

"Okay." Bel stepped toward the cot, unhooking his cuffs from his belt. Used them plenty of times on plenty of people, but never like this. Usually they were protesting their innocence the whole way, or plain old resisting. Bel wasn't sure he'd ever had anyone watch him like this, hold out his arm like that; trusting, hopeful, quiet.

He closed the cuff around Whitlock's right wrist and felt the guy's pulse flutter under his fingers. He almost hesitated when he saw the bruising on the skin under the cuff. But Whitlock hadn't asked for his sympathy or concern. Bel wouldn't've had much to give anyway. He closed the other end of the cuff around the bar at the side of the cot.

"Okay?" he asked softly.

"Thanks." Whitlock sank back down onto the thin mattress, his entire body relaxing. Bel hadn't even realized how tense Whitlock had been holding himself, until he wasn't. He exhaled, his eyes drifted closed, and his face took on that peaceful look that Bel remembered from years ago at Harnee's. "Thanks."

"Whatever." Bel's voice came out gruff.

His fingers tingled from where he'd felt Whitlock's pulse, and he flexed them until the sensation went away. Fought the crazy urge to touch Whitlock again, maybe trace the line of his jaw, or his throat, or his lips. Fought the dumb idea that cuffing the guy meant something more than giving in to his crazy for a bit, just to shut him up.

He went outside, closed the door behind him, and drank the rest of his coffee.

Bel pulled up at Dav and Jim's, shut the car off, and got out. His shoes crunched on the gravel drive. Inside the house, Stump barked. "Just me, Stumpy," he called.

The front door was open. He banged on the edge of the screen to warn whoever was inside. Stump raced across the wood floor and stood there barking at him. His front feet left the ground with each woof. Bel opened the door and walked in. "'Lo?" he called.

"In here," Dav called from the kitchen.

Bel walked in, Stump following. Dav was at the kitchen table with a pile of paperwork and her laptop. She typed faster than ought to be possible. He strode over and pulled a chair out. Turned it around and sat on it backward, folding his arms across the top. "Tell me," he said, his tone more brusque than he'd intended. "Tell me about what he's got."

"Hi to you too," Dav said. "What are you asking?"

"Whitlock. How come you believe him? You know something about his—whatever? His condition? You think people can do shit like he did in their sleep?"

Dav continued typing. "Why the sudden interest?"

"C'mon, don't play like that now. You're always telling me I ain't being fair to him, so tell me why I ought to be."

Dav closed her computer. Brushed her bangs out of her eyes and stared at him. "He sleepwalks. He does things in his sleep that he has no recollection of when he's awake. It's a real disorder, Bel."

"Yeah, and I looked that up. And I don't know what to believe."

"What do you mean?"

"I mean other nutjobs have been trying to get off on that defense when they kill somebody. But where's the proof unless they were hooked up to electrodes or something while they were doin' the murder?"

"Polygraphs. Whitlock took several."

"Ain't always accurate."

"Whatever Whitlock's dealing with, he's not faking it," Dav said. "I do believe people 'do shit like that' in their sleep. And I believe Whitlock's doing everything in his power to keep himself under control."

Bel swallowed, remembering Whitlock chained to the bed. Chained to his own bed. In his own house. If you could call that shack a house. If Bel hadn't come by . . .

Since when did he worry about what happened to Daniel Whitlock?

Since Harnee's. Since before Harnee's. Since he'd watched from his window at age twelve while Whitlock and the rest of the high school cross-country team jogged down his street.

Shit. The hope in Whitlock's expression when Bel had promised he wouldn't let anything bad happen while he slept. And he'd kept his promise. Whitlock had slept until dawn. Bel had quietly uncuffed him around seven, before the relief officer got there, and Whitlock had thanked him quietly.

"Just seems convenient, is all," Bel muttered. "You kill someone who fucks with you, then say you were unconscious when you did it."

"I don't think anything about Whitlock's condition is convenient," Dav said evenly.

Bel was silent awhile, tracing a crack in the table's finish.

"You heard what happened?"

"Jim heard. I haven't left the house all morning. All this paperwork." She paused. "You tried to save him."

"Tried? I *did* save him. Not that anyone'll thank me for it."

Dav stood, shaking her head. But when she spoke, it was just to ask, "You want coffee?"

"Nah."

"There's leftover ribs."

"Too early."

"Not for me. Had three for breakfast."

"Jesus. This is what you're like now, imagine how you're gonna be six months in."

"It's got nothing to do with me being pregnant. I just like ribs." Dav went to the fridge. Poured herself some juice.

"Gonna try and figure out who did that to Whitlock," Bel said.

"You need to figure?"

"I need proof."

Dav shrugged. "This is your territory. But I'd be out giving McAllister eight kinds of hell right now if I were you."

She was right, and Bel knew it. Just wanted to make sure he thought it through first, didn't just go looking for the obvious. Didn't want to railroad anyone, not even an asshole like Clayton McAllister. The whole department would have to tread carefully on this one, because most of the town would already be saying that Whitlock got what he deserved and it was only a shame he hadn't burned.

Bel rubbed his temples. "*Sleepwalking*. I can't even credit that."

"A jury of his peers did," Dav reminded him. She furrowed her brow. "Listen, I don't know about the science of it. All I know is they hooked him up to enough machines and took enough brain scans to prove it. If you ask me, it was lucky for him his lawyer got the trial moved out of town. Here, they probably would have burned him for witchcraft."

Bel snorted. "Yeah, probably."

"I feel bad for him, Bel. He's got no one. He's got nothing except for a condition even he doesn't understand, and I can tell it scares the hell out of him."

Yeah, Bel had seen that too. "So how come he ain't done nothing about it? Shouldn't he be committed or something? You get someone off on insanity charges, they still gotta be locked up. Just not in jail."

"Can't afford a hospital. No insurance. And he's not insane. I've told him his best bet might be to volunteer for sleep studies at the med center in Orangeburg."

Bel had a vision of Whitlock in a white bed with electrodes planted on his head, his eyes *Clockwork Orange*-wide.

"He almost died because he chained himself to his bed," Bel told her. "Then he wouldn't settle at the hospital until—" He bit that off too late.

"Until what?"

"Until I cuffed him." The memory still made him uneasy in a way he couldn't define. Whitlock, so willing to make himself helpless. So desperate. And so fucking relieved when the lock had clicked shut.

Dav raised her eyebrows.

Bel flushed. "Anyhow, even if it's true, it don't make it right, what he did to Kenny."

"I never said it did. It doesn't excuse it. But it explains it."

"That enough?"

"It has to be."

Bel made a face. "Maybe."

"Can't be easy," Dav said slowly, "being gay in this town."

"Dav." His warning tone.

They didn't talk about this. None of the family did. They knew, Bel guessed, even though he'd never come out and said as much. It added up though, didn't it? Strapping guy like him with no girlfriend. Once, he'd left a magazine out by accident at his place. Billy had seen it and pretended he hadn't. Then there was the clincher: the fact that Dav had been one of the best-looking girls to show up in Logan for years, and Bel had set her up with Jim instead of staking a claim himself.

Keeping quiet didn't eat him up the way Dav thought it should. His family kept quiet about plenty of things. Like Aunty Lu's drinking and his dad's gambling. Didn't have to be an issue unless you made it one. You liked cock in a town like Logan, you kept it to yourself. It was simpler that way. It wasn't like he'd be bringing anyone home to meet the folks anyway. Not when you took a look at the choice of guys in Greenducks. Hell no.

He thought of Daniel Whitlock. Good-looking guy, always had been, and he cleaned up nice. Madder than a cut snake, according to the whole town, but what if Dav was right? What if Whitlock's legal team and doctors had been right? And those twelve jurors, and the judge. Come to think of it, that was a good handful of people that believed Whitlock.

Bel had seen the need in Whitlock when he'd held out his arm to be cuffed. Unadulterated *need*. Like he'd been pushing himself too hard for too long, but didn't have anyone to catch him when he dropped. Like Bel was his savior in that moment, not just a cranky cop with a pair of cuffs. Like Bel was everything.

Would be nice to have someone look at him the way Whitlock had.

To have Whitlock look at him like that again.

Shit. Bel shook his head to clear it and realized he was disagreeing with something Dav was saying. "Sorry, what?"

"I said it's a shame you never went to college," Dav said. "Might have done you some good to get out of Logan."

"I like it well enough here." It was home. He'd never had any real desire to leave. Never saw the need. Being content was more than some people managed in their whole lives.

Except when he'd seen people like Whitlock and his sister and Tim Howard and Lauren Barber go off to college, sometimes he'd gotten a nudge of a feeling that he might like to at least vacation somewhere outside of Logan. A real vacation, not a weekend trip to Easley.

He stood. "Kinda disappointed in you."

"How come?"

"You always did a real good job of not giving a shit. Not letting it get personal."

She stared at him, and he almost winced. He might never get used to that look. "If I don't give some kind of shit, then what am I doing here?"

Uncle Joe had said something similar when Bel had started on the force. That it was easy to get bored in Logan, to get to where you hated people and their stale lives and petty disputes. But you had to remember why you were doing this. If you didn't want to protect, didn't want to *help*, then you were wasting your time. He'd managed not to sound corny about it either.

Bel sometimes doubted he'd ever helped anyone in any profound way. You had to think in the abstract—the guy you pulled over for speeding hated your guts, but maybe you'd saved someone else by getting the idiot off the road. A lame thought, but Bel had to think it, otherwise he'd go crazy.

Then, just when you thought your whole life would be spent writing tickets, you got a chance to save someone's life.

Part of Bel wished he'd had the presence of mind to enjoy freeing Whitlock. Saving him. But there hadn't been much time to process what was happening. Hell, it had barely even registered with Bel that Whitlock was in his underwear until they were outside. Bel had gotten a pilled blanket from the back of his car and let Whitlock wrap himself in it, and then they'd gotten in the cruiser and pulled the hell out of the driveway.

"You give a big ol' shit about Whitlock," he said, not sure why he was trying to goad Dav. "Just because he's handsome and young don't mean he gets special treatment."

Dav didn't rise to the bait. "Who're you talking to, me or yourself?"

That made Bel angry. Which wasn't fair, since he'd started it.

And since she was fucking right. "I'm outta here," he said. "Gonna go see if they've discharged Whitlock yet."

"On your day off?"

"Got nothing else to do. Might as well get started on the investigation."

"You could relax."

"Same to you. You're doin' work at home. Fuckin' get on YouTube or something."

She punched his shoulder as he walked past. Kind of hard. He rubbed the spot as he entered the front hall. Stump whimpered when Bel reached the door. Bel crouched and took the pup's face in his hands. "You be good, okay? You don't gotta be scared of guns, you know. Nobody's trying to shoot *you*."

He caught sight of the singed hairs on his arm. A feeling welled in him that he didn't understand.

When he straightened, Dav was leaning in the kitchen doorway, watching him with a slight smile.

"What?"

She shook her head. "Nothing. You'll be a good uncle."

He hitched up his pants. "Yeah. No pressure, huh?"

"No pressure."

He left and headed to the hospital.

CHAPTER FOUR

The cabin looked gruesome to Daniel in the daylight. There was a large purple-black stain on the front wall over the porch, like one of those birthmarks that covered half a person's face.

Or a bruise.

Daniel rubbed his wrists, where he had dark bruises that throbbed when he moved his hands. Part of him didn't want to go inside. He wasn't sure if it was fear or just the heavy depression that had settled over him since the Harnee's kid had left the hospital. The odds probably weren't in favor of another arson attempt tonight—though, who knew?—so he wasn't sure what he might be afraid of. It must be sadness. Not because he had any real love for his cabin, but because this was yet another stain. Because for so long he'd felt covered in shame, fucking graffitied in it. Like no one could look at him without seeing layers and layers of ugliness. Couldn't move without showing the world a worse side of himself. And now his cabin, the place most familiar to him—that was ugly too. Marked, ruined.

The sheriff had dropped him off here after their interview this morning. An uninspiring conversation during which they'd both agreed that a lot of people had reason to want to kill Daniel. Daniel forced himself to tell the sheriff about encountering Clayton McAllister out on the highway the other night. "But, uh, I don't remember what happened," he said. He waited for the sheriff to tell him that was bullshit, that he was lying. But Sheriff Joe only nodded. Maybe assumed Daniel meant he'd been too drunk to remember.

Sheriff Joe said he'd talk to Clayton McAllister before anyone else. The noose was gone from the mailbox post, and Daniel hadn't said anything to the sheriff about it.

He walked inside. Smoke damage mostly. To the walls and window trim and the bedsheets. The front windows had shattered. The fire department had told him he might want to find a motel for a couple of days. But a motel didn't have any of the things Daniel needed to sleep. He winced as he wandered into the bathroom and saw the plug still on the edge of the sink. Imagined what the fire investigator had thought seeing it.

What— Worried people might think you're a freak or something?

Back out to the main room. Belman's bolt cutters were on the floor. Daniel crouched, hugging his knees with one arm. Didn't pick the bolt cutters up, just touched them.

He'd have to get them back to Belman. And that might mean seeing Belman again. He took a deep breath. Remembered how it felt to breathe smoke. To know he was going to die.

No.

Remembered instead how it felt to hold his hand out to Belman to be cuffed. The look in Belman's eyes that Daniel couldn't read. Cuffing him was supposed to be practical—Daniel needed to be locked up; Belman had cuffs. And yet there'd been that moment, Daniel's pulse racing under Belman's hand. Marcus's voice in Daniel's head: *"You like what we do, don't you?"*

Daniel had wanted to. Had wanted to let himself like it. But he couldn't afford to have opinions about it one way or the other, not when it was so necessary. He picked his cell phone up off the bedside table. It seemed all right, just low on battery. As he wandered into the kitchen, the phone rang in his hand. He didn't recognize the number, and he figured he shouldn't answer it.

But he was so fucking lonely.

He took the call. "H'lo?"

"Daniel Whitlock?"

"Yeah."

"Officer Belman."

Daniel went still. "Hi." What did Belman want? Had they figured out who started the fire?

"I just . . . I got your number from the hospital. Just calling to let you know I still got your keys." Belman paused. "I came by to give them to you last night. Thought you might want your car back. It's still out behind Greenducks; I checked."

"Oh." Daniel glanced at the counter. There was a brown house spider by the sponge on the edge of the sink. "I can, uh . . . Maybe when I get a ride to town I can come by the station."

"You want me to bring 'em by? Then I can drive you to get your car."

Daniel flicked the spider into the sink. "You don't have to do that. I'll get a ride." Or walk. A walk would do him some good. Kill a few hours, too. "You've got plenty to do."

"It's my day off."

Daniel gave a small smile. Realized he was clutching the phone too hard. "Even worse." He watched the spider unfurl and start crawling again.

"I'll come by," Belman said. "I got some stuff to talk to you about. About the investigation."

"Pushy," Daniel whispered. But he was smiling just a little bit.

"What's that?"

"Nothing. You can come by. I'm just here. I'm not doing noth—anything."

"All right. I'll be by in a little while."

Belman hung up. Daniel lowered the phone slowly and hit End. He traced the bruise on his left wrist with one finger, daring to imagine for a moment that the touch was Belman's. He pressed the pad of his finger into the mess of flattened capillaries, holding his breath through the slight ache.

He's seen. He's seen you chained to your bed. He's seen you about to die. He's seen you in your underwear.

And he's known for years you're a murderer. That you don't belong anywhere. That you're a dangerous fucking animal. What would he say if he knew you wanted him to touch you? If he knew you thought about him last night? He'd hate you more than he does already.

Daniel eased up on the bruise. Let the smile return.

Ah, well. What's one more stain?

Bel drove Whitlock into town feeling as nervous and uncertain as he had his first day of work. He was in his regular car, a '92 gray Volvo—not the cruiser. So Whitlock was up front this time, and Bel actually had to turn his head to sneak glances instead of using the mirror. Whitlock didn't talk, which was okay by Bel. Bel didn't know what to say, despite what he'd told Whitlock about needing to update him on the investigation.

As they approached downtown, Whitlock finally spoke. "The other night . . . when you gave me a ride . . . you told me it wasn't smart to goad Clayton."

He didn't go on. "Yeah?" Bel prompted.

"What did . . . what did I say to Clayton, exactly?"

Bel threw a look at Whitlock. "You don't remember?"

Whitlock shook his head.

"You asked if he wanted to suck your dick. Called him a cunt."

Whitlock flinched.

"To be fair, he said some shit to you first. Threw a beer can."

"He hates me pretty well."

"Well enough to want to kill you?"

"I told the sheriff I don't know. Maybe. Maybe now that I said that to him. He was real good friends with Kenny."

Bel remembered Clayton on the witness stand. Those tears had been real enough. "Yeah, well, Kenny ain't worth being broke up over," Bel said before he could stop himself.

Whitlock didn't answer. Stared at his hands, which were folded in his lap. Bel glanced at the bruises around Whitlock's wrists.

"You lock yourself up every night?" Bel asked, because why the hell not? He was used to asking people questions they didn't want to answer.

"Yeah," Whitlock said. "Most nights."

"Because you do bad shit?"

"I don't know. Afraid I might."

"Were you asleep the other night? In my car?"

Whitlock was silent a while. "Woke up. Didn't know how I'd gotten there."

"You acted all right," Bel said, more aggressively than he'd meant to. "If I woke up in a cop car and didn't know how I'd got there, I'd freak out."

Whitlock cleared his throat. "Pretty used to it. Not cop cars. But waking up someplace and not knowing how I got there."

"Just don't seem very likely."

"No," Whitlock agreed. "It doesn't."

Bel hadn't expected Whitlock to agree with him. They pulled up in front of Greenducks. "How long's it been going on?"

"Since I was a kid."

"Jesus." Bel took a hand off the wheel to scratch his neck. "And you did, like, crazy stuff back then?"

"Not like what I do now."

Bel shut the car off and turned to face Whitlock. The Volvo had red leather seats and a velvet ceiling, like a hearse. Whitlock was pale except for twin spots of color in his cheeks. "So what happens if you don't use the cuffs? If you let yourself sleepwalk?" Bel could barely say the word; it sounded so ridiculous.

Whitlock stared at him, absently rubbing a bruised wrist. "I wander around like I'm tweaked out. I go to Harnee's. I cook. I fuck. And one time I did something a whole lot worse than any of that."

"You fuck," Bel repeated, knowing this was a dangerous thing to fixate on. That maybe they ought to talk about what happened with Kenny, or possible solutions for Whitlock's problem, but Bel wanted to know about the fucking.

Whitlock's color deepened. "Yeah."

"In your sleep? That ain't possible."

"It is, and I've done it."

"How do you know?"

"People told me." Whitlock's mouth trembled for a second before his expression hardened again.

"You know you sound crazy, right?" Bel asked. "How do you know you're not just crazy?"

"I don't fucking know!" There was that deep, jagged pain in Whitlock's eyes again, a sort of brutal disappointment, like something he'd hoped for had fallen through. He closed his right hand around his left wrist. "If I ain't crazy naturally, I feel crazy from not sleeping. So maybe I am crazy. Maybe I fucking am!"

"All right, settle down," Bel said, in what Dav called his cop voice. The one that was authoritative, calm, and brooked no fucking argument.

Whitlock glared. "You done with me?"

"I told you I'm off duty. This ain't an interrogation."

"Feels like one."

Bel felt heat rise in him, a sort of frustrated, half-stifled rush of *want*. Not for Whitlock. Not just for Whitlock. A want for things to make sense. For Whitlock to make sense, for his own feelings to make sense. He felt his hand drifting toward Whitlock's, because he wanted to be the one covering those bruises, and he only just stopped himself in time. The heat was in his throat and face, in his groin and fingertips.

"It's not," Bel said fiercely, his voice low. He leaned toward Whitlock, using his height, his broad shoulders, wanting to see if Whitlock would pull back. "You do whatever you want."

Whitlock leaned forward and kissed him. Just a brush of his dry lips over Bel's, and a brief press of Whitlock's forehead against his own. His eyes closed as he leaned against Bel, and it was a moment he was only able to steal because Bel was too shocked to move away.

The kiss had been electric, not because of passion or lust or any of that bullshit, but because it left Bel stunned, his body shivering with a strange current, a fear, a *need*, an uncertainty. Whitlock opened his eyes. Bel looked right into them, finding flecks of gold and green in the brown, wishing he didn't have to decide what to do next, wishing his only job was to look at those colors.

"You awake right now?" Bel asked, only half-joking.

"Wide awake," Whitlock whispered, and there was an intensity and danger in his eyes different from what Bel had convinced himself he'd seen those nights at Harnee's. This expression was calculated, almost playful, and it dissolved quickly, replaced by a soft vulnerability that pulled at Bel. "Guess I am crazy."

Whitlock wasn't the only one.

Bel ripped off his seat belt, lunged forward, and kissed Whitlock hard to show him he wasn't crazy—not right now, not for doing this. Bel cupped Whitlock's face with one hand, his other finding the man's wrist. He held it gently, running his thumb over the veins in the back of Whitlock's hand.

Whitlock gave a little sigh into Bel's mouth. He tasted like the hospital. Bel didn't understand how that worked, just that there was a combination of sterility and staleness and bland food on Whitlock's breath, and it didn't bother Bel a bit. Whitlock pulled back slightly, his lips still parted. His inhale moved his whole body in a series of small jerks. He glanced down, and Bel didn't know what he was looking at, but then Bel looked down too and his gaze fell on the front of Whitlock's pants, the swell there. Bel's own cock was full, his breathing ragged.

They caught each other's lips again, and this time Bel lost track of how long they stayed in their awkward embrace, Bel's elbow digging hard into the console, Whitlock's seat belt scraping the side of his neck. Whitlock's breaths turned into whimpers, and Bel rode a surge of desire, running his hand down Whitlock's chest, feeling his heart pound through his shirt. He continued down, stopping at Whitlock's belt. Whitlock tangled a hand in Bel's hair and pulled.

Bel drew back. "Someone's gonna see."

"I don't care."

"Maybe you don't . . ." Bel was panting hard.

"But you got a reputation to keep," Whitlock said.

"I wanna . . ." But Bel couldn't finish.

Whitlock leaned back in his seat. Took a few deep breaths. "I'll go get my car."

"Tonight," Bel said, because he couldn't stop the words. "You gonna stay out in those woods? By yourself?"

Whitlock looked uncomfortable. "Who else would I stay out there with?"

Bel tried to quiet the voice that was jeering, *You kissed Daniel Whitlock. You kissed Daniel Whitlock, a murderer. A psychopath, and you kissed him.* "You could stay in town. The motel."

"I wanna go home."

"'Cause you gotta lock yourself up?"

"Yeah." Whitlock wouldn't look at him now.

"It ain't safe. You gotta know that, after what happened."

"It ain't safe for anyone else if I don't do it."

"I don't get it. How's it work? How do you get out in the morning?"

"There's ice in the locks. When it melts, I can open the lock and get the keys to the cuffs." Whitlock said it without inflection, staring out the windshield. "I've tried other ways, but that's the safest. If the keys are anywhere I can reach them, I get them in my sleep and unlock myself."

"Shit," Bel said.

"Yeah."

"How long's the ice take to melt?"

"Three hours. I set the alarm so I get up and let myself out."

"You telling me you get three hours of sleep a night? No wonder you feel crazy."

"Sometimes I put another set of locks in the freezer. So when I get up I can replace the locks and go back to sleep another couple hours."

Bel leaned back. "Hell. Hell, I'd kill myself."

"Thought about it. Or figured someone would do it for me. But I don't wanna die."

Bel turned his head. "No?"

"No. You think I ought to want to?"

"Think whatever you like. Want whatever you want. Ain't my business."

"Yeah." They both stared out the windshield.

Bel's lips still throbbed.

"I'll come by," Bel said. "Someone ought to be out there until we figure out who tried to torch your place."

Heat in his face again. Whitlock could probably tell it was bullshit. Not that it wasn't a good idea to have someone out at Kamchee, but Whitlock would know Bel was volunteering. That he hadn't been assigned or anything.

"Probably best if it's me out there," Bel continued. "'Cause I already know what you got to do to yourself. You probably don't want to have to explain it to anyone else. If something did happen, I mean, and whoever was on duty had to come in."

"You think anyone on your force could think worse of me than they do?"

"I'm just saying I understand it. And I could help you, maybe."

Whitlock turned to him. "First of all, you don't understand it. Not even a little. And second, help me? What the hell does that mean?"

"You wouldn't have to lock yourself up. If you tried to leave the cabin, I could stop you."

"And what if I got violent?" Whitlock shook his head. "I'm not gonna risk it."

"Hell, Whitlock, it's kinda my job to deal with people who get violent, ain't it?"

Whitlock shook his head more vehemently. "Even a meth head's got more sense than I do when it comes to knowing when to quit. If I'm asleep and you try to wake me up, I might fight and not stop."

"Then I'll take the keys. I'll keep 'em till morning, and I'll let you out. That way you can sleep as long as you want."

Whitlock swallowed. Rubbed his forehead. "What's in it for you? Don't you have a job?"

"My job's working on this investigation. So I reckon that includes keeping anyone from killing you."

"Or you think I'll fuck you once I'm asleep?"

"What the fuck, Whitlock? I stay in the car, and you stay in the cabin." Bel scowled. "Best offer you're gonna get, so maybe you might want to think about it before you call me a fucking rapist."

Whitlock shrugged. "Not rape. I'd ask you for it."

"You ask me for it when you got less sense than a meth head, I'm gonna say no."

"You'd be the first."

"What about Kenny?"

Why the fuck couldn't Bel keep his mouth shut? Low blow, no matter what Bel thought of Whitlock. Whitlock's jaw tightened and he took another breath before he answered. "Yeah. Guess I was s'posed to take that as a no." He reached for the door handle.

"Sorry." Bel's stomach clenched. "Shit. I'm sorry."

Whitlock opened the door.

"I'll be there tonight," Bel said.

"If you got your heart set on it," Whitlock muttered, climbing out and slamming the door behind him. He walked around to the back of the bar and disappeared.

Bel struck the wheel. Then he turned the key and put the Volvo in drive.

"Ain't you still on a day off?" Uncle Joe grumbled at Bel when he turned up at the station with coffee.

"Yep," Bel said. "You going out to talk to Clayton today?"

"Yep." Uncle Joe reached for his hat and rolled his eyes. "Come on, then, if you're coming."

Clayton lived about fifteen minutes out of town. His father grew soybeans. They had a spot on a bend in the river, a nice place. The original farmhouse was set further back. When Clayton was in high school, his folks used to let him have parties in the old house. Bel had been too young to warrant an invitation, but Billy had gone a few times, and so had Jim. Those weekend parties were the talk of the school, except Bel never did find out what went on there. Probably nothing but a bunch of kids drinking and making out. By the time Bel was old enough to be going to those sorts of parties, Clayton had long graduated and the high school kids were back to hanging out in Harnee's parking lot.

A couple of dogs bounded out to meet them as they pulled up at the house. Mrs. McAllister followed them to the cruiser.

"You here to talk to Clay?" she asked. Her face was drawn, old before its time like so many of the folk around the place. Wasn't the first time the police had come looking for Clayton because of Daniel Whitlock. "He's around back."

He was in a shed working on a tractor when they found him.

"Sheriff," he said, wiping his hands on his coveralls. "Officer Belman."

"Got a few questions for you, son," Uncle Joe said.

"This about Whitlock?"

"S'pose so. You wanna tell me where you were last night?"

"Just riding around town, you know."

"You have anyone with you?"

"Just R.J. and Brock."

"You go out to the Kamchee Woods?" Uncle Joe asked. "Maybe head out there to pay Whitlock a visit? Spook him a little?"

Or try to kill him. Bel kept his face impassive.

"No, sir."

"You threw cans at him the other night on Main," Bel said.

"There a law 'gainst that?"

"Littering," Uncle Joe said placidly.

Clayton stared at Bel. "You heard what he said to me."

"Yup. And I heard what you said to him," Bel replied.

"You keep any gasoline in your truck, Clayton?" Joe asked.

"Sure," Clayton said. "So's most everyone." He grinned. "Heard someone lit his place up. Serves him right."

Uncle Joe rubbed the side of his face. "Can't have people going around taking the law into their own hands, you understand?"

"Yes, Sheriff," Clayton said. "Maybe whoever done it wasn't really breaking the law. Maybe they was *sleepwalking.*"

"Maybe," Uncle Joe said, his face betraying nothing. But Bel, who'd known the man his whole life, knew that Uncle Joe was pissed. At Clayton and his smart mouth, at all this shit starting up again, and probably at Daniel Whitlock for daring to stand up in court and claim something as stupid as sleepwalking. Played everyone for a fool, that did. "Okay, Clayton. You think of anything, you let me know."

"I will, Sheriff," Clayton smirked.

Bel scowled at him and followed Uncle Joe back to the car.

"Lying asshole," Bel muttered as he slammed the door shut.

Uncle Joe looked across at him. "Well, of course he's lying. That's what people do, Little Joe. Cops ask 'em questions, and they lie."

Daniel Whitlock hadn't lied, Bel thought. Sounded like one though: *"I wander around like I'm tweaked out. I go to Harnee's. I cook. I fuck."* Bel rubbed his face, aware of the heat rising there. Is that why he'd kissed the guy? Because he was good-looking, and because he said he fucked? It had been months since Bel had gotten anything more than a hurried blowjob in a dark bathroom, and maybe the thought of Whitlock wandering around town looking to get laid was too much. All of Whitlock's crazy sleepwalking shit aside, why did picturing him chained up on a bed also feel like a damned invitation?

Here I am. Do what you want. I can't stop you.

"So, on Main the other night," Uncle Joe said. "Anything that didn't make it into your patrol log?"

"No. It was Clayton who started it." Bel filled Uncle Joe in on what had happened. Didn't add the part about Whitlock apparently waking up in his car. Definitely didn't add what he and Whitlock had done in his car this morning.

Bel stared at the rows of soybeans as Uncle Joe drove back toward the main road. "When . . . when Whitlock got bashed, did you see him?"

"Yeah." Uncle Joe sighed. "Real mess."

"Maybe if Kenny had gone to jail for that, maybe he'd still be alive." And maybe Whitlock would be a victim then. Not blameless, not exactly, since he'd been the one who came on to Kenny, and everyone knew what Kenny was like—but not a killer either.

"Maybe," Uncle Joe said. "Except Whitlock refused to say what happened." Bel looked at him and Uncle Joe grimaced. "I know what you're thinking, but it wasn't like that."

Bel had seen it before in action. The way the cops talked people around. Hell, he'd done it himself. *If you want to make a complaint, I'll do that for you. You're gonna have to come in and make a statement, maybe more than one. Then you'll have to go to court. Don't know how long that will take, and he'll probably only get a fine. You want to think about it for a bit? We can always do it later.*

Only for small stuff, Bel told himself, for bullshit complaints. But who was he to judge that? Wasn't so crazy to imagine someone would have thought Daniel Whitlock's bashing was a bullshit complaint.

Uncle Joe shook his head. "You think I wanted to let those boys get away with bashing Whitlock? I don't give a good goddamn that Whitlock's a f—that Whitlock's gay. If those boys had smacked him in the mouth for what he did, fair enough, but it was beyond that. Way fucking beyond that."

Bel nodded.

"Was the prosecutor who wouldn't touch it, not without a complaint. Not in an election year." Uncle Joe shook his head and turned onto the road back into Logan. "So, that truck you saw last night?"

"What about it?"

"You sure you didn't get a look at it?"

"I already—" Bel clamped his mouth shut. Had a sudden feeling that wasn't what Uncle Joe was really asking, and didn't know how to respond. Wondered how sure he'd have to be that it was Clayton before he lied about it under oath. Wondered if it was something he could ever feel comfortable with, even if he *knew* it was Clayton.

"Well, maybe it will come to you," Uncle Joe suggested after a while.

"Yeah," Bel said, his heart thumping. "Maybe."

They didn't talk the rest of the way back.

Daniel was trying to choke down a late dinner when Belman arrived. He heard the gravel crunch in the drive and shoveled down the last few bites of his cereal, then put the bowl in the sink and hurried outside. "Hey," he said when Belman got out of the car. He tried not to sound too enthusiastic.

He's not here to pick you up for prom, asshole. He's here to watch you chain yourself to your bed and then sit in your driveway and make sure you don't try to murder anyone.

Not to mention that the last thing Belman had said to him was that awful comment about Kenny Cooper. Yet here was Daniel bounding out to greet him like a dog.

Belman nodded. "Hey."

"You can come in." Daniel moved back as Belman stepped onto the porch. He was a couple of inches taller than Daniel, and his shoulders were wider. Daniel liked that. Belman looked like a man with real power. Not a Kenny Cooper—overweight but still strong, too fucking strong—or a stringy rat like Clayton McAllister. Belman didn't have to *try* to look tough. Daniel held the screen door for him and followed him inside. "It's, uh . . . not the cleanest."

Idiot. Yeah, the whole almost-burned-down thing made a bit of a mess.

He watched Belman gaze around the room.

"I have your bolt cutters." Daniel picked them up.

"Thanks." Belman took them, still glancing around. "Cold in here." His gaze fell on the AC unit. Fifty-seven degrees.

"Yeah. Sorry. Guess I'm used to it. Keep it pretty cold in here. The ice melts slower."

Belman didn't say anything.

"So, uh." Daniel shifted. "I'll just change, and then I got some spare cuffs, and . . ." Just like that, Daniel was rigid with fear. Couldn't hardly breathe. Because what if Belman was playing him? What if he meant to drive off with the keys, leave Daniel chained to the bed? A sick practical joke.

Fuck. He'd been so stupid.

"What's wrong?" Belman asked.

Daniel's throat was dry.

Belman wouldn't. He could lose his job.

He's off duty. And who would blame him for doing it? The other cops would probably love it.

"Whitlock?"

Daniel turned. "I need you to promise me something," he said fiercely, trying to keep his voice from shaking.

"What?" Belman asked.

"Promise me you're staying."

"Staying?"

"Out there, till morning. That you're not leaving, even for a little while. It might seem funny to you, but it won't be funny to me, and if you're gonna do anything like that, then just go home. I'll use the ice locks."

Belman stared at him. The kind of look you gave a crazy person.

"How do you know you're not just crazy?"

"Maybe I am."

"I'm not going anywhere, Whitlock. I'll be right outside." Belman wasn't smirking. He just looked a little confused.

Daniel closed his eyes for a moment. "Thank you." He grabbed a pair of flannel pants and a T-shirt from his closet, trying not to feel self-conscious. "You want a drink or anything?"

"What happened to your feet?" Belman asked by way of response.

Daniel glanced down. His feet were still cut up from his walk from Master Beau's. Daniel hadn't checked his email since the fire. He wondered if Master Beau even cared what had happened to him. "Took a walk."

He hurried to the bathroom with his sleep clothes and shut the door. Changed quickly. Brushed his teeth. Grabbed a pair of leather cuffs out of the bag under the sink, plus a combination padlock. Took them out to the main room. Belman was standing next to the bed. Daniel swallowed, ducked his head, and walked over. He'd walked that way to Marcus sometimes, head bowed, flogger or ropes or paddle in hand. He set the cuffs and lock on the night table.

"I'll just . . ." Daniel pulled back the covers and swung into bed, pulling the comforter quickly over his body, as though he were naked.

"All right." Belman picked up the lock. It was brand-new, still in the package.

"Combination's on the back. Don't tell me what it is. Just hold on to it."

"There's no key?"

Daniel glanced at him. "No. You can let me out in the morning using the combination."

That way if Belman left, Daniel still had a chance. It might take a while to try every possible combination, but Daniel would eventually get out.

Daniel held still while Belman put the cuffs around his bruised wrists and locked them. He worked quickly, efficiently, as though he was afraid of letting his hands linger on Daniel any longer than necessary. He held on to the package with the combination on it. Set Daniel's phone within reach. "You text me when you wake up tomorrow. I'll come in and let you out."

"All right," Daniel said. He tried not to look at Belman. If he looked at Belman, he'd think about kissing him. If he thought about kissing him, he'd remember how pissed he ought to be at him. His cock stirred, and he shut his eyes.

"Whitlock?" Belman's voice was soft but still gruff.

Daniel opened his eyes. "Huh?"

"Sleep well."

Daniel almost laughed. "Thanks."

Belman turned off the light and clomped back out onto the porch. He shut the door behind him. And Daniel lay there alone, trying to get to sleep.

Bel had been on plenty of stakeouts before, but none of them quite like this. For starters, he was off duty, alone, and missed having someone to talk to. And usually the person he was watching didn't know he was being watched. And usually Bel wasn't imagining that person chained to a bed.

Bel tried to think about something besides Whitlock chained to the bed. He glanced at the empty passenger seat next to him and remembered Whitlock there, the feel of Whitlock's lips against his, Whitlock's soft whimpers. The heat of his breath. Fuck, he was gonna have to sit here all night with a hard-on if he kept this up. He had to think about something besides Whitlock. He started texting Dav, not telling her where he was, and they got into a discussion about some show they both liked, and that killed some time.

Near midnight, he took a walk to stretch his legs and take a piss.

Something rustled in the undergrowth nearby, and Bel shone his flashlight around but didn't see anything.

He sat on the hood of his car and stargazed for a while. He'd always liked that. Peaceful.

Got back in the car when he found himself staring too much at cabin, thinking about the cuffs around Whitlock's wrists.

Listened to some talk-back radio until it pissed him off. Went searching for music instead.

Around 1 a.m., Bel's phone buzzed. He looked at it, and his breath caught. It was like a horror movie—a text from Whitlock.

Why's that so weird? He's not dead, he's sleeping. Or supposed to be.

Bel looked at the text. It read: *Jeksfeiejkdd.*

Bel glanced at the dark cabin. Was it possible Whitlock was texting in his sleep?

Another text minutes later: *,sfn,jflemewm!!!*

Belman was troubled by the exclamation points. Were they intentional? Was Whitlock trying to ask for help? Belman looked at the cabin again. Whitlock wasn't screaming or anything. Belman didn't want to go into the guy's house without being asked.

A third text read: *ssselspsss Hel!*

Another exclamation point. And *Hel*, which could have been an attempt at either *help* or *Bel*.

Except Whitlock didn't call him Bel. Did he? Bel didn't know how Whitlock thought of him.

In the next few minutes he received a barrage of texts, none of them particularly coherent. Bel finally got out of the car, walked quietly to the porch, opened the screen, and rapped on the door. No answer. He turned the knob and pushed it open. Whitlock was lying facing the door, his eyes glinting in the darkness. Bel flipped on the lamp. Whitlock blinked. The expression on his face wasn't one Bel could read. Whitlock clutched his phone in one fist.

"Did you need me?" Bel demanded.

Whitlock didn't answer.

"Whitlock? You awake?"

Nothing.

"You been texting me. I thought you needed something. Or I wouldn't have come in." Bel stood awkwardly by the door.

"I need you," Whitlock said breathily. He jerked on the cuffs. Arched his back and raised his hips. He dropped the phone onto the mattress and grinned. "I'm glad you came in. Was getting lonely."

Jesus. Bel couldn't look at Whitlock sprawled on the bed like that, arms flexed, hips rolling, erection clear through his flannel pants. He looked away. "Now what'd I tell you? We're not doing any of that."

Whitlock gave a quiet chuckle. "We can. You want to, don't you? You kissed me. *Officer*."

Just like that first night. Cocky, unashamed. *Hot as fuck.*

Irritating as fuck.

"Whitlock!"

Irritating because Bel couldn't have him.

Whitlock laughed. "C'mon, *Officer Belman*. Lay down the *law*." He jerked the cuffs again, and the chains jingled. "Let me out, and I'll do something good for you."

"Daniel!"

Whitlock stilled. Lowered his hips onto the bed. Stared wide-eyed at the ceiling.

What the fuck?

"Daniel," Bel tried again, calmer. Didn't know why he was using Whitlock's first name, but hell, maybe it'd get through to him quicker. No response.

"You awake now?"

Nothing.

"You hear me? I need to know if you hear me."

Whitlock—Daniel—slowly raised a cuffed hand as high as it would go and pointed at something. "Look there."

Bel looked. Daniel appeared to be pointing to a soot stain by the busted window.

"Look there," Daniel repeated.

"I see it," Bel said, not sure if he was irritated or freaked out or both. How the hell did he know if Daniel was asleep or awake? He glanced at Daniel again and saw that his eyes were wet. That his jaw and throat were tight but quivering with the effort of staying quiet.

Shit. Bel definitely hadn't signed on for this. What the hell was Whitlock *crying* about? He should have stayed in the car. Daniel had managed sleeping chained to his bed alone for years, hadn't he?

Exactly why you shouldn't leave.

Bel glanced back at the stained wall. "That's seen better days, hasn't it?"

Daniel gave a soft sob. "Yeah."

"I guess we all have." Bel was afraid to look at him.

To his surprise, Daniel laughed. He looked, and Daniel was still crying, but he was trying to smile as well. "I guess we have."

Bel lowered himself into the chair. "You awake?"

"I don't know."

"You don't know, huh?" Bel kept the words soft, resigned. He put his elbows on his knees and clasped his hands.

Daniel's tears had stopped, and now he was smiling. Not the wicked, seductive grin of a few minutes ago, but an artless, beautiful smile. His smile stretched into a yawn, and Bel could see into his mouth, where two of Daniel's back left molars were absent.

"You got a couple of teeth missing," Bel said. A flash of anger he couldn't place, draining away to sadness.

"Yeah." Daniel's smile waned, but he still looked content. Peaceful. Bel couldn't help smiling a little too.

Ain't nobody in Logan knows what kind of freak show's going on here.

"You need anything?" Bel asked. "Before I head back to the car?"

"You can stay in here," Daniel said. Nothing suggestive about this invitation. It was earnest. "More comfortable, maybe?"

"You want me to stay?"

Daniel looked slightly fearful. "Please?"

Bel studied him. "You awake now, Whitlock?"

Daniel tensed. "Yes," he whispered.

"You're gonna go back to sleep, though." Bel shifted in the chair so he could reach the lamp. "I'm gonna turn off the light, and I'll be right here, and you'll go to sleep, okay?"

"Yes, sir."

Whoa. What the fuck? Bel'd been called sir plenty, and his cock had never reacted like this. He sat there like he'd been punched, willing the sensation, the heat, to subside. Two words, so soft, and Daniel's eyes, wide and a little nervous, and those chains that shouldn't fucking be there, because no one should have to sleep chained like a dog, but that looked so good on him. And Bel—maybe there was something Bel could do. Maybe that something was just being here, being here with someone who'd been alone too long. Maybe it was just switching off the lamp and saying, "Good night, Daniel."

And hearing the answering inhale in the darkness.

CHAPTER FIVE

For the first time in a long while, Daniel didn't flinch when he saw a police car. He was feeling better, sleeping better, and it was all down to Belman. Sooner or later the guy would get sick of spending his nights watching over him, or they'd catch whoever had tried to burn down the cabin, but until then, it was good. Yeah, he was a grown man who needed a babysitter, but this was the best he'd been in years. Even Rylan Davenport said so when he went for his appointment at the parole office.

"You're looking good, Daniel," she said.

"Thank you, ma'am."

He liked Ms. Davenport. She never gave him any trouble as long as he didn't give her any either.

"How's the job going?"

"It's okay," Daniel said. Cleaning the library in the evenings was hardly difficult work, but it kept him active and it kept him from being a total shut-in. Also, Belman had taken to stopping by if he was patrolling, just sitting in his car in the parking lot under the light where Daniel could see it was him. Waved sometimes before he left again. Felt a little less like a babysitter, and a little more like a friend.

Closest thing Daniel had anyway.

"I heard about your cabin," Ms. Davenport said.

"Smoke damage mostly. Those old cabins, the logs are thick as anything. Fire didn't really take. Lost the front windows, but everything else is good."

It still stank of smoke, but he was getting used to that. He'd scrubbed the walls, washed all his bedding and clothes. Used a whole can of air freshener, and guessed that time would take care of the rest.

"You're lucky Bel was there that night."

"Yes, ma'am." And every night since. Four of them so far. Sitting out front in his car, watching over the place. Watching over Daniel.

Ms. Davenport gave him a look he couldn't read, and then smiled. "So, have you thought about what we talked about before? Applying for other jobs?"

"No." Daniel fidgeted. "I do okay at the library. I do a good job. Why? Has someone complained?"

Probably that bitch Trixie. He knew she was the one who'd taped the box of matches to the door of the janitor's storeroom because of the way she looked at him after he'd seen. Thought she was hot shit just because she'd gotten a job in the town library, when back in school she could hardly string a coherent sentence together and had spent most of the day painting her nails. So nothing had changed there.

"Because you're a—" She looked at her computer. "A chemistry major. Not a cleaner." She lifted her coffee cup to her mouth.

"Well, the only call for my qualifications around here would be setting up some toothless redneck's meth lab," Daniel said before he could stop himself.

Ms. Davenport grimaced, clapped a hand over her mouth, audibly gulped, and finally burst out laughing. "Oh shit, Daniel! I almost spat that all over my keyboard!"

"Sorry," he smiled.

Ms. Davenport cleared her throat. "Anyway, you could do a lot better than cleaning."

"Yeah, I don't think that's true," Daniel said, his smile vanishing. "Not in this town."

Ms. Davenport shrugged. "Well, you're not going to be stuck in Logan for much longer. Once you're finished with me, you can go wherever you want."

Daniel looked down at the scuffed carpet. "I don't think that's true either, really."

"What do you mean?"

"Where could I go? Tried it before, and it didn't work out. I barely graduated because my grades were so bad. Messed up the only job I got offered, messed up a relationship, and came running back here. And we all know how that turned out."

"Listen, Daniel, can I be frank with you?"

He cringed inwardly. "Yes, ma'am."

"Okay," Ms. Davenport said. "I like you."

Daniel raised his eyebrows. He hadn't been expecting that. Mostly when people wanted to be frank with him, it was to tell him he should be dead.

"Most of the people who show up here, I know I'm going to see them again because they're drunks, or they're addicts, or they're just too plain stupid to go straight. But you're not like them. You can actually make something of yourself if you want to." She frowned at him. "Once we're done, I don't want to see you in this office again."

Daniel didn't know what to say. He fought against the stab of fear at not seeing Ms. Davenport anymore. She was the only person in Logan who'd talked to him like he was a goddamn human being, until Bel.

And it felt so fucking strange to have someone believe in him in some tangible way, after so long, that Daniel couldn't even manage a polite thank-you. Just stared at her, openmouthed, waiting for her to take it back. He wondered if this was really happening at all. Maybe he'd dozed off in the waiting room, and this was all a crazy fucking dream. He was probably at Greenducks right about now, with his hands down Jake Kebbler's jeans. And that thought was a hell of a lot less disconcerting than whatever this was.

"In the meantime," Ms. Davenport said, "keep doing whatever it is you're doing. You look better than I've seen you in a long time. Ever, probably."

Daniel flushed. "Yes, ma'am."

"See you next week," she said with a smile.

After his appointment with Ms. Davenport, Daniel drove the four blocks over to the library. He usually sat in his car until the place closed and waited until everyone had left, then took his keys from the glove compartment and let himself in.

He still had an hour to kill today, and it was hot inside his car. He got out, locked it, and decided to walk down the block to Harnee's. Get a bottle of water, even though he wanted something with enough sugar in it to rot his teeth from ten paces. He didn't eat junk food when he was awake, because he figured he was better off detoxing while his conscious brain was in control. Once, he'd woken up at college and found himself surrounded by empty pizza boxes. Wouldn't have believed he could eat so much until he was vomiting it up later.

He remembered Belman from his trial. Not a cop then, just the kid from the store. *"He would come in most nights and always get the same thing. Mountain Dew and a Twix."*

And, that one night, a lighter.

Daniel waited before crossing the road. There was a car he could have beaten, but half the time he didn't know if they would speed up or not. Sometimes they did, to scare him. He waited until it had passed before crossing.

At Harnee's, he took a bottle of water from the fridge, then stood awhile in front of the magazine rack. Tits and guns. And quilting. He probably had a paperback in his car somewhere, something to tide him over until he went into work. Of course, he could always just walk in when the place was open and take a book off the stacks. Except it wasn't worth the stares and the whispers.

He picked up a woodworking magazine and flipped through a few pages. There was a project on making mailboxes, which might be useful. He put it back anyway. Didn't matter if he made a new mailbox or not. Sooner or later it'd end up busted on the road. Most likely sooner.

He headed for the registers.

"Daniel!" A sharp intake of breath.

The sound of her voice was like a slap to the face.

"Casey." A meaningless word. A hollow sound.

She clutched her plastic basket to her chest and stared.

Daniel felt the overwhelming urge to apologize. For being here. For seeing her. For ruining her afternoon as surely as he'd ruined every other part of her life. "Wh-what are you doing back in town?"

She didn't answer.

"I just came in to get a drink."

She looked at the bottle in his hands as though she was trying to pick a lie from his words.

"You hear about the cabin?"

She nodded once.

"I'll fix it up," Daniel said. "I will, I promise. Make it nice again. You remember—"

She took a step back.

You remember when we used to go out there as kids, Casey? How we told scary stories about the watchers in the woods, how we held hands so we felt brave?

Everything was slipping away now. He could feel it. Belman's kindness, Ms. Davenport's strange belief in him; it all melted away under his sister's stare, and he remembered what he was. Dangerous. Crazy. A killer.

And whatever he did, however hard he tried, nothing would change that.

"Casey," he said, because it had been so long since he'd said the word. It threatened to break something inside him that Daniel didn't know could be broken again.

"I have to go," Casey said.

She put her basket down in the middle of the aisle and walked out the door.

Daniel stood there, arms at his side, trying to remember how to breathe.

Took a while.

When he could move again, he stepped over Casey's basket and went and paid for his water. The kid behind the counter didn't even look at him, but afterward, just as he stepped out the doors, Daniel heard him say "faggot freak," and the girl on the register next to his giggled.

Daniel stared at the ground as he walked back to the library, counting cigarette butts and beer cans.

"Hold my hand," Casey had whispered to him when they were little. *"Don't let go!"*

His throat hurt. He wanted to cry.

Fall break, he realized. Casey was probably in town to visit friends.

He climbed back into his car and sat there. Held the water bottle against his forehead until the cold gave him a headache. He watched as the staff left the library, then he headed inside.

When he was a kid, he'd loved the library. Thought it must've had every book in the world, except really it was just a couple of rooms of books, the small lobby, and the meeting room with the stained carpet. The stacks smelled a little of mildew. The Logan town library had the same books it had always had. Sometimes Daniel dug around in the tubs in the children's section and pulled out the picture books he'd loved. Sat on the floor and read them, and, if he dared close his eyes, could hear his mother's voice in his head. Not sharp. Soft and mellow. Filled with love. And Casey's giggle, bubbling up from her like it was overflowing.

He'd never have that again.

Daniel got the floor polisher out of the storeroom and plugged it in. He worked quickly, to keep his mind off Casey, and because he wanted to be home before too late, to meet Belman.

He trusted Belman.

Belman. Bel? *Joe?* That didn't sound right.

Everyone called him Bel, except Daniel, who'd managed to avoid calling him anything at all. At school he'd been Joe, Little Joe to some. Daniel guessed he'd always just thought of him as the youngest Belman kid. He'd known Billy better back then. Shared a chem class. And once, Mr. Sherman had made them lab partners. Lasted about a week. Daniel was serious about chemistry, and Billy Belman was more interested in drawing pictures of girls with exaggerated tits in the margins of his textbook and making fart jokes.

Billy had never been mean to him, but he was still one of the reasons that Daniel had been desperate to get out of Logan. Small town full of small minds. But so much for that escape plan. What he was chasing, what he needed, wasn't out there any more than it was here. For now he had Belman. After that, he didn't know.

Daniel's phone buzzed in his back pocket, and he turned off the floor polisher and reached for it. Shit. A message from Master Beau.

U gonna pussy out next time, slave? Gonna fuck u so hard you can't run.

Daniel stared at it for a long time, wondering how to respond.

Because when Belman was gone . . .

When Belman was gone, he'd have nobody.

He put his phone back without replying. Didn't want to see Master Beau again, but he also needed to keep his options open. He didn't have many left.

Bel jolted awake as the text message came through from Daniel. *Ftckme hhrd*. Which had to be some kind of a test. Maybe the text message equivalent of a Rorschach test, or a test from God. Because yeah, Bel knew exactly what he wanted it to say. And he wanted to go right into the cabin and *ftck* him. *Hhrd*. Daniel wanted it too, didn't he? Except to acknowledge that he wanted this, this thing that had come from his deep subconscious, Bel had to acknowledge that Daniel had wanted Kenny Cooper to die as well.

Earlier at work, he'd pulled the file. Not from the fire, but from Daniel's bashing. There'd been no complaint, just like Uncle Joe had said, but the initial report from the hospital was in there. So were the photographs.

Kenny, Clayton, and their buddies had fucked Daniel up real bad. Busted up some bones, and cracked his jaw so hard that he'd lost those two back molars. The photographs had been taken the day after the assault, and Daniel's face was so swollen and bruised, it looked like a lump of moldy dough.

Looking at what they'd done, it was easy to imagine that Daniel had wanted Kenny to die. Hell, Bel wished he was alive just so he could kill him himself. But you didn't do that. You wished it, but you didn't do it.

He got out of the car and walked up to the cabin. Place still smelled burned. He stuck his head around the door. "You texting me again, Whitlock?"

The moonlight streamed through the door and around the canvas that Daniel had nailed up over the busted windows. He was lying on his bed, his body bathed in it. All long, lean lines and silver planes.

"Hey, Harnee's kid."

Bel rolled his eyes. "I don't work there no more, Whitlock."

Daniel laughed, a low, breathy sound. "No, I know that. Want you to fuck me so I can't run."

"No, you really don't."

"Yeah." Daniel twisted his body. "Come on, please, Marcus."

That hit Bel like a bucket of cold water. "You want Marcus?"

"Yeah," Daniel said. "Not some fucking hillbilly. I want Marcus. You can do it right, Marcus. How I need it."

Well fuck. That hurt more than it should.

"Am I a hillbilly?" Bel asked.

"You got no right to call yourself a master."

Bel shook his head. "I got no idea what you're talking about, Whitlock."

"I'll try and come, Marcus, I promise."

Shit. Bel knew he shouldn't ask, but he couldn't stop himself. "You don't always come?"

"Gonna try." Daniel slumped back down onto the mattress and was silent for a long while. When he spoke again, his voice was softer. "Gonna fix this place up."

"Yeah, that's about the only good idea you've had so far."

Daniel smiled at him in the moonlight. "I'm caught up here. Help me out?"

"How are you caught up?"

The cuffs rattled on the bars of the bed frame. "I need to piss, man, real bad."

"You still sleeping?"

"I need to piss."

Bel studied him. Might be a trap. If he unlocked him, would Daniel try to leave? Would he fight if Bel tried to stop him? Bel figured he could take Daniel, if it came to that. He could bring him down safely.

"If I let you up to piss, you gonna come right back in here and go to bed?"

Like Daniel was a child. Jesus, that about killed Bel's hard-on. Except the way Daniel arched, eager, his breath coming faster, brought it right back. "Yeah," Daniel said. "Promise."

Bel sighed. Daniel had made him promise not to unlock him for any reason. But Bel wasn't gonna sit here and deny the guy the right to use the bathroom. He got up and walked over to the bed. Daniel looked up at him. That face—so hopeful and anxious. Daniel Whitlock could give Stump a few pointers.

Bel turned on the lamp so he could see to put the combination in. The padlock clicked open, and he set it aside. Daniel swung his legs carefully over the side of the bed. His erection was tenting the front of his pants. Bel watched him pad across the room to the bathroom, told himself to look somewhere besides Daniel's ass, but what was the point in even trying? Daniel didn't close the bathroom door all the way, and Bel listened to him piss—good Lord, he hadn't been kidding about needing to go—then flush, then wash his hands.

He didn't come out straightaway, and Bel started to get nervous. "Whitlock?" he called.

He heard the scrape and knock of a cabinet opening and closing. Then a muffled thud.

"What are you doing?" His hand went to his holster. Shit, what if Whitlock had a weapon?

The bathroom door slowly creaked open. Bel stood there, ready to draw if necessary. Daniel came out carrying a large shoulder bag. He crossed the room, his eyes on the floor, then went to his knees in front of Bel. He set the bag down. Pressed his forehead gently against Bel's right leg.

"What's that, Whitlock?" Bel asked, tensing at the contact. He didn't know if he wanted to jerk away or grab Daniel's hair and push his face onto his dick. "What are you doing?"

Daniel unzipped the bag. "You can use anything in here." He drew out something that reminded Bel of a giant lollipop, the head glinting in the moonlight. Bel took it. A paddle, he realized, looking at the holes drilled in it. And a fucking heavy one. Made of some kind of metal. Probably aluminum, and cold just like the room. Bel tried to imagine hitting someone with it. He was embarrassed by the way his cock swelled, because there shouldn't have been anything hot about this.

"That," Daniel said, handing Bel another paddle. This one was longer and made of wood, but the surface had a rubber tread on it, like a tire.

Jesus.

Daniel pulled out a strap next. Thick and wide and well-worn. He set it at Bel's feet. Scooted the bag closer to Bel. "Anything." He didn't look up.

"You want me to use this shit on you?" Bel still couldn't quite believe it. Though maybe he shouldn't be surprised. Whitlock was a fucking hazard—to everyone in Logan, including himself.

"Yes, sir."

"This what Marcus did to you?"

A nod.

"And you . . ." Bel didn't know what to ask. "You like it?"

No response.

Bel slapped the aluminum paddle against his hand. Daniel flinched but still didn't look at him. Didn't move.

Bel sighed. "Get up, Daniel."

Daniel held position. "Make me."

"We're not doing this tonight." *Tonight*? How about *ever*?

Daniel, kneeling on the floor with his knees spread and his back bowed, breathed heavily. An occasional twitch ran through him, his shirt rippling. "Can I stay like this?"

"You . . ." Bel's mouth was dry. "You need to get back to bed."

"Not tired. Make me tired."

Bel leaned down and took Daniel by the wrists, drawing him to his feet. "You must be tired, Daniel, you're sleeping."

"Am I?" He smiled at Bel, then his gaze drifted over Bel's shoulder. The smile vanished. "Look."

Bel twisted his head and stared at the front wall. "What?"

"Fire," Daniel whispered.

"Yeah." Bel walked him back toward the bed. "There was a fire. It's gone now."

"My hands." Daniel raised them, looking at his palms. "My hands are burned."

"They're not."

Daniel pulled back, shoving his hands under his armpits. He hugged his body, looking around the cabin furtively. "My hands hurt."

"You're sleeping, Daniel. You're dreaming it."

"My hands hurt," Daniel repeated. "There's fire in the walls. Washin' down like water. Didn't know it would do that."

"You're sleeping," Bel told him again, and reached out to grab him.

Daniel moved quickly. Threw a punch that Bel barely had time to block, and then he was . . . *fuck*, he was going for Bel's utility belt. Bel got a hand on his gun first, pushed it down into the holster the way he'd been taught, because if some nutjob was going for your firearm you had to get between them.

"Daniel!"

The guy could scrap, that was for sure. His hands were on Bel's, trying to lift his fingers, trying to get the gun. Bel lifted an elbow without even thinking and caught him right in the chin. Heard his jaw snap, and shoved him back. Fast and hard.

Daniel fell onto the bed, and Bel stood over him panting.

Fuck. Crazy.

Bel grabbed Daniel's right arm and cuffed it. No quiet trusting look in Daniel's eyes now. He struggled this time, twisting like a wet cat and spitting out curses. Bel got a knee on his chest and leaned over him to cuff his left wrist.

"Settle the fuck down," he ordered, straightening. "You ain't going nowhere."

Daniel bucked and thrashed.

Crazy fucker.

Bel went back outside, slamming the door of the cabin behind him.

Daniel woke up to Belman unfastening his cuffs. His jaw ached. The whole side of his face ached. He squinted in the early morning light, expecting to see Belman's uncomfortable smile. Got a frown instead.

Daniel sat up, carefully touching the side of his face. "What did—"

Shit.

Why were his paddles all over the floor?

He leaped off the bed and hurried over to shove them in his bag. "Were you going through my stuff?"

"No," Belman said. "I let you up for a piss, and you came back and told me you wanted me to use that weird shit on you."

Daniel burned with embarrassment. "I used to . . ." He closed his eyes. "When I was in school, I ran track. Trained like hell, every day, because it tired me out. In college, I didn't have time for that. But this one guy, he used to, used to do this stuff, and it kinda worked for a while."

"Marcus," Belman said.

"Yeah."

"But you didn't get off on all that."

Hell, Daniel should've known better than to think he had secrets. "Not like I was supposed to."

Belman's face was expressionless. "That where you got the idea for all this stuff?"

"Yeah. Doesn't work so good on my own though."

"I don't even know what half that shit is."

Daniel's hand shook as he zipped the bag closed. "The usual stuff."

"Usual for what?"

Daniel looked up sharply. "I don't expect you to get it, but he kept me under control, and it was *good*. Because for once I could wake up the next morning and not have to ask what the fuck I'd done, okay?"

"You do a lot of crazy shit, before Kenny?"

Daniel shrugged. "Yeah, enough. Never hurt anyone though, that I know of."

"That you know of," Belman repeated.

Daniel shoved the bag under the bed and stood. It hurt to move in front of Belman. Not physically, just . . . Hurt to think about what Belman knew about him. He'd come to love Belman's visits, which was incredibly pathetic. Shit, Daniel could remember being sixteen and investing all his effort in an online friendship with some kid from Texas because he didn't have anyone in his real life to talk to. This was sadder: some cop barely old enough to drink, who wasn't his friend, who only barely tolerated Daniel because it was his job to.

Who kissed me.

And you think that's ever gonna happen again, now that he knows?

"I better get goin'," Belman said.

Daniel nodded.

"I'll see you tonight."

Still?

Something like hope burned inside Daniel's chest. He fought to keep it out of his voice. "See you, then. Sorry about . . . about last night."

"Yeah," Belman said brusquely.

He left, and Daniel sat on the edge of the bed for a long time, trying not to think anything.

Finally he got up, dragged the bag out from under the bed, unzipped it, and dumped its contents onto the floor.

He threw the wooden paddle first, and it cracked against the soot-stained windowsill. Didn't break, though, so Daniel had to retrieve it and swing it against his ancient dresser a few times until the head snapped off. Then he sawed the leather strap against the edge of the trunk at the foot of his bed. He used his teeth, too, trying to tear the leather apart. He stomped on clothespins and hurled plugs against the wall. Why'd he keep this shit around anyway? Wasn't like Marcus was coming back.

He threw the broken paddle in the trash, and the mangled strap. Walked outside, intent on hurling the aluminum paddle into the woods. Hesitated. Drew back and struck his own ass with it. Fuck, the thing hurt. You didn't need another person swinging it to make it hurt. The aluminum was heavy, and Daniel could feel the ache deep down in his muscles. He hit himself again.

Asshole. You let him see. You showed him.

Daniel flung the paddle as far as he could, watching it land in the ivy that pooled around the trees.

You ruined it.

Ruined what? What was there to ruin?

Daniel walked back inside, stepping on the scattered clothespins again, kicking the straitjacket tangled on the floor. He picked up a nearby plug, pulled down his pants, and inserted it dry. His eyes watered at the burn, but he gritted his teeth and sat on the bed again.

You let him see.

You ruined it.

"You doin' all right?" Uncle Joe asked Bel.

Bel was in the station parking lot, leaning against his cruiser, and choking down some god-awful coffee. He could barely stay awake, and he blamed Daniel Whitlock. Blamed Daniel Whitlock and his own stupidity in promising Daniel he'd look out for him at night. What, was he gonna do this until Daniel was too geriatric to wander out of the house in his sleep?

It's just until we find the guy who set the fire.

Until we prove Clayton set the damn fire.

He thought about Daniel last night. *"My hands hurt."*

Sleepwalking didn't make you schizoid, did it? And yet Daniel seemed to see shit, hear shit that wasn't real. What was that about? Just part of being unconscious—you slipped into some kind of twisted nightmare world where your hands burned and you wanted someone to beat the shit out of you?

"Don't want to go under," Daniel had said, that first night in the hospital.

Bel couldn't do a damn thing to keep him from going wherever he went.

Bel thought about the pictures from Daniel's file. A face that wasn't even a face. Missing teeth. Broken bones.

Bel could look at those pictures and try to imagine the pain, but he couldn't begin to imagine the anger and the fear. Maybe that was what had stayed with Daniel, long after the swelling went down, the scars sealed split skin, and the bones mended. Stayed locked so deep under Daniel's conscious thoughts that maybe Daniel could almost believe he'd beaten them.

"'M all right," he told Uncle Joe.

Tired as fuck from babysitting a psycho. But all right.

"Be better if it wasn't so muggy," he added.

"Feels like summer," Joe agreed. He leaned against the hood of the cruiser next to Bel. "Wanted to talk to you about last night. The trailer park?"

Bel nodded. "Diggler radioed, but I was out near Kamchee."

"You patrol 601 at night."

"Yep. But I been swinging by Whitlock's cabin once a shift." Didn't say how long he'd been staying. "Just until we got someone nailed for the fire."

"Needed someone at the park last night. That eight-year-old kid who ended up with a busted face? Four stitches."

"Logan's two foot across. It was just bad timing. I got there as soon as I could, and I bet there was at least a couple guys coulda got there even sooner."

"You bet, huh?"

"Wasn't Avery out by First Baptist and the drive-in? He coulda been there in five minutes."

"Ain't the first time this week someone's radioed and you haven't responded right away." Uncle Joe cocked a brow. "You wanna tell me what's going on?"

Bel downed some more coffee. "Not really."

"Stay on your assigned patrol then. All right? I'll have Day make a pass through Kamchee tonight. His territory's closer."

Bel didn't look at Joe. *Fuck no.* He needed to be out there. Not Day. Had to stop himself from saying it out loud. The vehemence of his reaction surprised him, even if he was a little relieved. *Might not be a bad idea to take a break from Daniel.* "All right," he made himself say.

"All right." Joe patted the hood of Bel's cruiser. "I'm talkin' to one of Clayton's buddies—R.J. Hinton—today. I'll let you know how it goes."

He walked off.

Bel pulled out his phone to text Daniel. Hesitated, thinking about the ice locks. Wondered if this meant Daniel was reduced to three hours' sleep tonight.

He's managed years without you.

He started typing: *Can't come by tonight. Sorry.*

Thought about saying something else. *See you soon? Sleep well? You gonna be all right?*

Fuck it; when had he turned into Whitlock's mama?

He hit Send and pocketed his phone. Finished his coffee and got in his cruiser.

Daniel was still sitting on the bed when his phone buzzed. He must have been dozing, because the sound made him jerk, and he couldn't remember what he'd been thinking about the second before it happened.

He read Belman's text three times.

Set the phone down and went to the kitchen.

He'd used up all his anger throwing his BDSM shit, so he made some decaf tea and tried to warm up the knot of cold in his stomach.

Belman wasn't coming back.

Belman hated him, couldn't face him. And Daniel had been a fool to believe there was anything there besides a sense of obligation.

So it was back to the ice locks tonight. And for the next however long he lived. He shut his eyes. Wasn't gonna feel sorry for himself. He finished his tea and went back to the bed. Picked up his phone and checked his messages.

It was a risk, sure, but what the fuck did he care anymore? Belman wasn't going to look out for him. Stupid to think it would've lasted. He needed more than Belman was offering anyway. If he hadn't been such a coward with Master Beau, he'd be safe by now. Safely locked up anyway.

He was a coward now as well. He was too scared to ask outright for himself, but maybe he could leave it to chance. Chance, and whatever it was in his sleeping brain that fixated on Greenducks like it was magnetic north.

He typed out a text to Master Beau and sent it.

I'm at Greenducks most nights. Maybe I'll see you there.

CHAPTER SIX

Daniel was at a table with three guys. One was laughing, and Daniel couldn't remember what was funny, but he laughed too. He liked the way the air moved in here—it was heavy and it smelled bad, but the weight of it was comforting. He'd always liked feeling wrapped up. Used to sleep with all the covers on in the summertime and wake up sweaty. Hadn't minded the straitjacket or the body bag when Marcus had put him in those. It hadn't been sexy like Marcus had wanted it to be, but Daniel hadn't minded.

He laughed again. Shouldn't be thinking about Marcus. He tried to focus on the guy who was telling the story. He watched the guy's mouth move but couldn't hear the words. Maybe it wasn't air around him at all. Maybe it was water. Everything felt dull and muted and slow. Daniel felt weightless. He drifted a little.

The guy was still talking. Not a good-looking guy, but maybe it'd be all right to go home with him. Daniel needed a good fuck. He put his hand on the table. The guy ignored it. Daniel felt frustrated. He ran his palm through a ring of water one of the glasses had left on the table. Said something and wasn't sure what. But the guy stopped talking and looked at him.

That was a start.

The guy looked like he was about to say something to Daniel, but then the door opened and everyone turned, listening to the footsteps descending the stairs into the basement.

Daniel didn't turn, because he was looking at his hand. The back of it had red, scaly skin. Little purple marks. Was dry and cracking, lines appearing even as he watched.

He'd been burned. He was still burning.

That reminded him of something. Thoughts weren't connecting in his head, and they scattered each time he tried to pull them together. But he remembered Belman, wanted to ask the guy who'd been talking if he knew where Belman was. Maybe if he offered to blow the guy, the guy would take him to Belman. Then maybe he could offer to blow Belman.

Daniel licked his lips. Some reason that couldn't happen. Belman didn't want that. Hard to find Belman anyway. Had to wait until he showed up.

Daniel looked at his hand again and it didn't look so bad. Belman had told him the fire was gone.

Belman had saved him.

Saved him. Those two words took on a shape, a presence in his mind. They crowded everything else out. But Daniel couldn't hold on to them. He didn't even notice the man who'd come up behind him until a hand closed over his shoulder.

"Pussy."

Daniel heard the word, even if he didn't entirely understand who'd said it or why. The hand jerked him back in his chair, and he turned and saw a big guy. Balding. Stomach hanging down over his jeans. Master Beau.

The fear came into Daniel slowly, like a tendril of smoke. Wasn't even fear at first, just uneasiness. There was a shuffle in his mind, like a slot machine when you pulled the lever and all the pictures scrambled.

Belman, Marcus. The guys at the table. Master Beau. Greenducks and the cabin. Fire. A dark stain.

"Hi." Daniel tried to smile. Scooted his chair out and stood.

Master Beau raked a hand through Daniel's hair and grabbed a fistful in the back. "You gonna run from me again?"

Again?

"No, sir." Seemed like the best answer. Daniel's gaze drifted to the back of the bar, where there was a dartboard and board games no one ever played. He tried to tilt his head to get away from Master Beau's breath, but Master Beau tightened his grip on Daniel's hair and shook him.

"You thought I'd let you get away with that, Boy?"

The guys at the table laughed. Daniel heard one of them say something with "slut" in it. That was good. When guys started saying that, it usually meant Daniel would get fucked. His cock hardened.

"No, sir," he murmured again. His eyes suddenly filled with tears. Belman and the fire washing down the walls. Belman thought it was a good idea to fix the cabin up. Things were quieter with Belman. Belman didn't smell like this, and his voice wasn't so rough.

And Belman hated him.

With a grunt, Daniel slapped at the arm holding him. He planted both palms squarely on Master Beau's chest and shoved him away. Master Beau staggered back.

"I don't care!" Daniel screamed at him. It felt good to say that. "I don't care! I *don't care!*"

Terror flared through him as Master Beau stepped forward and grabbed his jaw. "You'll care when I'm done with you."

Daniel tried to shove him again, but the back of Master Beau's hand connected with Daniel's cheek. Daniel fell back against the table, almost into the lap of the guy sitting closest. He launched himself up and drew back his arm. Hit Master Beau as hard as he could, the crunch making him wince. It was too familiar—suddenly Daniel was lying in the slick grass, Kenny Cooper standing over him. Everything almost black, but some part of Daniel was still awake, begging *please leave, please leave.* He kept losing the full picture, as though someone were shaking a blanket out over him, and each time it billowed up, he could see the stars, the silver clouds, the universe, for just a few seconds. But each time it fell, he was in darkness again.

He was pleased and a bit alarmed when he saw blood pouring from Master Beau's nose. *I'm on my feet this time. Not on the ground. And you're the one bleeding, asshole.* He drew back for another blow. Someone grabbed his elbow. He twisted, trying to get free, trying to hit anyone he could reach. He was screaming again, and it hurt his voice, but he was glad for it. Another pair of hands grabbed him, and Daniel was forced into a chair. His arms were yanked behind his back. He screamed again and threw all of his weight to one side, falling out of the chair and sprawling on the floor.

He stayed there.

Felt a boot shoved against his dick, pressing harder and harder.

"Fucking pussy."

Daniel didn't notice the pain. Stared at the wall behind the guy. Watched it melt, and waited for the fire to come.

Water came instead, cool and fresh, soothing his burned hands. He was at the river with Casey and her friends, that summer before he graduated. That little kid was watching him. Well, not so little. Must've been thirteen, but already almost as tall as Daniel. Skinny, in his baggy shorts, bones sticking out everywhere like a half-grown pup. All elbows and knees.

"Hey," the kid said.

"Hey," Daniel answered. Didn't look up from his chemistry book.

"You coming in? It's real nice."

"No."

The Belman kid walked away again, leaving wet footprints on the grass.

Wet grass smelled like blood, didn't it? Blood and beer and sweat.

"Hey, Whitlock?"

Daniel smiled. Jake was kneeling over him. Jake was kind of cute. Daniel tried to reach up and touch his face but couldn't move his arms.

"He's fucked up, you guys. Hey, Whitlock, you good with this?"

"Yeah," Daniel said. Jake had nice eyes.

Jake disappeared, and then Master Beau was there instead.

Flick, flick, flick went the slot machine.

"Get him up. Get him over that table."

"Hold on now! You wanna fuck, you take it outside!"

"I wanna fuck," Daniel told the voice as he was hauled to his feet.

"Pussy," Master Beau said. "Slut. *Slave.*"

Flick, flick, flick. Jackpot. Daniel laughed.

Bel was writing up a ticket on the highway and getting a lot of pleasure from deflecting every obscenity thrown at him with a polite "Yes, sir." He'd learned from Uncle Joe that nothing pissed an asshole off more than a cop who wouldn't rise to the bait.

"Yes, sir," he said again as the driver told him he wasn't worth shit and why didn't he go catch a real criminal? "Well, speeding is against the law, sir, so I'm doing that right now."

"It's a stupid fucking law!"

"Yes, sir," Bel agreed. "You can write a letter to your congressman and maybe get that changed, but in the meantime I am going to give you this ticket."

The guy tore the ticket up, so Bel wrote him one for littering.

That was one of Uncle Joe's favorite tricks as well. And then, when the guy didn't pay either one of them, Bel would get the fun of arresting him and slinging his ass in jail for the weekend.

"You have a pleasant evening, sir," Bel said.

The guy looked like he was going to pop a vein in his temple, but he snatched the second ticket from Bel's fingers, wound his window up, and drove off.

Bel put his pen back in his top pocket and closed his ticket book.

His radio burst with static.

"Gonna need some backup on Main Street." Day's voice.

Bel swung back into his cruiser. Wasn't Day supposed to be out at Kamchee Road?

"What you got?" That was Ginny.

"Got a fight outside of Greenducks. Gonna need some more bodies here."

Bel waited until Ginny had responded, and then did the same. "On my way from the 601."

He hit the lights and siren, and headed for Logan.

The fight was outside Greenducks, like Day had said, but it was obvious it had started inside. The door was open, noise spilling out. Jake Kebbler was sitting cuffed in the gutter when Bel pulled in. Ginny was restraining some other guy, who maybe had more teeth when it started. Ginny was all of five foot nothing, but she packed a mean punch. The guy was struggling, but she got cuffs on him.

"It's still going on inside!" she shouted at Bel.

He headed for the steps, barreling down them into the gloom that was the dive's attempt at ambience. The music blared, so loud that Bel could feel it vibrating through him. It knocked him off-kilter for a second, then he hit the floor at the bottom of the steep steps and headed for the fight.

Day and Avery were pulling a pack of fighters apart, laying them on their assess one by one. They were mostly too drunk or too high to resist much, but that was often more dangerous. A drunk guy might not be the most coordinated fighter out there, but a lot of times he also didn't know when to stop.

Bel grabbed one of the guys by his belt loops and hauled him backward. Saw a pale face in the middle of the brawl.

Daniel! Jesus Christ.

"What the fuck you doing here?" he shouted, but Daniel didn't seem to hear him. Maybe it was because of the music and the yelling, but maybe it was because he wasn't even in the fucking room. Not really. That look on his face, that weird, spaced-out look. Bel knew what it meant.

Over by the bar, Mike finally turned the music off. Nothing then but shouting and grunting, and working at keeping the men apart.

"He wanted it," some asshole was yelling at Avery. "He fucking asked for it!"

"That's his fucking *thing*, man!" one of the others said. "Fuckin' freak."

"So why you all fighting like a pack of dogs?" Avery demanded.

Bel stared at Daniel.

"Okay, everybody settle down and we'll get this sorted out," Avery said. "Whitlock, you start this?"

"What?"

Avery glared at him. "I asked you if you started this."

"Burns," Daniel said.

"Ain't no good asking him." Mike wiped his bloody nose with his shirt. "Danny Boy's so fucked up he don't know what day it is. I told this asshole here to take it outside, but he wouldn't. He's the one that started it for real."

Bel looked at the guy Mike pointed out. Looked like a reject from the cast of *Deliverance*. Wasn't a local.

"Little bitch told me to meet him here!" the guy blustered. "Then he threw the first punch!"

"That right, Whitlock?" Avery asked.

Daniel smiled at him.

"Okay," Bel said. "Get over here, Whitlock."

Daniel trailed over, rubbing his face. Bel sat him down in a chair, crouched in front of him, and searched his eyes for any sign he was awake.

"Hey," he said.

"Hey." Daniel smiled.

"You need to wake up now," Bel told him. "Might be in some trouble here."

"Don't wanna get in any trouble," Daniel murmured.

Bel resisted the urge to reach up and touch his bruised jaw. So quiet and compliant like this, but Bel couldn't trust it. It could turn in a heartbeat. He'd seen that, hadn't he, when Daniel had gone for his gun and Bel had taken him down? "You punch that guy, Daniel?"

"He's got no right to call himself a master," Daniel said.

Bel looked at the guy again, his heart beating faster. *This* was the hillbilly Daniel didn't want to fuck? Not Bel? That probably shouldn't have made him as pleased as it did.

"What's a master, Daniel?"

"Supposed to lock me up, not let his friends gangbang me."

Jesus. Bel felt ice slide down his spine. "He do that to you?"

"Nah, I ran away. Pussy."

Bel sighed, relieved but still confused. "So what happened here tonight?"

"You went swimming in the river."

"That didn't happen, Daniel."

"Oh." Daniel exhaled slowly. "Was there fire?"

"Not tonight."

"That's good."

"Yeah, it is." Bel stood. "You stay here for me, okay?"

"Okay."

Bel walked back to Avery. "Got no sense out of him."

"Meth head," Avery muttered. "Well, Mike's not gonna press charges for this guy starting the fight, so long as he don't press charges on Whitlock."

"I don't want the fucking trouble," Mike said. "You're banned, asshole."

Deliverance guy glared at him.

"You're banned too, Danny Boy!" Mike yelled, then shook his head. "Makes no fucking difference. He never remembers."

Avery looked around the bar. "Anyone else want to complain about anyone else punching 'em, you sober the hell up and come down to the station in the morning. Y'all got that? Good, now get the fuck out. Bar's closing early tonight."

The small crowd cleared out.

Bel walked back to Daniel. "Come on, let's go."

Daniel stood and headed for the bathroom.

"Other way," Bel told him sharply.

Daniel turned toward the stairs.

Bel followed him up, watching his ass in those jeans. Thinking about it naked. Would be too damn easy to fuck him when he was like this, but then Bel would be no better than any other asshole in Greenducks.

He saw the outline of Daniel's phone in his back pocket. Reached up and took it, and Daniel didn't even notice.

Outside in the parking lot, Jake was still sitting in the gutter, bitching and moaning as Day unlocked his cuffs. "I didn't do nothing!"

"Shut up," Day told him.

"It's Jake," Daniel said, smiling again. He started toward him.

Bel caught him by the back of the shirt. "Go wait by my cruiser, Daniel." He pointed it out. "Go on, now."

Daniel shuffled over.

"That boy is high as a kite," Ginny said.

Bel couldn't tell if she was talking about Daniel or Jake. He nodded curtly.

"We all good?" Ginny asked. "I reckon I'll stick around here, make sure none of these boys try to drive."

"Yeah, I'll take Whitlock back to his place," Bel said. "Gonna get himself in more shit if he walks."

"Sure, Bel. See you later."

Bel loaded Daniel into the back of his cruiser, then sat in the front seat. Turned the air on, and went through Daniel's phone. Saw his own text message first: *Can't come by tonight. Sorry.*

Then saw the one Daniel had sent to the guy listed on his phone as Master Beau: *I'm at Greenducks most nights. Maybe I'll see you there.*

It had been sent this morning, after Bel had left. And Bel knew what Daniel's texts looked like when he was asleep. This one was coherent. Correctly spelled and punctuated. Which meant Daniel had most likely been awake when he'd sent it.

When Daniel woke up it was more than his jaw that hurt. It was his throat, like maybe someone had grabbed it too hard, and there was a bruise on his collarbone. And hell, his right hand ached like fuck. He flexed his fingers. The sunlight streamed in the back windows of the cabin. The canvas was still holding on the front ones. Maybe he ought to call someone to come and put new glass in.

Took him a second to notice there was someone sitting in the chair in the shadows. His heart stuttered, but he didn't know if it was from fear or something else. Bel looked good in his uniform.

"Thought you couldn't make it." Daniel swung his legs over the side of the bed and rubbed the knuckles of his right hand. "Did I punch you last night?"

"No," Belman said, leaning forward. "You punched some guy at Greenducks, got in a brawl, and got banned. I dragged your ass back here before you offered it to the whole town."

"Yeah, well."

"That all you got to say?"

Daniel ran his hands over his head. "What do you want me to say, Belman? I do crazy shit when I'm asleep."

"Yeah, you do." Belman threw something toward Daniel, who caught it on instinct. "You do crazy shit when you're awake as well. Want to explain that?"

His phone. Daniel looked down at the screen and saw the message he'd sent to Master Beau. Wondered if he'd been there last night. Probably. Wondered what sick shit Daniel had let him do. Mostly he wondered how to explain himself to Belman. It wasn't like he owed the guy an explanation. Not like Belman had any right to tell him how to lead his life. Not like they were anything.

But he was here, and he was listening, which was more than most people.

"You weren't coming," he said suddenly, wishing it didn't sound like an accusation. "And I need someone I can count on."

Belman narrowed his eyes. "You gonna count on that fucking freak before you count on me?"

"He was there, wasn't he?"

"Yeah, good for you. Good choice." Belman shook his head. "Avery ran his name. Your Master Beau tell you he spent eight years in jail for raping a fifteen-year-old girl?"

"No." The thought made Daniel sick to the stomach.

"That the kind of man you want touching you?"

"No!" Daniel dug his nails into his palms. "I don't know."

"You don't know?" Belman gave a disbelieving laugh.

"I killed a guy," Daniel said. "Pretty sure I don't get to claim any moral high ground."

"Maybe you don't. But maybe you need to stop being so goddamn stupid."

Fuck you. You got no idea what this is like.

"You don't . . . It's not that simple."

Belman stared at him. "Seems like it's real simple. You need someone to lock you up, and I'm telling you that a ped rapist is not your best option."

"He's my only option."

"No," Belman said quietly. "No, he ain't."

Daniel swallowed. "What do you mean?"

"I mean if that's what it's gonna take to stop you from doing crazy shit, I'll do it. Like we have been this last week, if that would work for you. Until we figure out some other way, I guess."

"But last night, you weren't coming."

"Yeah, sometimes that will happen. But I can tell you when I'm working, and we can schedule your sleep around that."

"Pretty sure this is a dream right now." Daniel couldn't remember the last time that anyone had gone out of their way for him, unless it was to spit at him or throw something. "Why would you do that?"

"You wanna question it, or you want to agree to it?"

"If—" Daniel sucked in a breath and tried again. "If you're looking for something in exchange, that's okay."

Belman gave a quick grin. "You offering me your ass, Daniel? That's the first time you've done that awake."

Daniel's face burned. "Yeah, well."

"Yeah, well," Belman echoed. "Well that's not what this is about, okay?"

So what's it about then?

"Okay, fine."

"I gotta head back into town now. I'll come back this evening and check in with you. You gonna stay awake until then?"

"Yeah," Daniel managed.

"You sure?"

"Yeah," Daniel said, stronger this time.

He could stay awake. He had a few tricks.

"All right," Bel said. He and Dav were sitting on Dav's front porch. Bel had a beer, and Dav had a cream soda. Bel was scratching Stump's neck, in that spot that made the dog twist his head and start kicking his hind leg. "So he ain't crazy. But he's got issues, huh? And maybe that's the problem. Maybe if his life's a little less fucked up when he's awake, he wouldn't do such fucked-up shit in his sleep."

Dav nodded. "Could be."

Bel took his hand away to scratch his own neck. Took a long gulp of beer. Stump whined until Bel started petting him again. "I mean, all the websites, they say, oh, sleepwalking ain't linked to having mental problems. But . . ."

"But maybe what you do when you sleepwalk is linked to your psychological health," Dav finished.

"Yeah," Bel said, relieved that she got what he was trying to say.

"Daniel and I have discussed therapy. I think it'd be good for him to start talking about what Kenny did. And about some of the shit that goes on with his family."

"What shit?"

"They've essentially disowned him. They weren't able to help him make sense of or deal with his sleepwalking as a kid." Dav glanced at him. "You know I'm not exactly Little Miss Care and Share—"

"Understatement."

"But it'd do him good. To talk."

Bel leaned back and watched the neighbor's kid, Joshua, roll his mother's yoga ball around the yard. "The websites say there's no treatment. Ain't that nuts? There's cancers they can get rid of, but they can't figure out how to make someone stay in bed for eight hours? Just 'establish a bedtime routine.' What the hell? Whitlock's got a routine all right, and it's fucked up."

"Well," Dav said. She didn't finish the thought for a while. "I think you're onto something. Attack the problem at the source. Figure out what's messing with him so bad when he's awake that he hurts himself in his sleep." She paused and swigged her soda. "Don't know who's gonna help him with that, though."

"Well, I ain't his therapist. I'm just sayin' maybe he should get one."

"I'll look into it. I know someone out of town who might help out."

"Whatever. I'm no expert."

"You asked Uncle Joe to put you on days."

Bel colored. "Yeah. So what?"

"So I think it's good you check up on him. And Daniel looks better than I've ever seen him."

Bel watched Joshua slam the yoga ball against the ground. Had a sudden vision of Kenny Cooper throwing Daniel to the ground. Beating the shit out of him.

You never knew, did you, with kids, what they'd turn out to be? Bel's mother had never liked him playing with Harvey Blake when they were little because she thought Harvey wasn't quite right, but now Harvey had a scholarship to some journalism program.

"What would you do?" he asked Dav. "If your kid turns out like Whitlock. Or like Cooper."

"Now there's a lovely thought. What the hell's wrong with you?"

"It could happen."

"Asshole. I'd love him. Or her."

"Even if he half beat someone to death? Or burned a guy's house down?"

"Probably. Yeah. I dunno, ask me when little Jim's on the news in an orange jumpsuit."

"You gonna name that thing Jim Jr.?" He couldn't picture Dav agreeing to that.

Dav grinned. "Hell no. I was thinking maybe Berkeley, if it's a boy."

"Why don't you just name him Wedgie Bait?"

"Shut up. *Bel*."

"I pull it off."

"Yeah, I guess you do."

They were silent a minute. "Dav?"

"Yeah?"

"I think I might try to help Daniel Whitlock. And I was wondering if you'd help me do that."

Joshua was rolling the yoga ball again. Bel and Dav both watched as he charged at a squirrel and laughed when it ran up a tree. It was a suicide mission, right? Rescuing a guy from a fire was one thing. Rescuing a guy from himself? Bel booked enough addicts and wife beaters to know people didn't change. Not really. Bel didn't even know what the hell he meant by trying to help Whitlock, what he planned to do, or whether it would work. He just knew he had to try.

He wasn't gonna watch Daniel burn.

Dav clinked her soda bottle against his beer bottle. "Welcome to the club. I haven't had anyone join in three years."

CHAPTER SEVEN

Daniel was helping Mr. Roan in the garden. A good way of keeping himself occupied until Belman showed up. Until he could sleep. Daniel kind of liked spending time with someone who was crazier than himself—though he didn't tell Mr. Roan that.

Mr. Roan planted vegetables by hurling fistfuls of seeds down like magic dust. Daniel kept half-expecting to see a ball of smoke fly from his hand, hit the ground, and burst into a bouquet of zucchini. Half of what the old man said didn't make sense, but Daniel nodded and agreed anyway. There were also random periods where Mr. Roan was totally coherent, and Daniel enjoyed hearing him talk about his brothers, his travels, and the history of Logan.

At one point Mr. Roan said something about the soil not having enough iron, and Daniel found himself talking animatedly about the chemistry of topsoil, something no one—not Marcus, not Casey, not Jeff—ever used to let him prattle on about. But Mr. Roan seemed to like the information, even if he didn't retain much of it.

"You know a lot," Mr. Roan said.

"I took a lot of bullshit chemistry classes." Daniel paused. Wiped his forehead on his arm. "Sorry. A lot of useless chem classes."

"Well, that's college for you. A lot of bullshit."

Daniel grinned. "I liked it okay."

"You have a feller in college?"

Daniel glanced at him warily. Just about anyone else in town, and Daniel would have assumed it was a trap. Could he count on Mr. Roan, at least, not to make a fag comment? "Yeah. I did."

"Me too."

"You . . . you too?"

Mr. Roan nodded. "A string of 'em."

Daniel glanced around, half-worried they were being overheard.

"I been alive eighty-two years," Mr. Roan said, following Daniel's gaze. "I don't care who knows I like cock."

Daniel burst out laughing. He felt simultaneously shocked, uncomfortable, and relieved. "I never knew that about you."

"Well, I don't advertise. But it ain't some dark secret."

Daniel's smile slipped. He thought back to Kenny. There had been no point in pressing charges after the assault, since he'd come on to Kenny. Since he didn't *remember* what he'd said to Kenny, and it didn't matter anyhow. It was Daniel's fault for not keeping his mouth shut. You didn't advertise, not in this town. Everyone knew that.

"Hey, Whitlock! Still wanna suck my dick?"

And Daniel, frozen at the edge of the field that stretched north from downtown, thinking why would he want to suck Kenny Cooper's dick. Bold and stupid enough to say so.

"Don't worry, though," Mr. Roan said now. "You're safe. Not my type."

Daniel laughed again. "Who is your type?"

Mr. Roan kicked the wheel of the wheelbarrow. "White hair. A real pretty head of white hair. And wrinkles. I like these ones." He pointed to the corners of his mouth, which had deep furrows down to his chin. He moved his fingers under his eyes. "I like just a slight bag right here." He grinned, showing his yellow teeth. "A nice, wrinkly dick that smooths out as it gets hard. And curly eyebrow hairs."

"You found anyone in Logan who fits the bill?"

Mr. Roan shook his head. "I'm working on it."

"Well, good luck. I advertise more'n I ought to, and believe me, the pickings are slim."

"I been here a lot longer than you, and I know it."

Daniel propped up a section of the fence that was sagging. Took his hand away and watched it sag again. "It's okay in a lot of places. Where I went to school, you could hold hands with a guy. No one fussed."

"Maybe you ought to go back there."

"Can't. Gotta stay where . . . where I know what's what."

Where I don't forget what I am, and that I don't deserve anything better. Would wreck anything better.

"I reckon that's what most of us think. But there's more strangers where you're from than in some sandland halfway around the world. And more strangers in your head than any place on the map."

Daniel laughed again. "Maybe so."

Ten minutes later, Mr. Roan was in a cawing match with some crows. Then he made a comment about Eisenhower, went inside, and fixed lemonade without any sugar. Daniel drank a whole glass anyway.

Beat the hell out of his own piss.

Daniel flinched as he released the tabs of the second clamp, letting the teeth sink into his right nipple. Increased the tension bit by bit. Five clamps—two on his nipples, two on his balls, one on his dick. The clamps on his nipples were clothespin clamps, and he'd screwed them as tight as he could without passing out. No way he'd fall asleep with these on. Just had to stay awake until Belman got here. He stood.

He'd felt all right since gardening with Mr. Roan. Being outside, being active, usually helped him feel centered. He was tired now, but in a good way—exhausted enough that he'd almost fallen asleep when he'd sat down for a minute, but at least he didn't feel quite so scared. And he was glad Belman was coming. Glad Belman wasn't so pissed about last night that he'd refused to have anything to do with Daniel.

Your fault anyway, Belman. You spoiled me.

Daniel almost grinned. Not that it was funny, what he'd done last night. And it sure as hell wasn't funny that he was becoming reliant on Belman—that would only lead to trouble.

But he wanted to smile. So fuck it, he was gonna smile.

He pulled up his boxers and went to the kitchen to make dinner. Chili. He made enough for Belman, too, in case he was hungry.

Just standing here in my clamps and boxers, making dinner.

The absurdity of the situation really was epic.

There was a knock at the door, and Daniel froze. Was Belman early? He took off the nipple clamps as quickly as he dared and shoved them in the spice cabinet. Almost doubled over as the blood came rushing back. He paused until the pain subsided. In the main room, he grabbed a baggy T-shirt and threw it on. It mostly covered his boxers. He thought about putting on pajama pants, but it would be too hard to get them on without jostling the clamps between his legs. And besides, he didn't mind Belman seeing him in his boxers. Didn't think Belman would mind either.

He opened the door and tensed instantly. Shit. Shit. Shit. His mom held a covered casserole dish. The corners of her mouth were turned down. In worry, or maybe disapproval at the state of the cabin, at the state of him. Daniel couldn't remember the last time she'd come out here. It had been so long that he'd forgotten what he should say.

"Hey, Mom," he managed at last. He could hardly bring himself to look at her: the lines, the gray hair, the hard cast to her features that he'd put there. Built it up over the years, bit by bit, until neither of them recognized her anymore.

"Hello, Daniel."

He opened the screen and stepped out onto the porch. He didn't want her in the cabin. Not with the cuffs on the bed. Not with the evidence of another fucking sickness lying there, out in the open, as stark as the scorch marks on the wall.

"I made you this." His mom handed him the dish. He peered through the glass top. Mac and cheese, it looked like.

"Thanks," he said numbly.

"Are you well?" She said it with as much polite concern as you'd muster up for a neighbor, or the friend of a friend.

"Sure." His throat ached.

"We heard about the fire."

"You and everyone."

Please leave, please leave.

Sometimes being near his mother was worse than the memory of Kenny Cooper standing over him.

And yet some part of him was still glad to see her. Didn't want her to go. He wanted to ask her if work was good, how her hydrangeas were doing, what she was reading at Cherry Hanson's book club this week . . . all those things that people in the street probably asked her every day, but Daniel couldn't.

She took a deep breath. "I've got some money together. To send you somewhere."

Daniel's heart became a heavy dark knot in his chest. "Send me where?"

"A hospital or . . . or somewhere." The plea in her words was evident. "Somewhere they can *help* you."

Help me, or hide me away?

Where had this idea of getting help been years ago? Would have been better for the whole fucking world if he'd been sent away somewhere when he was a kid. But no doctors. Just, *"Don't you lie to me, Daniel!"*

And he knew now that doctors couldn't do a damn thing.

I ain't going anywhere. Belman's gonna help me. Shit.

"Where'd you find money for that?" He knew money had been tight for his parents since the sawmill had closed. His dad's two shifts a week at the plant didn't go far.

"Borrowed it." She looked almost defiant. "It doesn't matter where from."

He shifted, and the clamps tugged between his legs. Five minutes ago, he'd wanted to laugh at how bizarre his life was. But no, it was just completely fucked up. *He* was completely fucked up. "Is that what you came out here to tell me?" Should have known it wasn't for mac and cheese. "I'm not taking your money. I'm not goin' anywhere."

Not another hospital. Not where they kept him on so many drugs he couldn't remember his own name. Couldn't tell the difference between his nightmares and reality even when he was awake.

"You get arrested again, though, that'll be trouble, won't it?" Her face twisted. "I hear things, Daniel, about how you . . . how you *behave*. It's disgusting. You need *treatment*."

"There's no treatment." Daniel heard his voice rising.

She took a step back. "Don't get mad at me. I want you to get help."

"By locking me up?" Odd to be getting mad, when locking himself up was exactly what he did anyway. But he did it on his terms, didn't he? He made the decisions.

"By keeping you . . . safe."

You mean keeping Logan safe from me.

"Do you think I ought to be committed?" he asked her.

She looked away.

"Do you?" he demanded.

She shook her head. "Not committed. No. But you could go somewhere . . . voluntarily. For help."

"What kind of help?" he shouted. "What kind of help am I supposed to get?"

She backed up some more. "Don't yell at me."

"Do you want to help me, Mom, or do you just want me to go away?" He clenched his fists, and her eyes widened.

He was scaring her. Shit, he wanted to scare her. But no, that wasn't a good idea. She'd leave now. And he'd be alone.

Sure enough, she turned away. "You shouldn't even say that."

Guilt bit at him, but it wasn't an answer, was it? It still wasn't an answer.

She walked toward her car. Didn't say good-bye.

"I love you, Daniel," she'd said twenty-two years ago, when they'd left the house for his first day of kindergarten. He remembered it so clearly. He'd been looking forward to kindergarten for weeks, but suddenly he'd been scared. He'd held his mom's hand the entire way there, listening to her tell him that he was such a big boy now, that he'd love it, that he'd make so many new friends. She'd made him feel so brave that he hadn't even cried at the front gate like some of the other kids.

What if he said it now? *"I love you, Mom."*

What if she just kept walking?

Can't love someone who treats you like that. Can't love someone who don't love you.

He wished he believed that.

He didn't say anything.

He thought of Belman. Why the fuck would he think of Belman? Belman had nothing to do with love.

He went inside and tried not to think about the money his mom had borrowed. *Borrowed.* She was that desperate to get rid of him. *Send you somewhere.* And maybe then she could pretend that he'd never existed at all.

His parole period wasn't up yet, but he didn't imagine he'd have any problem getting permission to leave Logan if it was to be locked up somewhere.

By the time Belman arrived, Daniel had left the clamps on his balls and dick way too long. He was in the bathroom removing them when the knock came. It was fucking hard to walk even the few steps across the cabin to the door.

Belman nodded at him. "Daniel."

Daniel liked hearing Belman say his name. "Hey." He stepped back so Belman could come in. "I made chili. You're welcome to some." He started toward the kitchen. Stopped. The pain in his balls was *awful.* "I haven't ate yet. Eaten."

"You all right?"

"Sure."

"Walkin' kind of funny."

"Stubbed my toe."

Belman grumbled. "Daniel?"

"Yeah?"

"Well . . . you wouldn't remember I guess. But if you . . . I mean, did you do anything with those guys last night? They do anything to you, besides push you around?"

Daniel shook his head. "Don't think so. You prob'ly know better'n I do what happened." He started to turn toward Belman, but thought better of it. "Sometimes the stuff I do to keep awake hurts a little."

"What do you mean?"

"I mean I use some of that stuff from the bag to keep me awake. You want chili or not?"

Belman cleared his throat. "I wanna see what's in the bag."

No. Fuck no. Don't do this.

"No, you don't."

"Why would I ask, then?"

"Ain't it enough? What you've seen already? You know I'm nuts, so let me do that stuff in peace. You don't have to see it."

"I don't want to see you do it. But I wanna know what you do."

"No." Daniel went to the kitchen and took two bowls out. Heaped chili into each one.

"And I don't think you're nuts."

"'Course you do."

"Damn it, Whitlock. I'm tryin' to help you."

"You can help me by locking me up at night and getting me out in the morning."

"You let Marcus do a whole lot more."

"Why're you so interested in Marcus? He's gone!"

"Well, you're the one who talks to him in your sleep."

"Why's it matter what he did? Huh? Why're you so interested? You like the shit you saw in my bag? You ever swing a paddle, *Officer?*"

"Bel. Call me Bel."

"This ain't an introduction. I'm yelling at you."

"I can hear that. So what's got you wound up?"

"You! Asking to know what I do. If I told you all I'd done, you'd never come back here." Daniel slammed the lid back on the chili pot.

"Try me."

Daniel faced him. "I drank my own piss. Few nights ago. Hid the spare key in it, thinking I wouldn't dare fucking drink piss, even in my sleep. But I did. And I unlocked myself and went to Greenducks. I got a plug I shove up my ass—sometimes I put stuff on it that'll make it burn while it's up there. Hard to go to sleep with your ass on fire. Tonight it was clamps on my balls."

Daniel realized he was still holding the ladle. He threw it in the sink. Went to the bathroom and grabbed the bag from the cabinet. He strode back into the main room, opened the bag, and started pulling out chains, locks, and cuffs, tossing them onto the floor. "This is all to keep me contained. I used to just put the locks on the doors, but my sleep brain always remembers where the key is." A coil of rope. The straitjacket.

Belman—Bel—picked that up. Daniel stopped breathing. Wished he could look away. Wished he could fucking *vanish*. "You use this?" Bel asked.

"Not without help. Marcus used it."

"Jesus."

"I didn't mind it," Daniel said defensively. "Felt good, actually. Knowing I couldn't move. Better'n the cuffs. The cuffs hurt."

Bel stared at the straitjacket.

"So what do you think, *Bel*?" Daniel spat.

"I think you're gonna be all right," Bel said, looking up.

"Huh?"

Bel dropped the straitjacket on the floor. "I said I think you're gonna be all right."

"Fuck you." Daniel tossed the bag at Bel's feet. "There you go. I'm wide awake, so it ain't rape or whatever you're worried about. Pick some toys. I'll show you what Marcus and I did."

"How many more times are we gonna play this game?" Bel sounded annoyed, and for a second, Daniel's bravado wavered. "You must really think I'm a piece of shit, huh? If you think I'm gonna like doing stuff to you that you hate."

"Who says I hate it? Maybe the reason I stay awake with clamps on my balls is I'm just getting off over and over again!" Daniel wished he could stop himself from talking, but it felt good. It felt good to yell at someone who'd *listen*.

"So do you get off on it?"

Daniel glared. "Sometimes."

"But not all the time?"

He could feel his anger dissipating, leaving fear in its place. An easy fear, familiar. "No."

Bel took a step closer. Daniel tensed, but Bel only picked up the bag, glanced inside it, then set it aside. "So what does get you off?"

Daniel drew on his last reserves of anger. "Anything you did would probably get me there in two seconds. But you won't fucking touch me."

"Not while you're asleep."

"I'm not asleep now."

"And while you're awake . . . well, I guess I think we should know each other better first."

Daniel laughed bitterly. "Why? I don't improve with time."

Bel smiled. That smile made Daniel ashamed of everything he'd said these last few minutes—it was soft and a little anxious. And real.

"Let's just wait on it, Daniel. It ain't that I don't want to. But let's just wait."

Daniel looked at the floor. Nodded. "Sorry."

"Me too. You forgive me enough to let me have a go at that chili?"

Daniel snorted. "I guess."

They went into the kitchen.

"I brought cards."

Daniel looked at him. "What cards?"

"Playing cards. You know Texas Hold'em?"

"It's been a while."

"I'll refresh you."

Daniel dropped spoons in the bowls and handed one to Bel. "I don't have anywhere to sit, really."

"How about the porch step?"

Daniel followed Bel outside, and they sat on the step. Played cards after they finished their dinner, Daniel finally relaxing into the idea of being here with Bel, of laughing at each other's dumb jokes, of not feeling like he ought to be apologizing every few seconds for making Bel come here. *He offered. Maybe for the town's sake and not mine. But he offered.* They went in once it got too dark and the mosquitoes got bad.

"How do you live without a TV?" Bel asked.

"How do you live with one? I don't need all that noise. I got enough of my own."

When it was time for bed, Bel fastened the leather cuffs around Daniel's wrists. Daniel was quiet. Tried to think of what he liked about being bound. Safe. Couldn't go anywhere. Safe to sleep.

Bel held on to his wrists for a moment after the cuffs were latched. Daniel squirmed. Mostly nerves, but maybe an invitation. He'd always thought some of the stuff Marcus and he had done *could* be sexy. If there hadn't been that other side to it. The side where Daniel had to push Marcus further than felt good, but Daniel was always afraid it wasn't going to be enough.

Bel waited until Daniel was looking at him. Then he squeezed Daniel's wrists gently. "Good night, Whitlock."

Daniel swallowed. "'Night, Bel."

"Gonna be in that chair, okay? Keeping an eye on you."

Daniel managed a grin. "That's pretty creepy."

Bel laughed. "You don't want someone watching you sleep?"

"Whole town's watched me sleep."

Bel laughed again, and warmth spread through Daniel. "Sorry," Bel said. "Maybe that ain't funny."

"No," Daniel agreed. "Sometimes it ain't. But right now it is."

Bel ran a hand briefly over Daniel's forehead. "Get some sleep."

"You too," Daniel said softly. "You look tired."

"I'm all right."

Yeah. I guess you are. More all right than most people I know.

Bel turned off the light, and Daniel closed his eyes.

Bel woke to screaming. At first he didn't know where he was, but he was on his feet in seconds.

The armchair. He'd been dozing in Whitlock's armchair, and now Whitlock was thrashing in the bed, screaming.

"Whitlock," Bel said sharply. "Daniel."

He went to the bed and turned on the light.

Daniel's eyes were wide, and he was arching up in his bonds like he was possessed. He'd kicked the covers to the floor. He let out another scream. Didn't seem to see Bel at all.

"Shhh," Bel said. "Shhh, shhh."

Daniel fell back, trembling. Opened his mouth, and shit, it was just like a possession, because nothing that came out made a lick of sense, just a few trembling syllables, and then another scream. The Devil and Daniel Whitlock, Bel thought. He finally caught one word: "Fire."

"There's no fire, Daniel," he said.

Daniel shivered again. Closed his eyes and keened.

Jesus. Bel sat on the edge of the bed and placed a hand on Daniel's chest. Daniel jerked. "No fire, Daniel. No fire. Come on now. Calm down."

He sat there awhile, murmuring nonsense, assuring Daniel over and over that there wasn't a fire, while Daniel struggled in his cuffs. Finally, Daniel lay still. Seemed to be listening to Bel's voice.

Bel glanced at Daniel's wrist. The tension in the chain made Bel wince. Daniel was gonna break his goddamn arm if he didn't quit pulling.

"Can't get out," Daniel whispered. "Trapped here."

He was, wasn't he? Maybe there was no fire, but that didn't change the fact that Daniel was a prisoner.

Bel reached over and undid the cuffs from the bed. Stupid? Definitely. But Bel wasn't exactly specializing in good decisions lately.

Daniel immediately rolled onto his stomach, drew his legs under him, and covered his head with his arms. He stayed huddled in a ball on the center of the bed, and Bel cautiously put his hand on Daniel's back and rubbed through his T-shirt, feeling the knots of bone, the heat and dampness beneath the fabric. "Easy, now," Bel said. "Whatever you think's happening, it ain't real." He paused. Wasn't sure what Whitlock thought was happening. "It's just me. I'm real. We're in your cabin and there ain't no fire, Whitlock. Come on, sit up and see."

He tried to urge Daniel up, watching Daniel's body closely for signs he might lash out. Daniel curled tighter as Bel ran a hand down his right arm, removed the cuff, and set it aside. Did the same with the left cuff. He stared at the bruises. Slowly worked his thumb around one of the worst spots. Daniel's hands were still clasped behind his head, his fingers laced tight. As Bel rubbed the raw skin of his wrist, he slowly moved up to pry apart Daniel's white fingers. "Daniel," he said softly. "Let go now."

Daniel let Bel unlace his fingers. Let Bel uncurl him. He sat up, still shaking, and tried to scream again as his gaze fell on the far wall. But his voice was gone. All he managed was a gulp and a slight whimper.

"Don't look," Bel suggested, pulling Daniel close to him. He shifted so Daniel was half in his lap, and pressed Daniel's head against his chest. "There you go. Just don't look at it."

Daniel's breath came in short, sharp gasps. Heat poured from his body even though he continued to shiver. He fisted Bel's shirt. Murmured something Bel didn't understand.

"We'll just stay here until things get better, okay?"

Bel didn't know what the fuck he was saying. They could stay here until Daniel's nightmare or whatever passed, sure. But things were never gonna get better for Daniel. Was Bel gonna hang around forever like a fool, hoping they would?

Maybe.

He rubbed Daniel's back.

Couldn't imagine letting him go right now.

Daniel woke to something tight around him. The straitjacket?

No. Bel. Bel was holding him. Bel was sitting on the bed, his back against the wall, Daniel's head pillowed on his chest. One of his hands was around Daniel's left wrist, not restraining, but rubbing the bruises softly with his thumb.

Fuck. For once in his life, Daniel wished he could stay under. Because this should have been a hallucination, but it wasn't; Bel really was holding him. And Daniel didn't want to find out why. Just wanted to stay like this.

The doctors he saw before his trial said he wasn't crazy, but Daniel didn't know if he believed that. They were paid to be on his side, weren't they? They said the confusion, the mood swings, the depression, even the lack of libido when he was awake, that all came from the fact that he didn't get enough proper sleep. The kind where his body rested, and not the kind where it went out and burned down houses with people inside. He was transferred to the hospital ward in the jail—wasn't crazy, but it was the safest place for him.

He'd been looking for another safe place ever since.

Waking up with Belman holding him felt like he'd found it. He remembered waking with Marcus's arms around him, years ago. Marcus climbing into bed with him after a scene. A hand on his back or in his hair. His lips against Daniel's. The pain almost worth it.

Bel's arms loosened. "Daniel?"

The jig was up.

"Hey," Daniel said. He shifted, sitting. Bel let go easily. Daniel didn't know what he'd expected—that Bel would try to hold on to him? "Sorry. What'd I— Did I get out?"

"You were having a nightmare or something. I undid the cuffs 'cause you were—"

Daniel nodded. "I get those sometimes. You just gotta ignore them."

"Pretty hard to ignore."

Daniel looked away. "Sorry."

Guilt swept through him, souring everything. What had it been this time? Kenny Cooper? His cabin burning? Hell? His shoulder was still brushing Bel's. He scooted away. "Don't even remember what I dream about, most times."

"The fire," Bel said. "You talk about the fire when you sleepwalk. And just now, when you were havin' the bad dream."

Daniel didn't answer. Didn't know what kind of answer Bel wanted. Yeah, he was freaked out by fire. Didn't know what to do about it except nut up.

"It ain't real. It's over."

"I know that," Daniel said quickly.

"I know you do. And I'm telling you now, while you're awake. You don't have to worry about it anymore."

Daniel tilted his head. Bel's tone was interesting—almost bossy, but not quite. Low, mostly calm, but with a slight edge Daniel wondered about. Was he pissed at Daniel for not getting it through his subconscious that his cabin wasn't burning down? Maybe that wasn't it. There was a feeling behind the words, but it wasn't anger.

"Well, I'll try to remember that," Daniel said. He stared at his wrists. They hurt.

Good. He hoped they would hurt worse when Bel put the cuffs back on.

"I'll get off your bed," Bel said, scooting forward. "You wanna go back to sleep?"

Fuck no. But what choice did he have but to try? "Rather not." Daniel tried to smile. "But reckon I oughta."

"We could take a walk," Bel said.

That startled Daniel.

"You got a nice big property," Bel added. He stood and stretched. "Bet it's pretty at night."

A moonlit fucking walk?

Daniel wasn't sure he liked pretending-to-be-nice Bel. Or maybe he liked him way too much, and he had to remember that pretending-to-be-nice Bel wasn't any more real than Daniel's dreams about the fire.

Maybe he likes you okay. Maybe he likes you okay enough to look after you a little. But he sure as hell doesn't want to take a walk with you in the middle of the night.

Daniel thought about how soothing the fresh air would be. How nice it would be to get out of this prison. But he couldn't. Bel needed sleep. Daniel needed sleep.

"No, thanks." He found the cuffs and started putting them on. "I'll be quiet now, I hope." He lay on his side and held his arms out for Bel to lock the cuffs.

Bel leaned over and picked up the combination padlock. Daniel swallowed. A part of him wished Bel wouldn't do this. That he'd insist on the walk. That he'd sit up with Daniel all night, playing cards or whatever, and Daniel wouldn't have to risk another night terror.

But Daniel appreciated Bel as much for his ability to be practical as for his kindness. He needed someone like Bel, someone who could see how much sleep hurt him, who could hear him screaming, see the bruises on his wrist—and would lock him up anyway.

Bel kept his gaze on Daniel's as he clicked the padlock shut. "Sorry," Bel whispered.

"Don't be."

"I am, though."

And that was all Bel said. He went back to the chair.

CHAPTER EIGHT

"Dad good?" Bel asked, the screen door clanging shut behind him.

His mama led the way through to the kitchen. "Not bad."

Strange how families talked in code like that. Bel's dad had a problem with gambling, but nobody came out and said it. Just asked if he was good, and checked that there was enough money for groceries that week. Bel could remember a few times when he was a kid, eating cereal for dinner or missing out on a school trip because even though his permission note was signed the money had vanished. And he could remember Billy and his dad coming to blows one night back when Billy was in high school, and Uncle Joe coming around and sorting them out.

"Uncle Joe," he'd asked when he was little, *"do you put bad people in jail?"*

"Well, I put people who've done bad things in jail."

"Ain't that the same thing?"

"Not exactly."

Uncle Joe and Aunt Marcy didn't have kids of their own, but they'd always kept beds made up for their nephews in case they needed them. Bel had bolted down to their place a few times when he was growing up, and barreled right in without knocking. Whenever that happened, Aunt Marcy would make him hot chocolate and open a bag of cookies, and Uncle Joe would head over to his house to see what was going on.

Families talked around things like that. Sometimes, so did whole towns. Everyone knew everyone's business in Logan. Mostly it didn't matter, since every family had a drunk or a gambler or a loon of their own. Sometimes you got into fights with other kids who talked shit about your folks, because you knew theirs were no better. But sometimes a family had a Daniel Whitlock in it, and nobody knew what to make of that.

"You dating Casey Whitlock?" their mom had asked Jim way back when.

"Yeah. So?"

"That family's trouble."

"That's bullshit, Mama," Jim had said. *"Her brother's weird, but she and her folks are okay."*

Weird. Bel hadn't known for sure what people meant back then. He liked to watch Daniel Whitlock run. A few times he'd seen him down by the riverbank, reading when the rest of the kids were swimming. He had a sinking idea that *weird* meant *fag*, and that he was probably weird as well. Then he heard about the time that Daniel Whitlock was caught looking into Bobby Grant's window for three nights in a row and claiming he didn't know nothing about it. Like Bobby was lying or something, but Bobby's sister saw him as well. And their mom.

Weird fag.

After that, Bel had kept clear of him. Didn't want to get tarred with the same brush. He wondered now if it would have made any difference if Daniel'd had a friend back then.

"Mama, you remember Daniel Whitlock when he was a kid?" he asked as he sat down at the kitchen table.

"'Course I do." She took a loaf of bread from the bread bin. "Want a sandwich, baby?"

"Yes, please. You got turkey?"

"I think so." She went to the fridge. "Why are you asking about Daniel Whitlock?"

"Someone tried to burn his cabin down last week."

"I heard about that."

Yeah, the whole town had heard about that. And everyone knew it was Clayton and R.J. and Brock, but the boys weren't saying anything. Just walking around with more swagger than usual, and proud grins plastered on their faces.

"Well, I've been talking to him a bit," Bel said. "Kind of got me wondering if anyone saw it coming. What he did, I mean."

His mother snorted at that. "'Course everyone did, but only in hindsight!"

"Yeah, I guess that's how it goes."

His mother set his sandwich in front of him. "Turkey and mayo."

"Thanks."

She sat down opposite him, cupping her hands around a mug of coffee. "Well, he was an odd one, always wandering around town when a boy his age should've been home in bed. There's worse things, I know, but I didn't want you boys hanging around him because of the drugs. Wouldn't be surprised if that's what scrambled his brain to begin with."

Bel had no reason to get defensive when a week ago he'd thought Daniel was on something as well. He took a bite of his sandwich. "What if it wasn't drugs though?"

His mother looked at him. "You don't believe that rubbish that he didn't know what he was doing, do you?"

"I think he knew what he was doing," Bel said. "But I think he was sleeping when he did it."

"That's nonsense."

"I've seen it, Mama. I've talked to him when he's like that, and when he wakes up, he don't remember. He's not lying, I know that."

"Exactly how much time are you spending with that boy, Little Joe?"

"It's for *work*, Mama." Not entirely a lie. "Anyhow, Dav's been saying for years she believes him."

His mother furrowed her brow. "Dav didn't grow up here, didn't know what he was like."

"Well, maybe that's a good thing. Maybe she's got no prejudice against him like the rest of this town."

"I love that girl like she's my own daughter. But she's plain *wrong*."

Bel pushed his plate away. "Maybe I'm plain wrong too then, Mama."

"I don't understand. Why are you getting all out of shape over this?"

This, Bel thought. *Him. Weird fag freak.*

"I dunno. Makes me wonder, I guess, if there was something wrong with me like that, if I'd be living out in the woods with my own family pretending I wasn't drawing breath."

His mother pushed her chair back and came to stand behind him. She put her thin arms around his shoulders. "No. That wouldn't ever happen, baby."

Bel leaned back into her embrace and sighed. "Thanks, Mama."

She held him for a moment longer, giving one last squeeze before she let him go. "Now, are you gonna spill the beans on Dav or not?"

Lucky he'd pushed his sandwich away, or he might've choked. "I don't know what you're talking about."

His mother leaned against the countertop, crossing her arms over her chest. "Don't you lie to me, Joseph Peter Belman."

"I ain't lying," he lied.

She huffed. "I was nineteen when I had Billy, but things were different then. These days, a girl can wait a while longer. Dav's got a career, a better one than Jim's, and twenty-five is too young to throw it all away on a baby."

She'd be singing a different tune when they told her, Bel knew.

He stood. "I gotta go. I gotta get some groceries and stuff."

"Little Joe," she said in a warning tone.

He showed her his palms. "Mama, if Dav and Jim have something to tell you, they'll tell you in their own time. Ain't no business of mine."

"Joe!"

Her voice followed him back down the hallway to the front door, where he made his escape into the sunlight.

"Fuckers! Inbred fuckers!"

Daniel thought it was the sound of his own screaming that woke him. That, or the smell of blood and wet grass. For a second, he saw Kenny Cooper looming over him and sucked in a breath for another scream. Then there was a hand over his mouth. They'd done that too. Put a hand over his mouth, blocked off his nose, and he thought he was going to choke. He'd tried to bite. Could still taste the cigarettes and beer and sweat.

"It's me," Bel said. "You're okay."

Bel's hand didn't smell bad. Didn't smell of anything at all, except Bel. Daniel relaxed and flicked his tongue against Bel's palm. Tasted good.

Bel pulled his hand back like he'd been stung. "You awake, Daniel?"

"I'm awake."

"Gonna turn the light on."

Bel knelt up, and a moment later the mattress rose as he stood up and headed for the light switch.

Daniel squinted when the light came on. "What'd you do that for? What time is it?"

"About three," Bel said. "You been flopping around like a landed fish for about an hour. I think maybe you hurt yourself."

It wasn't until Bel said it that Daniel felt it. He pulled his arms down as far as he could and twisted his neck to see. The cuffs had cut his wrists. "Yeah, stings a bit."

"You got a first aid kit?"

"No. Maybe got some iodine under the bathroom sink."

Bel snorted and shook his head. "You living out here in the woods and you got no first aid kit?"

"I got a pair of tweezers too!" Daniel said, and smiled at Bel's answering laugh.

When he came back, Bel sat on the bed beside Daniel with the iodine and a roll of toilet paper. He unlocked Daniel.

Daniel sat, resisting the urge to rub his stinging wrists.

Bel reached out for Daniel's hand and drew it onto his thigh. "This'll smart," he said, and dabbed it with iodine.

"Jesus fuck!"

Bel lifted Daniel's hand up, leaned toward it, and blew on the sting. "Better?"

Daniel couldn't remember the last time someone had done that for him. His mom, probably, when he'd skinned his knees as a kid. He nodded and gave Bel his other hand.

He hissed as Bel cleaned it. "Thanks."

"No problem." Bel didn't meet his gaze.

"Better put the cuffs back on now," Daniel said.

"Maybe that's not such a good idea," Bel said. "I gotta work early in the morning, and your yelling and twisting doesn't exactly let me get my eight hours, you know?"

"Sorry. If you wanna go, I got the ice locks. I already got a few hours, so it'll be fine."

"I ain't leaving you, Daniel."

That twisted his guts up.

"You lay there and get comfortable for once."

Daniel lay back with a sigh. "Bel," he said, as Bel rose and headed back to the bathroom to put the stuff back. He rolled onto his side. "You gotta lock me up, Bel."

Bel padded back and flicked the light off. "Shut up, Daniel."

Daniel scowled. "It's gotta happen! You can't fuck around with this. It's—" And clamped his mouth shut when the mattress dipped again. Bel pressed his warm body against Daniel's and wrapped his arms around him. "What're you doing?"

"Gonna hold you until morning," Bel said, his breath hot on the back of Daniel's neck.

Daniel bit back a whimper. He cleared his throat. "But—"

"Shut up," Bel said again, tightening his grip. "Just relax."

Daniel tried, but it was impossible with Bel's arms around him. Daniel was suddenly too hot. Itchy, uncomfortable. His dick was swelling, and he felt tight all over his body. Hadn't shared a bed with anyone he remembered in years. Awake, Daniel's body didn't want sex. Sometimes his cock reacted to an attractive guy, but there weren't many of those in Logan, and the desire never lasted.

But Bel kept breathing steadily, and soon Daniel couldn't do anything but breathe with him. His dick was hard, and the heat of Bel's breath was making him squirm.

"You always this antsy?" Bel asked.

Daniel's answer was a sharp inhale as Bel's groin pressed against his ass. "Can I . . .?" he whispered.

"What?" Bel's voice buzzed along the edge of his ear.

Daniel rolled over and faced Bel, wriggling against him. Threw one leg over Bel's hip and moved his lips toward Bel's.

Bel squeezed Daniel harder, making him grunt. He expected the kiss to be as hard as the embrace, but Bel's lips were gentle. Daniel kept one hand on Bel's chest and ran the other through his hair. Bel was wearing jeans, which was strange—the stiff denim against Daniel's soft flannel pants. He liked that Bel was dressed—it made him feel like if anything happened, Bel would be ready to take care of it.

He would have liked Bel better undressed, though. Was about to tell him so, except . . .

Except he never did this. Not awake. Yet his cock was throbbing, his balls fucking aching. He wanted anything Bel had to offer—Bel's hands on his wrists, Bel rolling him onto his stomach, forcing his hips up. He clenched his ass as he imagined Bel's cock sliding inside him. The burn of it.

Pain could be exciting. Daniel shivered at the thought. It could be, if it meant something.

He panted, taking gulps of air between kisses. Bel had pushed one leg into the V of Daniel's and was slowly moving it back and forth. Daniel gasped as the top of Bel's thigh grazed his balls through his pants. He moaned against Bel's cheek as he rubbed his cock on the front of Bel's jeans.

"There you go," Bel whispered, as Daniel found his rhythm.

Daniel wondered if he should offer to do something better than rutting against Bel like a horny teenager. Knew he couldn't manage a blowjob, but he'd make a decent effort with his hand. He started to reach for Bel's fly, but suddenly Bel was digging his fingertips into Daniel's back in quick pulses that matched the steady jerking of Daniel's hips. The pressure was just close enough to pain that Daniel forgot to think, forgot to worry, just fucking plunged into a dark fire that took his whole body, made him writhe and shudder.

"That's it." Bel kissed Daniel's chin. His tongue rasped along the stubble there. He bit lightly. Every few seconds Daniel had to stop thrusting and grind his cock against Bel's hip, clutching Bel as he did. Whenever he did that, Bel would press his hip against Daniel's groin, rubbing up and down, helping Daniel as best he could. Each time, Daniel felt closer to the edge, and he sucked in a breath and tried to let go. But each time he came up short, and finally he faltered.

"Come on," Bel urged.

Daniel let out the breath he'd been holding and tried one more time. Bel's hand slid down his back, and two of his fingers pressed Daniel's tailbone. Daniel imagined those two fingers pushing into his tight asshole, fucking him. The thought wasn't scary. With Bel, it wasn't scary.

Bel's lips closed over his again, his tongue skimming the roof of Daniel's mouth. A low groan from Bel that Daniel felt in the back of his throat, and then Daniel's balls tightened. He closed his eyes, tilted his chin up, and held Bel as hard as he dared as he came. Long, hot spurts of cum that covered the inside of his pants, dripped onto his thighs.

Daniel let his body go slack. Struggled to get his breathing back to normal. "Shit," he whispered.

Bel stroked his back. "You wore out yet?"

Daniel tried to laugh. The sound stuck in his throat, and he swallowed it. His face burned a little. "I don't, um, don't usually . . ."

"Usual ain't been helping you much," Bel said quietly.

"That what this is?" Daniel whispered, feeling the shame creep in. "You *helping* me?"

"What this is," Bel said, "is messin' around a bit. Ain't no big thing if you don't want it to be. Maybe you'll sleep without going nuts, and maybe you won't. I just wanted to see you come."

"I'm not so good with casual," Daniel admitted. He'd never had a casual relationship.

"You willing to let some stranger lock you up, but you ain't good with casual?"

Daniel wondered if Bel was talking about himself or Master Beau. "I mean, I don't know what the rules are."

"Why do there gotta be rules?" Bel rubbed his back.

"I don't know," Daniel said, trying to lie still. "I like rules."

I like being told. I like knowing there are boundaries. I like feeling secure.

"But you don't make the rules, do you?" Bel asked.

"No. That's not . . . that's not how it works."

Bel hesitated. "You want me to do it?"

Yes. Please, yes.

"If you wanna."

Bel was silent for a long while. Then he sighed, a gentle heat against Daniel's face. "Okay."

Daniel waited, but Bel didn't say anything else. A quick, cold bloom of fear. *What'd I do, telling him that?* "You want me to maybe . . . if you didn't come, I mean, I could maybe do something for you."

"Not tonight." Bel ran his fingers up the knots in Daniel's spine, rubbing against the soft material of his shirt. "Let's just lay here awhile, okay?"

Daniel closed his eyes, focusing on the touch, letting it quiet his body. "Okay." *Maybe it's okay. Maybe I didn't hurt anything.*

Sleep came much sooner than he expected.

Well, *shit*.

Bel stared at the image on his computer screen. A guy on his knees, with a tight ring around his cock and balls. Made them stick out and bulge like overripe fruit. Which wasn't even the worst of it. The guy had clothespins bristling from his balls.

Bel rubbed his hand over his forehead. Was that the kind of thing Daniel did?

He clicked onto the next picture. Saw blood dripping down some guy's hard cock, and clicked straight through. Did *not* want to know what the fuck was going on there.

He'd come home for lunch. He'd thought of going out to Daniel's, but he wanted to check this stuff out first. The stuff that Daniel was into. And no way was he going to use the computers at work.

Daniel wanted rules, and Bel had agreed to provide them. And there were a lot of rules. Like how a guy—a sub—ought to present himself on his knees. How he ought to mind his posture, how he ought to speak. How he ought to not come until he was told, as though there was any power in the universe that could stop a man from coming once those floodgates were open.

Bel thought of last night, when he'd encouraged Daniel into coming. Wondered if he'd get the same satisfaction from stopping him. He doubted that. So maybe he wasn't a dom or a master or whatever Daniel was looking for. And it was hard to look at these pictures and see Daniel as a sub or a slave. These guys were just . . . weird.

Bel didn't want Daniel wearing nothing but studded leather. Didn't want him to look foolish or debase himself. Didn't want him on display.

Shit, this was all wrong.

He clicked onto the next picture.

Fuck.

Just a guy in a pair of cuffs. Kneeling there, his hands behind his back. Naked, cock hard. And he was looking up at the guy standing over him, and he was smiling. Hell, they were *both* smiling. And it didn't look staged, and it didn't look weird, and it didn't look like they'd raided their Halloween costumes for the photo. It looked—Bel reached down and readjusted his stiffening cock—*hot*. It wasn't just the cuffs. It was their shared smile that looked like something more: hope, need, trust, comfort, *love*?

Bel snorted. Yeah, because two guys on a porn site were in love.

Except the longer he stared, the more real it looked.

He thought of the way Daniel had offered his hand to be cuffed in the hospital: so quiet and trusting. And remembered the way it had made him feel. Maybe it wasn't all about crazy costumes and crazier props. What did Daniel really want?

What did *Bel* really want?

He stared at the photograph. *That*. He wanted that. And Daniel wanted rules. So maybe there was a way to get there without the pain, without the props. Daniel had said himself that he didn't get off like that. Well, Bel wanted him to get off, because holding him last night when he rubbed against Bel until he came had been fucking amazing. Bel had been hard as well, but it didn't even matter. Okay, so he'd jerked off in Daniel's tiny bathroom when he crawled out of bed in the morning, but at the time, Daniel's need had seemed so desperate, so profound, that Bel had shoved his own onto the back burner. Never done that before. Never felt the obligation.

He wished there was some way he could keep this up with Daniel without having to *explain* himself to anybody.

"Went by your place last night," Uncle Joe had said when Bel had turned up to work. "Didn't see your car."

"I was out."

"Oh yeah?"

"It's complicated."

Uncle Joe had left it there.

It was more than complicated. Even disregarding the fact that Daniel was a killer and Bel was a cop, it was complicated. Bel wanted to give Daniel what he needed, wanted to fuck him until neither of them could walk straight too, but what did Daniel really want?

He wanted to be controlled. He wanted to be contained. He wanted Bel to make the rules.

Bel turned off his computer. Time he headed back to work anyway, and he had a feeling he wouldn't find the rules that Daniel needed on any website.

Daniel usually hated Wednesdays, because on Wednesdays he started work at four instead of five, which meant the staff was still in the library when he arrived. Usually he'd avoid them, but not today. Today Daniel went to work all but whistling.

"What's up with you?" Trixie asked. She seemed put off by his good mood.

"Nothing. Nice day, is all."

"Well, some kid puked in the ladies' room and didn't make it into the toilet. People been complaining for half an hour. So have fun."

Daniel barely noticed the stink of the vomit as he cleaned it up. He thought about his intro to chem class in college and the time the professor had taught them about the chemistry of vomit. Vomit contained a lot of hydronium, and when a person vomited too much, they risked potassium and chloride depletion. Useless facts, but hey. Daniel missed school. Wouldn't have minded going into a pharmacy program. Had thought about it a couple of years ago, but it was expensive. And with his condition, better to clean up vomit than be in charge of counting people's pills. Less risky.

He finally got the stall clean. Hell, now he *was* whistling.

Funny how much difference it made in his life, just having Bel.

Bel, who hadn't run, even when Daniel kept waking him in the night with sleep terrors. Even when Daniel had showed him what was in the bag. When Daniel had told him about the piss can.

Bel, who got that he was supposed to make the rules.

Bel would be good at giving orders. He had the right voice for it. It would be fine with Daniel if Bel bossed him around a little. Told him how to sit or stand. Told him what to do in bed. It'd been so long since Daniel had fucked while awake, he wouldn't've minded someone telling him how to do it. So long as Bel hurt him when he needed it.

Only problem might be if Bel wanted his dick sucked. And of course he would—who wouldn't? Still, Daniel could manage. If Bel ordered him to, he could.

Kenny Cooper's words were a hollow memory. Seemed like they shouldn't have any power left, like all that should have drained away over the years. *"Here's my dick, faggot."*

The edge of the barrel sliding between Daniel's lips. Clicking against his teeth.

"Suck it, cunt. I want you sucking it when you die."

Well, Daniel had showed him, right? Fucking showed him.

No. Not today.

Today, Daniel was happy. He was thinking about the chemistry of vomit. He was thinking about Bel. Wishing he could have at least gotten a look at Bel's cock last night.

But there was always tonight.

He wondered what they'd do when Bel arrived. If they'd go right to bed, or if it was only going to be sometimes that Bel joined Daniel there. Only when Daniel woke up screaming, maybe.

No. Bel liked him. Wanted to fuck him. And Daniel wanted to do more with Bel, even if he was a little nervous.

The rules would help.

Halfway through his shift, he started getting exhausted. At one point he slipped into the men's room and sat on the toilet and closed his eyes for a minute.

What are you doing? Can't fall asleep here.

He forced himself up and out of the bathroom.

Shit, he had to be careful. Couldn't let this buoyancy, this hope—*Bel*—make him reckless.

By the time he was done, he could barely drive himself home. It was almost time for Bel to arrive, and he briefly considered flopping on the bed and catching a nap, counting on Bel to arrive before the point where Daniel would normally start sleepwalking.

Instead he got out the seat cover he'd made for himself and put it on the armchair. It was a series of bottle caps glued—edges up—to a sheet of plywood. Sitting on it was a hell of an uncomfortable experience. But it was good for staying awake.

He stripped his pants and underwear off and sat, wincing. Every time he shifted, a new edge dug into his skin. Eventually he found himself moving on purpose, trying to get the bottle caps to cut a little deeper. As he did, he thought about Bel. Bel's voice in his ear, Bel's breath on his skin.

Daniel shivered as a frisson of pleasure skittered up his spine on the tail of the pain. It had been a real long time since that had happened. Not since the early days with Marcus, before he'd pushed Marcus to go harder and further. Before the pain he needed was so absolute that it drowned out any pleasure he was capable of feeling.

He'd never found his subspace, though he'd tried to fake it a few times so that Marcus kept going. In the end, he'd ruined it for both of them.

Daniel squeezed his eyes shut and ground down on the seat cover. Yelped.

Fuck, that hurt. Pushed him right back into the waking world, away from his memories and his fantasies and the sleep that was still calling him.

He breathed heavily. That was good.

That's what the pain was for.

CHAPTER NINE

Bel was anxious when he got to Daniel's that night. Like his heart was gonna tumble out of his chest and go clattering across the floor like a windup toy.

And Daniel barely gave him a chance to settle in before he asked, "You thought any more about what we talked about? About rules?" He sounded just as nervous as Bel felt.

"Yeah. I went online. And I saw a lot of pictures that kinda freaked me out."

Daniel stood there for a second with a stunned, horrified expression Bel saw sometimes when he delivered bad news to families of perps or victims. "Oh."

God, no. Don't look at me like that. I gotta be honest, or this ain't gonna work.

"And a couple that made me hard."

Daniel met his gaze.

"I don't know how to be a—be a dom," Bel said, trying to keep his voice steady. Fuck, maybe he should have practiced this. "I don't know shit about the equipment, or what I'm supposed to make you do. So if there's anything you want, you gotta speak up and tell me. But otherwise, here's the rules *I* came up with."

Daniel straightened.

"Except for Thursday and Saturday, I'm on day shift. So except those days, I'll come here at 9 p.m. Okay?"

"Okay."

"I'll expect you to be ready for bed."

Daniel's *what the fuck?* look almost made Bel falter. But he kept going. "Hey, now. You're the one who wanted rules. So you'll be ready for bed when I get here—showered, teeth brushed, and in your pj's."

"You want me to say my prayers, too?" Daniel asked flatly.

Bel's lips quirked briefly. "Maybe lose the attitude," he suggested.

Daniel stilled. Nodded.

"You can let me in, and then I'll expect you to kneel. Beside the bed." Bel thought again of the pictures. "Hands behind your neck. You know how to do that?"

"Yes, sir, I do." Daniel's tone was completely respectful now. He spoke quietly, and the "sir" pulled Bel's body tight, made him swallow.

"Show me."

Daniel went to his knees with a grace that surprised Bel. Bowed his head. Clasped his hands behind his neck. "Nice," Bel said, as though nice even began to cover it. The sight of Daniel in that position made Bel half-hard.

"You'll wait for me to tell you what to do next." *And I won't know what the fuck to tell you to do. But I reckon I'll think of something.* Shit, the things he wanted to ask Daniel to do . . . "Any questions?"

Daniel kept his head down. "Guess not."

"I expect you to be ready for bed. All right? Each and every night I come here."

"Yes, sir," Daniel said.

This wasn't so tough. Bel's mouth was still a little dry, but he felt less tense. He did shit like this every day, telling belligerent drivers he'd better not catch them speeding again. Telling the high schoolers fighting in Harnee's parking lot to lose the attitude. Giving orders came naturally to Bel, just . . .

Was this what you did with someone you were hot for?

Made sense to boss criminals around. Didn't make as much sense to boss someone you liked. Reminded Bel a little too much of the domestic disputes he handled out at the trailer park. Always, at the root of it, was some asshole who wanted to be in control, who wanted to make other people feel small.

I ain't like that. Don't wanna make him feel small. Want to make him . . . happy. I want to make him happy.

Didn't know if he'd ever seen Daniel Whitlock look happy. Even when they were kids.

"I'd rather you call me Bel. But if you like 'sir' . . ."

"I can call you Bel."

"During the day, you're gonna stay healthy. No caffeine, no junk."

"I already do that."

"Good. Then it won't be a problem."

"Guess not."

"There's another thing."

Daniel glanced up, then quickly looked down again. Breaking position—Bel had read about that. He wondered if this was supposed to be a test. Was he supposed to call Daniel on it? Fuck, this dom stuff was hard.

Speaking of hard . . . he had to get through this. Because what he really wanted to do was strip Daniel and explore his whole body with his mouth.

"Yes, Bel?"

"You're gonna text me. Every day at 2:30 p.m. No matter where you are or what you're doing. You're gonna start your text, 'Hi, Bel. It's Daniel.'"

"Aren't you gonna know it's me already?"

"That ain't the point."

"So the point's to make me jump through hoops?"

Definitely a test. Bel might be a BDSM novice, but he wasn't a novice when it came to people. He'd dealt with plenty of sass from guys in handcuffs. Daniel Whitlock was nothing new.

"Stand up," he said.

Now Daniel looked uncertain. He rose slowly, keeping his eyes mostly on the floor, except once when he flicked his gaze to Bel's. He kept his hands on his neck.

"Look at me."

Daniel looked at him.

"Now say that again."

"Say . . .?"

"What you just said to me."

"I said, 'So the point's to make me jump through hoops?'"

Bel stared at him. Daniel gazed back, his defiance overshadowed by a nervousness that increased with each passing second. "You didn't even let me finish," Bel said. "I had something to explain to you, and you interrupted."

Bel didn't say anything else. Another few seconds, and then Daniel said, "I'm sorry, sir. Bel, I mean."

Bel nodded. "All right. As I was saying. You text me. 'Hi, Bel. It's Daniel.' And then you tell me one thing. 'Bout how you're feeling or what you're doing or whatever."

"That's it? So I should tell you if I'm taking a shit? Or that I feel happy?"

"Whatever you want."

"These are weird rules, Bel."

"These are weird circumstances, Daniel."

Bel watched Daniel stifle a laugh.

"And what if I don't do what you say?"

"Then we deal with it," Bel said simply.

"How?"

Bel hadn't really thought that part through. He didn't know enough about Daniel to know what might be appropriate consequences for breaking the rules. "For me to know and you to find out."

Bel had a sinking feeling from Daniel's look that he was going to try to find out as soon as possible. Bel couldn't imagine using one of those paddles on Daniel. Or even his hand. Jesus, spanking was just . . . weird. And all right, maybe some of the pictures he'd seen of guys getting whipped had made him hot, but to actually think about doing that to another human being . . . Bel wasn't ready to go there yet.

"One other rule." Bel wasn't sure how Daniel was gonna react to this one, so he braced himself.

"Yeah, Bel?"

"You're gonna go see a counselor. Someone Dav knows in Ladson. Once a week."

"*What?*" Daniel curled like he'd been hit or was gonna be sick.

"Weekly appointments with a psychologist."

"For what?" He dropped his hands from his neck and stared at Bel. "What the fuck did I do?"

"To help you." Suddenly it was hard for Bel to remember the perfect rationale he'd had earlier. Daniel looked agitated. More than agitated—pissed. "You sort through some of the stuff that's going on when you're awake, and maybe it'll help you sleep."

"What stuff? What do I need help for? *You're* helping me." Daniel took a step back. "You want to get me committed, too?"

"I never said that." Bel wanted to reach out and touch him, to reassure him, but he didn't know if they were there yet. Shit. The guy had offered himself on a platter, and Bel didn't know if they were there yet? He had a right, didn't he? Had the right to make Daniel do whatever the fuck he wanted, to put up with any touch Bel chose to give him, because of this thing they were doing.

Was that what Daniel wanted?

"You scared of being committed, Daniel?"

Daniel barked out a laugh. "'Course I fuckin' am! What do you think?"

I think you'd get to wear a straitjacket as often as you wanted.

"Thought you liked being locked up," Bel said. He showed Daniel his palms. "I ain't trying to fuck with you, just trying to figure some things out."

Trying to figure you *out.*

"Was in the hospital ward in jail for a while," Daniel said, his voice wavering. "They put me on drugs. Didn't make it better, just made it harder to tell the difference between awake and asleep. I started to see shit even when I wasn't sleeping. I think maybe some other stuff happened." He looked at the wall. "Told them what this other inmate did to me in the night, and they said I dreamed it. I don't know."

"Come here," Bel said. He held his arms open, and Daniel stepped forward, stepped into them and rested his head on Bel's shoulder. "You ain't crazy. I know that. But there's no shame in talking to someone. You'll do it, won't you?"

Daniel didn't answer. His muscles went hard under Bel's arms.

Bel firmed his voice. "It's a rule, Daniel."

"Okay." Daniel's breath was hot on Bel's throat. "I'll do it, so long as they don't put me away. I gotta be safe, Bel. Gotta know what's going on."

"I get that," Bel said. He gripped Daniel by the shoulders and pushed him back gently. Needed to see his face. "I won't do that to you. I'm trying to understand here, and I'm gonna need you to be patient with me, okay? Because I'll ask dumb questions and I'll say the wrong things, because I ain't never done anything like this. You okay putting someone like me in charge here?"

Daniel bit his lip and nodded. "Yeah, I think so."

Bel allowed himself a smile. "Good, 'cause I've got a couple of ideas already."

Daniel looked half-terrified, half-delighted. "You do?"

"Yeah." Bel let go of his shoulders. "Why don't you show me again how you kneel? Only this time I wanna see some skin."

Daniel stared at him. Was Bel supposed to say something else? *What do you want to see?*

"Take your shirt off."

Daniel reached around and grabbed his T-shirt by the back, then pulled it over his head and tossed it aside.

Bel took a minute to admire Daniel's chest. No rush here. Most of Daniel's muscle was in his legs, from running. But his chest was well-defined, his torso lean and smooth.

Bel wanted to see those runner's legs, though.

"Now your pants."

Daniel's chest moved in and out. He bent, and Bel watched his arms flex as he unbuttoned his jeans and slid them down. Stepped out of them. Kicked them over to join the shirt.

"You hard?" Bel asked, keeping his tone casual.

Daniel laughed uncertainly. "What?"

"You hard?" Bel repeated. "C'mere and let me feel."

Daniel stepped forward.

"Put your hands behind your head, like you were doing earlier."

Daniel obeyed.

Bel reached out and stroked the bulge in his underwear. "Not all the way, huh? You'll get there."

Daniel tipped his head back as Bel continued stroking him. Shifted his weight once, then forced himself still. Bel could see what an effort it was for him not to move.

"Kneel down, now."

Daniel went down onto his knees, looking almost relieved to break their contact.

Bel wondered at that. Did he want to be touched or didn't he? He probably didn't know himself.

"That's good," Bel said.

Bel walked around behind him. He looked at the muscles bunching in Daniel's shoulders and reached out to touch him. Daniel jerked as Bel swept a hand down his back. Bel made a shushing noise, gentling him like he was a skittish animal or something.

A part of him missed sleeping Daniel—smiling, sluttish, up for anything. But a part of him knew he was getting what none of those assholes at Greenducks ever had: the real thing. That was worth working for. However much he wanted to kneel behind Daniel, rip those briefs off, and shove his cock into his ass, Bel wasn't going to fuck this up. He couldn't imagine that this was ever going to happen again—that some hot guy would ask Bel to take charge like this. It seemed like the sort of thing that would only come along once in a lifetime, so Bel wanted to take his time with it. Wanted to draw it out, see where it went.

"Spent a long time on that website today," he said, watching Daniel breathe.

Daniel bowed his head. "Some of the stuff that freaked you out..."

Bel tugged gently at a curl of hair on Daniel's nape. He needed a haircut. "Yeah?"

"I've probably done most of it," Daniel whispered. "That matter to you?"

"Wouldn't be here if it did," Bel said. "You really like it though? The stuff that hurt?"

A beat. "Yeah."

Bel tugged harder on his hair. "You telling me the truth, or you telling me what you think I want to hear?"

Daniel shifted slightly. "I like it when I'm too hurt to move, but I don't get off on it if that's what you mean."

Bel stared down at him. "There a middle ground with you, Daniel?"

Daniel was silent for a while. "I don't know."

That was okay. Bel cupped his hand over Daniel's clasped fingers. "We'll figure something out, I guess."

Daniel relaxed.

Bel moved around in front of Daniel again and crossed the room to sit on the bed. Daniel darted an uneasy glance at him, and Bel smiled. "I want you to do something for me now, okay?"

Daniel waited.

"Want you to show me how you bring yourself off."

Daniel opened his mouth, closed it, and opened it again. "Been a while."

"It's been a night," Bel reminded him, watching the blush rise on Daniel's face.

"That was . . . that was you helping me," Daniel whispered. "Telling me."

Bel glanced at Daniel's briefs and saw the way his cock was still pushing against the fabric. "You're hard enough. And I'm still telling you. C'mon now."

Jesus, it was excruciating to watch as Daniel slowly unhooked his hands from behind his neck. His left hand balled into a fist. His right hand slid under the elastic of his briefs, and cupped his cock. Bel wanted nothing more than to haul his ass onto the bed and touch every goddamn inch of him. But he also wanted to see this. To see Daniel do something that so obviously made him uncomfortable, just to see if he would.

"Don't hide it from me," Bel said.

Daniel nodded and shoved his briefs down. His cock rose, dark against the pale skin of his abdomen. He wrapped his fingers around it and started to stroke. Closed his eyes, frowning. Hating it maybe, but he didn't stop.

Fuck. If Bel knew nothing else about what they were doing here, he knew that one day he wanted to see Daniel do this with nothing on his face but pleasure.

"That's good, Daniel," Bel said, shifting to ease the pressure on his own cock. "Real good."

Daniel sucked in a quick breath. He rubbed his thumb over the head of his cock, spreading the moisture to the shaft. Kept working it, lifting his chin now.

Bel wondered if he would open his eyes. Wondered if he ought to tell him to, or if that would break the spell.

Something did.

Bel heard it before Daniel did: the sound of an engine getting closer and the crunch of tires on dirt. Then the blare of a horn.

"Stay there," Bel said, as Daniel sprawled backward and tugged his briefs up. Bel headed for the window. He saw the glare of headlights around the edge of the canvas. Not just headlights, but spotlights too. The sort of array that Clayton McAllister had on his truck.

And every second guy in town.

The horn blared again, and Bel went to the door.

"Don't go out there!" Daniel said, his voice pitched high.

Bel paused with his hand on the doorknob. "They ain't gonna mess with me," he said, and then realized he had no idea if that was true or not. If they saw him here like this, off duty, what would they see first? The cop or the fag? Didn't matter. No way was he gonna hide inside the cabin.

"Don't! Let 'em have their fun and they'll be on their way. Don't make it worse."

Bel could hear whooping now, and laughing. They must've seen his car. Must've known Daniel wasn't alone. He wondered if they knew the car was his, and if it would make any difference. Fuck it. He wasn't a coward.

"Bel!" Daniel was suddenly right beside him, holding his arm. "Don't."

"Someone tried to burn this place down with you in it," Bel reminded him.

Daniel leaned against the door, flinching at the sound of smashing glass from outside. "Just a bottle, probably. Yeah, someone did, but they were quiet about it. This is probably just kids or something."

Bel thought about asking just how many people in Logan took the time to terrorize Daniel, then figured he really didn't want to know.

Please, Daniel mouthed. He reached out and caught Bel's hands.

It took everything Bel had not to push him out of the way.

"I don't want any more trouble," Daniel whispered.

Too bad. Trouble was already there. The floorboards underneath them vibrated as several sets of boots pounded up the steps onto the porch. Bel heard laughing and loud shushing noises. Daniel was probably right; probably just kids. Didn't mean they had a right to do this sort of shit.

When Bel was a kid, there'd been a man who lived on Gable. Creepy guy, lived all on his own. All the kids told stories about him and filled in the blanks with what was speculation one day and gospel truth the next. Made him a monster. They used to sneak by his house and watch the curtains twitch. The guy never came out through, which just *proved* it. Proved everything they ever made up about him. Bel wondered what it would be like to grow up and discover that you were that guy.

There was a thunk. More stifled laughter. Somebody howled like a wolf.

"That's it." Bel pushed Daniel gently to the side and threw open the door. Shoved the screen as hard as he could. It hit something. There was a shout, then footsteps pounding in the drive. Bel ran out of the cabin, stumbling on whatever the thing was. He glanced down. Eyes glinted. Ears like slabs of deli meat. A pink snout, a dark mouth half-open.

A severed pig's head.

Fuck. Bel almost called to Daniel to stay back, not to come out. But he had to catch the culprits. He ran past the head and off the porch.

"Outta here! Get the fuck out!" They were already in the truck, tires shooting gravel as they backed out. They nearly hit a clump of bushes, and Bel wished they had.

The truck had to be Clayton's. Looked like the one he'd seen on the highway that night he'd taken Daniel home from Greenducks. Bel ran after it as it pulled onto the road. He was trying for a glimpse of the license plate, a glimpse of the people inside.

He couldn't remember running this fast in a long time. He was no Daniel Whitlock, all long legs and easy grace. He could tackle a guy okay, but he wasn't too quick. As the truck sped through an open patch of moonlight between the trees, Bel could see the driver had his arm out the window and was giving Bel the finger. Bel stopped, hands on his knees, and watched it disappear.

It was too dark to pick up all the broken glass, but Daniel dropped the biggest bits into a trash bag along with the pig's head. He'd take it to the dump tomorrow morning, because he didn't want it to stink the place up and there was no garbage collection this far out of town.

He could hear Bel talking to someone on the phone, his voice low and tense, but didn't know who he was talking to.

Daniel dropped the trash bag on the ground. He glanced back at the cabin, but it was too dark to see what the graffiti said. He wouldn't know until Bel came back with the flashlight. He figured it wouldn't say anything too original anyway.

Bel came striding back, pocketing his phone. "Don't know if it was McAllister. I didn't get a good look at them." He glanced at the trash bag. "This sorta shit happen to you a lot?"

"Nothing I can't handle," Daniel said.

Bel flashed the light around, checking their cars. "Ain't safe out here, Daniel."

"It's safe enough."

Bel shone the light on the cabin. Yep. The words were about what Daniel expected. He was glad when Bel pulled the light away from them.

"Get dressed and get in my car," Bel said. "We ain't sleeping here tonight."

Part of Daniel was relieved, didn't want to argue. The other part of him panicked. "Where we going?"

"My place."

"I can't—"

"Daniel." Bel didn't raise his voice, but his tone shut Daniel up. "Who'd you put in charge?"

Daniel nodded. Went back into the cabin and put on his clothes. Grabbed Bel's keys from the table beside the bed.

He didn't speak in the car. They passed downtown and headed east, finally pulling up to a small split-level.

Bel's house. Daniel had never given much thought to where Bel lived. He'd pictured Bel living in the house the Belmans had occupied when Daniel was growing up—half of a duplex near downtown. A birdbath on the front lawn.

But Bel was an adult now, with his own lonely little house. Inside, decorations were spare—nothing on the walls but a calendar in the kitchen. The carpet was old and soft; the furniture all leather and wood in neutral tones. Bel gave Daniel a brief tour, then made coffee. Decaf.

Bel took a long drink. "There's some twisted fuckers in this town."

"Poor pig," Daniel said.

Bel didn't answer. Daniel wondered what happened next. If they were gonna finish what they'd started back at the cabin. His cock had lost interest, but he bet he could get hard again for Bel.

"How often does this happen?" Bel asked. "People coming to the cabin to bother you?"

Daniel cupped his mug, feeling the warmth. "Not too much. Most people'd rather forget about me. Just once in a while . . . And maybe now because . . . because I saw Clayton that night . . ."

"Saw the noose," Bel said. "Night I tried to bring your keys back."

The night of the fire.

Daniel felt a familiar rage starting in him.

Fuck those animals.

I want to fucking show them.

Dangerous thoughts. Had to make himself quit.

"Can I use your shower?" he asked. "I still smell like that pig."

"'Course."

By the time Daniel got out of the shower, smelling like Bel's shampoo, Bel was in bed. Daniel's mood had improved considerably. He was glad to be out of the cabin, in a new space. There were times these past few years he'd have given anything for the chance to sleep somewhere else, to be able to rent a motel room just for a night or two. But he'd never risked it. And now here he was, in an unfamiliar place that still felt safe.

The bed had brown sheets and a dark-blue comforter. It was bigger than Daniel's, queen-size, enough space for both of them. Bel had laid out sweatpants and a T-shirt for him. Daniel dressed self-consciously, keeping the towel around his waist. Bel didn't say anything about it. Just patted the bed when Daniel was finished. Daniel climbed up next to him, and Bel held up the covers while Daniel eased himself under.

Daniel leaned his head against Bel's shoulder and waited for his breathing to match Bel's.

"What's that?" he asked, nodding at a stack of papers on Bel's nightstand.

"A new addition to the manual at work. Policy about officers from other jurisdictions. We're supposed to read it for the next meeting."

Daniel grinned. "Homework?"

"Something like that."

"You read it in bed?"

"Puts me to sleep faster'n anything."

Daniel's grin broadened. "Well, that's not right, Bel. You gotta take pride in your job."

Bel snagged the sheaf of papers, cleared his throat, and read: *"When responding to an incident involving a police officer from another jurisdiction, the same procedures apply as those set out in Section V, paragraph B (1-3) of this policy. The on-site supervisor must notify the highest-ranking member of the department or the designee."* He glanced at Daniel. "You asleep yet?"

"Almost." Daniel nestled closer. "You got a nice voice."

"No I don't. I sound like a hick."

"You still got a good voice."

Bel snorted. "We can't all go to fancy colleges in the city. You talked just like me when you were in high school. Now you sound almost like a city boy."

"I tried to stop saying 'ain't' in college. It comes out when I'm mad, though." Daniel patted Bel's shoulder. "Keep goin'. I like this."

"You're crazy," Bel said. Daniel didn't even flinch. He knew Bel was teasing; knew Bel hadn't even thought about his word choice. Bel looked back at the page and read some more.

Daniel closed his eyes. He didn't give a shit about the content, but he really did like Bel's voice. He concentrated on the rhythm of it. Smiled whenever he heard Bel stumble over a word.

Bel stopped.

"Why'd you quit?" Daniel murmured.

"'Cause it's boring. And you can't be enjoying it."

"Well, I am."

"If I'm gonna read, we can find something better than this."

"Maybe next time. This is good for now."

Daniel didn't open his eyes, but he could feel Bel watching him. He sighed against Bel's neck and felt the breath bounce back to his lips.

"Didn't know you were into bedtime stories, Whitlock."

Daniel laughed. "Didn't know either."

Bel went back to reading. Daniel lost track of how long he read. Felt the hum of Bel's voice through his body and Bel's. Drifted, glad to be somewhere safe, unchained and unafraid. He was hazily aware of Bel putting the papers aside, turning off the light. Bel shifted down, pulled the covers over them and tucked the comforter tight around Daniel's neck. He traced Daniel's body until he located Daniel's hand and twined their fingers.

"Good night, Daniel," Bel whispered.

Daniel was too tired to answer with anything but a smile Bel probably couldn't see in the dark.

CHAPTER TEN

Daniel should've known Ms. Davenport wouldn't come right out and ask about therapy. She'd ask how things were going, and if he just said *pretty good*, she'd wait, busying herself with her notes, until he came up with something better.

It still made him nervous that Ms. Davenport hadn't just organized his therapy, but that she knew his therapist, John Frommer. They were friends, she'd said. Even though John assured Daniel everything about their sessions was confidential, Daniel sometimes imagined John gossiping to Ms. Davenport. That was why he was careful about what he told John. Especially if John asked about Kenny Cooper.

So far he and John had mostly just talked about his job. And a little about his parents, of course. It was therapy.

"John's pretty nice," he said to Ms. Davenport.

She ticked something on the page she was working on. "I like the free tea in his waiting room, personally. You still mad you have to go?"

Daniel flushed. "I wasn't mad."

"Bel—Officer Belman—says I gotta see a therapist." He'd told Ms. Davenport two weeks ago.

Ms. Davenport had cocked her head. *"He told me you were interested in seeing one."*

"He's a liar. I ain't interested. But I'll do it if it's paid for."

He'd worried all last week that he'd somehow clued Ms. Davenport in to the kind of relationship he and Bel had by suggesting Bel was making him go to therapy. He didn't want to tell her or John or anyone about the rules. Didn't want to tell them Bel came over each night and made sure Daniel was safe. Read to him—not the police manual, but actual books—talked to him, played cards with him. Made him come. Drove him way out on 601 a couple of evenings last week, and they parked in the apple orchard and watched the moon rise.

Now, on an impulse, he told Ms. Davenport, "It's better than being locked up somewhere."

She set her papers down and met his gaze. "No one's going to lock you up if you don't go. If seeing John's not beneficial to you, you don't have to do it."

"I know that." He forced himself to continue. "But my parents, they want me to go off somewhere and get treated. They got together money and everything. And I'm just saying, I'd rather talk to John."

Ms. Davenport frowned. "Where do they want you to go?"

"Don't know. Away from here."

"I don't think your parents realize how well you're doing."

"'Course not. I never talk to them." Then, to discourage any questioning in that direction, he said, "I painted the cabin this week. The outside."

"What color?" she asked him with a smile.

"Just white. Took a few coats, but it looks good now. Got the windows fixed too."

"That's good," she said. "Keeping busy is good."

Daniel went for a run when he got home, then made dinner and watched some stupid movie on his computer. Tried not to be bummed that it was a night Bel worked.

The nights Bel couldn't stay over, they still had a routine. Bel had gotten Daniel a set of hospital restraints—big, soft cuffs that didn't bruise his wrists or cut the skin. They had a long strap between them that threaded through the bedrails, so Daniel didn't have to keep his hands above his head when he slept. He'd also brought Daniel a sleeping bag—lightweight and not too warm for the muggy fall nights, but still padded and comfortable. It was mummy style too, tapered at the legs and with a wide hood that extended from the top. The top of the bag had a drawstring. Once Daniel was inside, Bel would pull the string until the sleeping bag was snug around Daniel's neck. Daniel liked being in the bag. The implications were less creepy than the straitjacket, and when he fell asleep he could almost believe it was Bel surrounding him. Almost.

Bel usually arrived early on these nights, too, so that he and Daniel could play a little before he bound Daniel for the night and went to work.

Daniel was finishing up the movie when Bel arrived. As soon as he heard the car, he started to turn the computer off so he could get in position. Thought for a second. Stayed where he was.

He hadn't brushed his teeth, since he'd been working his way through a package of crackers as the movie played, so he figured he was in trouble anyway. Got a little jittery, wondering what Bel would do, but he made himself relax. Nothing to be scared of with Bel.

Hi, Bel, he'd texted at two thirty today. *This is Daniel. I feel bored.* Bel's reply, five minutes later: *We can take care of that tonight.*

Daniel liked the texting ritual, though he wished sometimes he could come up with more creative things to say. He didn't think Bel cared that he felt tired or that he'd just gotten his hair cut or that he liked chicken.

Daniel was still in his chair, focused on the laptop, when Bel came in.

Bel had a plastic bag with him; Daniel listened to him set it down.

"Daniel." Bel's tone was casual, but Daniel caught the underlying edge to it. "Where're you supposed to be?"

"Just a minute," Daniel said, staring at the screen without absorbing any of the movie. His pulse jerked.

"Not just a minute. Turn that off now, put it on the table, and kneel."

Bel didn't raise his voice at all, but Daniel still tensed. Turned off the movie and shut down the laptop like some supernatural force was compelling him. He placed the laptop on the table and kneeled, clasping his hands on the back of his neck.

Usually when Bel came in and found Daniel kneeling, he touched him. Stroked his hair or cupped Daniel's face and ran a thumb over his lips or reached down to gently twist a nipple. Tonight, he didn't touch Daniel. Just sat in the chair Daniel had vacated and put his hand on the laptop.

"I'll be taking this with me," he said, "and keeping it for the next three days."

Daniel willed himself not to protest. "I get bored."

"You want to use it, you can come to my place and ask permission."

Daniel looked up, startled. "You don't mind?"

Bel shook his head. "My spare key's under the mat. Real original, I know. If I'm at work, you can text me permission to go in and use it."

Daniel stared. This was punishment? Then why was he so fucking thrilled? Permission to go to Bel's house—to go *inside* Bel's house when Bel wasn't there? Daniel couldn't believe Bel trusted him that much. "Yes, Bel."

Bel leaned back in the chair. "So what do you have to say for yourself?"

"I was into the movie. Didn't hear you come up." Daniel kept his tone cool.

"Oh really? Don't you know when to expect me by now?"

"Lost track of time."

"Not cutting it." Bel snapped his fingers. "Undress."

Daniel obeyed, shucking his clothes then kneeling again, a little closer to Bel.

"You said you were bored earlier?"

"Yes, Bel."

"Is this how you make a little fun? By not doing what you're supposed to?"

Daniel didn't answer.

"Aha," Bel said.

"I'm not gonna have any fun tonight anyway, with you gone," Daniel muttered. He couldn't keep the resentment from his tone.

"Daniel Whitlock." Bel's voice held a trace of amusement, but it was still hard enough to make Daniel jolt. "Stand up."

Daniel stood. *Maybe this is it. Maybe this is where he finally takes off his belt and lays into me.*

So far Bel hadn't touched a paddle or a strap or anything like that. Of course, Daniel hadn't really pushed Bel into punishing him until tonight, but still, Daniel could tell Bel felt uncomfortable with the idea of hitting him.

Bel spread his legs and patted his left thigh. "Come straddle my leg. Face away from me."

Daniel glanced at him. No anger in Bel's expression. He turned and slowly lowered himself onto Bel's thigh, so that Bel's knee jutted between his legs. Bel was wearing his uniform pants. *Hot.* Daniel couldn't help skimming his fingertips along the dark fabric. His cock went from half-hard to fully erect as Bel reached around him and gave it a couple of pulls. "You're bored and I'm bored." Bel ran a palm down Daniel's back to the top of his ass crack. "Why don't you put on a show?"

Shit.

Bel had homed in pretty quick on Daniel's nervousness about giving himself pleasure, and he exploited it. He loved making Daniel jerk himself off. Loved making Daniel tell him when he was close to coming. Loved making Daniel beg for permission to let go.

Bel jiggled his leg. "Don't use your hands. Just ride me. Make yourself come."

Daniel was glad Bel couldn't see his expression. He had a feeling Bel would consider it attitude. "That could take a while."

"That's okay. I got time before my shift starts. Go on now."

Daniel slowly shifted his hips forward. "I'll mess up your pants if I come."

"I got another pair in the car."

Daniel rolled his eyes.

"This ain't much of a show," Bel noted.

"I don't want to hump your damn leg."

Bel caught Daniel's hair and tugged, forcing his head back. "I want to see it so bad," he whispered. "Can you want it for me?"

For Bel? Okay, fine.

Bel released him, and Daniel started to move his hips. Slowly at first, then faster as fluid appeared at the tip of his cock. It was frustrating. In order to get friction on his cock, he had to lean far forward, and he hated thinking about the view Bel was getting of his ass when he did that. His balls mostly got in the way, and his ass cheeks felt raw after a few minutes of rubbing against Bel's pants. He needed something more—a hand on his cock. Something up his ass.

"I can't," he said finally, panting. He was still riding Bel's leg, but his rhythm was jerky, ineffective. He was tired, and he felt silly, and he wondered not for the first time why he and Bel had been playing for *two weeks* and Bel hadn't fucked him yet. "I can't get off this way, Bel."

Bel stroked Daniel's sweaty back. "Shy, I think. You ain't doing half of what you could be doing." Daniel could hear the smile in his voice, and worked up as he was, Bel's amusement irritated him a little.

"I'm not shy, I just . . . this isn't enough."

"Turn around."

Daniel obeyed, re-straddling Bel's leg from the other direction. He looked at Bel's face, and the expression he saw banished any irritation he'd felt.

Holy shit. He really does like watching me. He really does want a show.

Bel put two fingers in his mouth and sucked them. Withdrew and reached behind Daniel. Worked his wet fingers down the knots of Daniel's spine. "What do you need?" he asked. His fingers reached a slick of sweat and slid the rest of the way down, to the top of Daniel's crack. Bel dipped one finger into the cleft. "This?"

Daniel leaned forward, lifting his hips slightly. His face was inches from Bel's. His breath caught as Bel's finger traveled further, brushing his hole. He lifted his hips higher, straining. "Please," he whispered. "Okay . . . please."

Bel tapped Daniel's asshole. Daniel let out a shuddering breath against Bel's cheek as Bel worked his finger in. It burned with so little lubrication, and Daniel kissed Bel's jaw to distract himself from the pain. Once Bel was in, Daniel slowly sank back. Lifted, then sank back again. "You like that?" Bel whispered.

Daniel dropped his head and nodded into Bel's shoulder.

Bel pushed a second finger in. Daniel groaned, lifting his hands to Bel's shoulders. He shifted his weight on the balls of his feet. He was so fucking tight, and Bel was slowly, *slowly* stretching him open. Bel slid his fingers in past the last knuckle, and Daniel grunted and arched, pressing his cock against Bel. Bel's fingertips grazed his prostate. Daniel closed his eyes. "Fuck!"

Bel did it again. Left way too much time between strokes. Daniel wiggled, not so self-conscious anymore. He bit down on Bel's shirt to keep from crying out.

"How's this?" Bel asked.

Daniel released his mouthful of fabric and gave a strangled whimper.

"More?"

"No, no, no, no," Daniel whispered as Bel crooked his finger again, sending heat through Daniel's body. "You don't have—don't have to do this."

"I'm doing it, though, aren't I?" Bel asked calmly. He rubbed the sensitive spot, and Daniel bucked, cock leaking on Bel's shirt.

"Could do something for you?" Daniel suggested, desperate to get the spotlight off him.

"You are doin' something for me."

Daniel forced a laugh. "This ain't . . . I don't know what this is."

"No shame in coming in front of me, is there?"

"I don't know," Daniel admitted breathlessly as Bel continued the light pushes on his prostate. Wouldn't have been any shame if Daniel was hot shit. He'd felt that way once in a while during college. But there was something pathetic about a broken, used-up freak like him rubbing himself off on someone like Bel.

Nobody in Logan wanted to see Daniel getting pleasure. If they fucked him, it was for the novelty of fucking a freak, a monster, someone who deserved to be used.

"Show me. Show me what you need."

Why do you want to see?

Daniel twisted his hips, got a better grip on Bel's shoulders, and began to raise and lower himself on Bel's fingers. He let out the breath he'd been holding and moved faster.

"That's right. Fuck yourself on me."

Daniel's face burned, but he did what Bel said. Bel began crooking his fingers in time with Daniel's thrusts. Daniel tipped his head back, a hoarse gasp forcing its way through his throat. He moved one hand to the front of Bel's pants. Rubbed sloppily at the bulge there, until Bel was panting too. His palm chafed against the fabric, and that not-quite-hurt in combination with Bel's increasingly rough jabs sent Daniel over the edge.

He came all over Bel, too focused on trying to breathe to be embarrassed. He continued to rub Bel's cock through his uniform pants, until Bel lifted his hips, threw his head back, and groaned. He sat down hard.

"Okay," Bel said a little desperately, as Daniel kept rubbing. Daniel could feel the wetness through Bel's pants. He collapsed forward against Bel, pressing his lips to Bel's neck and ear. "Okay," Bel repeated.

They stayed like that awhile, Daniel draped over Bel, Bel tracing Daniel's hip bones with his thumbs.

"So that was my punishment?" Daniel asked finally.

"Let that be a lesson to you," Bel murmured.

Daniel sat up, grinning as he planted another kiss on Bel's jaw. "I think you better change before work."

Bel laughed, a low chuckle that vibrated through Daniel. "If you got a shirt I can borrow, I won't say no."

Bel changed shirts and Daniel cleaned up. When Daniel was tucked into the sleeping bag, his wrists bound with the hospital restraints, Bel said, "I got something for you." He grabbed the plastic grocery bag he'd set by the door and pulled out an iPod and a speaker deck. He set the speakers on the table, plugged them in, and attached the iPod. "Since I can't be here tonight."

"You gonna play me some mixtape you made?" Daniel teased.

"Nah. It's an audiobook. Some sci-fi thing—the library didn't have much of a selection. But the whole thing's on here, so you can listen all night if you can't sleep."

Daniel stared at Bel. Jesus fucking shit. No one had ever done anything like this for him before. "I'd rather hear you," he said softly.

"Wish I could stay." Bel finished with the iPod and reached out to brush Daniel's hair off his forehead. The narrator started reading, his voice low and rich but nothing like Bel's. "I'll see you in the morning, okay?"

"Yeah."

Bel moved his hand to the sleeping bag. Stroked Daniel's shoulder. "I won't be too far away. You got your phone in there?"

Daniel nodded, throat tight. He curled his fingers around his phone.

"Anyone bothers you; anyone comes onto this property—you call me. You need to get out—you call me. Got it?"

"Okay. Good night, Bel."

"'Night, Whitlock."

Bel swung into the parking lot at the trailer park. Avery was waiting there, leaning on the hood of his cruiser. He waved a sheaf of papers at Bel. "Just gotta serve these on Grish, and figured he might not like it much."

"I got your back," Bel told him.

Grish was okay, it turned out. Must've hit that magic number of beers between angry sober and belligerent drunk, where he mellowed out, smiled a lot, and sang along to Willie Nelson on his beaten-up old stereo.

"You wanna meet up at the diner for breakfast?" Avery asked as they walked back to their cars.

"What time?" Bel asked.

"About three?"

"Sure," Bel said. "I'll see you there."

He watched Avery drive off and walked around the parking lot for a while, shining his flashlight into cars to make sure they were secure. Nothing much else to do.

He thought about Daniel and hoped he was still in the cabin. Hoped he hadn't wormed his way out of the restraints and the bag, and he hoped no one had gone out to Kamchee to mess with him. They were getting somewhere, he and Daniel, even if he wasn't sure where it was. They were different than a few weeks ago, that was for sure. And sooner or later he was going to fuck Daniel—hopefully sooner. Bel had told himself that he was a gay man living in Logan—he was no stranger to doing without. His right hand had been his best friend for years. Except it was difficult to remember that when most nights he was sharing a bed with a hot guy, also gay, who Bel had been fantasizing about since middle school.

Bel looked up sharply as he heard footsteps approaching.

"Whoa!" The guy put his hands up in front of his face as Bel's flashlight blinded him. "Someone said there was someone checking out all the cars, is all!"

"And you didn't see the police cruiser parked right over there?" Bel asked, angling the flashlight away.

The guy squinted. "What?"

Brock. Brock Tilmouth. One of the guys who had set fire to Daniel's cabin. Probably.

"Oh, hey Officer Belman." Brock emphasized the 'officer,' like he was making a joke of it. Like they were still in school, and Brock thought he was hot shit because he could throw a football. Like he wasn't some unemployed bum living in Logan's trailer park.

"You not out riding with Clayton and R.J. tonight?" Bel asked him.

"Uh, no." Brock spread his arms. "I'm right here. Obviously."

Bel didn't react to that. "Thought maybe you boys might head out to Kamchee Woods, try to finish what you started."

"Didn't start nothing." Brock narrowed his eyes.

"Is that so?" Bel rested a hand on his firearm. "Not what I heard."

"Fuck, man," Brock snarled. "We didn't do nothing, and who the fuck cares if Whitlock burns anyhow?"

Bel fought his own rage. "You go near Whitlock's place again, or Whitlock himself, and there will be consequences."

"That faggot killed my friend," Brock said. "He deserves anything that's coming to him."

"Not your job to decide that," Bel said. "The law is done with Whitlock. You oughta be done as well. And if you ain't, then next time we talk it'll be at the station. You understand me?"

Brock's mouth tightened.

"You understand me?" Bel asked again.

"Yeah," Brock said, scowling. "I got you loud and clear, *Officer*. Kenny's dead, Whitlock's walking around, and I gotta let it go. That's the fucking law."

"Yeah, that's the law."

Brock stared at him for a moment. "Ain't no wonder people take it in their own hands then, is it?"

Yeah, Bel thought as he watched Brock slink away like a stray cat. *Ain't no wonder.*

It was no good wasting his breath on Brock Tilmouth. Nothing Bel said would change the man's mind, nor the rest of the town's mind neither. Hell, a few weeks ago, Bel would have agreed with Brock.

You killed a man, you didn't deserve to be free.

You beat a man for being gay, you were a fucking waste of air, but you didn't deserve to burn to death.

But Christ, it worked the other way too, didn't it? You come on to the wrong guy, you didn't deserve to be beaten almost to death. You didn't deserve to live your whole life after that afraid and angry and alone. Bel thought about the rare occasions Billy'd snuck Bel into the Shack when Bel was still underage. Watching Billy hit on girls who wanted nothing to do with him. Those girls had never dragged Billy into a field and beaten the shit out of him for daring to think he had a chance.

There were no winners here. Not Kenny, not Daniel, and not the law. They were all wanting, every one of them.

CHAPTER
ELEVEN

Bel got to Kamchee earlier than he'd expected the next morning.

Daniel's cabin never felt safe or welcoming. Bel's memories of the place were of Daniel struggling in his cuffs while smoke filled the room. Of broken glass and the pig's head and helping Daniel scrub graffiti off the front. Daniel's hallucinations, his bruised wrists, the tiny, isolated room where he'd imprisoned himself for years.

Yet Bel loved coming down the dirt road and catching his first glimpse of the cabin—if only because it meant he was going to see Daniel. Was going to kiss him while he was still tied down and taste him before Daniel could duck away to the bathroom to brush his teeth.

Daniel was still sleeping when Bel let himself in. Holy shit. When was the last time that had happened? Bel closed the door quietly and went to Daniel's kitchen to grab a glass of water. Came back and sat in the armchair, watching Daniel sleep.

Daniel slept through most nights now. Once in a while he got up, and when that happened, Bel tried to do what the internet suggested and calmly lead Daniel back to bed. Sometimes Daniel didn't want to go, and he and Bel would sit up and have an entire conversation with Daniel still asleep. Or they'd play cards. Daniel wasn't always coherent when he was sleepwalking—and he cheated at cards; though Bel suspected he sometimes did this awake too. Bel had learned not to panic when he encountered unconscious Daniel. Not to try to wake him, not to allow himself to go cold with fear when Daniel hallucinated. Just to engage him, comfort him, and try to encourage him to lie back down.

Bel didn't want to give himself credit for Daniel's improved sleeping habits, but he couldn't help preening a little. What other explanation could you give besides the fact that Daniel felt safer? He followed a routine, listened to Bel, trusted him, and as a result, he was sleeping better. His hallucinations were less frequent. His night terrors had all but stopped.

Bel wanted to suggest they get out of the cabin more, that they spend more nights at Bel's house. But he wasn't sure how Daniel would feel about that. He was curious, now that he'd commandeered Daniel's computer, to see if Daniel would come over to use it.

Bel was still trying to figure this whole dom thing out. He spent a lot of time online, reading about rules and punishments and daddies and boys and sirs and subs, compulsively deleting his history as he went. He'd read an article just the other day on revoking privileges as a means of disciplining a submissive. Sounded like a bizarre thing to do to a grown man, but Daniel hadn't seemed to mind. But was that good or bad? Was Daniel supposed to mind more?

The punishment part of his and Daniel's relationship didn't appeal to Bel nearly as much as the being-in-charge part. He liked the idea of leading, of protecting, of looking after Daniel. And he wanted Daniel to follow because it made him feel safe and happy—not because Bel would punish him if he didn't.

And so far, that seemed to be how things were working. Except there were those moments Bel knew Daniel wanted more. Wanted pain.

Bel could never imagine wanting pain himself, but the more he read, the less the idea of masochism bothered him. What bothered him in Daniel's case was the *why*. Over the last few weeks, Bel had seen pictures and videos of guys getting whipped and apparently loving it. But Daniel never asked Bel for pain in the moments he was relaxed, caught up in pleasure. He asked when he was anxious or angry. He asked when he felt shitty about something he'd done. He'd never broken Bel's rules until last night. But he'd asked Bel to hurt him the day he overheard his coworker Trixie call him a psychopath. The day he saw his father in town and his father hurried on without talking to him.

So Bel hadn't hit Daniel at all yet. Needed to figure out first if it was gonna fuck with Daniel to do stuff like that. If it was gonna fuck with *Bel* to do stuff like that. And they hadn't done much more in bed than jerk each other off. Bel had tried to blow Daniel last week, but Daniel had seemed weird about it, so they'd gone back to handjobs.

That same night, Bel had woken when Daniel slipped out of bed. Daniel went to the bathroom, and at first, Bel had thought he was awake and just taking a piss. But when Daniel didn't come out after a few minutes, Bel got up and knocked. Still nothing, so Bel had gone in and found Daniel digging in his palm with tweezers, blood sliding down the heel of his hand.

"What're you doing, Daniel?"

"Got a splinter. Look."

Daniel had showed him his hand, but all Bel could see was blood. *"No splinter. You're sleeping. Let's rinse that out and go back to bed."*

"Gonna fuck me if I go back to bed? Gonna use your cock?"

Daniel had grinned wickedly, and the idea of fucking this man who was standing in the bathroom, asleep and bleeding from his efforts to remove an imaginary splinter, made Bel sick. Then Daniel had stepped forward and tried to grab Bel's cock, and Bel had shoved him back harder than he'd meant to. *"No, Whitlock! Don't you ever fucking do that. You hear me? You ain't awake. Rinse your hand and go back to bed."*

Bel hadn't told Daniel about it the next morning, and though he saw Daniel studying his injured hand, Daniel never asked what had happened.

Now Daniel stirred. "Hey," he mumbled, turning to face Bel.

"Hey yourself," Bel said.

"You have a good night?"

"I've had better. How about you?"

Daniel nodded and yawned. "It was okay. Liked the book."

"Good. You can keep that here." Bel gestured to the iPod and speakers. "I never use it."

Daniel smiled. "So I lose my computer but I get your iPod? I'll have to get in trouble more often."

Bel grinned back. "Don't even think about it."

"You ought to give me a real punishment. Use your belt or something. I'd behave then."

Daniel was still smiling, albeit awkwardly, so Bel gave himself permission not to take the comment too seriously. Even though he had a feeling Daniel meant it seriously. "Who's in charge here?" Bel asked, walking to the bed and leaning down to kiss Daniel.

"You are."

"That's right." Bel raked his fingers through Daniel's hair and tugged lightly. "So who decides when and if I take my belt off?"

"You do."

"That sounds about right." Bel patted the sleeping bag, right over where he figured Daniel's cock was. Daniel gave a tiny gasp. Bel reached up to loosen the drawstring. "Let's undo you."

Daniel pulled his arms out of the sleeping bag and let Bel unfasten the restraints.

"Now get up and get dressed. We're going into town. New bakery there I want to try. You been?"

Daniel sat up, rubbing his wrists. "No. I don't really go into town. Awake."

"Well, today I'd like you to go with me. If you want to."

Daniel looked uncertain. "Not a good idea, Bel."

"I think it's a great one."

"You sure you don't mind being seen with me?"

"You spend too much time shut up here, and I want a donut." Bel tossed a T-shirt at him. "Get dressed and come on."

Daniel pushed himself from the sleeping bag and swung out of bed. "Bossy."

Bel couldn't hold back another grin. "I am, ain't I?"

"Wasn't a compliment." Daniel turned to face the bed and pulled on the T-shirt.

Bel walked up behind him. Put his hands on Daniel's shoulders and slid them down Daniel's arms, to his wrists. Pushed himself against Daniel and bent him forward slightly, hands braced on the bed. "Wasn't it?" he whispered.

Daniel turned his head slightly toward Bel, his eyes downcast. "Might have been," he admitted.

Bel squeezed his wrists. Pressed his lips to the back of Daniel's neck. "You like rules." He kept his voice low, little more than a release of breath against Daniel's skin. "Here's a rule: you walk through this town like you got every right to be here. You don't mind about how anyone looks at you, what they say to you. You got it?"

Daniel arched, trying to roll his shoulder against Bel's lips, seeking more contact. Bel pushed his thumbs against the insides of Daniel's wrists, feeling the pulse there. Daniel finally exhaled. "I'll try, Bel."

Bel kissed him again, leaving his lips on Daniel's skin for several seconds before releasing with a small pop. "That's all I'm askin'."

Daniel went into Logan every weekday for work, but that didn't count. He parked at the library, sometimes walked to Harnee's to buy groceries, and drove out of town again as soon as he was done. He didn't talk to people, and he sure as hell didn't saunter down the sidewalk like he had as much right to be there as the next man. When Bel pulled up a good two blocks from the new bakery, Daniel thought about refusing to get out of the car.

"Maybe I'll just wait here," he said.

"You're coming, Daniel," Bel said, and that was it.

It was morning. The school bus rattled down the street, heralding in what passed for Logan's peak hour. Which was a couple of trucks and a few stray dogs, mostly. Daniel almost smiled at the thought, until he remembered he was living in a cabin in the woods and had no right to look down on Logan at all, one-horse town or not. Those couple of years away in college counted for nothing now. Not with where he lived and what he was. So what if he'd once ordered Thai takeout every Friday afternoon and ate it while Jeff's girlfriend tried to get him to come to the Student Socialist Alliance's screening of some grainy Eastern European film with subtitles? He wasn't exactly urbane now, was he?

He didn't get to look down on the people in Logan, because they were already looking down on him.

Daniel could feel every fucking stare as he walked with Bel. Could imagine the whispers that followed them. If it hadn't been for Bel, he would have cut and run. Although *shit*, it was stupid to draw strength from the guy who'd forced this on him in the first place. If it hadn't been for Bel, he would've been safely hidden away in his cabin.

He couldn't remember the last time he'd just walked down Main Street, counting the same cracks in the sidewalk that had been there since he was a kid. He could remember skipping over them, swinging from his mom's hand. Could remember her laughing at him when he told her he didn't want to break her back by stepping on one.

Even now, he didn't like to step on them. The childish superstition had turned into a habit somewhere along the way. Burrowed into his subconscious and made a home there. Didn't matter. Of all the things in his subconscious, it was the most harmless.

The morning was warm, edging a little toward humid. There was enough of a breeze to keep it pleasant. When Daniel was a kid, the breeze from the west of town had smelled like freshly cut timber, the same as his dad's clothes. He'd loved that smell. The sawmill had been closed for a few years now though. It had employed over a hundred people. A closure like that hurt a town as small as Logan. There were a few empty storefronts on Main Street nowadays. The bakery they were heading for had been a shoe store when Daniel was a kid.

He pulled up short when Bel stopped.

"Thought we were going to the bakery," he said.

Bel pushed the diner door open. "Can't have a donut before breakfast."

Fuck. Fuck fuck fuck.

Daniel followed him in.

Must've been about six customers in the place. Daniel kept his gaze on the floor as he followed Bel to a free booth. Heard conversations stop as he passed and then pick up again, full of whispers.

He slid into the booth opposite Bel. Picked at a blemish on the shiny veneer of the table.

Bel opened a menu. "What do you fancy? I might get bacon and eggs, and a milk shake."

There was a sign on the counter of the diner promising the best milk shakes in Logan. Which was true, given the only other option was the machine at Harnee's. They still made milk shakes the old-fashioned way at the diner, with real milk and ice cream.

"Not that hungry," Daniel said quietly, but took a menu anyway and read it to keep his face down.

"I'll order for you if I have to," Bel said, "so you might as well pick something you want."

The waitress appeared. "What can I get you, Bel?"

"I'll have the bacon and eggs, Sue-Ellen," Bel said. "And a vanilla milk shake."

Vanilla, Daniel thought. No surprises there.

Sue-Ellen tapped her pen on her notebook. "And what about . . . what about you?"

"Same, please," Daniel said, his voice rasping.

Bel reached over and plucked the menu out of Daniel's hand. He put it with his own and passed them back to the woman. "Thanks, Sue-Ellen."

She moved away.

Daniel stared fixedly at the table. "Wish you hadn't brought me here."

"Gotta leave the cabin sometimes," Bel told him. "Look at me."

Daniel lifted his gaze. Bel's face was serious, his eyes dark with concern.

"You got every right to be here, Daniel," Bel said. "You know that, yeah?"

"I guess." Knowing it and feeling it were two very different things.

Daniel wondered what people would make of seeing him eating breakfast with Bel. Couldn't be good for Bel. Daniel wondered what sort of courage it took for Bel to do this, or if Bel had done it without thinking it through. Or maybe he knew exactly what sort of shit would start flying, what sort of sneering rumors this would start, and he didn't give a damn. Was it possible anyone was that confident? Bel was just stupid, maybe.

It had been a long time since Daniel had eaten a decent breakfast, or at least one that was more than toast and peanut butter. Their plates were heaped high when they arrived. Daniel's still was fifteen minutes later, but Bel had demolished his.

"Not hungry?" Bel asked.

"If I eat any more, I'll be sick," Daniel said.

"Yeah, probably a good idea to save room for the donuts, anyway." Bel reached out and speared a piece of Daniel's bacon with his fork. Put it straight in his own mouth.

Daniel's face grew warm. He couldn't help glancing over to the counter where Sue-Ellen was watching. You didn't do something like that—take the food off a guy's plate—unless you were friends. Or more. It was the sort of careless intimacy that said too much.

Bel flashed him a grin. "Stop thinking so hard. You got that same look on your face you did that summer before you graduated, when you were walking around with your head stuck in that chemistry book."

Daniel wrinkled his nose. "You remember that?"

Long days at the river, when he was supposed to be watching Casey. Watching she didn't disappear with Jim Belman, probably, although their mom hadn't specified that. Daniel had studied instead, ignoring Casey and her friends the way they'd ignored him. Except for that one kid.

"You coming in?" the skinny kid had asked, dripping from the river and dappled with sunlight. *"It's real nice."*

"I remember," Bel said with a smile.

Daniel played with his straw. "You were a nice kid, worrying I was being left out."

"Nah," Bel said. "Just wanted to see you take your shirt off."

Daniel couldn't stop the laugh that escaped him. Then he realized what he'd done, and his heart beat faster.

On the other side of the diner, someone's cutlery clattered to the floor.

Fucking murdering freak faggot, Daniel thought, coming in here and *laughing*.

"I gotta—" He slid out of the booth. "I gotta use the bathroom."

He hurried away from Bel, keeping his gaze down again—safest that way, safest to not make any eye contact—and pushed the door to the bathroom open. Went into a stall, locked the door, flipped the toilet lid down and sat there.

Sat there and made himself breathe.

Five minutes passed, maybe more, and then the bathroom door squeaked open.

"Daniel?"

Daniel sucked in a breath. "Yeah, Bel?"

"Your breakfast's getting cold."

"I'll be out in a minute." He closed his eyes and waited to hear the door squeak again. It didn't. "You still in here?"

"Yep."

Daniel opened his eyes again. "You can wait outside. I'll be out soon."

"I'll wait here." Silence. "You want to tell me what happened just now?"

"No."

"Maybe you don't want to, but you're going to."

Daniel made a face at the stall door. "You think?"

"Yep."

Fucker. Daniel sighed. "I *laughed*, Bel."

"Is that a problem?"

"Yeah, it is." Daniel picked at a thread hanging from the hem of his shirt. "I came into their town, where I killed a guy, and I *laughed*."

"This is your town too, Daniel."

"No," Daniel murmured. "No, I don't think it is."

"Come on out and finish your breakfast," Bel said.

Daniel didn't want to. He wanted to stay in the stall, away from people looking at him and whispering about him, but it wasn't going to happen. Not with Bel pushing. Dumb anyway. He'd have to get up and walk out at some point. Might as well be now.

"Can we just go back to the cabin, please?"

"No. We're eating breakfast, getting donuts, and going for a walk first. Then we'll go back to the cabin."

"I don't want to do that."

"You ain't in charge, Daniel. Remember?"

Daniel's stomach clenched. "Yeah."

"So open the door," Bel said. "Right now."

Daniel stood and opened the door. He stared at Bel's face, searching it for signs of anger and finding nothing. "I'm sorry, Bel."

Bel reached out and curled his hand around the side of Daniel's neck. "Nothing to be sorry about."

Daniel let the warmth of the touch soothe him.

"You good?" Bel asked.

Daniel nodded and followed him back into the dining area.

Daniel was jittery, Bel knew, but the longer they stayed at the diner the more relaxed he got. Or maybe it just wore him down to the point where he didn't care anymore. Bel couldn't even imagine what it would be like to have every stare land on you like a threat.

After the diner, they walked along to the bakery. Bel got half a dozen glazed donuts for later, and two for now. Daniel didn't get anything except a bottle of water.

"You watching your figure?" Bel teased him when they were back outside.

"Already had enough sugar to last the whole day," Daniel answered. They walked.

There wasn't much to see. One day soon, Bel thought, they should go down to the river and check it out. Make it a school day, when they wouldn't be gawked at by teenagers who thought they owned the spot. Find a place in the shade under the old railway bridge and relax there for a while.

"You need anything from Harnee's?" Bel asked as they walked.

Daniel shook his head.

They turned off Main Street, passing the police station. Daniel dropped back a few paces, and Bel wondered why that was. He didn't care if anyone saw him walking with Daniel. This was Logan—the whole town would know in a few hours that they'd had breakfast at the diner together. Daniel had done his time, so there was no reason at all that Bel couldn't be his friend. Didn't Uncle Joe play poker every week with that guy who'd held up the store over in Goose Creek in the '80s? So maybe Tyrone had found Jesus inside jail—He was always in the last place you looked—but it would be on his record forever. Same as for Daniel. The difference, Bel supposed, was that Tyrone hadn't killed anyone.

The more they walked, the more easily Daniel spoke and moved.

The more this could be *normal*. Just two guys wandering around town on a sunny day, talking and smiling. It was nice. It was good.

Until their path brought them to the church, and the sign out front on the board with the wonky letters: *Friday night. Vigil for Kenny Cooper. Always in our prayers.*

If it hit Bel in the guts like a blow, then how must it feel to Daniel?

Daniel was wearing almost the same faraway look he did when he was sleepwalking. He flicked his tongue over his lower lip, then bit it. Hard. Turned his lip white under his teeth.

"Daniel?" Fuck, was he bleeding?

Daniel wiped his mouth with the back of his hand, smearing blood over his chin. "Can we go now, Bel? Please?"

"Yeah." Bel lifted the hem of Daniel's shirt to his mouth, cleaning him up like he was a little kid. Maybe this had been a mistake after all. Too much, too soon. Because sure as shit it would take a long time before he saw relaxed Daniel again. Before he could pretend again that anything about this was normal. "Okay, let's go."

Bel took him back to his house. He was quiet, which Bel had expected. Daniel got on his computer, and Bel left him in the living room while he went to shower. He wasn't sure what to say. As a cop, he had to give bad news, talk to people about a lot of awkward things. But if he offered comfort, it was almost always surface level. He said the words he'd been trained to say: *"Sorry to tell you this." "Take all the time you need." "There's resources available if you need them." "We'll do everything we can."*

He wasn't so good at figuring out what to do or say for people he cared about when they were hurting. Much as he loved his mother, she worried too much, and it made Bel uncomfortable not knowing how to reassure her. He preferred to hang out with Dav, who, if something went wrong in her life, dealt with it head-on. Didn't ask for help.

Yet there was some part of Bel that wanted to protect, wanted to reassure, wanted to be needed. It was why he'd become a cop, and it was maybe why he liked being in charge with Daniel.

Fucked that up, though, didn't you? Bein' in charge don't mean you get to push him to do whatever you think's good for him.

He wondered how far back the trip to town had set Daniel.

But what if Daniel needed to be pushed? Wasn't that why he'd given Bel this control?

Thinks he needs to be contained, but that ain't what he needs.

Daniel needed to be pushed to accept freedom. To reclaim his place in the world. He was an odd mix—self-sufficient to an extreme, strong, angry, and alone. And more in need of help—of *company*—than anyone Bel had ever met.

And now what was Bel supposed to say?

"Sorry your whole town still prays for the guy who beat you half to death."

"Sorry, but there's gotta be some consequences for you killing him."

Shit, that wasn't fair. Daniel lived with the consequences every fucking minute. His nightmares. His fear of going out. His shitty—no pun intended—janitor job, when he had a college degree. The noose, the fire, the pig's head, the whispers. Daniel was paying. And Bel was half-terrified to realize he'd all but forgiven Daniel Whitlock for committing murder.

Bel finished toweling his hair and put on some sweatpants. Headed downstairs to where Daniel was doing something on his computer.

"I'm gonna sleep awhile," he told Daniel. "But make yourself at home. Food, drink, anything."

"Gotta go to work in a few hours," Daniel said. "Sorry. Shoulda had you take me home. I wasn't thinking."

"Wasn't saying it to get rid of you," Bel said. "Just, after night shift, I tend to crash real fast. Only so much that a sugar high can do, you know? I meant what I said. You're welcome to stay. I'll be up in time to take you to work."

"Don't want company, do you?"

Bel felt a rush of heat in his groin. He couldn't think of anything more appealing than Daniel joining him in bed. He also knew if that happened, he wouldn't be getting any sleep. "I'd love company. Just figured you were sick of sleeping."

Daniel gave him a tentative smile. "Got years of sleep debt to pay off."

"All right, then. Come on."

Daniel shut his computer, but before they could head to the bedroom, there was a knock at the door.

Bel went to the hall and answered it.

Jim stood on the porch. "Hey."

"Hey," Bel said.

"This a bad time?"

"It's all right. Whatcha need?"

"Wanted to see if I could borrow your mower. I got the truck here."

Bel glanced past him at the big navy-blue pickup in the driveway. "Sure. It's in the garage. Thought you and Dav fixed yours."

"It quit again."

Jim had his thumbs hooked in his belt loops and was shifting back and forth. Bel had never quite understood his brother—got along with him without getting him. But he knew that look and had a feeling Jim hadn't come just for the mower.

"Sue-Ellen said you was at the diner this morning."

"Yep. Daniel Whitlock and I went over." Bel figured it was better to go ahead and say it like there was nothing weird about it than watch Jim try and figure out how to ask.

Jim's eyes widened for a moment. "Oh. I didn't know you—didn't know you knew him, really."

"Mm-hmm," Bel said.

"Well, uh. Obviously Sue-Ellen wasn't the only one who saw you. Couple folks saw you on Main Street, out by the church." Wiping Daniel's bleeding lip. Keeping his hand on Daniel's shoulder as they went back to the car. Bel stared at Jim. "Just wanted to let you know there's some talk."

"It's Logan. I'd be disappointed if there wasn't." Bel glanced over his shoulder.

"He here now?" Jim asked.

"Yeah," Bel said, trying to sound nonchalant. Not quite succeeding.

Jim's face colored. "All right. Sorry to bother you. I'll grab the mower."

Bel nodded.

Jim turned and headed for the garage. Bel shut the door. He felt a little funny, but overall, he was all right. Of course people were gonna talk. Talk about Bel hanging out with Whitlock the killer and talk about Bel hanging out with Whitlock the fag. Talk about Bel the fag. So fucking what?

The pictures of Daniel after Kenny Cooper had beaten him flashed in Bel's mind. You took a chance in a town like this, because people could be cruel. But no point in lying. Hiding.

He returned to the living room. Daniel was still sitting on the couch. He looked at Bel.

"My brother," Bel said. "Wants to borrow the mower."

"And people saw us in town?"

So Daniel had overheard. Bel tried to smile. "Like a celebrity sighting, huh?"

Daniel twisted his mouth. "Not exactly."

No. Bel's smile faded. Not exactly.

CHAPTER TWELVE

Bel polished his boots for Kenny Cooper's vigil and scraped the bugs off the grill of his cruiser. Not that the police were invited—after Daniel's lenient sentence, most people in Logan were wary of any representatives of the law when it came to Kenny Cooper—but Uncle Joe liked to put a few cars along the route just to show some respect.

The vigil started with a church service, then people walked the four blocks down to the park on Main where they waited until their candles burned out. Far as Bel could tell, that was the extent of it. Mostly it was quiet, decent folk who remembered that Kenny had been a good-looking kid who played high school football and missed out on a scholarship to college because he'd wrecked his knee. In another life, he could have been a football star. Stayed in Logan instead, took a job with his dad, and then got burned to death by Daniel Whitlock. Mostly that was the only side of the story people remembered.

There was the other side, too. Bel didn't know if people had forgotten on purpose the sort of man Kenny Cooper had been, or if the horrible way he'd died had magically cleaned his slate. You didn't speak ill of the dead, Bel knew, but why lie about it? Kenny hadn't been anything special. He hadn't been a good person. Kenny had beaten the shit out of Daniel, given him nightmares that lasted to this day. Didn't deserve to die the way he had, but what was the point of pretending he'd been a saint?

Maybe he did *fucking deserve to die that way.*

Bel had been having more and more thoughts like that lately. Scared him to realize he might have felt this way all along.

Bel parked on Main, at the intersection of Cartwright. They'd come this way as soon as they were done at the church: Kenny's parents, still hanging onto their grief, reliving it freshly every year like a scab they got to pull off over and over again, and his sisters, and his friends, and the sort of people who hadn't known Kenny that well, or at all, but knew the law had fucked up Daniel Whitlock's prosecution. Bel's mother would be in the group somewhere. She'd once worked with Kenny's mother. Billy would be there as well, not because he'd been Kenny's friend, but he'd been a classmate, and that was enough. Showing their respect, same as Bel.

Except this year, showing respect felt like a betrayal.

Daniel's message earlier hadn't given anything away: *Hi, Bel. It's Daniel. I'm digging the garden. Might plant onions.*

Sounds like a good idea, Bel had sent back, when he'd really wanted to ask Daniel if he remembered what day it was. What he'd done, four years ago. How he'd walked into Harnee's, and Bel had sold him a lighter with his Twix and Mountain Dew.

Bel could still remember hearing about it the next day. He hadn't believed it, not at first, and then he'd been horrified, he guessed. And something else. He'd felt a strange vicarious thrill from having touched the lighter that crazy Daniel Whitlock had used to kill a man. Like a brush with a celebrity might feel, given that Whitlock was the closest thing to famous that the people of Logan were ever going to get. Logan was a small enough town that everybody had some story about Daniel or about Kenny, but Bel was the only one who'd sold Whitlock the murder weapon.

Bel had recounted the story exactly twice—once for Uncle Joe, and once at trial. Because he was going to be a cop, not a fucking gossip. So that thrill he'd felt, he'd kept it all to himself and got the bonus of feeling sanctimonious as well.

Bel got out of the cruiser.

It was just dusk, so they ought to be winding up at the church soon. Bel wondered if Clayton and R.J. and Brock would be there, wearing ties and trying their hardest not to cuss in church. And he wondered if they'd ever told Kenny's family what they'd done to Daniel Whitlock to make the need to hurt Kenny run bone deep in him, or if it was something Kenny's parents already knew. They had to know. Daniel claimed not to have seen his assailants, but everyone *knew*. Had Kenny's parents forgiven their son for his crime? Or had they convinced themselves that Daniel had deserved it? That all Kenny had done was put a fag back in his place?

Bel had thought not too long ago that Daniel had deserved a smack in the head for being stupid enough to come on to Kenny and giving the homophobic asshole ammunition. You kept your head down and your mouth shut. You didn't draw attention.

Now here he was thinking he'd probably have torched Kenny's house himself, if he'd been in Daniel's place.

So much for not taking sides.

There was no point even pretending now, was there?

He was on Daniel's side. Couple of people suspected it: Dav and Jim, his mom, Uncle Joe. Everyone who'd been in the diner that day. Pretty soon the whole town would know it, if they didn't already. There were no secrets in a place like Logan. Sometimes there were things that people didn't talk about, but there were no real secrets.

Mrs. Henley? Got beaten black-and-blue every time Mr. Henley's team lost, as though she had something to do with it.

That girl in tenth grade who acted weird? You knew her daddy was doing something.

Mr. Pickering? You didn't go into his house alone.

It seemed arbitrary to Bel, the things that were talked about and the things that weren't. Bel had always tried not to give people anything to talk about. Until now, he guessed, because he'd taken a side.

He'd stand here and watch Kenny Cooper's mourners pass, and he'd feel sorry for them because they'd lost someone they loved. Didn't mean that Bel couldn't acknowledge the truth: to the rest of the world, Kenny Cooper wasn't worth mourning.

I'm digging the garden, Daniel had texted Bel, but it was a lie. He hadn't slept the night before—couldn't, not with the knowledge of what day it was. Surprised him that he'd almost forgotten about the vigil until he'd seen the church board. Had been too busy with Bel to think about it. But since that moment, hardly a second had gone by without seeing the date on his mental calendar circled with a big red pen. Red, like blood. Like fire. Like whatever, but it was enough to keep Daniel from sleep. Wasn't going to go under, not when it was all so fucking close again.

The police had woken him. It was like a crazy dream. They were lying to him, or something, except his hands hurt. Why the hell were his hands blistered like that? What did they mean Kenny was *dead*? Kenny couldn't be dead, because Daniel wasn't a killer. Couldn't be.

Because if he didn't know that about himself, how could he know anything? Killing wasn't something you should be able to forget, to *sleep through*.

He'd been too keyed up to sleep last night, too afraid because Bel was working . . .

Too fucking reliant on Bel.

Couldn't expect another man to save you, not when the thing you needed saving from was inside. That was too much of a burden. His parents hadn't been able to stop him from painting the living room green when he was a kid, and Marcus hadn't been able to stop him from wandering every time. Wasn't fair to expect Bel could keep him on a leash when he couldn't keep himself on one.

Daniel didn't need a caretaker or a boyfriend. He needed a fucking jailor.

He sat on his bed, holding up the cuffs that Bel had gotten him from the hospital: thick, padded, soft. The sort they made for crazies, not fetishists. Daniel probably should have been wearing them for years, instead of looking for something in leather, right?

I'm not crazy.

He'd almost believed it, up until Kenny.

Daniel closed his eyes for a moment and drifted before he realized. He felt himself falling and pulled himself back with a jolt.

He was dangerously close to sleep. So close that it took a moment to climb back up into awareness and make sense of his surroundings. His bed, his table, his tiny kitchen, his bathroom door. His cabin, that still smelled a little of smoke overlaid with fresh paint. Everything just where he'd left it.

Except that can of bug spray on the table.

He'd put that beside the sink, hadn't he?

He stood. Stared at the can.

Hadn't he?

Fuck, he couldn't remember. Easy to confuse himself when he was this tired. What was crazier? Not remembering where he'd put the bug spray, or thinking someone had been in here and moved it?

Someone?

Clayton.

No. No proof of that. Daniel could have moved it. Could have gone to sleep and done it without realizing.

He stared around the cabin.

The bug spray had moved. So had the magazines on the table. He'd left them stacked, and now they were fanned out. Daniel rose from the bed and went over to them. One of them was open. A glossy picture of a naked guy with an erection. Someone had scrawled the word *faggot* over the guy's cock in stark, angry capital letters.

It wasn't Daniel's handwriting. He thought it wasn't, but *fuck*, he couldn't be sure. He'd once drawn the Bridge of Sighs in his sleep. He'd once killed a man in his sleep. He couldn't be certain of anything.

He closed the magazine. Wouldn't look at it again. Wouldn't jerk off to it. It was ruined now.

He unlocked the door, went outside, and checked the nail under the porch railing. The spare key was still there. No one had taken it, at least. He brought it inside. He couldn't leave it out there anymore.

Had he left the cabin unlocked? He wouldn't have. Had someone gotten in without a key?

Were the magazines really there? He checked again.

Still there. He touched the cover of the ruined one. This was real. He was awake. He went back to the bed and sat down. Picked up the cuffs again.

Faggot.

Daniel had never hated being gay, just wished that he'd been normal enough to do what other guys could: keep it quiet until he was out of Logan. But he couldn't, even in high school. Because everyone said he'd stared through Bobby Grant's bedroom window, even though Daniel didn't remember doing it. And when he was awake, he'd stolen glimpses he shouldn't have; glimpses he was sure would be followed by shouted accusations.

Faggot.

So fucking hard not to look, when you were a teenager. When your whole fucking life was hormones and hard-ons and jerking off. When everyone else got to look at who they wanted to fuck, even if they hadn't figured out the mechanics yet, but you didn't because it was dangerous.

Faggot.

In high school, he'd had wet dreams about Kenny Cooper. A hundred different variations that usually started with Kenny, in his football gear, telling Daniel to get on his knees and suck his cock.

Four years ago, he hadn't understood when Kenny and the others had cornered him that night: *"Hey, Whitlock! You still wanna suck my dick?"*

How the hell could Kenny know about those dreams? But then, just when he was wondering how the fuck he was supposed to respond, the truth hit him: he must have *asked*. He'd asked Kenny if he could suck his cock. Not in a dream, but in his sleep. And there was nothing—absolutely nothing—he could say to defend himself.

After the beating, he told the police he didn't remember what happened. They knew anyway—whole fucking town knew. Strange. He'd been going to tell the truth, going to tell everything, right up until his parents came to visit at the hospital, and his father had held his hand, carefully because of his broken fingers, and said, *"Daniel, what did you do?"*

Your fault. Your fault. Your fault.

So he kept his mouth shut, pretended he'd never seen his attacker. Told himself he hated himself as much as he hated Kenny and his buddies, and almost believed it too. Except he hadn't tried to kill himself when he was sleeping, had he? No. He'd gone and found some gasoline, bought a lighter from Bel, and driven over to Kenny Cooper's place.

Woken up the next morning with blistered hands, and the police knocking on his bedroom door.

Daniel hunched over. The memory hurt. Not like the twinges and aches he still got when his body remembered his injuries, but in a different way. Like nausea. It sickened him. There was something monstrous inside him, something that he couldn't control, and it wasn't fair to expect Bel to control it either.

Maybe . . . maybe that sleep clinic.

Daniel threw the cuffs onto the floor.

Fuck that. They'd just want to try him on a new drug or something. Daniel had been down that path before, and his parents knew it, so why the hell had his mom turned up on his doorstep and told him they were going to give him money to go? Maybe they were just sick of him hanging over them like a fucking pall.

Daniel closed his eyes and tried not to see Kenny Cooper's face.

Tried not to think about how, right now, a bunch of people were lighting candles for Kenny.

In prison, Daniel had thought about killing himself. Not when he was still frightened, or confused, or crying so hard he couldn't say his own name, but later. Days and weeks later, when the first shock had worn off. When it still felt crazy and unreal, but less sharp around the edges somehow. When killing himself seemed like the only recompense he could make. A life for a life, and all that. He might have done it as well, if he hadn't suspected the real truth lurking under that simple equation: he wasn't thinking of atonement, he was thinking of escape. And he didn't fucking deserve to escape. He'd made this nightmare, and he deserved to live in it. Then, when his lawyers called in the doctors and the doctors started asking about his sleepwalking, Daniel had felt hopeless all over again. It should have been good news. *Mom, Dad, guess what? I'm not crazy after all.*

Too bad he was already a killer.

Too bad he was . . .

Daniel felt himself falling and flinched awake, his heart beating rapidly.

Too close to going under.

Shit.

He climbed off the bed and paced the cabin for a minute.

He remembered reading something about that sensation of falling. When he was a kid, a cousin or someone had told him that if you dreamed you were falling and you didn't wake up before you hit the ground, then you died for real. Which was probably the same bullshit about swallowed chewing gum staying in your stomach forever and ever, until you got old and dropped dead. The sensation of falling, he'd read, came from some part of the brain that remembered when people still lived in trees. Some ancient piece of monkey memory that warned you to grab hold of something before you fell.

Daniel went into the bathroom and dug around in the cabinet under the sink.

He found a pair of nail clippers and teased the metal file out. It was old and rusty, but the hooked point was still sharp. Daniel stood, leaned against the wall, and dug the end into the heel of his hand. The sharp sting brought him back to where he needed to be—the here and now—but as soon as he let up the pressure, his weariness flooded back in again.

Daniel pushed the file in deeper.

There was always a moment when his courage failed. Always a moment when a voice in the back of his head told him he didn't have the guts to do it. Daniel clenched his jaw and pushed harder. An excruciating moment of resistance, then the file split his skin. Blood welled.

Daniel sighed in relief and closed his eyes.

Wasn't going to sleep.

Wasn't.

Just had to make it hurt until Bel got here.

Bel must've been a mile out of town when he saw Daniel walking on the side of the road. Daniel didn't react at all when the headlights on Bel's car hit him. Bel braked, backed up, and swung the cruiser around. He would have hit the siren if he thought it would make a difference.

He drove past Daniel, pulled over, and got out and waited for him.

"Daniel, what're you doing?"

"Hey." Daniel smiled. "It's you."

"You call me the Harnee's kid, and I reckon I'll have to use lethal force."

Daniel's smile widened. "You messin' with me, Bel?"

"I guess I am."

Daniel stepped closer, shoving his hands in the pockets of his jeans and swinging his hips. "You wanna mess with me for real?"

"Maybe later," Bel said. "Get in the back, and I'll give you a ride home."

"No, there's fire there." Daniel frowned. "And a pig's head. And the bug spray, Bel."

"You're not making any sense." Bel kept his voice even.

"And Kenny's there. Wrote 'faggot' on the guy's cock."

Bel reached out and touched him gently on the shoulder. "None of that's there."

Daniel leaned into his touch. "Yeah, it is. Tonight it is." He pulled his hands out of his pocket. "I burned my hands."

Bel took his hand. "What'd you do?"

"Burned 'em."

Bel squinted at the wound on Daniel's hand in the gloom. "This isn't a burn. This is blood."

"I don't wanna go back," Daniel said. "Kenny's there."

The vigil. Maybe tonight, Kenny was there, whenever Daniel closed his eyes.

"Okay," Bel said. "You want to stay at my place tonight?"

"Yeah," Daniel said. He leaned his head on Bel's shoulder. "Wanna go home."

Bel stroked his hair, staring off at the roadside. "Where's home, Daniel?"

"Dunno."

"Get in the back," Bel said gently. "Lie down on the seat and I'll take you to my place."

Last thing anyone needed was for someone to spot Daniel in the back of a police car tonight. Not when the whole town was saying prayers for Kenny Cooper.

Daniel could see every face but Bel's. There was a tribunal staring at him—his mother, his sister, his father. Kenny Cooper, his face burned, charred skin hanging off. The sheriff. The officer who'd booked Daniel after he'd been arrested. Ms. Davenport. And Bel. But Bel was turned away. He wouldn't look at Daniel.

A wall of flames went up between Daniel and the people staring at him. But Daniel wasn't scared. Just a magic trick. He needed Bel to turn, needed Bel to see him. He walked right through the flames.

And then the fire was gone, and everybody but Bel vanished. Daniel put a hand on Bel's shoulder, but Bel just groaned.

The bed. They were on a bed. The slot machine shuffled images in Daniel's mind: the cabin, his old dorm room, Bel's bedroom, his mother's house.

Daniel crawled over Bel and slid off the mattress. The floor was cold. He went to the kitchen, got a box of crackers, and ate a few. Went back to the bedroom and turned on the light. Bel was lying on his back with his head facing the doorway, one arm under the pillow. Daniel could see Bel's face now. That was good. Bel's face was beautiful. He was young. Twenty-three was real young, but Daniel didn't mind. He smiled at sleeping Bel. Then he picked up some papers he found on the floor. There was a pencil in a cup on the night table. He had to lean over Bel to get it. He backed up and settled cross-legged on the floor a few feet from the bed.

Then he started to draw.

He kept stopping to look at Bel. He'd sketch for a few minutes, then stop and just watch. Bel was a quiet sleeper—no snoring. Daniel's cock was hard, and usually that meant he should leave the cabin and get in the car. Tonight it meant he should stay near Bel.

He couldn't go into town. Tonight was for Kenny.

His hand hurt. He looked down at it. Flexed it.

Hurt. Bel had put a bandage on it.

He drew Bel's face—that quiet face. He shaded the lips, but Bel shifted, and Daniel couldn't get the nose completely right. And then he couldn't take it anymore. Bel was too beautiful to just sit here and draw.

Daniel set the paper and pencil aside. Climbed on the bed and peeled back the comforter. Bel was in just his boxers. Daniel's cock ached, and his whole body felt prickly, like he had to move, had to find a way to scratch an itch beneath his skin. The slot machine tried to give him Marcus, a boy named Steve from his freshman year of college, then a brittle-skinned guy from Greenducks who was missing a canine tooth. But it landed on Bel, three Bels in a row.

He reached into the slit of Bel's boxers and caressed Bel's cock with his fingers. Felt it stiffen. Bel's breathing hitched, but he didn't open his eyes. He pushed his hips toward Daniel. When Bel was hard enough, Daniel slowly lowered Bel's boxers and took his cock in his mouth, pushing his tongue down the length of it. He closed his eyes and hummed. This was perfect.

This was how he would worship Bel.

Daniel opened his eyes a minute later because Bel's hand was twisting in his hair, pulling. It hurt. A loud sound, an angry voice. Footsteps? Not footsteps. Tires squealing outside. The smell of gasoline. Of smoke. Broken glass. Not real, though. Bel said that wasn't real.

Daniel lashed out, striking Bel's arm.

"Daniel!"

Daniel's eyes were already open, and yet it seemed like they opened again, like there'd been a second set of lids keeping reality hidden. Bel was pulling his hair, saying, "No," and "Cut it out."

Daniel's memory of the last few minutes shrank to a black pinprick and disappeared. He froze, his mind scrambling for something to hold on to, some memory of what he'd been doing.

The hand in his hair hurt. He wanted to struggle, wanted to fight. But instead he concentrated on Bel's voice.

"Wake up, Daniel. Wake up, right now."

Daniel whimpered as Bel shook him. He tasted salt in his mouth. Bel's boxers were pulled down to his thighs. He was with Bel, in Bel's bed, except he didn't remember how he'd gotten here.

"You awake?"

Daniel tried to nod.

Bel let go of Daniel's hair. Took him by the shoulders. He was angry.

"You know what you just did?"

Daniel looked at Bel's cock, hard and wet against his belly. Felt the ache in his own jaw. Wasn't too hard to figure out. Daniel closed his eyes.

"What were you thinking? Were you asleep?"

Daniel didn't know whether to apologize or not. Seemed like there were worse things he could have been doing than sucking Bel's cock. But maybe that wasn't all he'd done.

"Daniel? You can't do that. You understand me?"

"Sorry," Daniel said. "I didn't mean to." He looked down at himself. He had a few cracker crumbs in his pubic hair. *Shit.*

Bel swung his legs over the edge of the bed, lifting his ass off the mattress so he could tug his boxers back up. "Not while I'm asleep, and not while you're asleep. What the *fuck*? Did you do anything? Besides what you were doing to me?"

How should I know? Daniel glanced around the room but saw no signs of destruction. "Must've ate some crackers."

Bel rubbed his forehead with the heel of his hand. "I leave you alone for a few hours, I find you wandering on the roadside after you've gouged your own fucking hand. I go to sleep, I wake up to you blowing me."

Daniel forced himself to breathe. He hadn't seen Bel this upset in a long time. "You should've let me finish," he tried to joke.

"I don't want that from you. Not while you're sleeping. You know that." Bel's voice was sharp enough that Daniel flinched.

"Don't see why not," Daniel muttered, rubbing his wrist—where a cuff would have been if Bel had any sense. If Bel had done what he was supposed to and locked Daniel up. What was Bel doing blaming Daniel when he was the one who'd fucked up? Tonight was Kenny Cooper's fucking vigil, and Bel had left him alone.

"Because it ain't right," Bel almost shouted. "It ain't fucking right!"

Daniel didn't respond. He felt as miserable as he ever had.

When Bel spoke again, it was several minutes later, and his voice shook. "I'm sorry. Shit. I didn't mean to yell. Just, it scares me. To see you . . . You really don't remember?"

Daniel shook his head.

Bel put a hand between Daniel's shoulders, and they stayed like that for a minute. Then Bel hoisted his legs back onto the bed and settled against the pillow with a sigh. "Can't believe I didn't hear you get up. I'm dead tired."

"At least I didn't leave," Daniel pointed out.

"Yeah," Bel said. "At least."

"Probably stayed 'cause of you." Daniel leaned down to kiss between Bel's pecs. Bel's erection wasn't quitting, that was for sure, and Daniel's hadn't flagged. Maybe there was a way to save the situation. They were both awake now, weren't they? "Better I tried to blow you than some guy at Greenducks."

"Jesus, don't talk like that."

"Don't like stories about me being bad?" Daniel stroked Bel's chest, running his finger around Bel's nipple and watching it tighten.

Bel glanced at him and gave him a slight smile. Ruffled Daniel's hair but also pushed Daniel's head away. "Try anything again when we ain't both awake, and I won't let you come for a month."

The threat stung, even if it was a tease.

I can't fucking help it.

Yet part of him was thrilled at the idea of Bel punishing him for what he did in his sleep. The excitement wasn't even sexual. It came more from a sense of relief.

Maybe the only way to control what he did when he was asleep was for people to hold him accountable. His parents had tried to when he was a kid, then had given up. Kenny Cooper had made to teach him a lesson, and it had worked, for a while. Daniel hadn't gone into town for months afterward, even once he'd healed enough to. Then he'd burned Kenny, and he'd almost gotten punished for that, except the law had knocked the charges down.

"Do it." There was a hard challenge in Daniel's voice.

"What?"

"Punish me. Make me sorry." He crawled toward Bel. "You said you'd be in charge."

Bel looked uneasy. "What're you doing? I don't want to play this game right now."

"Come on!" Daniel shouted, striking the pillow by Bel's head. "You're a fucking cop, ain't you? What're you so scared of?"

Bel put his hands up. "What the fuck, Daniel? Lie down and go the hell to sleep."

"I can't." Daniel got up on his knees. "Look how hard I am. You're hard too, and we're both awake. Tell me what to do, Bel. I need it. And don't tell me to go to bed. I can't sleep tonight, I don't *want* to, not this fucking night, okay?" Daniel knew he was rambling, knew he sounded crazy. Didn't give a fuck. "I'll do anything you say."

Bel's face flushed, and his breathing quickened.

Fuck yes. You want to play. You want to stop being so fucking careful with me. You want to treat me like an animal. You want me to know what I am.

Daniel's cock *hurt* it was so full.

Bel leaned forward. "That what you want, Daniel?"

Daniel stared right at him, seeing the darkness and fire in Bel's eyes and hoping whatever Bel did, it would hurt, would leave Daniel without any thoughts of his own. Without any thoughts of Kenny Cooper or the fucking vigil. "Yeah," he whispered.

"How bad?" Bel's voice was low, savage, and Daniel almost laughed, not sure if he was delighted or scared.

"So bad. Stop fucking asking me questions, Bel."

"I'll give the orders here." Bel pulled down his boxers. His cock was dark and full. "Finish what you started."

Daniel hesitated only a second, then plunged toward Bel's cock. Kissed and licked Bel's stomach, working his way lower until his lips touched the thatch of hair around Bel's dick.

Froze.

Fuck.

He pulled his head up.

Just do what he says. You were doing it anyway a few minutes ago. It ain't a gun, obviously, so just wrap your stupid brain around that fact and do it.

Daniel slid his hand down Bel's stomach. Rubbed the head of Bel's cock with his thumb, spreading wetness around the ridge.

Bel grunted. "Quit teasing and get to it."

Daniel had only tried sucking dick while awake twice since Kenny. Once he'd made it all the way through—though he'd shaken for hours afterward—and once he'd left the guy in the restroom with his pants down and fled home. He wished his subconscious could be smarter, more subtle. Instead of some goddamn psychological paint-by-numbers picture: *Guy made me suck his gun. Now I hate sucking dick.*

Look at that—he didn't even need therapy.

He scooted down the bed. Ran his palms down Bel's legs, then pushed his hands inward, watching Bel's muscles tense and quiver. He wanted this. Wanted to do it for Bel. He lowered his head and planted a kiss right below Bel's navel.

Stalling.

"Fucker. I'm gonna shoot down your throat."

It was too easy to imagine what it would be like to have a bullet go through the back of your throat when you had a gun in your mouth. Daniel had thought he could sense precisely what places would be torn apart; could feel, in advance, how much it would hurt; could count how many seconds it would take to die.

Couldn't get his mouth open. Jaw was broken. When the gun went in, so did more blood, and that was what choked Daniel, not the gun itself. He sprayed the barrel with it when he coughed.

He sucked in a breath, trying to get enough air to stay conscious.

"Daniel?"

He wasn't sure what happened. One minute, his lips were against Bel's skin, the next he was lying with his head pillowed on Bel's stomach, tears running down his face. He could feel Bel's muscles contracting under his cheek. He tried to open his mouth. Was relieved when he could.

'Course you fucking can. This is now.

"Daniel," Bel whispered, his hand on Daniel's hair, stroking.

Daniel couldn't answer. The tears kept flowing. His mouth worked silently.

"Hey. Come on, sit up for me."

Not a chance. Bel finally dragged Daniel up the bed until Daniel's head was tucked under Bel's arm. Daniel buried his face in Bel's side.

"You're all right. We ain't doing anything now. It's okay." Bel smoothed Daniel's hair. "It was a bad idea."

"I want it." Daniel forced the words out. "I want you to make me."

"No," Bel said. "Not like this."

Anger and despair tore at Daniel, twin sets of claws dragging down his insides, leaving everything open and ruined. "Can't suck dick while I'm awake. Can't suck dick because of the gun. I had to suck the gun," he said in a rapid monotone. "So he could shoot down my throat. Too fucked up for you, Bel." He started to choke. "Sorry. I shoulda figured . . ." He pressed his lips against Bel's ribs, almost a kiss, but more a way of keeping back the sounds that wanted to come out of him.

"Don't be stupid." Bel ran his hand over Daniel's hair and down his neck in long, gentle strokes. "You ain't too anything for me."

They were silent a long time. Daniel tried to be quiet. Bad enough Bel'd gotten involved with someone who attempted blowjobs while he was unconscious. Didn't need to add *cries when he tries to give one awake* to the mix.

"You think you slayed your demon," Daniel murmured finally. "And it turns out he's built a whole wall of himself around your life."

Bel didn't say anything, but he didn't stop touching Daniel.

Daniel swallowed. "Sometimes I don't regret doing it. Killing him. I think if I had more guts, I'd've done it awake." He paused. "But I pay for thinking like that. I pay because he's not dead."

"Yes, he is," Bel said firmly.

"Then why's he always here? Why can't I get a fucking second of rest?"

Bel didn't answer.

"I do forget him sometimes. Go hours without thinking about what I did. And then it makes it ten times worse, because eventually I remember. And then I hate myself for the time I spent away from it." Daniel looked up at Bel, willing him to understand. "When I sleepwalk—maybe that's the only time I really rest. Because I'm someone else. Someone who *does* something about the shit that scares him and doesn't feel bad."

Bel frowned, but he didn't look pissed—just like he was trying to make sense of it.

"I go out and fuck," Daniel continued, "even though when I'm awake I can't do that—too chicken. And Kenny Cooper—never had the guts to do anything about him awake, but once I was asleep . . ."

"Stop," Bel said sharply. "Don't talk like that. You shouldn't've done it."

Daniel's rage flared. "He shouldn't've fucking beat me!" He struggled up onto his hands and knees, then sat back on his heels. "The problem's what *he* did. What *he fucking did*! Only reason he didn't kill me was someone was coming, and he didn't want to get caught."

"But he *didn't* kill you."

"No, but God, sometimes I wish he had," Daniel said, voice breaking.

"Quit it!"

"Shut up, Bel. It's the truth sometimes." Daniel slid off the bed.

"Where're you going?"

"Sleeping in the chair."

"Why?" Bel demanded.

"Because you ain't on my side! And because if I spend another second near you, I'll hit you. I'll hit you wide awake."

"I am on your side. But I believe in the law. I've got to."

"Well, the law says I done my time. So quit tryin' to make me serve some personal sentence for you." Daniel sat in the chair and drew his legs up, wrapping his arms around them. "And what the fuck did the law ever do after Kenny bashed me? I said I didn't know who did it. I said I never saw the guy's face. I said that so he wouldn't come back and *kill* me, but God, Bel, I hoped the cops would figure it out and fucking *do* something. 'Cause it wasn't like the whole town didn't know. That's the law you believe in? Fuck you."

They sat without speaking.

"What am I supposed to do?" Bel asked after a while.

Daniel didn't respond. Fuck him, for being too young, too scared, or too stupid to even *want* to understand.

"Inside," Bel said quietly. "Inside, the only reason I wish you hadn't killed Cooper is so I could kill him myself."

Daniel pressed his face against his knees until he saw blue and purple shadows on the backs of his eyelids, like he was bruising himself from the inside.

"But outside, I gotta believe in the rules. You know that. You like rules too."

"The fucking *rules* say something shoulda happened to Kenny."

"Yeah. You're right. You're right, but if the rules fail sometimes, does that mean we chuck 'em out altogether?" Bel didn't say anything else for another few minutes, and Daniel wondered if that was it. His heart was still pounding, and he sort of wished the fight would keep going. He hadn't said half the rotten things he wanted to say to Bel yet. But when Bel spoke, it was just to say, "I wish you'd come back to bed."

"I wish you'd stop being a fucker."

Daniel heard Bel's sigh and wished he was feeling it against his throat as Bel worked his cock with his hand. Wished a movie director would step in with a clapboard and they could take this night again from the top. But he couldn't stop.

"I'll bet you're not even out, are you?" Daniel demanded. "Bet you're scared to tell anyone you like cock. Bet you hate yourself, and that's why part of you's on Kenny Cooper's side."

"Would you quit with the what-side-I'm-on bullshit? I'm on your side. Or I wouldn't be here."

And maybe he was right. Because Daniel had a bandage on his hand that Bel had put there. Bel had taken Daniel to the diner and told Daniel this was his town too. And he *was* here. Every fucking night, except when he worked.

Maybe Bel *was* on his side.

Maybe that was what hurt so much.

After another minute, Daniel heard the bed creak. Bel came over and crouched beside the chair. Daniel glanced down at him suspiciously. More than anything, he wanted himself and Bel on good terms again. Bel settled on the floor, his back against the chair. Daniel couldn't see his face.

"There ain't words," Bel said, "for how sorry I am about what Kenny Cooper did to you. Ain't words for how angry it makes me. I don't know what to do sometimes with that. It scares me, how glad I am he's dead. How much I *like* to think about him burning."

Daniel forced himself to breathe. Slow and steady.

"I don't know if it's okay to feel like that."

Something about Bel's tone—helpless, anxious. *Young*. Still figuring shit out—made Daniel feel better. Even though it scared him a little to realize Bel didn't have all the answers, couldn't *fix* things, he was glad to know he wasn't the only one who was confused.

"Me either," Daniel whispered.

Bel tipped his head back to look at Daniel. "I'm sorry," he said.

Daniel nodded.

Bel's hair brushed Daniel's knee. "You wanna get some sleep?"

"I wanna forget this whole night."

Bel pushed himself to his feet. Offered his hand. "C'mon."

Daniel started to give Bel his injured hand, but Bel reached down and took the other one instead. He pulled Daniel up, and they stood facing each other. Daniel wanted to touch him. Was almost afraid to—not afraid of Bel. Just . . . afraid. A new kind of fear that wasn't familiar, that was alive and sharp. That wasn't *of* Bel but came from him. Afraid of Bel's power, not to hurt him, but to give him something to hold on to.

Bel reached out and brushed Daniel's jaw with his fingers. "Remember when I said I'd need you to be patient with me?" he asked. "Because I'd do the wrong things?"

"Yeah."

Bel pressed his forehead to Daniel's. Gave a long, slow exhale that Daniel felt against his nose, his lips, his eyelids. "I wanna keep this. Be patient. I'll learn."

Daniel closed his eyes. Licked his lips as he tried to figure out how to answer that. He gripped Bel's shoulders. Felt all that warm, hard muscle. "I don't have the right," he said finally, "to give second chances. I don't have the right to be anything but patient."

"That ain't true." Bel jostled him. "That ain't true. You got a right. Talking like that—everything's about punishing yourself, ain't it? Because that's easier than figuring out how to be a whole man again, now that you done your time." Bel's voice was fierce. "It's all about pain with you, huh?"

"It's gotta be," Daniel said. His eyes were still shut, but he could feel Bel's breath quick and warm against his face, could feel how much Bel's words would change him, if he let himself think too hard about them. If he let them be the truth. He pushed against Bel, gripping his shoulders tighter and tighter, trying to make him understand. He opened his eyes and stared right into Bel's. "That's all that keeps me awake."

CHAPTER THIRTEEN

Bel pulled his phone out of his pocket when it buzzed, and smiled at the text message.

Hi, Bel. It's Daniel. I miss you.

I miss you too, he sent back. *See you tonight.*

Bel had big plans for tonight. He'd already been to Harnee's and bought condoms and lube, and fuck whatever the smirking kid on the counter thought. Didn't cops deserve to get laid too? Except it wasn't as simple as that. Half the town was probably already saying he was fucking Daniel, and the other half was probably thinking it. So what? It wasn't *wrong*.

He was less worried about what the town thought he was doing than what Daniel wanted him to do. Bel didn't want to hurt him, and he thought that a part of Daniel didn't want to be hurt. He said he needed it, but there had to be another way. They were working toward one, weren't they, with the sleeping bag and the holding? Bel didn't want Daniel to go back to pain. Hell, he didn't even want him to use the cuffs if there was nobody there to look out for him.

He stared at the pile of paperwork on his desk. Some file he had to get ready for the prosecutor, a couple of warrants to chase up, and a report that Uncle Joe had sent back to him with all his misspellings underlined. Uncle Joe was a stickler for shit like that, and being his nephew did not give Bel a free ride. Not that he wanted one.

Ginny came in from out back with a blast of warm air. She pushed the door shut again. "Hey, Bel. You coming to the Shack tonight? They got that band playing, you know, them high school kids. They're pretty good."

If you liked country. Bel had watched them last time. Swore the kid on the bass guitar was dying to burst into something alternative, but maybe that was just the eyeliner he wore. Bel couldn't imagine any boys wearing eyeliner when he'd been at school. Fashions changed fast, he guessed, but attitudes didn't. Wondered how much shit the kid took for doing that.

"I got plans tonight," Bel told her.

"Okay." Ginny headed down the hall toward the locker rooms. "Starts at eight, if you change your mind."

"Thanks."

Bel reached down for his backpack and unzipped it. He grabbed the sheaf of papers that he was supposed to have read by now and reached for his folder of operating procedures. He'd put them in there and get around to reading them properly at some point. Daniel might like to hear him read it as a bedtime story, but it was boring as hell. He opened the folder, pulled the lever arch open, and lined the pages up.

Then saw it.

On the back of the first page, someone had drawn a picture of Bel sleeping.

Someone. Bel snorted. *Daniel.*

He turned the pages over and spread them out on his desk.

Shit. Pages and pages of them. And they were good. Just pencil drawings, but they were really fucking good. Bel didn't have an artist's eye and couldn't remember much from art classes at school except for perspective and shading, and cross-hatching. Daniel had used all of those, and other stuff that Bel had forgotten the words for. The drawings were—well, strange to call a thing beautiful when it was your own face on them, but Bel didn't have another word for it. They were the sort of drawings that you looked at and wished to hell you'd been born with a fraction of the same talent. The sort of drawings that should have been framed and hanging on a wall somewhere, not shoved in a folder full of standard operating procedures.

Daniel never said he could draw.

Bel ran his fingertips over a page, feeling a blemish where the pencil had dug in and snagged on the cheap paper.

Did Daniel do this when he was sleeping? That was crazy, but no crazier than killing a man.

He bundled the pages up again and slid them back into his backpack. No way were they staying in the station. He wanted to keep them at home.

Maybe he ought to drive over to Goose Creek and check out the stores there, see if there was anywhere that sold decent art supplies.

God knows Harnee's didn't run to anything like that. A proper sketch pad, with good, thick paper. And maybe some pencils and charcoal. Because when it came down to it, Daniel shouldn't've been playing poker when he was asleep. Not when he could be drawing like this. And Bel would love to watch him.

"You got a minute?"

Bel gave a guilty start. He hadn't even realized Uncle Joe was standing there. "Yes, sir."

"Come on into my office."

Well, that was never good. Bel kicked his backpack under his desk and followed Uncle Joe down the hall.

"Sit down," Uncle Joe said, doing the same. Then he cut straight to it. "You been seeing Daniel Whitlock?"

"I seen him around," Bel said.

"That ain't what I asked you, Little Joe."

Great. So this was how he was coming out to his family? Bel squared his shoulders. "Is there a problem if I am?"

"Won't be easy," Uncle Joe said, "being the first gay cop in this town."

"I got my suspicions about Avery." Bel knew even before he said it that the joke would fall flat.

Uncle Joe snorted. "C'mon, we can talk about this man-to-man, can't we?"

"Depends which man is asking. My uncle, or the sheriff."

"Same man," Uncle Joe told him.

"I ain't ashamed of what I am," Bel said. "Are you?" He held his breath.

Uncle Joe looked at him steadily. "Nope. But like I said, won't be easy for you."

"I can handle it."

"I don't doubt that. But you've gone and put a millstone around your neck, haven't you? Whitlock will drag you down, Little Joe, make no mistake."

Bel frowned, thinking of Daniel's smile, of his trust, and that look on his face when he came. He wasn't ready to give him up, not yet. Maybe not ever. "He's done his time."

"Yeah, he has, according to the law. And you know as well as I do what low account some people around here hold the law in. You want to be the gay cop, that's hard enough. But you want to be the gay cop sleeping with a killer, well, whole town's gonna turn against you."

"I can handle it," Bel said, less sure this time.

"I been in this job for thirty-five years," Uncle Joe said. "Back when I was new, one of the boys married a black woman. Now you can do the math and tell yourself that it shouldn't have mattered even back then, but I promise you, it mattered. If the town's against you, you can't do this job."

"You firing me?" Bel asked, his voice wooden.

"I ain't firing you. I'm just warning you that whatever decision you make, you're gonna have to live by it."

Bel nodded sharply.

Uncle Joe's expression softened. "Now go on out there and write me some tickets."

Bel stood. "Yes, sir."

He left the office.

The rest of Bel's shift went slow. Too fucking slow when he wanted to be out at Daniel's cabin, watching him and touching him instead of just reading that one text message over and over: *Hi, Bel. It's Daniel. I miss you.*

After work, he changed out of his uniform at the station, tossed his cuffs in his backpack, and left before anyone could talk to him.

The drive out to Kamchee Woods wasn't long enough to settle his nerves. He was still on edge when he pulled up at the cabin, walked up the steps to the sagging porch, and opened the door.

Daniel knelt there, his hands clasped behind his neck, *smiling.* "Hey, Bel."

Bel felt a smile spread across his own face. "Hey yourself."

"Missed you today."

Bel dumped his backpack on the floor. "Yeah, you said something about that. Why don't you come over here and see what's in this bag for you?"

Daniel shuffled forward on his knees, and damn, if that wasn't one of the hottest things Bel had ever seen. He sat down on the edge of the bed and pushed the backpack forward with the toe of his boot. Daniel reached it, unclasped his hands, and unzipped it.

"This?" he asked in a croaking voice as he pulled the bottle of lube out.

"Yep. There's more."

The box of condoms followed. Daniel's face was red. His chest rose and fell quickly. He dug around in the bag again. "And *these?*"

The cuffs.

"Just for you." *If you want. Jesus, tell me I ain't done an idiot thing, thinking you'd want that.*

Daniel gazed up at him, and for an instant Bel was completely lost. Had no idea what Daniel was feeling. Then he saw that look again, the one he'd seen at the hospital. Hopeful. Trusting. "How do you want me, Bel?"

Any way I can get you. "Naked. On this bed, on your back, right now."

Daniel stood, pulling his shirt over his head. His track pants and underwear were next, and he was clambering onto the bed before Bel had even gotten his boots off. Bel grinned at his eagerness. Hell no, he wasn't done with Daniel. Fuck what anyone thought.

He raked his gaze over Daniel's slim body, finding the path he wanted to trace later with his tongue: the hollow of his throat, down his pecs to the dip in his sternum, those abs that were tight without being overly defined, and that sparse trail of hair that led from Daniel's navel down to his thickening cock. Fuck yes. All for him. But first . . .

Bel removed his socks and pulled his own shirt off, then his belt, but kept *his* jeans on for now. Rubbed his cock through the denim, arousal overriding embarrassment or uncertainty. He stooped to pick up the cuffs. "Ready for this?"

"Yes, Bel." Daniel's voice was soft but urgent.

"Hold the bars for me," Bel said, and Daniel reached up to wrap his fingers around the rails of the headboard. Bel knelt on the bed. "You look so good when you're like this, Daniel."

"What, turned on?" Daniel asked with a breathy laugh.

"No." Bel thought back to the hospital again. "Trusting."

Daniel sighed as Bel clicked the cuffs shut. "I like to be restrained."

"I know you do," Bel said. "That's a thing you like that doesn't hurt, isn't it?"

"Yeah," Daniel whispered.

Bel leaned down and brushed his lips against Daniel's. Tasted toothpaste. "Well, we're gonna find plenty of other things you like that don't hurt."

"Are we?" Daniel lifted his head for another kiss.

Bel obliged him, this time touching his tongue against Daniel's, deepening the kiss and swallowing the noises that Daniel made underneath him. He curled his fingers in Daniel's hair and tugged gently before kneeling back again.

Daniel panted, shifting restlessly on the bed.

"Used to watch you running track," Bel said. "Wanted you, even back then. Wouldn't've known what to do with you if I'd had the chance, but I know different now, don't I?"

Daniel nodded. "Yeah."

"So I guess," Bel said, reaching out and splaying his hand over Daniel's wildly thumping heart, "I can do whatever I want."

Daniel arched toward his touch.

Bel smiled as Daniel's nipple hardened under the palm of his hand. "You like that?"

"Yeah." Daniel swiped his tongue over his lower lip. "I like that, Bel."

Bel swelled with pride. Felt good to touch a man like this, to be in charge. None of that awkwardness of past hookups where you had to figure out who was putting what where, and whether the answer might mean the whole thing was a bust. Didn't have to worry about that with Daniel.

"Fuck me," Daniel said, his voice straining. "Please, fuck me, Bel."

No, didn't have to worry at all.

"We got all night," Bel told him. "Ain't you much for foreplay?"

Daniel made a face. "Past few weeks have been foreplay. I've been to the edge so many times, I've got the goddamned T-shirt. Just stick your cock in me already."

Bel laughed. "I might be new at all this, Daniel, but I know you're not in charge." He slid his hand down to Daniel's abdomen, feeling the muscles undulate under his palm. "Are you?"

"No." Daniel exhaled, his hips jerking. "You're in charge."

"Okay then," Bel said.

Daniel closed his eyes.

"Lucky for you, I'm more than ready to get straight to the main event."

Daniel's eyes flashed open. "Fuck, yeah. *Please.*"

Bel laughed again and rose from the bed. He shoved his jeans and underwear down and stepped out of them. Picked up the lube and condoms. Climbed back onto the mattress, and knelt in the space that opened for him between Daniel's legs. Actually licked his lips at the sight of Daniel's hole, small and tight.

Bel opened the lube, drizzled it on his fingers. "How many you want?"

This, this was a hurt he'd be willing to give him.

"Two," Daniel said. "Start with two. I can take it."

"Yeah you can." Bel slid his fingers up Daniel's crease, circling that tiny opening and then pushing in.

Daniel jolted like he was caught on an electric fence, all his breath whooshing out of him, his body squeezing the hell out of Bel's fingers.

"You okay?"

Daniel gasped for breath. "Yeah. It's good. Keep going." His body jerked again, less violently this time, and he rolled his hips. Found Bel's rhythm and matched it. "Yeah, fuck, yeah."

Bel felt Daniel's muscles loosen and scissored his fingers inside. Watched Daniel's face—his eyes closed, a tense line between his drawn brows, his jaw clenched—and watched the way he pulled against the cuffs, his muscles cording. So fucking hot.

Bel withdrew his fingers and ripped a condom open. Rolled it down his aching cock, and slathered himself with lube.

"Gonna—" His voice hitched. "Gonna fuck you now."

Daniel took a deep breath. "Yeah, Bel."

Bel shifted closer on his knees, his hands under Daniel's ass. Lifted him slightly, tilted his pelvis up. Wondered if this was what submission looked like: Daniel, restless with anticipation as Bel arranged him how he wanted him. He shifted Daniel up more, getting his knees under him. Hooked his elbows under Daniel's legs. Held him there for a moment, just to see what he'd do.

Daniel tugged on the cuffs. "Please."

"Open your eyes," Bel said, shifting so that his cock nudged Daniel's hole.

Daniel obeyed.

"That's it," Bel said. "Want to see you, Daniel."

He pushed in.

Daniel's body arched toward him like a bow. The cuffs rattled against the rails of the bed. His body shook.

"So tight," Bel groaned.

"Fuck me," Daniel whispered, eyes wide. "Fuck me hard."

Might have been a good time to remind Daniel that he wasn't calling the shots, but Bel wasn't inclined to disagree with him at that moment. Fuck him hard? Hell yes. They'd been stepping around this for weeks now, for too damn long. Now that it was happening, now that he was finally inside Daniel's ass, there was nothing that could stop Bel from giving them both what they needed.

Bel went as hard as he could, his first thrust pushing a moan out of Daniel. His second, something that was more like a yelp.

"Yeah, right there." Daniel gasped.

Bel angled his hips to hit the spot again, and Daniel arched his spine and shook his head from side to side. Squeezed so tight on Bel's cock that Bel gasped as well. No way was Bel going to last. He dropped Daniel's left leg, and Daniel hooked it around his hip. Bel grabbed for Daniel's cock, hard and leaking against his abdomen. Bel wrapped his fingers around it and jerked it in time to his thrusts.

Daniel shuddered. "Jesus, Bel!"

Bel grunted at him. Must be nice to have enough breath to form words. Next time he'd lie back and make Daniel do the work. At the moment, it was taking all of his energy to keep thrusting, and to stop from coming too fast.

"Fuck," he groaned. "You need me to tell you . . ."

Daniel writhed underneath him.

Bel thrust again into the tight heat of his body. "You need me to tell you to come?"

"Gonna," Daniel managed. "Gonna, real soon."

"Hurry up then." Bel grunted, tightening his grip on Daniel's hot shaft. Daniel's body tensed, froze, and then he came all over Bel's hand.

Bel managed one more thrust, then a second one, and tried for a third before he was coming as well, buried deep in Daniel's ass.

Daniel slumped back down onto the mattress.

Bel withdrew slowly, easing himself carefully to his shaking legs. He stumbled to the bathroom to dispose of the condom, then lay back on the bed beside Daniel. Wiped the mess off his belly with the sheet.

"You want me to uncuff you now?" he asked when he'd caught his breath, nuzzling against Daniel's throat.

"Want you to do anything you want," Daniel whispered, his eyes fluttering closed.

Bel propped himself up a little.

"Think I'd like to leave you cuffed," he said, leaning down to kiss Daniel. He ran his palm over Daniel's chest, then slowly down his torso. "Just let me touch you awhile."

Bel slid his fingers over Daniel's hip. Drew small circles on the top of Daniel's thigh. He kept his gaze on Daniel as he touched him, watching the subtle shifts in Daniel's expression, noting when Daniel tensed or squirmed. Cataloged hitches in his breathing, moments where he arched into Bel's touch. He wanted to learn this body.

He brushed his fingers over Daniel's now-soft cock. Daniel jerked, then slowly exhaled.

"All right." Bel leaned over and snagged the key to the cuffs. Let Daniel out. Daniel kept his arms above his head. Bel smiled. "You look real good like that."

Daniel smiled too. "I like it when—" He stopped himself.

"When what?"

"When it's because I want to, not because of what I might do when I'm asleep."

Bel took his wrists and gently guided his arms down. "I like that, too." He kissed Daniel's shoulder. "Roll over."

Daniel obliged. Bel ran his hand from the base of Daniel's neck down his back. Daniel shivered. Bel did it again. After a few more strokes, he let his hand continue over the hard muscles of Daniel's ass. Daniel spread his legs slightly without any hesitation. Bel's chest tightened. There was trust there. Unless it was just habit. Bel frowned as he ran his hand down the back of Daniel's leg and massaged his calf.

Was always gonna be hard, wasn't it, to figure out what Daniel really wanted versus what he'd trained himself to want?

Bel draped over Daniel's back, rubbed a hard circle on his side, feeling his ribs. He placed his lips close to Daniel's ear. "You're incredible."

Daniel stiffened under him. Bel didn't budge, just kept touching him. After a minute, Daniel relaxed.

Bel wasn't sure when they drifted off to sleep. He woke once in the night to find Daniel on the floor drawing. Daniel didn't stop when Bel got up, but he also didn't fight when Bel leaned down and gently took the pencil from his hand and guided him to his feet. "That's beautiful," Bel said, taking the picture and setting it on the table. He kept one arm around Daniel and whispered against his neck, "Beautiful work, but you need to sleep."

Daniel didn't say anything. He was usually coherent during his sleepwalking episodes, but every now and then there'd be one where Daniel didn't speak at all.

Bel led him back to bed.

"Well, look at you," Ginny said when Bel walked in the police station the next morning. "I know that look. Belman got laid!"

Bel rolled his eyes but couldn't stop the telltale smile from tugging at his lips. And why the hell not smile? He was entitled. Last night had been fucking incredible, and waking up beside Daniel this morning had felt pretty damn good as well.

"You can't tell that just from looking at a guy," Diggler protested from his desk.

"I can," Ginny said. "I'm an expert. Also, he's wearing the same clothes he left in last night."

Bel clapped her on the shoulder. "Do some fucking work, Ginny."

He headed down to the locker room to get changed and have a proper shave. That bathroom in Daniel's cabin was next to useless. It was pokey, and the mirror above the sink was tiny. It would have been nice to shower together, except there was no way the pair of them would have fitted. Would have been nice to eat breakfast together as well, sitting down at a table instead of on the front porch steps although that had been all right. Sharing a plate of toast with peanut butter since Daniel had nothing else in his kitchen, their hands knocking together when they reached for a slice at the same time.

Daniel had been shy this morning, and Bel liked that. Liked the way his smile had been hesitant until Bel had reached for his hand, tugged it, and said, "Can't wait until my shift is done and I can see you again."

Daniel's smile had widened then. Matching Bel's.

It was the sort of smile that Bel wanted to come home to at the end of every shift.

Bel changed into his uniform, laced on his boots, and fastened his utility belt. Then he headed back out into the office to check his emails and tasks for the day.

"Hey, Bel," Ginny said. "You gonna be free around midday?"

Something in her tone warned him. He glanced at Diggler, who shook his head urgently.

"No, I got an interview coming in," he said warily.

"Goddamn," Ginny groaned.

"Why?" Bel asked.

She made a face. "I gotta go give a road safety talk at the elementary school, and they want me to bring Petey."

Petey was the department's Road Safety Ambassador, a talking dog. He'd been around long enough that Bel could remember him from when he was in elementary school. The costume smelled of mothballs and, for some reason, cough syrup.

Bel snorted. "Oh, hell no. You can definitely find someone else."

He'd made the mistaking of agreeing to be Petey once, back when he was still the rookie. Never again. There was just something about a grown man in a dog costume that triggered the attack response in kids.

"I'll find someone, I guess," Ginny said.

Diggler grabbed his keys and bolted.

Bel laughed and began to check his emails. His phone buzzed. A text from Daniel.

Hey, Bel. It's Daniel. It's not 2:30 yet, but I wanted to tell you I'm happy.

Bel read it twice.

I'm happy too, he sent back.

Was that the sort of thing a dom would send? Well hell, too late now to change his mind. He *was* happy and didn't see the point in acting all strict and dour just to stick to some role that he didn't really understand in the first place. Just because he was the one making the rules, didn't mean he had to be some sort of hardass, did it?

He hoped that wasn't what Daniel was expecting.

He set his phone on his desk so he wouldn't miss Daniel's reply.

Later on, he might head to Harnee's and pick up some bacon and eggs so they could have a decent breakfast tomorrow. Maybe he'd even make pancakes. That probably wasn't the sort of thing a hardass dom should do either.

Bel had been checking it out online again. Reading about subs who were subs even outside of scenes. Subs who kept the house clean and had dinner ready on the table, and were always looking for ways to please their man. Like 1950s housewives, except for the kink. And it seemed weird to Bel. The height of hypocrisy. He couldn't remember the last time he'd mopped his kitchen floor, so why the hell would he expect someone else to do it for him?

Kink was kink. Lifestyle was . . . too much?

Bel was overthinking it, probably. There was nothing to suggest that Daniel wanted anything like that. There was nothing to suggest he was even as hard-core as his gear might indicate. It was just unsettling to Bel, knowing so little about what he'd gotten into. Knowing that he was supposed to be in charge when really it was Daniel who understood more about what they were doing.

But last night. Last night had been amazing, so they were doing something right. That had to count for something.

Bel smiled when Daniel's text came through: *I'm glad you're happy too.*

CHAPTER FOURTEEN

"I'm drawing again," Daniel said to John a week later. "Bel . . . um, Officer Belman said I should tell you that."

"You don't need to use any titles in here," John told him. "He's your friend, I know that."

John's tone said he knew a lot more than that, and Daniel flushed.

"Do you like drawing?" John asked him.

"I don't know," Daniel said. "I only do it when I'm sleeping. Stopped for a while, but it's back now."

"That scares you, huh?"

John wasn't like any other therapist Daniel had ever spoken to. The others had been inside prison or hired by his defense team. It didn't feel so official, sitting in John's home office drinking tea.

"Yeah," Daniel said. "If that's back, what else is? Bad enough when I was bending over for any asshole in Greenducks, but at least I wasn't—"

"At least you weren't what?"

"Least I wasn't killing anyone."

There, he'd said it, but if it was any kind of breakthrough moment, John didn't comment on it. Just showed Daniel that same encouraging smile he always did, as though Daniel didn't scare him at all. And waited.

"Last week was Kenny's vigil," Daniel muttered.

"Mm-hmm," John said. "How'd you do?"

"Always makes me feel sick. Don't know if it's because I hate Kenny or hate myself."

"Which do you think it's more of?"

"It's both." Daniel paused. "I think . . . because I'd imagined doing it before—just fantasized, you know? About getting him back for what he did? If I hadn't let myself think about that, ever, maybe I wouldn't've done it. And I worry I should have known. Should've known I was dangerous. Just, I never hurt anyone before. Hit a couple of people who tried to wake me up. That's it. I didn't know that I could do something so bad."

Daniel stared at the African violet on John's windowsill.

John shifted in his chair. "In the days leading up to Cooper's death, did you notice anything different about yourself? Any change in mood, behavior, or thought patterns?"

John asked the question easily, without any censure or suspicion. Daniel had been asked similar questions before, but always by people trying to get him to admit he'd known what he was going to do. That he'd planned it. And Daniel wasn't sure whether he was relieved or pissed by John phrasing it "Cooper's death." Not "Cooper's murder," just "Cooper's death"—as though Kenny might have died of illness or in an accident. As though Daniel might not have been involved at all.

"I don't remember," Daniel admitted. "I wasn't sleeping very much. And when I did sleep, I was sleepwalking. I got to where I honestly couldn't tell when I was awake or not. And I kept seeing things. It was like I really was crazy."

"Did you find yourself thinking about Cooper during that time? Or don't you remember?"

Daniel hesitated. "Yeah. Sometimes. I have these—nightmares. Really bad ones. And usually I don't remember them. But I had some the week before I set the fire that I remembered."

"What happened in them?"

"'Bout him beating me up, I guess. Hard to even want to go to sleep, because I knew I'd see him."

Can see him now. Shit. Don't want to talk about this.

"And after Cooper died, did you still have those nightmares?"

"I slept fine the first two nights in jail. Slept like a fucking baby. During the days I was a wreck, but at night I was fine. Fuck!" He squeezed the arm of his chair, forcing himself to calm down. "Sorry."

"You can say fuck in here," John said.

"Anyway, now a lot of the dreams are about fire. Either fire or being on the ground with Kenny Cooper standing over me." He glanced at John. "So what's that mean?"

"What do you think it means?"

"That I'm fucked up."

"Or maybe that you still have a lot of fear—both of what Cooper did to you and what you did to Cooper?"

"I guess." Daniel pressed the spot on his hand where he'd dug the nail file in. It was almost healed. He wished Bel was here. Hoped Bel would fuck him rough tonight. There was even stuff he could do to himself before Bel arrived, to make sure it hurt.

"I'd like to go back to the drawing," John said. "You said you did that mostly in college?"

"I did it some when I was younger. But yeah, college was when I did it most."

"What did you draw?"

"Stuff in the dorm. People in my roommate's photos. I did a still life once with his computer and a bag of chips and one of his shoes."

John smiled. "And you've said you liked college?"

"I liked staying busy. College kept me pretty tired out."

"And you had a steady boyfriend there?"

They hadn't talked much about Marcus yet. Daniel hadn't told John anything except that he and Marcus had dated for a couple of years. "Yeah."

"You look like you're thinking," John said after a minute.

"I'm just waiting to see what you'll ask me."

"Is there something you hope I won't ask you?"

Daniel snorted. "There's a bunch of stuff I hope you won't ask me."

"You can tell me anything you want about Marcus. Or we can move to something else."

John never pressed him. That was good. Daniel took a minute to gather his thoughts. "Marcus was a pretty good guy. But we wanted different things. I drew him a lot," Daniel added, suddenly eager to change the subject back to drawing. "Well, not a lot. I didn't draw as much when I was with Marcus, because I slept through the nights better with him. Just like I sleep better now with Bel." He watched John warily.

John didn't even flinch. "So it helps not to be alone?"

It helps when someone else is in charge.

"Maybe. I think it ain't gonna last, though. Not, I mean. It's not gonna last."

"Why do you think that?"

"Because I killed someone and I do crazy shit in my sleep and I have nightmares like a goddamn kid. And Bel doesn't have time for that."

John leaned back. "Bel's told you he doesn't have time for that?"

"N . . . no. But he'll figure it out. He just likes to fuck me because I'm better looking than the Greenducks crowd." John's eyebrows rose slightly. "You said I could say fuck."

"You really believe that?" John asked. "That's all Bel wants from you?"

Daniel thought awhile. "I don't know," he said finally. "Really. I don't know."

When he got back to Logan, Daniel felt as tense and exhausted as he had at the end of any interview he'd been subjected to in prison. Even though John hadn't pushed him or judged him or threatened him, he felt wrecked.

It was only one fifteen, but Daniel didn't know if he could wait until two thirty to send Bel his text update. He'd been late last week with a text. As punishment, Bel had read him the instruction manual for the toaster that night instead of the next chapter in the thriller they'd been working through. Wouldn't've been so bad, except they'd ended on a cliff-hanger the night before, and it was all Daniel could do not to beg Bel to read the book.

He'd been early once, and Bel hadn't minded.

You could just shoot him a regular text now, then do the official text at two thirty.

But what Daniel wanted right now was the reassurance of their ritual. When Daniel and Bel texted for fun, Bel might tease him, or Bel might reply sarcastically, or Bel might even wait awhile to respond. But the two-thirty text Bel always answered right away, honestly and seriously, no matter how dumb Daniel's update was.

Daniel got into his car and pulled out his phone.

Hi, Bel, it's Daniel. He paused. For all his impatience to text Bel, he didn't have anything in particular he wanted to say. He typed: *I don't know anymore.*

And hit Send.

He buckled his seat belt, feeling guilty. He didn't want to worry Bel. Fuck, what if Bel thought Daniel meant he didn't know anymore about seeing Bel?

Was that what he meant? He wanted to keep seeing Bel more than anything. And yet it was so obviously a bad idea. *It's gonna hurt him, in the long run, to be associated with me.*

He picked up his phone to text Bel again, but before he could, the phone buzzed. A text from Bel.

Taking my break by the river in 15. Near the launch. Meet me there?

Daniel's stomach clenched. He wanted to see Bel, but he was nervous that might mean more talking. Hadn't he done enough of that with John? He'd basically come out and told John he was sleeping with Bel, for Christ's sake. But why had he texted Bel, then, if he didn't want to talk? If he wasn't looking for a little reassurance?

He drove to the river, stopping briefly at Harnee's, where he ignored the clerk's stare and bought two glazed donuts.

I got as much right to be here as you, asshole.

Bel was on a bench near the canoe launch. He grinned when he saw Daniel, and for a second Daniel's worry vanished. He smiled back and hurried over to Bel.

Bel stood and hugged him, and Daniel flushed with pleasure and just a little bit of fear. There wasn't anyone around, but there could have been. *Fuck it.* Daniel squeezed him back.

"C'mon," Bel murmured. "Let's take a walk."

They walked down river a ways until they found a secluded spot—all sunlight and warm grass and patches of shade, the water sparkling in front of them. Bel sat and patted the ground beside him. They took off their shoes. "What's up?"

"Got you this," Daniel said shyly, holding the Harnee's bag out to Bel.

Bel took it and peeked inside. Grinned again. "I ain't some cop stereotype, you know."

Daniel laughed. "I just know you like donuts."

"I do. There's two here, so you gotta eat one."

"All right." Daniel reached into the bag. "We'll eat 'em at the same time. Last one to finish has to fuck the other one tonight." Daniel began cramming the donut into his mouth.

Bel threw back his head and guffawed. "In that case, I'll savor mine." He cuffed Daniel playfully on the back of the head. "Wish I was in that tight ass right now."

Me too.

Daniel finished first then sat watching Bel. As soon as Bel was done, Daniel reached out, grabbed Bel's wrist, and guided Bel's hand to his mouth. He sucked the glaze off each of Bel's fingers, and though Bel laughed at first, by the time Daniel reached his ring finger, he was breathing harshly, his gaze locked with Daniel's.

Daniel slowly released Bel's hand, still staring at him. He had a vision of lying by this river years ago, and of the skinny kid whose shoulders were starting to broaden, dripping river water. *"You coming in?"*

"Take your clothes off," Daniel said softly.

Bel looked uncertain. "Might get a call."

"Or you might not." Daniel leaned forward and kissed him, unbuttoning Bel's uniform shirt. Bel undid his own fly while Daniel worked, and slid his pants down. Kicked them off.

"What about you?" Bel asked. He nipped Daniel's upper lip.

"Undress me." Daniel finished sliding Bel's shirt off, then lay back on the grass while Bel removed his own undershirt, then bent over Daniel and pulled Daniel's T-shirt up. He licked and kissed Daniel's stomach until Daniel squirmed. Tugged Daniel's shirt over his head and tossed it aside.

He stuck his hand down Daniel's pants and rubbed his cock. Daniel arched into the touch, lost in a haze of pleasure. Let Bel roll him onto his stomach. A blade of grass went up Daniel's nose, and he almost sneezed. Bel pulled his hips up, reaching under him to unsnap his fly. Yanked Daniel's pants off so hard Daniel got grass burn.

Daniel lay there in just his boxers, his hard cock pressing into the warm earth. When he didn't feel Bel's hands on him again, he rolled onto his side.

Bel had stood and was stepping out of his briefs. Daniel couldn't do much more than stare, admiring the hard planes and ropy muscles of Bel's body. The sunlight hit his skin and gave it a warm flush. Bel's cock was full and thick, surrounded by dark hair.

"Well?" Bel cocked an eyebrow at him. "You coming in?"

Daniel slipped off his boxers and stood. He followed Bel to the bank. They waded out together until the water was up to their chests. The surface of the water was warm, but below were cold pockets. Daniel treaded closer to Bel until their legs brushed. Put his arms around Bel, and they shared a long, soft kiss.

"What don't you know?" Bel whispered when they parted.

"Huh?"

"Your text."

"Oh. Just a little confused, I guess."

"Happens," Bel said, kissing him again.

Daniel watched a drip of water fall from Bel's chin. Bel had pretty eyes. Bel and Daniel didn't spend enough time outdoors for Daniel to have figured out what those eyes looked like filled with sunlight. They were brown with specks of gold. And they were kind.

It had been a long time since anyone had looked at Daniel like they wished good things for him.

"Sometimes it feels like it'd be easier to be like I was before than to try to figure all this out."

"What's all this?" Bel asked.

Daniel held Bel tighter. *Don't leave. Don't hate me.*

"Bein' alive again, I guess. Not spending every moment of the day thinking about how I'm gonna keep myself from doing anything in my sleep." He paused. "Figuring out how to make this my town again."

Bel pressed his chest to Daniel's. His teeth grazed Daniel's jaw. "You're doin' all right, far as I can see. You really think it was easier, locking yourself up every night?"

Daniel shook his head. "This is tough in a different way."

"Don't think so hard," Bel suggested. He smiled. "Let's just be here."

He kissed the tip of Daniel's nose, then released Daniel, dove under the water, and swam away. Daniel had a moment of panic watching him go. He swam after Bel, catching him in a few strokes. Bel rolled onto his back as Daniel surfaced beside him. "You're fast."

"I know." Daniel pounced on him, and they wrestled for a few minutes in the water. Bel laughed so hard, so uninhibitedly, that he got Daniel going, and soon they were both out of breath. Bel found a clump of riverweed and set it on top of Daniel's head. "There. You look perfect." Daniel shook his head and sent the weed flying onto Bel's chest with a wet slap. That set them both laughing again.

From the bank, Bel's radio crackled and a woman's voice came through.

"Fuck," Bel said, paddling toward the bank. He climbed out, dripping, his ass flexing as he scrambled for the radio. Daniel got out slowly and knelt on the grass. Watched Bel pull on his clothes. Saw Bel's socks lying there all balled up and grabbed them.

"It's this lady's fucking dog," Bel told Daniel, rolling his eyes. "It gets out every couple of weeks and digs up the neighbor's flowers, and the neighbor calls the cops. Complete waste of time, but I gotta go give her another warning." He looked around—probably, Daniel imagined, for his socks. "Where the hell . . .?" He looked back at Daniel, who tried not to smile.

"What's behind your back?" he demanded.

"Nothing," Daniel said innocently. He was kneeling naked on the bank with his hands behind his back, Bel watching him, and it felt perfect.

"Show me your hands."

Daniel dropped the socks on the ground behind him and held up his hands. "See?"

Bel darted around him. Daniel grabbed the socks and tried to turn to keep them hidden from Bel, but he ended up sprawling.

"Whitlock, you devil," Bel said, reaching down to snatch up the socks.

Daniel lay on his side, snickering. Yelped in surprise when Bel swatted his bare ass. The blow barely stung, and yet it sent heat through Daniel's entire body.

"I can't take you anywhere."

Daniel sat up and gazed at Bel. "Wish you could take me everywhere."

Bel looked thoughtful. "C'mere," he said.

Daniel scrambled up. Bel reached out and trailed his fingers down Daniel's chest. Daniel held still. He did wish he could go places with Bel. Wished he wasn't so freaked out about spending time in town.

"Put your clothes on. And then I got an idea."

Daniel dressed, aware the whole time of Bel's gaze on him. Bel had put on his shoes but stuffed the socks in his pocket. Now he held out his hand. Daniel took it and they walked back toward the launch. When they got closer to the parking area, Bel let go of Daniel, and Daniel followed him over to the cruiser. Bel glanced around, making sure they were alone. "Hands behind your back," he said softly.

Daniel crossed his wrists behind his back.

"Turn around."

Daniel turned to face the car, reveling in the warmth of Bel's body behind him, at how his muscles ached—from laughing, he realized—at the way the sun was pulling the moisture from his clothes. He felt something soft around his wrists. One of Bel's socks. Daniel tried to ignore his stiffening cock as Bel bound him. "You want to ride with me?" Bel asked.

"Yeah," Daniel whispered, tugging at the sock, still not sure what was going on. Bel opened the back of the cruiser.

"Get in. Lie down on the seat."

Bel kept a hand on him to steady him so he didn't fall as he climbed in. Daniel lay curled on the seat with his arms tied behind his back, his heart quick, too quick—everything too quick for a second. He took a deep breath. He was Bel's. Bel had bound him, and now all Daniel had to do was be still and listen to Bel. He spent so much time out of control, doing bad things, that it was a relief to find moments like this, where he could show that he could control himself. Could behave. Bel shut the door and got in behind the wheel. Threw a look back at Daniel. "Now, you understand, if I gotta put anyone back there for real, you better be ready to get the hell out."

Daniel grinned. "Okay, Bel."

"But seeing as it's not likely to be anything more than loose dogs and speeding tickets today, you can stay back there till my shift ends. Long as you're quiet."

"Yes, Bel."

Bel shook his head. Turned the key and put the car in reverse. "Whitlock, I've mentioned you're pretty damned incredible, right?"

Daniel didn't answer. Incredible seemed like the last thing he was. But Bel was in charge, so who was Daniel to argue? His smile broadened, and he closed his eyes.

CHAPTER
FIFTEEN

Bel slipped into Greenducks and ordered a cheap draft beer. He didn't really want it, but he needed something to kill the time until Daniel was free. He sat nursing the beer until the basement started to fill. All the usual suspects—Larry Hilton, Martin Ferris, Bob Locke. The guy with the receding hairline; Bel could never remember his name, but everyone called him Stubbs. Matt Lister showed up. Biggest tweaker of them all; his uncle used to have a meth lab outside of town. And then Jake Kebbler.

They'd all been wary of Bel when he'd started coming into Greenducks every once in a while. Now they tolerated him, though they rarely acknowledged him beyond a nod. It was an unspoken rule—you didn't tell who you'd seen at Greenducks. Even if you saw a cop, or your doctor, or Jim Hines, the lawyer with a wife and three kids who made a big show of voting Republican. There were guys the whole town knew sucked dick, and there were guys who passed for straight. But even if you were one of the obvious homos, one of the guys who had nothing to lose by admitting you'd been at Greenducks—you didn't tell on anyone else.

Bel kept an eye on the group until Larry waved at him.

"Belman," Jake called cheerfully.

Bel nodded.

Jake and Larry turned back to each other and talked in low voices. There was a bark of laughter from Jake. Bel sipped his beer. Jesus, he hated Greenducks at the best of times, but lately he'd been getting strange looks from people at the Shack, and it didn't take a genius to figure out what that was about. Daniel. He'd hoped he'd get a reprieve in Greenducks.

It was Daniel's sister's birthday, and he was at a family dinner. Bel could only imagine how that was going. He was irrationally jealous of the claim a bunch of strangers suddenly had on Daniel. Because that's what they were, weren't they? Strangers. Bel may have known the Whitlocks a little growing up, but the only thing he knew now that counted was they treated Daniel like shit. Bel hadn't tried to talk Daniel out of going to the dinner or anything, but privately, he thought Daniel was setting himself up for trouble. Yet Daniel had seemed tentatively pleased to be invited to the dinner. He'd promised to text Bel when he was done.

Bel wasn't sure which idea he liked less—that Daniel's family would treat him like dirt and leave him shattered, or that Daniel would have a great time and would be too tired to do anything with Bel tonight.

Then Bel felt guilty, because of course he wanted Daniel to have a good time.

Just if other people start treating him decent, you don't get to be his savior.

Bel took another gulp of beer. He hadn't asked to be anyone's savior. But it was almost intoxicating to be needed the way Daniel needed him.

"Ain't seen Whitlock around in a while."

Bel whirled. It was Larry who had spoken, and he was looking at Bel.

The other guys laughed. "We miss him," Matt said.

"Crazy fucker," Bob agreed. "No one he wouldn't bend over for. Worse'n ol' Jake here."

Jake had been trying to signal the bartender, but now he turned suddenly. "I got more standards than Whitlock."

Bel gripped his beer glass.

"You tried him, Belman?" Bob asked. "Or you're not into crazy?"

Bel got off his stool and walked over to the group. "Gentlemen. This is not a conversation I mean to have."

"'T's all right, Officer," Matt said. "We don't fuck and tell here." His eyes were too wide and the left one was bloodshot.

"I don't neither." Bel took a swig of his beer.

"Just bein' friendly," Larry said.

"You all," Bel said, trying to keep his voice even, "ought to think good and hard about what—"

"I always think good and *hard*," Jake said. There was a pause, then he laughed at his own joke until he hiccupped.

"—about what makes you go after someone who obviously ain't right."

Fuck. That wasn't how he'd meant to put it. He'd only meant that Daniel wasn't in any state to be having sex when he was asleep. And why had he started this conversation when it couldn't lead anywhere productive? Daniel was safe now in Bel's care. He wouldn't come back to Greenducks. So why the hell did Bel mind what this group said or did?

Larry's gaze was stony. "Well shit, Officer. Maybe the system didn't fuck him hard enough. So we're making up for it."

"You fuck each other while you're tweaking. I get that. But Whitlock . . . when he comes here, he doesn't know what he's doing, okay? It's a medical thing, and it's pretty fucked that you all go after him."

"Officer Belman." Bob slid his glass back and forth on the bar. "You saying you believe his sleepwalking bullshit?"

"I'm sayin' he's got a medical condition he can't control, and if he ever comes in here again, you're gonna leave him alone. No matter what he says to you."

Jake laughed again. Bob didn't. Bob just kept sliding his glass. "You'd prob'ly be surprised how many of us said no to Whitlock. I ain't ever fucked a freak. A killer. And I ain't gonna."

And damn if that didn't make Bel burn just as bad as the idea of this lot fucking Daniel without caring that he was unconscious. Why the hell *shouldn't* they want to fuck Daniel? Any one of them would be lucky to. "Well," Bel said coolly. "I suppose that's somethin'."

"I'd fuck him any day," Matt said. "He's hot. And he'll do some fucked-up shit."

Bel slammed his glass on the bar, still a third full. He was sweating and angry and he wanted to get the fuck out of here.

Matt grinned. "Just because he ain't right don't mean he can't have a little fun."

Larry cuffed Matt on the back of the head.

Jake leaned across the bar. "Whitlock's my superhero," he said in a stage whisper. "Getting rid of Kenny Cooper. Cooper used to give me all kinds of shit in high school. I fuck Danny to thank him."

There was a power Bel felt in certain moments—a power that came from being a cop. An authority that came with a uniform and badge. And then there were moments like this when he knew his badge meant nothing, when he felt outnumbered and useless. He thought about the mourners at Cooper's vigil, and how he'd tried to feel sorry for them. There was an anger in him now that he couldn't even begin to sort through.

"Well, he's righter'n the head than any of you," Bel snapped. He tossed a five onto the bar and left.

His cell said it was only nine. Felt later. No word from Daniel yet, which was probably a good thing.

Bel got in his car and drove awhile.

He ended up way out on 601, halfway to Goose Creek. Far away from town and far away from Daniel, who might text or call any minute. Bel drove partway into the apple orchard, stopped, and got out of his car. Walked over to one of the skinnier trees and sat down with his back against the trunk.

What do you want, Bel? A relationship you gotta keep defending? With someone you gotta keep protecting—from himself most of all?

But when had Bel really protected Daniel? Daniel had been on his own for years before Bel.

Does he really need you?

Do you really want him to?

Bel didn't know what he wanted to be. Daniel's hero? Daniel's dom? Daniel's *boyfriend*? He'd never dated anyone. Had never bullshitted himself that one day he'd fall in love with a man. But neither did he bullshit himself that he was gonna pretend to fall in love with some woman and settle down. True, a single man in Logan would get talked about, especially as he got older. But the nice thing about being a cop was you had an excuse. The long hours. The commitment you'd made to serving the public. People still preferred you had a wife and kids, but they cut you a little slack.

So was it enough? Was it enough to spend a lifetime in Logan arresting his former classmates for taking baseball bats to mailboxes or for turning up in their underwear in a ditch, high as the river in spring? Needed something more than that. And maybe that something more was Daniel, but Bel was scared. How many more nights could he spend with his arms around Daniel before something had to give? Before Daniel had to get better, or worse? Before Bel had to decide what he was to Daniel, and what Daniel was to him?

I ain't gonna leave him.

Bel was slowly starting to feel the weight of what it meant to take sides. To make himself an outcast in the town. And the best way to ease the fear and the pressure was to strengthen his tie to Daniel. People ended up together for a lot of reasons, and very rarely was one of those reasons the kind of kissing-on-a-mountaintop-at-sunset bullshit you saw in movies. Mostly people were just too chickenshit to walk through the world alone.

It was ten thirty, and still no word from Daniel. Bel didn't know if he was upset or relieved.

He sat under the apple tree and picked a stick into splinters. Thought about the guys he'd seen online who wore leather and had their partners on leashes or strapped to crosses or kneeling at their feet. Thought of the stuff he'd read about how all this bondage and leather shit was consensual. That it was really the guy who was being whipped who ran the show. Traffic light safewords—red, yellow, green; did Daniel know about all this?

It wasn't that Bel didn't believe it was consensual. He had known a guy in Goose Creek who liked to take it real rough, and another guy who'd visited Logan from out of town who'd wanted Bel to call him a whore about every two seconds. Had *asked* for it. Told Bel just how to say it too.

The trouble was that Daniel was so obviously *not* the guy from that online photo, kneeling at his dom's feet. Okay, maybe that wasn't true. Daniel was capable of looking that adoring, that lost in his own pleasure, that *submissive.* But Bel had also seen him look scared as fuck—when he was cuffed to the bed, hallucinating fire. When he was dreaming about the beating he'd taken from Kenny Cooper. Bel had trouble figuring out how tying Daniel up or whipping him wasn't going to fuck with his mind after all he'd been through.

So what was the right thing to do? Tell Daniel that what he was asking for wasn't all right, that he needed to find a better way of dealing with whatever was going on in his head?

I like being in charge.

Didn't even know I would, but I do.

Bel loved tying Daniel up. Loved seeing Daniel kneel—loved stroking Daniel's hair while he knelt and having Daniel press his forehead against Bel's thigh. He sure as hell liked fucking Daniel. He might not even mind giving Daniel a licking, if that was something Daniel wanted.

But something bugged him about the whole situation. And maybe if he knew more about BDSM—what it meant, for instance; he could never quite remember all the words the letters fucking stood for—he'd know what to do. But he was ignorant. Which was a big problem when it came to dealing with Daniel.

Bel jumped when his phone buzzed. Checked the text.

Heading to your place now.

Time to head back and meet Daniel at the house. Daniel knew where the spare key was. He could let himself in. Or . . .

Maybe it was time to be less ignorant about Daniel.

At the orchard. Get your ass out here.

He hit Send before he remembered that Daniel might be out of sorts after that family dinner. Might not be in the mood for *Yes sir, No sir* games.

Shit.

He texted: *Please.*

A little politer, at least.

Bel sat back and waited.

There'd been a time when a family birthday meant they'd all go out to dinner, or that the house would be full of people. Not for a long time now. Now it was just the four of them, sitting around the dining room table and trying to think of things to say to one another.

"How's Charleston?" Daniel asked Casey.

"It's good," she said. "Expensive sometimes, but I got a nice place. Next semester, I'm gonna share with Aiden."

"Oh." Daniel had no idea who that was. A boyfriend, he guessed, from his mom's disapproving frown.

"Did you buy your sister a birthday present, Daniel?" his mom asked.

"I—I didn't expect to get invited," Daniel said.

His mother stared at him. "Don't make this all about you."

"Jean." His father's voice was quiet.

"It doesn't matter!" Casey said too brightly. "I don't need a present."

"Oh, honey," their mom shook her head as though Casey was being a martyr to Daniel's selfishness. She reached over and squeezed her hand.

"Mom." Casey pulled her hand away. "Really. I don't need a present."

A silence settled over the dining room.

Daniel had been happy in this house once, but with every visit, it got harder and harder to remember those times.

"I'm going to meet some of the old gang at the Shack," Casey announced over dessert.

"At this hour?" their mother asked.

"Sure."

"You should take the car," their dad said.

"It's my birthday, Dad." Casey smiled. "I'm gonna be drinking!"

"I'll drive you then. How are you getting home?"

"I'll get someone to walk me home after," Casey said. "And Daniel can drive me there, right, Daniel? I mean, you gotta go down Main to get home."

Daniel looked up from his pie, startled. "Um, yeah, sure."

He was planning on going to Bel's, but the family didn't need to know that. This was Logan. Not like anywhere was more than five minutes out of the way. Why did Casey want him to drive her? Foolish to hope maybe she wanted to spend time with him, but he couldn't help himself.

Casey pushed her plate away. "You want any help washing the dishes, Mom?"

"No, honey. But let your father drive you to the Shack."

"Why?" Casey asked, jutting her chin out. "Why shouldn't Daniel drive me?"

Their parents exchanged glances that Daniel couldn't read. In the sudden silence, Daniel pushed his chair back. "Thanks for dinner. I gotta go."

"I'm coming with you," Casey said.

She followed him outside to his car.

"You really want a lift?"

"'Course I do." She wrenched the door open and climbed inside. "They like that all the time with you?"

Daniel adjusted his seat belt. "Dad's okay. Mom . . . Mom's not okay."

Casey sighed. "I was a bitch to you in high school. I mean, I was a bitch to everyone, but you especially. You ruined my life back then, you know?"

"I know." Daniel started the car.

Casey reached out and touched his shoulder. "Yeah, but *anything* would have ruined my life. The wrong color nail polish, last season's jeans . . ."

"A freak for a brother."

Casey was silent for a while. "That time in Harnee's, you took me by surprise. I didn't know what to say, and I'm sorry. Mom said you never come into town, 'cept for work."

"You asked about me?"

"Of course I did. You didn't *die*, Daniel. You didn't just vanish after you went to prison. You're still my brother."

Daniel fixed his gaze on the road. Didn't want to Casey to see he was tearing up. "Thanks."

Casey turned her head and stared out at the passing houses. "Why do you stay in Logan?"

"Parole board says I gotta."

"You gonna leave when that's done?"

"I don't know," he lied. "No. I—I almost got a handle on things here, Case. As good as I'll ever have."

"You could do better," Casey said. "Why stay in a place where everyone hates the sight of you?"

Cut deep and hurt bad coming from her, even if it was mostly true.

"Got the cabin," Daniel said. "Got a job. Got a routine."

Got Bel.

He doesn't hate the sight of me. You don't know everything, you or anyone in this town. Think I can do better? I am doing better.

"You oughta come and visit me in Charleston when you can," Casey told him.

Daniel turned wide onto Main. What the hell was she trying to do? Coming here, playing nice, saying he should *visit* her? Did she feel guilty? Was that it?

He felt his phone buzz in his pocket, but he didn't take it out. "That probably wouldn't work."

"Why not?"

"Because I still do it," Daniel said bitterly. "Still sleepwalk. Still wake up not knowing what I've done. You don't want me in your town, Case, not even for a bit. You know what I can do."

"I know exactly what you can do," Casey said as they pulled up outside the Shack. "I miss you, though. I miss the way we used to be friends."

Daniel didn't remember that. He remembered fighting with her. Remembered that any time their parents had to take sides, they took hers. Remembered her making friends at school and ignoring him as much as possible.

But there'd been more to it than that. Casey could be sweet, sometimes. Just because the good times weren't what stuck with Daniel didn't mean they hadn't existed.

He'd been convinced everyone had written him off. Hadn't occurred to him he might have shut people out too. Hadn't occurred to him he had that kind of power.

When he'd moved back here after college, he'd stayed inside as much as possible, sure that his parents were embarrassed to have him in Logan again. After Kenny Cooper'd beaten him, he'd spent weeks in bed. His mom had done his grocery shopping, cooked for him, and he'd treated her coldly. His self-loathing and fear were great enough that he'd needed to project some of it onto her.

But he'd never known what she really felt. Maybe she'd pitied him, and maybe she'd cried for him. Maybe she'd hated Kenny Cooper with a force that scared her. Daniel had never looked at her with any hope of seeing love or sympathy. He'd needed to see loathing, disgust—*deserved* to see it—and so he had.

And maybe he'd done the same to Casey. Disregarded the complexity of her feelings for him in favor of an easy verdict: she hated him, and she wanted to forget he existed.

"That was a long time ago," Daniel said.

"So?" Casey unclipped her belt. "You want to come in for a beer?"

"No. Can't do that."

"Why not?"

Daniel almost smiled. Same old Casey. Always asking her bullheaded questions. "Because it's your birthday, and you don't need your freak brother starting shit for you." He did smile then. "Go and have fun, okay?"

She stared at him, and Daniel felt a flash of fear. She was judging him, he knew she was. Just wished he knew what she saw.

She shrugged suddenly. "What do I know? I'm just your little sister. But you ought to stop hiding on account of everyone else, okay?"

"I'm not hiding. It's just easier this way."

"You're letting people push you around. Just like when we were kids."

"I didn't—"

"Remember when I had to punch Cody Miller for throwing rocks at you?"

"You didn't *have* to do that."

She snickered. "I really enjoyed it though."

"And then you punched me."

"For being a chickenshit." She looked at him. "You gotta fight back," she said quietly.

Because that turned out so well with Kenny.

He'd fantasized about retaliation for months after Kenny had attacked him. If only he'd been conscious when he'd actually gone to get his revenge. If only he'd stopped short of killing him. If only he hadn't been such a coward, letting his subconscious do the dirty work.

Can't fight back. I'll always lose.

He scratched the back of his neck and tried to smile. "All right. Go on."

"Okay." She opened the door, then turned back and surprised him with a hug. "I'm heading back tomorrow. But you email me, okay? Promise me."

You mean that? God, please don't say it if you don't mean it.

"Okay," he said, releasing her. "I . . ." He stopped, his momentary joy dissolving. "I don't know your email."

Don't know how to contact my own sister.

"Oh." She smiled awkwardly. "Right. Give me your phone."

He handed her his phone and watched her type.

"There you go," she said. "Number and email."

"Thanks." He took the phone back.

He sat in the car and watched as she walked inside. Some things in his life were broken beyond repair. Other things, well maybe they weren't in as many pieces as he thought. Maybe some things were actually starting to come together.

He got out his phone. Read Bel's texts and looked up, through the windshield, at the light from the Shack and the dark road beyond.

Things were definitely coming together.

He texted a reply and headed for the orchard.

Bel's phone buzzed.

He'd gotten back a *:)*

What the fuck did that mean? Was Daniel coming or not?

Took twenty minutes for an answer to that—twenty minutes for Daniel to arrive at the orchard, which probably meant he'd sped. Bel made a mental note to look out for Daniel's car in town over the next few days and to pull him over if he saw him. Just for kicks.

Bel's cock showed considerable interest in Daniel's arrival. Bel had to remind himself to let Daniel make the first move, if there were moves to be made.

Daniel looked all right when he got out of his car. Walked over, knelt at the base of the tree, and kissed Bel, which got Bel's cock all the harder.

"You have an okay time?" Bel asked.

"Actually, yeah."

When Daniel didn't elaborate, Bel's bizarre jealousy returned. Would it have killed Daniel to fill him in? "No one gave you trouble?"

Daniel shook his head and scooted closer. There wasn't enough room against the tree trunk for both of them, so Daniel leaned on Bel. "Mom was a little awkward. Dad was okay. It was funny, though—my parents had a hell of a time getting Casey to visit. She'd already celebrated her birthday with her Charleston friends and wanted that to be it. I kept wanting to shake her—*you know how lucky you are?* Don't know if my folks will ever celebrate my birthday again."

Daniel didn't say it like he was sorry for himself. In fact, the way he was talking, he sounded more animated than Bel had heard him in a while. Maybe ever.

"But we talked a bit. So, it was okay."

"That's good," Bel said. His jealousy dissipated, and he shook his head, trying to clear the memory of what the guys at Greenducks had said. Bel loved Daniel like this—stable, lively, unafraid. He'd been here all of three minutes and Bel already felt calmer, more anchored. There was something about Daniel that did that—brought all the scattered parts of Bel's mind together. A beautiful, quiet energy that was even more perfect because it came from a place Daniel didn't control.

Same place that had killed Kenny Cooper. Same place that made those drawings.

"What'd you do?" Daniel asked him.

"Had a beer then came out here to sit."

"Pretty out tonight."

"You're prettier." Bel bumped Daniel with his shoulder. He felt lame saying it, but he liked teasing Daniel. And besides, it was true.

Daniel laughed. "Aw, come on. Big tough guy like you doesn't want a pretty boy."

"How do you know?"

"Say I'm handsome or something."

"You are. Handsome and pretty both."

Daniel snorted. "Yeah right."

"You callin' me a liar? I'd hate to go all tough guy on you."

"I'd like it."

"Would you?" Bel checked him hard with his shoulder, and Daniel fell sideways. Had to put an arm down to catch himself.

"Jerk!"

Bel grinned and leaned over, pushing Daniel to the ground. He got on all fours, his hands on either side of Daniel's head, pinning him.

Daniel made a pretty pathetic show of struggling. He raised one leg as if to kick Bel, and instead rubbed his knee over Bel's groin. Bel swooped down to kiss him, refusing to give Daniel even a second to breathe. Daniel kept thrusting his tongue into Bel's mouth, so Bel finally caught it between his lips and sucked hard on it. Daniel was panting when Bel was through. Bel sat back on his heels and undid his belt.

"Roll over," he said.

"Make me," Daniel whispered.

Bel hesitated. Stared at Daniel's face in the darkness and read the expression there. Made sure they were on the same page, his belly tightening with anticipation when he saw they were. Then he moved. He took hold of Daniel and tried to roll him, but Daniel wouldn't budge. On an impulse, Bel grabbed the front of Daniel's pants. The jeans were loose enough that it took Bel a minute to find Daniel's balls through the denim, but he did, and he gripped them tightly.

Daniel hissed.

"Roll over, boy," Bel said. *Roll over, boy who's got four years on me.* Bel liked saying it, though.

Daniel tried to clamp his knees around Bel's arm. Bel squeezed his balls tighter.

"Roll over, or I'll make you jerk me off, and I won't fuck you, and you won't come."

"Oh, come on," Daniel said, voice strained.

Bel gave Daniel's balls a little more pressure. Daniel gasped. Shut his eyes and writhed.

"Okay . . . okay . . . Bel."

Bel let go.

"You asshole," Daniel muttered as he started to roll onto his stomach.

Bel flipped him the rest of the way. Leaned down, still straddling Daniel, and said into his ear, "I'll remember that." He slid one hand behind him and patted Daniel's ass. "I'll remember that when I'm deciding how long, and how hard, and how *raw* to fuck you."

Daniel's breathing was so rough it made Bel wild. He wanted to hear Daniel struggling for breath, choking on what little air he managed to draw. "Good," Daniel whispered defiantly.

Bel lifted off Daniel a little so he could reach under him and undo his pants. He turned so he was still straddling Daniel but facing his feet, and then pushed Daniel's jeans down to his ankles. Daniel helpfully kicked them the rest of the way off. He wore gray briefs instead of his usual boxers. Bel stroked his ass through the cotton. "Looking good, Daniel."

Daniel squirmed under him.

Bel finished removing his belt, letting Daniel hear it jingle as he pulled it through the loops. He was pretty sure Daniel stopped breathing. He climbed off Daniel and got to his feet. "C'mon." He grabbed Daniel's ankles and pulled him back until his legs were on either side of the thin trunk of the apple tree.

"What're you doing, Bel?" Daniel's voice was thick, his breath coming in sharp gulps.

"Making sure you stay put." Bel reached around the tree and pulled Daniel's ankles together. Used his belt to bind them. It was harder than he'd figured—not much light, and the leather was thick and didn't tie easy. But he got it good enough that Daniel wasn't going anywhere. Daniel kicked the ground, and Bel slapped his ass, pleased when Daniel bucked.

He moved in front of Daniel and pulled Daniel's shirt over his head. Now he was naked except for his underwear, his legs tied around the tree trunk. His breath moved his whole body, and he was digging his fingers into the earth. Bel placed his fingertips at the small of Daniel's back, then dragged them down to tease at the elastic of Daniel's briefs.

"Gonna fuck you right out here in the middle of nowhere," Bel said.

Daniel wriggled against the ground. "Yes."

Bel took a condom out of his pocket. "You're gonna feel it for days. And you're gonna remember this."

Bel wasn't quite sure Daniel's reply was a word. It sounded like "yeah," but it also sounded like a whimper and a gasp together.

Bel undid his pants and pushed them to his thighs. Didn't put the condom on yet. He hooked his fingers in Daniel's waistband and tugged his briefs down, exposing that taut, muscular ass. He slid them as far as they'd go down Daniel's legs before he hit the tree trunk.

"Get your legs as far apart as you can."

Between the belt and the briefs, that wasn't very far, but Daniel made a good effort, bending his knees awkwardly so he could open himself for Bel. Bel leaned over and parted Daniel's cheeks with one hand. He bent closer, gathering saliva in his mouth, and then he spat. It fell in one long string, landing just above Daniel's hole and dribbling down. Daniel arched his back, pushing his ass up as Bel spit again.

Bel trailed a finger through the wetness. When he reached Daniel's hole, he slipped inside. Daniel grunted and clenched around him. Bel added a second finger almost immediately. Heard the catch of Daniel's breath. He played for a while, not actively searching for Daniel's prostate, but finding it just often enough to keep Daniel whimpering. Mostly he worked on stretching Daniel, and when Daniel felt relaxed enough, he added a third finger.

"Please, I don't need this," Daniel whispered. "I can take your cock. Please."

"You don't like this?" Bel thrust hard with his fingers.

"Ah! No, I do, I just—need *you*."

"This *is* me, Daniel." Bel thrust again. "You know, we really got to do something to help you remember who's in charge."

"Sorry, Bel," Daniel mumbled, the words almost lost against the ground.

"You say that. But next time you want my cock up your ass so bad you can't stand it, you're gonna beg, aren't you? You're gonna try to tell me what to do."

He skimmed Daniel's prostate. Daniel jerked. "I won't! I promise, Bel. I'll listen."

Bel pressed the tip of his pinky against Daniel's entrance. "Gonna do four now. Breathe."

Daniel groaned as Bel pushed the fourth finger in. Bel felt Daniel's muscles spasming, the damp heat of him. Reveled in his sounds of arousal and frustration.

"'Bout half my hand inside of you." Bel was trying to formulate a plan for the rest of the night, though it was pretty hard to concentrate with Daniel writhing and moaning, and Bel's cock nudging through the slit in his underwear.

"How hard do you like it, Daniel?"

Daniel hesitated. "Um . . . up to you?"

That wouldn't do. Wasn't what Bel had meant by Daniel needing to let Bel be in charge. "When I ask you a question, I want the truth." Bel rubbed Daniel's prostate and spread all four fingers as far as he could, pushing against the walls of muscle. Daniel cried out, hips coming off the ground.

"Hard, Bel. I like it hard. Please." Daniel's voice was ragged with need.

Bel fucked Daniel harder, then harder still when a plea met every thrust. Amazing, to look down and see Daniel stretched around his fingers. He liked the moonlight on Daniel's skin too—a good look for him. The fabric of Daniel's briefs strained as Daniel struggled to keep his legs wide enough to accommodate Bel.

"There?" Bel asked, grazing his prostate again.

"*Fuck*! Yes." Daniel hadn't quite managed to get his hips back on the ground. It was all right, though. Bel liked him with his ass up like this.

"Get your knees under you."

Daniel tried. Bel hooked his free arm around his hips and helped him, slowly withdrawing his fingers as he did. Daniel's moan might have been disappointment or relief—or both. Bel scooted back a little so that he straddled Daniel's shoulders, facing his upturned ass. He rose onto his knees and spread Daniel's cheeks to look at his hole, loose and wet.

Bel leaned forward, lowered his head, and stuck his tongue in.

He'd never eaten a guy out. Had wanted to try it on a couple of occasions when he was really horny, but most of the time he was ambivalent. Right now, though, he wanted it so bad he could feel the need through his entire body. Daniel's startled gasp, the way he contracted his muscles and pushed his ass higher, it all fueled Bel's hunger. Maybe there was an art to this, and maybe Bel would take the time to master it later, but right now, he was going on instinct.

Their position made things a little difficult, but Bel managed. He pushed his tongue in as far as he could, then withdrew to lap at Daniel's hole before plunging in again. Bel got a cry from Daniel with each stab of his tongue, plus the satisfaction of watching Daniel thump his feet on the ground and strain against the belt, chafing his calves on the tree trunk.

Bel clamped his thighs against Daniel's sides and reached down to give Daniel's cock a couple of pulls. Then he put his hands back on Daniel's ass cheeks and held them spread while he licked circles around Daniel's hole. Daniel tried to kick again, and Bel gave his ass a light slap, more sound than sting. But the moan that came out of Daniel stopped Bel dead. Heat raced through him, and he had to stop and stroke his own cock for a minute.

Daniel kept moving, humping the air, and Bel slapped him harder. "Stay still."

Daniel didn't listen, but Bel was too lost in his own pleasure to do anything about it. He leaned forward and licked the top of Daniel's crack, jerking himself harder and faster while Daniel bucked under him. He let his moans echo Daniel's until he came across Daniel's lower back.

Bel sighed and sat back on Daniel's shoulders, watching his cum slide toward him. He reached behind him and stroked what he could find of Daniel's hair. Daniel was breathing fast enough to hyperventilate. Bel heard a wet, rhythmic sound and realized Daniel was working his own cock.

"Uh-uh." Bel glanced around and saw a small branch from the apple tree. He picked it up and gave Daniel's ass a flurry of light taps. "Get your ass on the ground."

Daniel let go of his cock, lowered himself onto his belly, and straightened his legs out behind him. Bel gave him another few whacks with the switch, letting these ones sting a little more, just because it was fun to see Daniel flinch and wriggle, to know his cock was still hard and trapped between his body and the ground. The twig snapped, and Bel tossed it aside. Reached around the tree and undid the belt. Traced the indentations left in Daniel's skin by the leather.

Bel didn't move for a minute. Wasn't sure what he was going to do now. Daniel hadn't come—didn't have to, Bel knew. But Bel wanted him to.

Just Bel was tired. And not sure the best way to proceed.

He stuck a finger back inside Daniel and fucked him while he thought. Daniel grunted, squeezing each time Bel thrust, trying to rub his cock against the ground.

Bel had an idea. Thought it might work pretty well. He climbed off Daniel and retrieved the condom from the ground. Put it in his pocket, pulled his pants up, and fastened them. Daniel's back was still wet with Bel's cum. His breathing had slowed, but not much.

"Roll over."

Daniel didn't. He kept trying to rub against the ground.

Bel sharpened his voice. "Daniel."

Daniel rubbed faster. Bel picked up his belt, doubled it, and snapped it across Daniel's ass. Daniel gave a muffled yelp and rolled onto his back. That felt good. Better than Bel would have expected. Better because he knew Daniel wanted it—pain for the sake of it, for the pure *sensation*, instead of some fucked-up desire to be crippled by it—and because he imagined Daniel could have come like that, humping the ground while Bel whacked his ass. They were both of them here in this moment, where nothing else existed apart from flesh and need and moonlight. A place Bel had tried to imagine when he'd been scrolling through those sites on his computer, but it wasn't by studying any pictures that he'd gotten here. It was by studying Daniel.

Daniel's eyes were wide as he looked at Bel, and his hand strayed to his cock.

"Don't you dare," Bel warned.

He straddled Daniel once more and kissed him hard. Moved his lips down Daniel's throat to his chest. He licked Daniel's left nipple into a hard point, then sucked on it, biting down every few seconds. Daniel arched each time he felt Bel's teeth, fighting back whimpers. *Fuck yeah.* Bel reached behind him and gave Daniel's cock a few quick strokes, just enough to get his hips pumping, then let go and worked the other nipple with his mouth.

Bel alternated sides until both nipples were so sensitive that even the slightest brush of Bel's tongue made Daniel cry out. Bel sucked and bit until the pain started to wilt Daniel's cock—at which point Bel jacked him until he was hard again. But he didn't stop what he was doing to Daniel's nipples. Daniel was begging incoherently when Bel finally quit. Bel kissed Daniel on the mouth again, and Daniel kissed back so hungrily that Bel knew he was doing the right thing—wasn't taking this too far.

He cupped Daniel's cheek, then climbed off him. "Get up," he whispered.

Daniel rolled onto his side and got unsteadily to his feet, his cock jutting, legs trembling. He started to pull his underwear up. "No," Bel said.

Daniel froze.

"Bend over."

Daniel hesitated, then bent at the waist, automatically clasping his ankles. Jesus, he was perfect. Bel picked up the belt and cracked him with it, pretty hard. Daniel gave the slightest gasp but didn't move.

"I'll tell you when you can pull those up."

"Yes, Bel."

Bel started collecting Daniel's clothes. Daniel held position until Bel smacked him with the belt again. "Walk to the car."

Daniel went obediently. His back was a mess of dirt and grass and cum.

Bel opened the backseat of the Volvo. Whipped Daniel again—still not near as hard as he could have, but the sound was satisfying. "Get in there. All fours. Ass up. Just like you were a while ago."

Daniel complied, climbing onto the seat and thrusting his ass toward Bel. Bel gave Daniel's ass a couple more licks, watching his muscles clench and a faint blush appear on his skin. "You're gonna stay in position, aren't you, Daniel?"

A muffled answer. Bel licked him again. "Didn't hear you."

"Yes, Bel." Daniel's voice was hoarse.

"You're gonna tell me if anything's wrong. If you don't want to play anymore. Right?" *Can I trust you to do that for me?*

"Yes, Bel," Daniel replied, clearly and promptly.

Bel whacked him anyway. Just because it was fun. "Good."

Bel shut the door and got in the driver's side. Set the belt on the passenger's seat. Daniel didn't speak, not even to ask what they'd do about his car. Bel started the Volvo, then turned to look in the back. Daniel's face was pressed against the seat, his ass in the air, his briefs still around his ankles. God help them if they got stopped. Or had to brake suddenly for a deer or some shit.

"Daniel?"

"Yeah, Bel?"

"I want you to reach behind you and get at least three fingers in your ass. Four if you can."

Daniel hesitated only a second, then spit on his right hand, put it behind him, and started working his fingers into his ass.

"Good," Bel said, his voice gentler. He watched, enthralled, as Daniel pushed three fingers in. Daniel took a deep breath, then squeezed his eyes shut and added a fourth. "Very nice." Bel reached out and stroked Daniel's bare shoulder. "Keep them in there. I'll drive careful."

Bel pulled out of the orchard and onto 601. It was a long, silent ride to town, Bel's cock slowly hardening as he watched Daniel in the rearview mirror. Daniel was trying hard to control his breathing. Trying not to fuck himself—because Bel hadn't said to do that. Had just said to keep his fingers in there. Shit, Bel couldn't believe how good it felt to have this kind of control. To be *allowed* this kind of control.

When they reached the first traffic light in Logan, Bel reached back and pinched Daniel's left nipple. Daniel's breath hitched, and he let out a soft moan. Bel continued to roll and pull his nipple, digging his nail in at one point. "That hurt?" Bel asked.

"Yes, sir. I mean, yes, Bel." Daniel's voice was tense.

"You like it?"

"I do, Bel."

"Fuck yourself until the next light."

Bel listened until he heard the quick, wet slide of Daniel's fingers moving in and out of his ass. Fuck, if they didn't get home soon, Bel was gonna blow another load just listening to Daniel.

Logan was dead. Almost midnight on a Thursday—no one was around. Still, Bel kept an eye out for cops or late-night wanderers.

At the next light, he turned and started stroking Daniel's cock. Daniel gasped and panted, still finger-fucking himself. Bel figured his neck and shoulders must be getting tired. "Take your fingers out," he ordered. Daniel did so with obvious reluctance, slowly and with a groan that made Bel's balls ache. Bel pinched his nipple as a reward.

The next light was green, but Bel stopped anyway. Turned, slapped Daniel's ass, and kept driving. They were done with traffic lights after that, but Bel stopped a couple more times to roll Daniel's balls, stroke his dick, or pinch or slap him. Daniel took it all.

When they reached Bel's house, Bel parked in the garage and put the garage door down. Then he got out of the car and opened the back door. Couldn't even take a minute to appreciate Daniel's ass, he was so eager. He yanked his pants down, fished the condom out of his pocket, opened it, and rolled it on. Daniel heard what he was doing and whispered, "Please, Bel. Please."

Bel tried to climb onto the seat with Daniel, but he didn't quite fit. He pushed Daniel down into the seat well, guiding Daniel's upper body onto the center console between the driver's and passenger's seats. When Daniel arched his back, his ass was just above the level of the backseat. Bel crawled onto the seat, spit in his palm, and guided his cock into Daniel. He braced his hands on the front seats and started rocking his hips. Daniel was loose now, but he still clenched every few seconds, sending shocks through Bel.

"That's good," Bel murmured. "You're so good."

He took his right hand off the headrest, reached under Daniel, and made a fist around Daniel's cock. Bel pounded Daniel's ass, imagining how Daniel felt with his aching nipples rubbing against the console, his ass already raw from the fingering. Daniel thrust into Bel's fist a few times and came, and Bel followed a minute later.

Bel closed his eyes.

Shit. Just . . . holy fucking shit.

He pulled out. Eased himself off the seat and out of the car. His legs would barely hold him, but somewhere he found the strength to help Daniel out too. Drew Daniel in for another kiss, stroking Daniel's back as he did, not minding the mess.

"Inside," Bel whispered, kissing the sweat from Daniel's upper lip. "Let's get cleaned up."

Daniel pressed his forehead to Bel's and nodded. Followed Bel into the house.

CHAPTER SIXTEEN

"**N**ext few months'll go by fast."

Daniel didn't answer. Ms. Davenport's office was neat as always. She had a card on her windowsill and he wondered who had sent it and why. Birthday? Get well? There had been occasions where he'd almost fooled himself into thinking he and Ms. Davenport were friends. It was a dumb thought, but it had helped him when he'd felt like complete shit, utterly alone and hated by everyone. Ms. Davenport had believed him. She'd spoken to him, not like he was crazy or dangerous, but like he was just a regular guy who'd ended up in temporary trouble.

"Any idea yet what you want to do after?"

Daniel almost smiled. People had asked him that when he was getting ready to graduate from college. Now someone was asking him what his plans were post-parole. "Might go on vacation."

"I feel you." Ms. Davenport rolled her eyes. "I'd give anything for a break from Logan right about now."

"I was kidding," Daniel said. "Don't have a clue where I'd go, even if I did want a vacation."

Ms. Davenport nodded. "Well, it's not like you have to have any big plans. But you'll have options now."

"Don't know what to do with 'em."

"Enjoy them." She paused. "I can't order you to get out of Logan, but it sure would make me happy to know you were doing something better than cleaning up the library."

"Not much else I'm good at."

"That's bullshit." At Daniel's startled look, she added, "Sorry. Should I be more professional? I think that's baloney."

Daniel felt a cold sadness settle in his guts. "Well, maybe I'll figure something out someday. But right now, I'm here."

"Fair enough." Ms. Davenport placed a hand over Daniel's file. "I suppose we're done here."

Daniel hesitated. He didn't like that Ms. Davenport was frustrated with him. It made him frustrated with himself. "How would I . . . how would I get a job anywhere else? With my record? Feel like I'd be worse off in some other town. At least here, people are sort of used to me." His face heated, but he went on. "They still talk about me here, but it's the same old stuff. Somewhere else, it's gonna be a whole new set of rumors, a whole 'nother set of gawkers to get used to."

Ms. Davenport got up and placed his file in her cabinet. Came back and sat across from him. She leaned back and clasped her hands over her belly and just *stared* for a minute. God, she was ten times more intimidating than Bel at his wickedest. If Bel could learn to do that stare, Daniel'd be a goner. "Maybe some people'll talk wherever you go," she said. "But why would you let that stop you? There's places that aren't so goddamn bigoted. You ever been to New York?"

Daniel shook his head.

"Nobody there gives a fuck who you are or what you've done. You can walk around wearing a garbage bag, and people just stare straight ahead."

Daniel thought about it. USC at Aiken hadn't been quite that anonymous, but it had been better than Logan, where you couldn't sneeze without someone telling their neighbor about it.

Maybe I want to stay. Maybe I don't want to let myself forget what I did. Need to be around people who'll remind me.

But that wasn't quite right either.

Maybe I want to stay because now I got something worth staying for.

"There'd be better treatment options for your condition, somewhere else."

"There's no cure for it," Daniel said a little too sharply.

"I know that. But there might be ways to make it better."

Daniel didn't answer.

"Give it some thought," Ms. Davenport said. "You've done your time. It's not really my business, but for someone like you, I think staying here would be a life sentence."

"Bel likes it okay," Daniel said, before he could stop himself. "I just mean . . . he and I got some things in common, and he's happy here."

Ms. Davenport tapped a pen against her desk. "Bel's never known anywhere else."

"Well, neither have I, really."

She shrugged. "It's not that I have anything against Logan. A little too much Jesus and not enough forward thinking, but I don't think it's horrible. So do whatever you want to do. I'm sorry I stuck my nose in."

"It's okay," Daniel said, getting up. "I wish someone would tell me what to do sometimes."

Like Bel does. Wish we could both stay here and he could tell me what to do. Why's it got to be more complicated than that?

He thought of Clayton. Of the pig's head. The noose. The fire.

Because if Daniel stayed here, it would never be finished.

If he stayed, he'd always be surrounded by hate. A hot strike of fury hit him. Clayton and his buddies had wanted to watch him die. They'd *laughed*. And it wasn't only other people's hate he had to live with. There was his own too. And that well ran fucking deep. Deeper than Daniel wanted to acknowledge.

There were those moments where everything disappeared but his rage, and he knew he'd meant to kill Kenny Cooper. Knew Cooper had deserved it. Knew Cooper would have killed him, back in that field, if someone hadn't happened along.

"Can you speak? What happened? Can you stand up?"

Daniel didn't even know who it was.

"Can you stand up?"

So much blood. The glow of a cell phone screen. The man trying to explain to a 9-1-1 operator where they were.

The cold.

"Say something."

And somewhere in there, he'd slept.

Woken in the hospital. The questions.

"Who did this?"

Cooper would finish the job if Daniel told. And Daniel had thought death wouldn't be a bad idea. He'd been ready to tell, except then, his father: *"Daniel, what did you do?"*

Healing. The swelling going down. He could open his eyes. His jaw was wired. Couldn't afford dental work. Nothing to be done about the missing back teeth.

"Did you see the guy? Was it more than one?"

People had figured out it was Kenny and his gang. Maybe Kenny had bragged.

Had a gun, Daniel wanted to tell them. *Was going to kill me.*

Casey was right. He wanted to fight back, sometimes. That feeling rose in unexpected moments, but ebbed when he thought about what he'd done to Kenny. Gone beyond revenge.

Or had he?

Because he'd ended up hurting himself in a way that went deeper, lasted longer, than anything Kenny had done to him. Kenny had left him with nightmares.

But murdering Kenny had left him alone.

"If I thought you wanted to stay in Logan because you loved it, I'd let you be," Ms. Davenport said. "But I think you're staying because you think you don't deserve a life anywhere else."

Daniel shoved his hands in his pockets. "You're worse than John."

Ms. Davenport grinned. "He tell you the same thing?"

Daniel didn't return the smile. "I think it's weird that all you liberal people come here just so you can look down on us."

Her grin fell away. "Excuse me?"

"What are you doing in Logan if you think all the 'smart' people who could do a lot better ought to move somewhere else? What are you, like those missionaries that go to Africa and try to get people to be Christians? You're forward thinking. You've been to other places. And you want to settle here where you got to drive twenty minutes to get to a movie theater? You want to keep doing parole for addicts and dealers and wife abusers? I lived in the city, and there was nothing that great about it."

He was lying. Well, not exactly lying. There'd been more to do in the city; there'd been better food and a feeling that he could breathe. The city had felt like a destination rather than a crossroads. And yet, it hadn't changed his life. People weren't *better* there. Just had some different ideas. He'd been so excited to leave Logan when he'd been in high school. And then he'd come crawling back.

This is my home now.

This is what I am.

Where I belong.

This is where I have some crazy, fucked-up kind of hope.

Ms. Davenport looked at him evenly. "I've got my reasons for being here. And I'm sorry. I guess it was rude of me to think you don't have yours too. I don't look down on anyone here. Well, maybe some people. But I'm not a missionary."

"Sorry I went off," Daniel muttered. His heart was going fast. It had been pretty stupid of him to lecture his parole officer.

"Not a problem. Consider the subject dropped."

Daniel wasn't sure he wanted to drop it. He wished he could believe in a place where people didn't hate him, didn't care what he'd done. Where he could go to a pharmacy program and get a decent job and live in a space bigger than one room.

Maybe Bel would come with me.

For some reason, that idea didn't seem crazy.

Daniel went to work that afternoon, and all he could think about was Ms. Davenport saying, *"Sure would make me happy to know you were doing something better than cleaning the library."*

And he wanted to say fuck her. Wanted not to think about what she'd said. But he couldn't stop imagining a place where people didn't stop to stare at him. Where no one threw bottles at his house or left nooses on his mailbox post. There was a pharmacy school in Charleston. There were people there who didn't hate him. Didn't even know him.

If I paid my debt to society, then is it okay to start answering just to myself? I won't forget what I did.

Casey said it was okay to fight back.

He let himself imagine a little further. A place where he could breathe. Where he felt safe.

Where he and Bel—

He stopped.

He and Bel. Would Bel ever leave Logan? Why would he? Why give up his home—his life—for Daniel?

But the thought made him so genuinely fucking happy that he let himself have it. He left Logan, and Bel came with him, to the place where the world didn't seem like an endless night he wandered through, awake and on edge. It had color and beauty, which were his as much as anyone else's to appreciate.

Could that place *be* Logan? It seemed strange to even think it, but what if Bel kept helping Daniel, and Daniel got stronger? Strong enough that the stares didn't bother him. That he could feel good walking through the town with Bel.

What if Daniel made Logan his home instead of his prison?

He swept between the children's literature aisles. It wasn't that simple. He was locked up in all sorts of ways.

But for now, he'd imagine. He'd think about Bel in the orchard. About how with Bel, Daniel had become the person Marcus had wanted him to be. Strong, using the pain to anchor himself, to move forward. To take and to give and to be something other than trapped.

A knock at the side door startled him. He glanced around, not sure where Carl, the security guy, was. He'd probably gone out to smoke and had ended up wandering over to the gas station for a sandwich. Daniel walked toward the door.

Clayton McAllister stood on the other side of the glass.

Daniel froze. Clayton was gesturing for him to open the door. He pounded on the glass, looking over his shoulder every few seconds.

Fucking hell.

"Open up!" Clayton yelled. "Please!"

What, did the guy have a sensor or something? Could tell when Daniel was starting to feel some hint of happiness, and was coming to wreck it.

Daniel glanced around the library again. "Carl?" he called.

No answer.

"Please!" Clayton was yelling on the other side of the door. "It's an emergency."

No way in hell was Daniel going to open the door for Clayton. What the hell kind of emergency could involve Clayton needing to get into the library? Clayton had probably never used a library in his life.

But shit, if Clayton was on the run from a maniac or something—sweet justice though that would be—and Daniel didn't let him in . . .

Clayton wouldn't stop pounding, wouldn't stop begging Daniel to open up.

Clayton wasn't going to try anything in a public building. Carl would be back any minute anyway. And Clayton was gonna break the glass if he kept at that.

Daniel pushed open the door. "What the hell do you—"

Clayton shouldered his way into the building, followed by R.J. and Brock.

"Get the fuck out of here," Daniel said, shoving Clayton in the chest before he could really think about what he was doing. Fear and anger warred for dominance in him. "What do you mean, coming in here?"

"Left my phone in here earlier," Clayton said. He didn't look panicked anymore. There was a grin pulling at his lips. "Need to look for it."

"You're lyin'. What would you have been doing in a library? Can you even read?"

"Ouch, Whitlock."

Brock laughed.

Clayton took a step toward Daniel, and Daniel backed up. "You're right. I didn't lose my phone. Just came to talk to you."

Brock and R.J. crowded closer to Daniel. "'Bout what?" Daniel demanded.

"'Bout you showing your face in my town," Clayton said casually.

Breakfast with Bel. Walking around town that morning like he belonged there. He'd known it was a bad idea. Known it would cause trouble, even though he wasn't wrong for doing it. Cold dread snaked through him. But he willed it to stop, and it did.

"My town too," Daniel said.

"That what you think?" Clayton's voice was soft. "Think you can show up at the diner with your cop friend and expect people to treat you like you ain't a murderer?" He paused, watching Daniel. "Are you a murderer, Whitlock?"

Daniel stayed quiet. Wasn't like he could deny it.

Clayton nodded. "Right. I wanna talk about how things go from here."

R.J. reached out and pinched Daniel's arm. Daniel staggered back, hitting a shelf of picture books and knocking several to the floor. R.J. and Brock laughed, but Clayton didn't. "The hell do you mean?"

Daniel stepped forward, anger finally overtaking fear. What the hell did Clayton think he was doing, coming in here and ruining Daniel's first good dream in years?

"I mean the law didn't see to it you paid for what you done to Kenny. So I'm gonna."

"You can fucking try," Daniel snarled. "But I done my time, and this is as much my town as yours. And you don't know shit. I paid. I paid more'n you think."

Clayton gave a lifeless smile. "Fuck you, Whitlock."

It was then that Daniel recognized the hollowness in Clayton. Daniel had felt that himself in the months after Kenny had attacked him. And he'd felt it again after Kenny's death. After the trial. After his jail sentence. Sometimes there was loss without grief. Sometimes the person you were mourning was yourself.

Maybe Clayton had grieved for Kenny, but Kenny was gone now. Clayton had had years to come to terms with it. But he was still running on an old anger.

Sometimes it's a slow burn, ain't it, Clayton? Sometimes you don't even see how it's ripping you open new every day. Sometimes you live with it for years. And then one day, you snap.

It was never going to be over. Not for Clayton. Not for Daniel. Not if Daniel stayed here. Logan would never be his home as long as there was this much hate burning in both of them.

"I think you'd better leave," Daniel said. "If we're gonna settle this, it ain't gonna be here."

As if on cue, they heard the back door to the library creak open, and then Carl called, "Daniel?"

Clayton looked at Daniel. "Gonna have to finish this one day, Whitlock."

And Daniel felt a strange peace at those words, a calm that shifted beneath his anger. At least they understood each other.

At least they agreed on something.

The guys edged toward the side door. Carl showed up just as they reached it. He looked from Daniel to Clayton, confused. "What's going on here?"

"Thought I'd left my phone here," Clayton said, jamming his hands in his pockets. "Whitlock let me in to check."

"You find it?" Carl asked.

Clayton shook his head. "Nope. Gonna try some other places." He nodded at Carl, then he and R.J. and Brock went out the side door.

Carl looked at Daniel. "Library's closed. You ought to've had him wait outside while you looked for the phone."

Daniel stared at the door. Listened to the truck start up in the parking lot.

Tires spinning in gravel.

The thud of the pig's head on the porch.

Crack of gun against bone.

A whoop.

"Yeah," he said at last. "That was dumb of me."

Bel woke in the middle of the night to find Daniel sitting in the armchair, drawing. The kitchen light was on, but the main room of the cabin was still gloomy. "How c'n you see?" Bel murmured.

Daniel didn't answer. Bel got up slowly. Daniel glanced at him, then went back to sketching, the pencil making soft noises on the paper.

"Not drawing me, are you?" Bel asked.

"Yeah, Bel."

Bel flipped on the lamp and walked over. Sat on the arm of the chair.

The drawing was of Bel, but Daniel hadn't been drawing from life. In the sketch, Bel was sitting on the edge of the bed, hands beside him, looking at something off to the side. He was in three-quarters profile, and there were dark patches on the skin of his face. "You gave me the plague or somethin'," Bel commented.

"No." Daniel's voice was soft, dreamy. "Those are your burns."

"My burns?" Bel's heart clenched.

Daniel kept drawing without looking at him. "From when you saved me."

"I didn't get burned saving you."

When Daniel spoke again, his voice shook. "So sorry, Bel. Your face."

Bel put a hand on Daniel's shoulder. Didn't jostle him. Didn't want to spoil the drawing. Just squeezed lightly, hoping to get Daniel's attention. "I ain't burned, Daniel. Look at me a minute."

Daniel turned slowly. Looked at Bel's face.

"See?" Bel said. "No burns."

Daniel shook his head, as though he wasn't quite believing this. "He was right."

"Who was right?"

"He said you wouldn't. Said the fire couldn't hurt you."

"Who said that?"

Daniel worked around the words for a minute. His jaw trembled. "Um, Kenny. K-Kenny Cooper. He said, um . . ."

"Take it easy," Bel said, sliding off the arm of the chair and sharing the seat with Daniel. "Kenny ain't here. You're sleeping."

"You're hurt, though. Aren't you? Even if I can't see?"

Bel took Daniel's hand. Brought it up to his face. "Feel."

Daniel gently stroked Bel's cheek. Started to smile. "Oh, yeah," he said.

"I'm not hurt. No burns."

Daniel's brows drew together. "You saved me though?"

"I got you loose. The night of the fire."

Daniel leaned against Bel, and Bel wound his arms around him.

"We ought to get you some proper art supplies," Bel said. "Maybe take a trip to the store in Goose Creek. How's that sound?"

Daniel didn't answer. He took Bel's hand and guided it to the back of his head.

"Feel that."

Bel smoothed Daniel's hair. "What's that?"

"Feel!" Daniel insisted.

"What am I supposed to be feeling?"

"My brains," Daniel said very seriously. "They were gonna fall out."

"I'm not sure what you're talking about."

"He hit me. And they were gonna fall out."

Bel went cold all over. Stroked Daniel's hair again, trying to keep calm. "You're all right now. Your head's fine. See?"

Daniel gave a shaky laugh. "Not after what he did."

"Kenny?"

Daniel hummed.

"What'd he do to you, Daniel?"

Daniel laughed again. "Hurt me. With his gun. It *hurt*, Bel."

Bel wasn't sure what else to say. He fucking hated it when Daniel got like this. He didn't want to remember how fucked up Daniel was. And yet, Bel's fear and repulsion were overshadowed by how much he cared about him. Deep breath, he reminded himself. *He needs you to be in control.* Bel slid his palm down Daniel's back. "That must've been really scary."

Daniel shook his head.

"No?"

Daniel's eyes were wide and blank, the pupils just tiny dots. "Suck my dick, cunt. I'm gonna shoot down your throat." Bel's stomach twisted. Wasn't that what Daniel had yelled at Clayton that night on Main? "Suck my *dick*, cunt." Daniel kept saying it, his voice getting louder. Hadn't been goading Clayton that time, Bel realized. He'd been remembering.

"All right. That's enough," Bel said, holding him close. "You're all right."

But Daniel wouldn't stop. "Suck my dick, cunt. Suck it. Suck it till I shoot, you fucking faggot *cunt!*"

Bel thought it was Daniel trembling, but he realized Daniel's body was perfectly still, rigid. Bel was the one shaking. "Daniel, that's enough. It ain't happening anymore."

Daniel started to struggle. His elbow caught Bel hard in the ribs. "Let me go. Let me *go!*"

"I can't till you settle down." Bel tried to keep his voice gentle. Tried not to panic. But Daniel was fighting hard. Bel stood them both up and got Daniel so he was pinned by his own arms, his back to Bel's front.

"Let me go!" Daniel screamed. "No! *Please* let go!"

"I need you to listen." Bel's voice was firm but quiet. "Are you listening? You know I'm in charge and that you need to listen, right?"

Daniel stomped on Bel's foot, but Bel ignored the pain. "I need you to take a couple of deep breaths, and I need you to stop yelling. We're gonna get through this. Okay?"

Daniel wasn't listening. He writhed against Bel, gasping and shouting.

"Daniel," Bel said sharply.

"You fucker," Daniel yelled. "Gonna have to finish this one day."

"Wake up. You hear me, Whitlock? Wake up right now!"

"I am awake. I'm *awake*, you fucker!" Daniel turned and tried to bite Bel's shoulder.

Bel attempted to change positions, tried to get Daniel to where he could see his face. Because something in Daniel's voice made him wonder if it was true. If Daniel *was* awake.

"If you're awake, Daniel—if you understand what's going on—I need you to calm down."

"Why should I?" Daniel's voice was high-pitched, shredded, furious. "Why the fuck should I? I'm allowed to get mad, Bel! I'm not asleep; I just fucking—*hate* this!"

Bel manhandled Daniel over to the bed. Tried to keep a hold of Daniel with one arm while he searched for the hospital restraints under the mattress. Pulled them out.

"No," Daniel shouted. "No! Don't leave me!"

"Shh. Shh." Bel wrapped both arms around Daniel again. "I ain't leaving. Gonna help you. You like these, right? They make you feel safe. I'm gonna put them on you." Bel's voice was hoarse, as though he'd been the one screaming.

Daniel stilled for just a second. Then he started thrashing again. "No! I don't want them! I'm tied down, he can get me. He can *get* me!"

"You're asleep, Daniel."

"No!" Tears streamed down Daniel's face.

Bel studied him. He couldn't tell. He couldn't fucking tell if Daniel was awake or asleep, and either way, this was too much.

"He can get me," Daniel repeated, arching against Bel.

"But not if I'm here," Bel said. "And I'll be right here. We can read a little. And nothing'll get you."

Fuck, there was a lump in Bel's throat he could hardly swallow around. Daniel didn't stop fighting, didn't stop yelling, and yet somehow Bel managed to get one of the restraints around his wrist.

Daniel pulled away from him as he fastened it. Backed up until he was at the front door of the cabin. Bel held the other cuff, the strap taut between them, Daniel pulling so hard Bel could barely hold his ground.

"You're gonna hurt yourself," Bel warned.

Daniel banged on the door of the cabin. "It's an emergency," he said. "Let me in."

The panic spilled over, pouring down Bel's whole body. What if Daniel had snapped for good? If he was awake and having these delusions, then nothing Bel did was gonna make a difference, was it? "Daniel..." Bel didn't have the breath to reason with him anymore. He pulled on the strap, reeling Daniel toward him like a fish. He drew the other cuff through the bedrail, and when Daniel got close enough, Bel shoved him onto the bed, no longer worried about being too rough. He just needed to get Daniel contained. Then they could sort this out.

Somewhere in his mind, though, a voice was saying, *Nothing you can do.*

Bel climbed on top of Daniel. Daniel was losing energy, and Bel took advantage of this, strapping the other cuff around Daniel's wrist.

"No..." Daniel's eyes watered. "Please, no. Don't leave, Bel."

Bel held Daniel against the mattress, but used his thumbs to rub gentle circles on Daniel's upper arms. "You know it's me, don't you? That's good. You know it's me, and I want to help you. I love you, and I'm gonna help you."

He kept murmuring to Daniel. It wasn't nonsense, what he was saying. It was true, though Bel didn't have time to worry about how the "I love you" had gotten in there, or what he'd meant by it. Finally the lump in his throat hurt too much, and he had to quit talking.

"Bel?"

"Gonna let you go now," he whispered. "You're tied to the bed. Don't hurt yourself."

He climbed off the bed and stood in the center of the small room.

"No." It wasn't a shout now, just a pathetic whimper. "Don't go." His voice was getting louder again. He pulled against the cuffs. "Don't leave me here."

"I'm not leaving. Just—just stay still a minute." Bel's voice cracked. *Shit.* Wasn't gonna do any good to fall apart in front of Daniel. "I'm gonna help you. Just— I need a minute." *What if it's too big for me? What if this never fucking gets better?*

Daniel was staring at him, dry-eyed, his breathing a little slower. "Bel?" he said again.

Bel nodded.

"I'm sorry."

Bel shrugged. "Nothing you can do." He ought to get back in bed with Daniel. But he couldn't move. His hands were shaking. He tightened them into fists.

"You think that's true?" Daniel whispered. "Nothing I can do?"

"I don't know," Bel said wearily. "You're the one who said there's nothing to be done for it."

"Except you can keep me under control."

No. You can't count on that. Because what if I can't? "Maybe." *Maybe I can't. Maybe I can't do this each time. How many times are there gonna be?*

"You do."

"I try."

Daniel's eyes watered again, but he nodded. "Not forever, though."

Bel sat on the edge of the bed. Picked up Daniel's hand and stroked it.

"Sorry I didn't listen," Daniel said.

Bel shook his head. "Quit. None of this is your fault, okay? You get that I'm not—not mad at you. Right? I just don't know what to do."

"Yeah, Bel." Daniel kept looking at him. That same hope and wariness Bel remembered from their first days together.

"I am *not*—you hear me? I am *not* gonna leave."

Daniel didn't answer.

"Tell me you hear that."

Daniel was silent for a long moment. "You might, though."

"I won't."

"If you have to, it doesn't make you bad. I'd leave me if I could. Walk right out of this body. Shit." Daniel almost smiled. "I've tried. So many times. But I'm always here."

Bel tried to take a steady breath. "Good. Because I'm here too."

"You wanna be with me?"

"Yeah." Whatever that meant. Now or forever or in love or just on Daniel Whitlock's side. He'd rather be here than anywhere else.

He climbed onto the bed and settled beside Daniel.

CHAPTER SEVENTEEN

Bel took three days off work. Knew Uncle Joe would have something to say about it, but right now, Bel didn't care. He wasn't going to leave Daniel.

Except once Daniel nodded off each night, Bel couldn't sleep with all the thoughts jumbled in his head. Could he really stay with somebody who might need this kind of supervision long-term? What if Daniel needed more than Bel could provide? If Bel did have to leave this—this relationship for any reason, what would become of Daniel?

Not gonna leave him.

Some things you just know.

If he knew so much about his feelings for Daniel, then why was he sitting awake asking himself the same questions over and over?

Said "I love you." The fuck was that about?

How the hell could I know I want to stay with him? There's a whole fuckload of future that ain't happened yet.

But just as Daniel had occasional access, when he slept, to some brilliant, violent, and primal part of himself, Bel had a part of himself too that was reckless, passionate, and stupider yet somehow better than his conscious self. And that part of him knew it loved Daniel. Knew even if that love wasn't the kind of shit Shakespeare wrote about, it was real and it ran deep. Chained the two of them together in some weird underworld.

After the third day stuck in Daniel's cabin, Bel said, "Get dressed. We're going out."

Daniel lay sprawled in the chair. "Didn't go so hot last time, Bel," he said to the ceiling.

"Yeah, well, this is another try."

Daniel shifted. "Don't want another try. Let's fuck."

"I'm all fucked out. Get up."

Daniel continued to gaze at the ceiling. "I made you miss work."

"You didn't 'make me' do anything."

"You didn't have to stay."

"Said I would, didn't I?"

"Yeah." Daniel's voice was soft. "You did." He knocked his head lightly against the back of the chair.

"Can you quit moping and get dressed?"

Daniel reached between his legs and stroked his cock. "You like me undressed pretty well."

"Yeah, I do. But a guy needs a change of scenery now and then."

Daniel didn't move.

"Thought I was in charge?" Bel said.

Daniel got up without a word. Went to the bathroom, shut the door, and stayed in there a long time. Bel felt frustrated. Then cold with panic. "What're you doin' in there?"

"Not carving my fucking eyeball out or anything, don't worry," Daniel called back.

"Daniel. Come on. I got an idea for a way we could actually have a nice time, if you'd quit acting like this."

"We could have a nice time here."

Bel sighed and leaned against the wall. "Come out here, or I'll—"

The door swung open. Daniel gazed at him coolly. He was wearing jeans and a T-shirt. "You'll what?"

Bel grabbed him before he could duck back in the bathroom and kissed him. Daniel started kissing back immediately. Got in Bel's car without any further protest, and they headed out to the interstate.

"Where we going?" Daniel asked.

"Wait and see."

"You mad at me?"

"Nope. You mad at me?"

"I was," Daniel said. "A little."

"Mmm."

"I didn't want to go."

"I know."

Silence. "But I ain't mad now."

"Good. Neither of us is mad. That's a start."

"But I reckon we're not real happy."

Bel shot him a glance. "Speak for yourself. I got you in my car. I'm feeling pretty good."

He didn't miss the smile Daniel tried to hide by looking out the window. "Shouldn't I be tied up in your backseat?"

"Don't tempt me."

Something was a little off about Daniel's demeanor. Bel supposed he could put it down to the episode the other night, or too long spent in the cabin. Or maybe the fact that Bel had said he loved Daniel. Neither of them had brought that up, which Bel thought was for the best.

They drove to Goose Creek. Bel pulled into a plaza with a couple of chain clothing stores, a Chinese buffet, and a craft outlet.

"What're you doing?" Daniel asked.

"Goin' shopping."

"For what?"

"Art supplies."

"What the hell? For who?"

"You, dummy."

Daniel stared at him. "I don't . . ."

"Don't what?"

"Don't need any supplies."

"You draw like a fucking genius. Unfortunately, it's on the backs of my reports and training manuals. So let's get you some paper. And some real pencils or pens or whatever you want to use."

"I don't even *know* what I use."

Bel was already out of the car. "You use pencils mostly."

Daniel didn't budge. "I can't afford it."

"This is my treat." Bel tried not to let Daniel's reluctance unnerve him. He wanted to do this, wanted to give something to Daniel—damn it, why couldn't Daniel just deal with that? "You like me well enough to let me give you a gift, don't you?"

Daniel gave a half smile. "I think you feel sorry for me."

"Are you getting out of the car or not?"

Daniel shook his head. But his smile broadened a little. "Guess I got to. I put you in charge."

"Smart move."

"We'll see."

As soon as Daniel was out of the car, Bel came around and swatted his ass. Didn't care who the fuck saw. Then he put his arm around Daniel and they walked in together.

It felt good to listen to Bel. To know that he meant something to one person in this world. To know that Bel wanted to get him a *gift*. Which, it was stupid, but it had been so long since anyone had wanted to give him anything—besides maybe a pig's head or a noose—that Daniel's pleasure at the prospect had overridden his pride. The pride he knew he ought to have, the pride that should have made him say he'd buy his own damn supplies—if he needed supplies, which he didn't.

Daniel wandered through the aisles of the craft store, trying to pretend he had any idea what to look for.

Bel stayed. Stayed with me for two days.

Bel seemed just as uncomfortable as Daniel. He picked up a black velvet poster of two kittens playing with a ball of yarn. It came with a set of markers so you could color in the kittens and the yarn. "People really do this shit?" Bel asked.

Daniel laughed.

I freaked out. I was awful. And Bel stayed.

Bel was examining bottles of glitter paint. Daniel glanced around. They were alone in the aisle. He placed a hand between Bel's shoulder blades. Bel straightened and turned to him. Daniel loved Bel's face—a little round, a little boyish. The skin was darker and rougher than Daniel's. There were just the faintest traces of acne scars under Bel's right cheekbone. So faint, Daniel could only see them in bright light like this. Bel's chin was stubbled, and he had his usual serious expression. Sometimes that expression held a sense of genuine authority, and sometimes, like now, it looked like the face of a kid playing a cop. Daniel liked those moments. As safe as authoritative Bel made him feel, slightly lost Bel made him feel safer. Because then Daniel knew he wasn't alone, wasn't a freak. Wasn't the only one who just couldn't fucking figure things out sometimes.

"What're you smiling about?" Bel asked softly.

Daniel leaned forward and gave him a quick kiss.

Bel smiled. "Shit. You better hurry and pick out your stuff. I need to get you home."

"You said you wanted a change of scenery."

"Yeah, and now I want to fuck you."

"Well, too damn bad. You had your chance."

They made their way to the aisle of drawing supplies. "Honest, Bel, I don't know what to look for. I don't know what I need when I'm asleep."

"How about these?" Bel picked up a package of pencils in different shades of gray and black.

Daniel took the package from him and looked at the price tag. "Maybe if I was actually gonna *do* somethin' with these drawings, it would make sense to pay that much for pencils."

He started to put them back, but Bel caught his wrist. Squeezed gently. It wasn't a threatening gesture, more of a reassurance, a reminder. "Daniel." Bel's voice was low. "I don't want to hear another word about price. You understand me?"

Daniel gripped the pencils. Felt them shift in the package. "Yeah, Bel."

Bel slid his thumb from Daniel's wrist to the heel of his hand, running it lightly over the still-tender spot where Daniel had dug the nail file in. Daniel swallowed. "You get what you want. I'm gonna get one of those velvet kitten posters for myself."

Daniel snorted. "Maybe that's what I need too."

Bel raised Daniel's hand to his lips and kissed it before letting go. "We'll get a couple. Have craft time some night when you're sleepwalking."

Daniel shook his head. "You're so weird. You're the first person since my college roommate to act like—like what I do's just a funny thing about me. No big deal."

He tensed. He hadn't meant to imply Bel thought his sleepwalking was no big deal. Obviously Bel thought it was sick and wrong that Daniel had killed Kenny Cooper. Still, Daniel's sleepwalking encompassed a hell of a lot more than that one night he'd burned Kenny's house. And hadn't Bel said he hated Cooper, was glad he was dead?

"It ain't a big deal except when it hurts you," Bel said simply.

Daniel couldn't look at him. He put back the pencils and picked up a smaller pack—seemed better to start with less variety, since he wasn't even sure he'd know how to use the things. Didn't hurt that this pack was cheaper, either.

Bel was trying to be nice. And Daniel appreciated it. But it *was* a big deal. Not just when it hurt Daniel. When it hurt other people. And ever since the episode two nights ago, Daniel hadn't been able to stop thinking about Clayton. Clayton hadn't forgotten how Kenny Cooper died. Hadn't consigned him to quiet memory. It was hard to lay a man to rest when you knew his last minutes had been spent in terror: fighting and choking, desperate and afraid. And Clayton wanted to make Daniel pay for that.

Daniel understood. He would carry his guilt over Kenny Cooper's death for as long as he lived, but he was through being a martyr to it. So fuck Clayton.

He picked out a sketch pad—well, Bel picked it out. It had a sketch of two spheres on the front, intricately shaded to make them look three dimensional, and a pyramid behind them. "It's like a cock and balls," Bel said.

"You got a dirty brain."

"Not me. Whoever designed this. It couldn't've been an accident."

They got some charcoal too, and an eraser, and then Daniel said he was done. Bel took them back through the aisle with the black velvet posters and got a kitten one and a unicorn one. "You're not serious," Daniel protested.

"Deadly," Bel said. He grabbed a small package as well, but Daniel couldn't see what it was. Bel said it was just extra markers for the posters, but he had a smirk that Daniel didn't trust.

They drove back to Logan. Daniel was silent while they waited at a fast-food drive-thru for a lunch he wasn't hungry for. He took out his phone. It was two twenty, but he figured that was okay. *Hi, Bel, it's Daniel*, he texted. *Thanks for the gift.*

He sent it, and a second later, Bel's phone buzzed. Bel dug it out of his pocket and looked at the screen. Smiled. He reached over and placed a hand on Daniel's cheek. Daniel turned and kissed his palm.

At Bel's place, they barely made it through the door before Daniel turned and started kissing Bel. Bel dropped the bag of art supplies and pulled Daniel hard against him, cupping his ass. "I'll get cleaned up," Daniel whispered.

"Later," Bel said. "I want you to strip and kneel for me."

Daniel flushed, his groin tightening, a smile spreading across his face. "Yeah, Bel." He stripped quickly and knelt at Bel's feet. He wanted to look up at Bel, but he made himself bow his head.

"That's nice." Bel placed a hand on Daniel's shoulder. Ran his nails in light circles between Daniel's shoulder blades. Daniel's whole body prickled with pleasure. "You wait here, okay?"

Bel left the room. Daniel heard him in the kitchen, running the sink. When Bel came back, Daniel snuck a glance at him. Watched him go over to the bag of art supplies, but didn't get to see what he took out, because Bel looked up, and Daniel bowed his head again.

Bel was opening something. A minute later, he was right behind Daniel, kneeling on the carpet. Daniel heard a small *click*, and then something pressed against his back. "Pay attention," Bel said softly. "See if you can figure out what I write. Then do it."

Daniel barely had time to process that before Bel was drawing a wide curve on his shoulder with a—a marker? Shit. Daniel tried to pay attention. An unbroken serpentine. An *S*. The next letter was a T. That was easy. The marker didn't tickle, just felt nice. Daniel almost lost track of the letters as he relaxed into the sensation. Bel must have run out of room—the last two letters were squished next to Daniel's armpit. STAND UP. Daniel started to do what he thought Bel had told him to, but Bel kept him in place with a hand on his shoulder. "And . . ." Bel whispered. He wrote what Daniel was pretty sure was KISS ME across the middle of Daniel's back.

Daniel waited a second to be sure Bel was finished. Then he stood and turned, pressing his lips to Bel's. Bel kissed him slowly, deeply, and Daniel's cock gradually hardened. He wound his arms around Bel's neck.

Bel slid a hand down his back and patted his hip. "Go lie on the couch. On your back."

Daniel did. Bel gathered the package of markers from the floor and climbed onto the couch, straddling Daniel's legs. He looked almost giddy. "Body markers." He showed Daniel the package, which had two kids with their faces painted the colors of some sports team. "Maybe you ain't the only one who can create a masterpiece. Put your hands above your head. Wrists crossed, like you're cuffed."

Daniel obeyed. He was intrigued by this new game, by Bel's excitement over the markers—an excitement that was contagious.

Bel drew for a while on Daniel's stomach. Daniel tried to look down to see what he was doing, but he finally gave up and stared at the ceiling, enjoying the way the markers tickled, the way Bel's free hand rested on his hip. "Hold still," Bel kept telling Daniel, because Daniel's stomach muscles kept fluttering and tightening.

"Feels funny."

"You're messin' up my art."

Finally Bel sat back on his heels. "Okay. This is a start."

Daniel lifted his head and glanced down at his stomach. He saw two green stick figures. And a few blue squiggly lines. That was about all he could make out. "What is it?"

"That's me tryin' to get you to swim in the river." He pointed to a red square on one stick figure's arm. "That's your damn chemistry book."

Daniel laughed. "I can't believe you really remember that."

"Don't you?"

Daniel met his gaze. "Yeah. But I didn't think you would. You had plenty of friends, Harnee's kid."

Bel leaned forward and nipped his jaw. "Well now the memory is preserved in ink."

Bel picked up the green marker again.

Twenty minutes later, Daniel's body was covered in ink. There were pictures of blocky skyscrapers on Daniel's chest that were supposed to represent Aiken, where Daniel had gone to college— never mind that Aiken didn't have skyscrapers. A picture of a police car. An angry-looking rabbit just above his left pec. Bel's drawings were childish, but Daniel loved them.

Bel moved on to words. He wrote Daniel's name down one side of his ribcage. Then KICKS ASS down the other. The word HOT appeared just below his navel, with an arrow pointing down to his cock. BEAUTIFUL on one thigh, the letters warped a little by

Daniel's leg hair. SMART on the other. Daniel had to work not to let it mean anything. *Just a game. He's just playing.*

"What the hell does that say?" Daniel looked at the word Bel had tried to write on his arm.

"S'posed to be 'Michelangelo,' but I dunno how the fuck to spell it."

Daniel tried to laugh. "I ain't Michelangelo."

"Who said you were? Maybe I just like his name."

"You done yet?"

Bel grinned. "If you want me to be. I was gonna draw something here, though." He rolled Daniel's balls in his hand, then slid his palm up Daniel's cock. Daniel groaned. Bel kissed his forehead and rubbed his cock until he came quietly, gasping and whispering Bel's name. Bel wiped his hand on his shirt, then picked up the blue marker. "Hold still."

He tipped Daniel's head back and wrote something across Daniel's throat. He had to get Daniel to turn so he could finish it on the side of Daniel's neck. "What's it say?" Daniel asked.

"C'mere."

Bel helped him up. Daniel winced at the stickiness coating his abdomen, blurring the marker drawings. Bel led him to the bathroom, to the mirror. Daniel studied his body, covered in Bel's pictures and words. Tried to read the words on his throat. "What's it say?" Bel asked him.

"I don't know. Your writing's shit, and it's backward."

Bel looked a little hurt, so Daniel tried harder. His throat got tighter as he read. His face burned, but the heat seemed to go deeper than his skin, into his skull, and gathered behind his eyes. It was a game, just a stupid game they were playing, and it didn't matter what Bel had written. Bel was just trying to cheer Daniel up, right?

But he kept staring, turning his head, reading the words over and over. Memorizing the scrawl of Bel's writing.

In a dark band around his neck, it said, BRAVEST MOTHERFUCKER IN LOGAN.

CHAPTER
EIGHTEEN

In the morning, after Bel left for work, Daniel washed the sweat-smudged words and pictures off his body, sorry to see them vanish from his skin under the spluttering shower. Bel's sheets were covered in colorful smears. Daniel bundled them into the washing machine. He felt better than he had in days. He was afraid of how much he was relying on Bel, but he wasn't going to think of that this morning. He was stronger because of Bel, but he could be strong on his own too. He'd promised Casey he'd try.

After hanging the sheets out to dry, he walked down to Main Street. And reminded himself he had every right to be there, whatever Clayton and R.J. and Brock thought. Whatever his parents thought. Whatever the whole damn town thought. And it didn't hurt to know that Bel was patrolling somewhere nearby. He was the bravest motherfucker in Logan, wasn't he? Yeah. Yeah he was.

Right until he stopped at the gas station for some gum he was.

He needed to piss, so he went into the bathroom. Just two stalls, both of them covered in graffiti, but more or less clean. He was just finishing up when he heard footsteps and laughter.

"Hey, Whitlock?"

Daniel froze.

"I seen you come in here, Whitlock," Clayton called. He banged on the door of the stall, rattling it. "You looking for a— What's it called?"

"Glory hole," R.J. said. "You on your knees, Whitlock? You come in here to suck off truckers?"

Someone whooped with laughter. Brock, Daniel guessed.

He clenched his shaking hands into fists.

Where the fuck did these guys get off, doing this to him? Didn't they have anything better to do? 'Course not. Nothing so pressing on their schedules—drinking beer, driving around in Clay's truck, shooting squirrels, and talking about pussy—that they couldn't rearrange if they saw Daniel walking down the street. He hated them. They were fucking *worthless*.

"Come on, Whitlock, don't be shy," Clayton called. He rattled the door again. "Answer me."

"Maybe he's sleeping!" R.J. said.

Daniel leaned against the wall of the stall and closed his eyes tightly. God, if only that were true. Because then Bel would walk through fire to save him, and he would look down at his burned hands and watch in amazement as they healed. Except he knew this was no dream, because in his dreams, he never questioned if he was sleeping or not.

And there was no fire.

"I told you not to come into town again, didn't I, faggot?" Clayton called.

I got as much right to be here as you. But Daniel wasn't dumb enough to say it. He kept his eyes closed and slid a hand into the pocket of his jeans for his phone. He wanted to be strong. He wanted to prove to himself, and to Bel and Casey, that he could be. For the future. For the times when Bel wouldn't be there. For the time when Bel looked at him the same way Marcus had, and told him they were done.

He wanted Bel so much. Wanted to keep him in his life. But how could he, when *this* was his life?

"Say something, Whitlock!" Clayton beat on the door so hard that Daniel was afraid the hinges would break.

His eyes flashed open. He struggled for breath. He willed his voice to stay steady. "Get the hell outta here, Clayton."

And shit, he realized there was a hole in the wall between the stalls after all. Not a glory hole—too high for that—but probably where someone had put their fist through the wall. And R.J. had found it. "I see you, Whitlock!"

Daniel stared back at him, his heart racing, his guts clenched.

"He's got his phone out, Clay," R.J. said.

"You gonna call Belman?" Clayton taunted. "You can't face us like a man, Whitlock? You gotta get your pig boyfriend in on this?"

Brock laughed, a high-pitched nasal sound. "Pussy!"

Clayton smashed against the door again, and Daniel jumped. R.J. roared with laughter. "You got him scared now, Clay!"

Daniel's fingers shook as he lifted his phone. "I'm gonna call the cops unless you leave right now."

"Pussy!" Brock called again.

"I'll be seeing you, Whitlock!" Clayton punched the door one last time.

R.J.'s eye vanished from the hole in the wall, and Daniel heard the three of them laughing as they headed outside again.

Daniel flipped the toilet seat down and sat. His stomach churned and he swallowed bile.

Jesus.

He squeezed his eyes shut.

Breathe. In and out. In and out.

He became aware he was humming. He was fucking *humming* every time he exhaled, and if he lost control of the sound it'd be a whimper or a sob or a panicked scream in the space of a heartbeat.

He put his head in his shaking hands and breathed until his heart rate slowed again. Until the noise subsided.

What if they were waiting for him outside? What if they followed him back to the cabin? What if they got him alone, this time without any door to protect him?

No.

No more.

Fuck this.

Daniel sucked in a deep breath and held it. Rode out the burn in his lungs. Rode out his panic and his fear.

He was done being scared. They had no right, no *fucking right*, to keep hounding him this way.

"It's all right to be scared."

Maybe so, but he was goddamn sick of it.

The rage swelled again in the pit of his stomach. If they weren't going to stop, he'd have to find a way to fucking *make* them stop.

Dangerous thoughts? Maybe, but it was nothing his subconscious didn't already know. He wanted those animals gone. This was his *life*, and he wasn't going to stand for this.

He got up and walked outside. Squinted in the sunlight. No one there.

But at some point, there would be. And he'd have to be ready for them.

Fucking animals.

He'd do what Clayton said. Next time he'd face them like a man.

"Goddamn, Diggler, are you serious?" Bel sighed into the radio. There was no answer for a while, so he clicked it a few times. "Diggler?"

"Sorry, Bel." Diggler sounded a little breathless, like he'd been laughing. He wasn't sorry at all. "You have fun now."

Bel shook his head and turned his cruiser around. Headed for the intersection of Gable and Hatcher. There was a silver sedan parked up there, the door open, and two women standing in the street.

Bel pulled in behind the sedan and got out. Put his hat on, adjusted his utility belt, and walked over to them.

Sometimes walking into a job felt like walking onto a stage, something Bel hadn't done since he was the angel in the school's Christmas play in fifth grade. *Hark*, he'd been supposed to say, but the kid operating the cable had swung him out too fast and too wide, and he'd ended up screaming for his mama instead. Took longer than the Christmas vacation to live that one down. But sometimes there was a hushed pause when Bel arrived someplace, when people stopped and gave him room to make his entrance. When they leaned toward him in anticipation, waiting for him to make his opening speech. Which was never as momentous as they expected.

"Ladies," Bel said, touching the brim of his hat. "What's happened here?"

Old Mrs. Pritchard began to wail, but got the story out amid her sobs. She pointed at the front of the car, and Bel stepped around to get a look. Saw Poppet the fluffy dog lying dead on the road. He'd been torn up pretty bad. Bel grimaced.

Well, that's what you got for not keeping your damn dog inside. How many times had Bel been called out to lecture Mrs. Pritchard when Poppet had gotten into the neighbor's flowerbeds? Bel glanced across the street to Franny Harman's place and saw the curtains twitch. He bet Franny was loving this.

"I'm real sorry, Mrs. Pritchard," he said, walking back to her.

She sobbed into her liver-spotted hands.

"He . . ." The second woman drew a deep breath. "He just came out of nowhere. I wasn't speeding."

Bel looked at her properly for the first time. Shit. It was Jean Whitlock. Daniel's mom. "Accidents happen."

She had Daniel's eyes.

"Are you okay to drive?" Bel asked her. She looked a little shaky. Bel tried to concentrate on that, rather than anything else.

"I—" Her gaze slid to his name badge and her voice faltered. "I'm fine."

Bel ushered her away from Mrs. Pritchard. "Okay. Don't worry too much about it. The dog was always getting loose. Could have happened to anyone."

Jean nodded, her gaze flicking up to his face. "You're . . ."

Fucking your son?

"Mary's youngest," she said at last.

"Yes, ma'am," Bel said, wondering which one of them was gonna break first. The whole town knew by now that Bel was seeing Daniel. Whole town had an opinion about it as well. Bel wondered what Jean Whitlock's was.

When Bel was seventeen he'd taken Amy Peterson to prom. She was the preacher's daughter, which made the whole thing even more excruciating. Her daddy had sat Bel down in the living room while Amy and her mom fussed with her dress upstairs, and given him a whole lecture on respect and gentlemanly behavior and what he called urges. Only urge Bel had felt was to get the fuck out of there. But he'd nodded and said "yes, sir" a lot, and eventually her parents had let Amy leave the house with him. Hours later, parked down by the river, Amy had blamed her daddy for Bel's unwillingness to dive in under the layers of her pretty tulle dress, but she hadn't known that the whole night Bel had been sneaking looks at guys' asses instead.

Now Bel found himself wanting to hear a parental lecture from Jean, just so he could assure her that he was a decent guy and not looking to take advantage. Mostly though, he wanted to tell her that he was treating Daniel well, that they were doing okay, and that last night he'd written BRAVEST MOTHERFUCKER IN LOGAN around Daniel's throat and that together they were proving those words true.

Jean drew a deep breath and didn't say anything. She stared at a point over Bel's shoulder.

"Okay," Bel said, regret creeping in. "You take care, Mrs. Whitlock."

She nodded at him and murmured her thanks.

Didn't climb into her car though.

"Listen," Bel said, lowering his voice. "About Daniel."

She looked at him sharply.

"He's doing okay, is all." The words felt inadequate. They didn't even scrape the surface of what Bel felt for Daniel.

Jean searched his face. "We tried," she said at last. "We didn't *know*. Not how bad it was. Not until . . ."

Until Kenny Cooper.

Bel nodded. He swallowed, and it hurt.

"Some kids are just trouble," Jean said. Her mouth compressed into a thin line. "Just trouble."

She got into her car and drove off.

Bel stood there, feeling a chill despite the heat of the day. How many times had he heard that before? How many times had he agreed with it? But Daniel wasn't some wayward kid he was dropping back at his mom's trailer after he'd been arrested again for shoplifting. He wasn't some kid who'd punched a teacher or crashed his daddy's car when he was drunk.

Daniel had been the kid who'd roamed the streets at odd hours, and who'd stared into Bobby Grant's bedroom window. Who'd tried to deny it when he was caught. He was the kid your parents had warned you to steer clear off. The weird kid. The freak.

Just trouble, unless you looked closer.

He wondered if it would have made a difference if Daniel's parents had done that.

Bel fetched an old towel from the trunk of his cruiser. He gathered up Poppet and wrapped him in it, trying his hardest not to actually look at the broken little body. Then, even though he'd hated that damned dog, he carried him back to Mrs. Pritchard's yard, took a spade from the garage, and dug a hole to bury him.

"You good, Bel?" Diggler asked him as he was shoveling the dirt back in.

Bel leaned on the shovel and reached for his radio. "Yeah. Be another few minutes here, then I gotta go home and change."

"Ewww. Copy that."

Bel put the spade back in the garage, let Mrs. Pritchard fix him a cold drink, and then drove home to shower and change.

There was a note sticking out of his mailbox. Bel tugged it free and unfolded it.

FAGGOT PIG.

He stared at the words for a while, trying to feel offended. Oddly though, he wasn't. He'd expected it, and Uncle Joe had warned him it was coming as well.

Bel tucked the note into his pocket and headed inside.

He just hoped that when he was done burning all his bridges, he was left standing on the same side as Daniel.

"Saw your mama today," Bel said as he did the dishes in Daniel's tiny kitchen.

"Oh yeah?" Daniel stared out the open front door into the darkness. He was nervous. He'd been nervous all day, waiting for Bel to get back from work, and, when he had, somehow it wasn't enough. There wasn't enough of Bel to fix what was wrong with Daniel, to patch over all the holes gnawed in his insides.

"Yeah. She ran over Mrs. Pritchard's dog."

That caught his attention. Daniel turned his head and stared at Bel. "She did what?"

Bel made a face. "Dog was real messed up. I buried it."

"Oh." He stared out the door again, into the trees, into the night. The bed dipped as Bel sat beside him. His warm hand slid up Daniel's thigh. Daniel didn't look at him. "I'm real tired tonight, Bel."

"You look it." Bel squeezed his thigh. "Early night, I guess."

Daniel glanced at him. "That a problem?"

"No." Bel showed him a crooked smile. "No problem."

Tired like this, unsettled like this, sleep should have been an escape. Never was though. Daniel watched as Bel stood up and crossed to the door. Closed and locked it, as though there was any lock in the world that could stop Daniel when he was fixed on getting out.

"You okay?" Bel asked him, his face creased with worry.

"Yeah." Daniel lay down on his side and listened to Bel in the bathroom. Brushing his teeth. Taking a piss. Thought of his mother, running over a dog. Thought of what she'd said to him at Casey's birthday dinner.

"Don't make this all about you."

It hurt that she'd said that. He'd wanted to tell her that it hurt, but that would only prove her point. He wondered if she was upset about the dog. She would be, he figured. She'd loved animals. Probably still did. That was the sort of thing that didn't change, did it? He'd thought the same of her love for him, once.

His eyes closed, and the fire came.

His mom was there, standing behind it. A curtain of fire. It shimmered. So pretty, but Daniel couldn't cross through it. Couldn't reach out and touch her.

"Mom?"

"It's okay." Bel's voice. Bel's arms around him.

"I gotta get through the fire, Bel," Daniel said. He turned, but couldn't see Bel. Could still feel him though. Solid. Warm.

"You don't gotta do that," Bel told him. "You just stay here, with me. Okay?"

No. Daniel couldn't do that. Had to get through the fire alone. Without Bel. Had to show Bel he could.

"Where are you?" The cabin came back into focus. It was on fire. His mom was gone. "Bel, where are you?" Panic rose up in him, twisting in his guts and clawing in his throat like it was a living thing inside him. Devouring him. But he cut it away. *Gotta turn it into something else.*

Anger.

Daniel watched as the fire grew. So bright. So hot. The air cracked. God. He'd burn. Any second now and it would touch his skin and he'd burn. But he wasn't afraid of that anymore. He hoped he'd burn—if he burned, if he made it through, he'd be much stronger than those animals. He'd destroy them.

He stared as a figure loomed out of the flames.

"Kenny."

"Suck my dick, faggot," Kenny said.

"Your face," Daniel said. He reached out to touch it. The charred flesh crumbled away like dust. There wasn't a grinning skull underneath though. There was a boy's face, with freckles. It scowled at Daniel.

"We gonna work on this geography project or what?"

The fire receded, and Daniel was in his bedroom. In his parents' house. There was a movie poster of *Jurassic Park* on the wall.

"Hey," Kenny said in a voice that hadn't broken yet. *"We gonna work on this geography project or what? You can draw the maps. You're good at drawing."*

Daniel sat cross-legged on the floor with his book in his lap. "I'm real sorry."

Kenny scrunched up his face. *"What for?"*

Daniel looked around. Confusion washed through him. He picked up his colored pencils. "I don't know. For the . . . for the fire?"

Kenny snorted.

"Will you tell them to leave me alone?" Daniel asked.

"Who?"

Clayton and Brock and R.J. The kids from his class. Daniel stared at the baseball cap hanging from his bedpost and couldn't remember why he wanted them to leave him alone. Last week, Daniel hit a home run at Little League, and Clayton whooped and gave him a high five.

They were okay.

They were his friends, weren't they?

Unease crept up on him, but Daniel pushed it away.

It was okay, here. He'd watch Kenny, and he'd learn how you made an animal scared of you.

He watched as Kenny picked through his colored pencils, looking for blue for the Atlantic Ocean. Daniel dropped his green pencil. It rolled over the carpet and onto the grimy tiles of the gas station bathroom. He picked it up and stared through the hole in the wall. The hole grew bigger. It shimmered somehow, seemed to fold in on itself, and Clayton stepped through.

"Bel!" Daniel yelled into his phone. "Bel!"

"I'm here. I got you."

"Don't fucking *need* you! This is my fight."

"Then why'd you call?"

A flickering light at the bottom corner of the bathroom stall caught Daniel's attention and held it. It bloomed into fire and swallowed the stall. Daniel gasped as it caught Clayton, and he dissolved silently into ashes. Then Bel stepped through the flames.

"Hey, Bel," Daniel smiled.

"Hey. You awake?"

"Yeah." Daniel watched the flames wash over the walls.

Bel kissed him on the forehead. "No, you ain't."

Daniel twisted his head away. "Where's Kenny?" Then, "Where's my pencil?"

The world shifted, and Daniel found himself sitting on the cabin floor, a pencil in his hand and his drawing pad open in front of him. He leaned back against Bel, and felt Bel's arms come around his waist. Daniel drew his knees up. He rested the drawing pad on them.

"I'm good at drawing."

"Yeah." Bel's breath was warm against his neck. Warmer than fire. "You are."

Daniel relaxed as the flames died.

He began to draw.

Bel stared at the picture on the floor.

Clayton McAllister. Daniel had drawn Clayton McAllister lying in a field with a shadow spreading all around him. And a figure—*Daniel*—was standing over him, his dripping fists clenched. Blood? And Jesus, the look on Daniel's face. His mouth was stretched into a snarl, his eyes narrowed to slits. It made Bel sick just looking at it.

What the hell was this? Wish fulfillment?

Bel ran his finger along the side of the page and wondered if this was the sort of thing that John Frommer should know about. Maybe he already did. Whatever Daniel's subconscious spewed out, it wasn't . . . it wasn't *evidence*. Bad enough that the rest of Logan judged Daniel by his actions when he slept; Bel didn't need to start doing it again.

The picture didn't *mean* anything.

Bel looked up at Daniel. He was curled on the bed, murmuring something in his sleep. Something that made him smile. Bel didn't like to think that he was holding so much rage inside him, so much potential for violence. But Kenny Cooper was proof of that.

It wasn't fair that it hurt to look at Daniel. It wasn't fair that at the start of this thing with him, in the part where Bel should have been the happiest, the most secure, it still fucking hurt. Bel knew shit about relationships, but wasn't there supposed to be a honeymoon period? Wasn't there supposed to be a time when you were blind to the other guy's faults?

Or maybe that was all bullshit.

He knew who Daniel was, knew what he'd done. And it didn't matter, because Daniel was more than his actions, more than his dreams, and more than this fucking picture.

Much more.

Bel tore the page out of the pad and crumpled it in his fist. Shoved it in his backpack so he could dispose of it in the morning without Daniel seeing it.

Then he climbed back into bed with Daniel and held him until dawn.

CHAPTER NINETEEN

Daniel started seeing John twice a week instead of once.

Ms. Davenport had dug up some info on cases where sleepwalkers were treated psychologically by identifying the triggers for their sleepwalking episodes, and Bel couldn't seem to get that stupid idea out of his head, so Daniel went along with it.

He still didn't know who the fuck was paying for all this, but Bel said Ms. Davenport had worked it out with the state and that Daniel shouldn't worry about it.

The first time John had said, *"Tell me about your parents,"* Daniel had laughed.

"You sound like the therapists in movies."

John had made it into a regular joke now. About halfway through each session, he would lean back, cross his legs, lace his hands around his knee, and say, very seriously, *"Daniel. Tell me about your parents."*

Therapy wasn't what Daniel had expected it to be, mostly because John was so normal. He *didn't* sound like the therapists from movies, most of the time. He laughed and made jokes and came in pissed off once in a while because he'd been having car trouble. That usually led to a discussion with Daniel about what car John should get when he finally bought a new one. Daniel didn't know a ton about cars, and his knowledge mostly centered on the chemistry of hybrid vehicles, but he still liked these conversations. He often found that even when he came to John's office tense and determined not to share anything, those first five minutes spent talking to John about stupid stuff usually relaxed him.

But now they talked about Daniel's parents every time. It scared Daniel because he never knew what he was going to spill. Sometimes he just told random anecdotes from his childhood. He half hoped John would get bored and end the conversation early. But sometimes, especially after they'd been talking awhile, Daniel found himself revealing things it hurt to talk about. He never had one of those sobbing breakdowns you saw in movies. But sometimes he got pissed off, or he reached a point where he knew if he kept talking, he'd lose it, so he shut up. He hadn't totally shed his fear he was going to say something that would convince John he really was crazy.

John didn't pry, didn't push. Just kept reminding Daniel that most adult neuroses were rooted in things that had happened during childhood. That it was important to work on finding triggers for Daniel's sleepwalking episodes.

So now John knew about Daniel painting the living room when he was a kid. About his dad pretending to punish him with his belt for Daniel's mom's sake, but really taking him to the garden to let him work until he was exhausted. John knew about the devil. Knew about a lot of the fights Daniel had had with Casey, who had been the first person to call him a freak. Knew about the times Casey had been sweet to him, too—assuring him he'd get better. Singing him a lullaby. Once she'd pretended to be a therapist and had tried to hypnotize Daniel, dangling a necklace over him while he lay on the floor, telling him he was getting very sleepy. Another time she'd tried to perform an exorcism.

Telling stuff from his childhood got to Daniel sometimes, but mostly it was easy. He felt a disconnect from that life, from the person he had been before Kenny, and he could almost imagine he was telling someone else's story. But trying to talk about his relationship with his family now was awful. Usually pissed Daniel off or shut him down. One time John had suggested Daniel talk to him as though John was his mother. Daniel had refused.

"That's totally a cliché." Daniel had tried to laugh. *"You're better than that, John."*

They also talked about sex, much to Daniel's chagrin. About how Daniel had started to fuck guys while he was asleep after Marcus had broken up with him. About the wet dreams he used to have about Kenny Cooper. Apparently John had no fucking sense of privacy whatsoever. And apparently all those degrees didn't make John particularly smart, because he once asked Daniel how he felt about Kenny Cooper now.

"Well, he tried to kill me, and then I murdered him, so . . . yeah, the wet dreams are pretty much over."

They didn't talk about pain or about how Bel was in charge of Daniel in the bedroom. Daniel didn't care how confi-fucking-dential this was; he wasn't going to talk about that.

Therapy was confusing and weird and sometimes left Daniel feeling worse, not better, but he couldn't deny he saw progress. John had taught him some grounding techniques to use when he felt panicked or empty. Breathing exercises, focusing on one particular object, saying aloud whatever was on his mind. All stuff Daniel had made fun of at first. But it did kind of help. He made lists now, too. He'd said hell no to journaling when John had suggested it, so John said maybe lists were a better option. He could list anything—how he was feeling, what he was going to do that day, things he was worried or happy or pissed about, stuff he saw written in the restroom stalls at the library. Daniel had tried it without much enthusiasm and found it sort of helped.

But what helped Daniel even more than lists, more than sessions with John, was Bel. Bel's belief in Daniel, his patience, his authority—fuck, Daniel would have done anything to make him proud. It would have been pathetic, except for the moments where it seemed like Bel felt the same about him. Bel wanted to please Daniel, wanted to give him what he needed, and occasionally Bel became the kid he still was—foolish and eager in his efforts to impress Daniel.

Since the night in the orchard, Bel had been less cautious about hitting Daniel. They'd waded through the ivy outside the cabin to hunt for the aluminum paddle Daniel had thrown out there weeks ago. They'd finally found it, and Bel had made Daniel pick it up, carry it back to the cabin, kneel down, and hand it to him. He'd used it lightly, and Daniel had been turned on at first, begging him to use it harder. But Bel had stopped as soon as Daniel went soft from the pain, and they'd fucked instead.

Daniel could tell it still bothered Bel the way Daniel simultaneously craved and hated pain. The balance was hard to find. Bel had found it in the orchard—a few whacks with a belt, some pinching and biting, and a rough fuck. But Daniel, inclined to push Bel the way he'd pushed

Marcus, often didn't even recognize the moment when he slipped into the place he feared. The place where the pain was too much, but a voice in his head was telling him he needed it, needed more of it if he was going to sleep. He didn't want to be a coward, didn't want to tell Bel to stop. Because pain could always be worse than this, like that night with Kenny, and Daniel had to be ready in case that happened again, had to know he wouldn't break . . .

He had to be *strong*.

Bel usually recognized that moment, though, and Daniel was glad Bel was the one in charge. Because Bel could say they were stopping, and Daniel had to listen. Didn't make him a coward.

The one thing that was never a problem was rough sex. Bel seemed to love it just as much as Daniel, and it left Daniel plenty exhausted. Bel did some research and seemed to have a new idea every night for how to position Daniel. Sometimes he tied him up, and sometimes he made Daniel hold the position on his own. Bel never seemed interested in toys—plugs, clamps, gags. Anything in Daniel's bag except for cuffs and locks seemed to confuse Bel. "The hell's this?" he asked one night, holding up a large ring gag.

"You gag me with it. Keeps my mouth open, and you put your cock through the ring." Bel's brows went together. "I don't use it anymore," Daniel added quickly. "Not since . . . but Marcus used to . . ."

Bel tossed it aside. "What do I want with gagging you? I like hearin' you."

Daniel still felt guilty about not being able to give Bel head. Wished he could do that for Bel, since Bel seemed willing to do anything for Daniel. Once of Bel's favorite activities was teasing Daniel to the brink of orgasm and telling him if he moved or came, he'd be punished. But the bastard never played fair, never gave Daniel a break, just kept working him until there was nothing Daniel could do to hold back. The punishment was usually to do Bel's dishes if they were at Bel's house—and Daniel swore Bel kept them piled up just for him. Or, once when they were at the cabin, Daniel had to sit backward on Bel's cock and use his ass to make Bel come, despite Daniel's own post-orgasm exhaustion. And he'd had to listen to the extremely self-satisfied smirk in Bel's voice each time he gave an order for Daniel to move faster, clench harder.

It had been worth it, though, to hear Bel getting closer to coming, to hear him lose the smirk, lose control, start begging instead of ordering. Daniel had slept well that night. Now and then, when Daniel felt relaxed enough, he'd lick Bel's cock, or suck on the head. But he just couldn't put Bel's cock in his mouth. And Bel never asked him to.

At the end of a month, Daniel was sleeping through most nights. When he did sleepwalk, Bel got up with him and helped him find his sketch pad and pencils. He had a huge folder of drawings now, which he stashed under the bed. During the day, Daniel felt more relaxed and focused. He didn't wake up each morning with a sense of dread, wondering how he was going to fill all those hours. He was excited to wake up next to Bel, excited to fuck, excited to get online and look at pharmacy schools, like Ms. Davenport and John kept suggesting.

What didn't go away, though, was the anger. It didn't come often, but when it did, there was nothing he could do, no way to stop it. It took over everything, and he imagined Clayton on the ground, Clayton screaming, begging. R.J. and Brock, all of them, dying while Daniel watched.

He'd jerk out of those moments as if from a dream, sweating, panting, disoriented. The anger would diminish and leave him feeling alone, abandoned. Wanting.

When Bel wasn't working, they went into town a few times. Daniel practiced walking through Logan like he had as much right to be there as anybody. When Bel stopped to talk to somebody, he included Daniel in the conversation. And Daniel got used to participating, even if the other person was looking at him like he was a grizzly that Bel was walking on a chain. One time they were walking down Main, and Daniel saw Clayton, R.J., and Brock on the other side of the street. The guys were whispering and snickering, and Daniel could have thrown up on the spot. He was afraid for a different reason now—not so much of *them*, but of how much he wanted them *gone*. But Bel took his hand, squeezed it once, then let go.

Got as much right to be here as you, Clayton.

So stay the fuck away, if you know what's good for you.

But the fear didn't lessen. It was as sharp and overwhelming as it had been that day in the gas station. Or that night in the field. He was afraid of what Clayton could do to him, but just as scared of what he was capable of doing to Clayton. He couldn't keep on living like this. Something had to give.

Moments like that made Daniel think more and more about leaving Logan. Going somewhere he wasn't hated, yes, but more importantly, going someplace where there wasn't anyone he wanted to hurt.

But leaving Logan meant leaving Bel, and that hurt too much to think about right now. Something had to give. Daniel just didn't want it to be him.

Daniel walked out of the library. The parking lot was empty except for his car and a rusty truck. Someone was sitting on the truck's tailgate, but that barely registered with Daniel because he was too busy staring at his car.

Blood, all over the hood and nose of his sedan.

Smeared over the headlights.

He panicked. *Whose blood? I didn't do anything, didn't kill anyone. Whose blood is that? I didn't do anything.*

He took a deep breath. He was tired. Not thinking straight. Not seeing straight. Maybe it was just paint. Or if it was blood, perhaps it belonged to an animal. He closed his eyes and clenched his fists briefly, then turned his attention to the guy on the truck. He already knew who it was.

"What'd you do to my car?" Daniel demanded.

Clayton slid off the tailgate. The red stuff was on his hands, his jeans, and his shoes. He walked toward Daniel, but Daniel didn't back up.

"Don't you fuckin' touch me!" Daniel ordered, as Clayton got closer.

"I wouldn't, faggot, not with a ten-foot pole. Bet you'd like me to, though, wouldn't you? Want my cock in your mouth? It feels a lot like Kenny's. Difference is, *I'll* actually shoot." Clayton was quieter than when he was with his buddies. No whooping. No laughing. Just that hollowness Daniel had seen the evening Clayton had come into the library. He wasn't putting on a show. This was his hatred, the raw heart of his grief exposed only to Daniel.

"Get out of here!" Daniel shouted. "You're gonna fix my car, you fucker! You're gonna pay to get it fixed."

The car wasn't the real issue here, but shouting about the car was better than shouting about how fucking scared he was. Of the way his and Clayton's hollownesses had matched once, before Bel. Of how Daniel was slowly leaving that behind, while Clayton sank deeper into it—and maybe that wasn't fair. Maybe they ought to both be sinking.

He wanted it all to stop. He wanted to go back and start over and be a different Daniel Whitlock.

Doesn't even have to be a complete do-over.

I'd go back to that day by the river and get in the water with Joe Belman.

Because maybe if Daniel'd had Bel then, he would have turned out all right. Maybe he wouldn't have ended up in a bar hitting on Kenny Cooper. Wouldn't have ended up in a field tasting his own blood. Wouldn't have bought a lighter at Harnee's. Wouldn't be standing in this parking lot today with someone who wanted him dead.

He was a kid, idiot. You couldn't have counted on a kid to rescue you. And you can't now, either.

Clayton looked at Daniel's car, then turned back to Daniel, his face screwed up with puzzlement. "What are you on about, Whitlock? Nothin' wrong with your car."

Daniel shook his head. Clayton was faking. There was blood all over the car and all over Clayton. Anyone could see.

"The blood," Daniel said, pointing. "The red stuff you put on my car, right there, all over the hood."

Clayton glanced at Daniel's car again, then at Daniel. His expression was so bewildered that a familiar disquiet slunk through Daniel's body. "What the *fuck* are you talking about?"

"It's all over you too, so quit your act."

Clayton looked down at himself. He laughed, the sound half-disbelieving, half-mocking. "You really are a lunatic. *There's nothing on your car.* Or on me." He straightened. "Crazy fucking Whitlock!"

The fear wound around Daniel's ribs, pulling tight, jerking him forward a step. For a second, he imagined the car as it should have been—clean from the rain two days ago. Nothing on it but a scratch from sideswiping a parked van years ago. And he imagined Clayton with nothing on his hands but dirt and tobacco stains, his clothes free of dark patches. What if that was how things really were? What if the blood was the part Daniel was imagining?

"Yes there is," he said slowly, refusing to let the fear choke him like it had in the gas station bathroom. "And you're gonna fix it. That's my property you fucked with. *My property*, you hear?"

"You don't have a right," Clayton said, voice low, "to call *anything* yours."

He was so close, Daniel kept expecting him to make a move—to grab Daniel, or try to punch him. But Clayton kept his hands balled at his sides. And Daniel, who'd never been one to throw the first punch, found himself struggling not to beat the shit out of Clayton. *Yes I do. I have things that are mine. Things you'll never have. You don't get to ruin those things for me anymore.* "I'll fix *you*," he said, voice rising. "I'll fix you myself. I'll fix you good, you fuck!"

Daniel's stomach clenched as soon as the words were out. Of course Clayton would take them as a threat—they were—and if Clayton told the police what he'd said, the cops would probably figure Daniel was planning to murder Clayton.

And maybe he was.

He saw a flash of fear in Clayton's expression, and that was enough. The anger was like a rush, and he let it come, this time. Like someone had finally given him permission. Like he'd given *himself* permission. Was this what he'd felt the night he'd burned down Kenny's house? This righteous fucking fury that welled up from deep inside him? Something had to give. Somebody had to back down. But it wouldn't be Daniel. Not this time. Not again.

Clayton held up his hands, his red palms facing Daniel. "Better chain yourself back up, Whitlock. 'Fore you hurt someone."

No, Clayton. Maybe I ought to let myself free. Ain't ever really *hurt no one who didn't deserve it.*

"I seen the setup you got out at Kamchee," Clayton continued. "You're either a more fucked-up fag than I thought—"

"You shithole!"

"—or else you're at least smart enough to know you gotta be chained up like an animal."

"You were in my house? You crazy piece of shit— It was you. I *knew* it was you!" Daniel raised his fist and lunged. Clayton sidestepped.

"You wanna hit me?" Clayton taunted.

Daniel dropped his arm, breathing hard. *No. Can't hurt him. What would Bel say? Ms. Davenport?* "More'n anything. You better watch I don't forget I'm on parole."

Clayton grinned again. "That's the spirit, Whitlock. What do you say we sort this out once and for all?"

"Yeah, I'll sort you out," Daniel muttered. "I'll sort you out, you fucker. What the fuck do you mean? Huh?"

Clayton stared at him. He smelled like cigarettes and mustard. "A fair fight. Just us two. Bolton Farm. Behind that old barn that's falling down."

Daniel grinned too, ugly, savage. He wasn't afraid of Clayton right now. Just relieved. Because he'd had so many nightmares about this, about the people who wanted to hurt him and what it would be like when he finally had to face them. And here was the moment, and it was suddenly *easy*. He could fight Clayton McAllister and win. He could do fucking *anything*, because he was the bravest motherfucker in Logan, and because he'd finally gotten in the river with Bel. Even if he couldn't fight for himself, he could fight for that.

Shouldn't, a voice warned. *Even if you win, you'll lose.*

Don't care. Fucker was in my *house. Messed up* my *car. Kept me out of* my *fucking town for way too long. He doesn't get to touch anything else that's mine. Doesn't get my* life.

"Right now?" Daniel said.

"Tomorrow. No weapons. We don't tell anyone what we're up to. You win, I leave you alone for good."

"And if you win?"

Clayton's grin faded. "If I win, Whitlock, you don't show your face in Logan. Ever again. I don't care what you have to do—quit your job, get your fuckin' groceries delivered, jump off a bridge—whatever. If me or any of my buddies see you, we'll finish the job we started, okay? It'll be that cop's head you find on your porch, right before we burn you to the ground!" He shoved Daniel's chest, his palms leaving faint red prints on the fabric of Daniel's shirt.

Daniel's rage was too big for his body. It split him as it poured out, hurt him so bad, he let out a high-pitched sound, somewhere between a scream and a snarl. He shoved Clayton back, harder. "You leave Belman out of this. This is between you and me, and I'll be there tomorrow. You name your time. I won't lose, you fucker, you animal. You thought I lost last time, but I didn't, did I?" He was inches from Clayton's face, and he saw that fear again. *That's right. That's right, you don't fuck with a killer.* He lowered his voice. "*I'm still fucking here.*"

Clayton took a step back. "Won't even be enough left of you for that pig to fuck, when I get done." He planted his palm on Daniel's chest and dragged it slowly down his shirt in a fucked-up parody of the way Bel might have touched Daniel, the heel of his hand grinding over Daniel's nipple. Daniel didn't flinch. Didn't fucking blink. Refused to back down as Clayton left a faint trail of red from just above Daniel's heart to the end of his ribs. When he was done, he deliberately held Daniel's gaze for a moment.

Then he spat on the ground, turned, and walked back to his truck. "Three o' clock," he called.

Daniel spent the rest of the day in a state of numb panic. Reminded him of the nights he couldn't sleep, couldn't do anything but lie awake and worry. He'd worry this was how his entire future would be spent—chained to a bed and waiting for nightmares. He'd worry about his parents, his sister, worry about Kenny Cooper's family, because even if Kenny had been evil, his family had probably loved him. Sometimes his biggest worry was that his own family still loved him, deep down, and that they'd be better off letting that go.

There was rarely any sharpness or definition to the panic, it was just an even layer of fear Daniel couldn't get out from under.

That was what he felt right now, and he hated it. If he had to be afraid, had to be angry, he wanted to feel the bite of it. He wanted to *hurt*.

Bolton Farm was only a couple of miles from the field where Kenny had tortured him. It was near the river too—not the part Daniel had gone to as a kid with Casey and her friends, but the south end where the water was darker, dirtier, full of rocks.

"You coming in?" The echo of Bel's voice.

Bel believed in him. Bel didn't think he was an animal or a monster. If Bel knew Daniel was planning to meet with Clayton, he wouldn't let him go. Wouldn't matter what Daniel told him about wanting to fight this fight, about needing to settle things with Clayton. Bel wouldn't understand. He was too young, and—Daniel felt a flash of anger—he didn't *know*. Didn't know what it was like to try to beg for your life with a broken jaw and a tongue cut nearly in two by your own teeth. Didn't know what it was like to wake up and be told you'd killed someone. To live in fear for years of what you are. To have nightmares each night, to be hated by everyone, to drink your own piss, to *need* so much and be given so little, *fuck*, *shit*, he just didn't *know*.

Bel cared about Daniel, but he didn't know what it was to love. To love fiercely and constantly, to have love be your lifeline, the only thing pulling you up when you were being dragged under again and again.

Daniel knew that kind of love.

And that was why he had to face Clayton without Bel. Because if there was one thing that might redeem Daniel in this world, it was his love for Bel. Maybe there was a God and maybe there wasn't, but Daniel had to trust that if he was meant to live a life free of Clayton McAllister, a life with love in it, then he'd win tomorrow. And if he wasn't meant to, well . . .

Maybe there won't be enough left of me to regret.

It wasn't just Bel, either. If Ms. Davenport found out he'd been in a fight, there went his parole record. If Casey found out, or his mother . . .

They're already ashamed. And Ms. Davenport's just doing her job—she doesn't really care about you. Bel's the only one you can still lose. And if you win tomorrow, you get to keep him. And Clayton won't bother you anymore.

It occurred to Daniel that Clayton was hardly someone Daniel could trust to keep his word.

Gotta put the fear of God in him. Gotta win big. Make him scared of me. Can't just win—gotta break him.

Daniel took a hose to his car. The paint came off pretty easily—and it was paint, not blood. Clayton had *lied*, and that spurred his rage in a way nothing else could have. Daniel wasn't crazy. What Daniel had seen was real, and Clayton would pay for making him believe otherwise, even for a moment.

There were a few spots where it had been laid on thick and Daniel couldn't get it all off. He ended up pulling the car up closer to the cabin to hide the front of it and hoped Bel wouldn't look too closely.

He went inside and tried to work on his computer until Bel arrived, but he couldn't concentrate. Kept thinking about lying to Bel, keeping secrets from him. Losing him.

Fuck you, Bel, get over here already. Fuck me. Hurt me. Please, fucking please make it hurt. I deserve it. I need it. Tell me, Bel. Tell me I'm getting what I deserve. Make me sleep. Hurt me 'cause I can trust you to do it. You don't hate me.

If you don't hurt me, I'll do it. I'll kill him.

Daniel was suddenly lying on his back on the bed, stroking his cock. When the hell had that happened? He blew out a shuddering breath. "Hurt me," he whispered to the ceiling.

Bel wouldn't hurt him. Bel would fuck him rough, but Bel wouldn't *hurt* him. Bel would feel too guilty.

I could help him. If he doesn't know he's hurting me, he doesn't have to feel bad about it.

Daniel stood and went to the bathroom. His legs shook. He pulled the bag out from under the sink. Found the biggest plug he owned. Black silicone, over two inches in diameter at the widest point, not the best-made product. The core was slightly lopsided, which had always made getting it in harder, even when Marcus did it slowly, with lots of lube.

Daniel stared at it. He hadn't used it in ages. And he'd never put it in dry. He'd fucked himself dry with other stuff, but this . . .

Too big.

He could use something smaller.

But I ain't a coward. I want it to hurt.

*Could use a little lube. Some spit, at least. Don't want it to take too
long to heal.*

He'd just have to be careful tonight not to let Bel figure out what
he'd done. He'd keep the lights off. Get Bel to fuck him facedown, so
if Daniel had to cry or muffle a scream, he'd be able to without Bel
seeing.

Wasn't the most appealing idea, but Daniel didn't know any
better way to make sure every thrust hurt the way he deserved to hurt.

He took the plug back into the main room and set it on the bed.

"You telling me the case is closed?" Bel asked.

Uncle Joe gave him the same look he'd given him the time he was
three and rode his tricycle into the back of a parked pickup truck. "I'm
telling you that there's no forensic evidence, no confession, and no
witnesses."

Bel rested his hands on his utility belt. "No witnesses? Maybe I
saw Clayton's truck the night of the fire after all."

Uncle Joe looked around to make sure there was nobody close-by.
"I think the window of opportunity's closed on that, Little Joe."

Bel frowned, but he knew Uncle Joe was right. You didn't
remember a thing like that weeks afterward, and not once you'd
started sleeping with the victim. "They get away with setting that fire,
they'll try something worse next time."

"I know that." Uncle Joe drummed the desk. "Listen, you talked
to your folks yet?"

"'Bout what?"

"What do you think?"

"I think it ain't nobody's business but mine," Bel said.

Uncle Joe narrowed his eyes. "Thought you were smarter than
that, Little Joe. No, not smarter. Tougher."

"Nobody's business but mine," Bel repeated. "Whole fucking
town knows anyhow."

"Well maybe your parents oughta hear it from you," Uncle Joe
said. "What are you ashamed of?"

"I'm not ashamed!"

Uncle Joe folded his arms over his chest. "Is that so? Tell me this then, if it was some other man you were seeing, would you tell them?"

Bel opened his mouth to answer and couldn't. *Shit. I would. I'm not ashamed of being gay, but I'm ashamed of being with Daniel Whitlock.*

"That ain't fair, Uncle Joe," he said. "You know what this town is like, what it thinks of him. Hell, I thought it myself not so long ago."

"I know I've shut my mouth every time Dav spoke up about him," Uncle Joe said. "'Cause it ain't worth the hassle. I'm not a crusader like that girl, but I saw Whitlock after he was arrested. Interviewed him a few times. Knew there was something not right about him." He showed Bel his palms. "Knew he wasn't lying when he said he didn't remember what happened, I mean. Figured he was crazy, and figured a good lawyer would show the court that. But then they said he ain't crazy, he's *sleeping*. Well, hell if I know the difference, but I tell you one thing: you can sometimes cure crazy. Can't cure sleeping."

Bel thought about Daniel the night of Kenny's vigil, insisting that he was awake, and yet begging Bel to protect him from phantoms. Thought of how the night before Daniel had been drawing furiously, talking furiously, and laughing at something only he could hear.

Bel wasn't sure he could tell the difference between crazy and sleeping either.

Uncle Joe put a hand on his shoulder. "Little Joe, you got no future with him. Not in this town."

Bel flinched.

"Make of that what you will," Uncle Joe said. "And then head on home. I ain't paying overtime for this."

Bel, still smarting, headed for the locker room to change out of his uniform. He'd known what being with Daniel would do to his reputation, and kidded himself that it didn't matter. Avery was in the locker room getting ready for his shift.

"Hey, Bel," he said, but didn't look at him.

Hard to know if it was because he was lacing his boots, or because he just didn't want to make eye contact.

And that's how it's gonna be now. You'll second-guess every goddamn interaction you have. You put yourself on Daniel's side, now you're gonna see what it's like for him.

Bel changed quickly, slammed his locker shut, and headed outside to the parking lot. It was just on dusk. Maybe he ought to swing by Harnee's and pick up something he and Daniel could microwave for dinner, since neither of them were much for cooking. Or maybe he'd just drive straight out to the cabin and worry about food later.

"Little Joe, you got no future with him."

Well fuck the future. He needed Daniel now. Maybe they'd get the markers out and he'd write the word across Daniel's heart that he'd only ever had the courage to say when Daniel was sleepwalking: love.

You gonna call it that already, Bel?

Bel gripped the steering wheel and frowned at the road. But what the fuck was *already*? How old did a thing have to be before you put that label on it? And why did the word have so many expectations? Didn't matter how it started. Didn't even matter if it crashed and burned. It was still what it was.

Except what if it was just his own stubbornness pushing him into thinking it was love? What if it felt like more than it was because the town had forced him to pick a side? If nobody gave a fuck, would it still feel as intense?

Would be nice to find out.

Bel pulled up in front of the cabin just as the dusk was softening into darkness. The lights were on inside. Bel didn't even knock before entering, just opened the door to find Daniel kneeling there.

"You're a sight for sore eyes," he said.

Daniel looked up. "Bad day?"

"Long day," Bel said. "Spent most of it looking forward to this."

Daniel smiled.

"You gonna stand up and show me how glad you are to see me?" Bel asked.

Daniel rose awkwardly.

"You okay?"

"Yeah." Daniel stepped into Bel's embrace and kissed him. "I'm good, Bel."

"You're wearing too many clothes," Bel told him, catching Daniel's belt in his hands and tugging it open. Fuck, but he liked this. He liked being aggressive like this. He liked telling Daniel what he wanted as much as Daniel liked being told. He popped the button on Daniel's jeans, pulled the zip down, and reached inside to grip Daniel's cock through his underwear. "You hard for me yet?"

"Getting there," Daniel moaned, his breath hot against Bel's throat.

"Yeah, you are." Bel guided him over to the bed and pushed him down. He tugged Daniel's jeans and underwear off, and Daniel squirmed out of his shirt. Bel stripped quickly, grabbing a condom and lube from the drawer beside the bed. "You ready for me?"

"Yeah." Daniel reached up for him. "Right now."

Bel knew Daniel liked the sting when they fucked hard and fast. Went off like a firecracker. Bel rolled the condom on, slathered himself in lube, and knelt over Daniel. Daniel hooked his legs around Bel's ass, urging him closer.

"Fuck," Bel whispered as his cock breached Daniel.

Daniel flinched underneath him, his breath hitching.

Bel stilled. "You okay?"

Daniel squeezed his eyes shut. "Yeah. Keep going."

Bel stared at Daniel's drawn face, and at the tears caught in his eyelashes. Something wasn't right. What the *hell*? He pulled back.

Blood. Blood on Daniel's ass, now smeared all over Bel's cock. Blood and lube, shiny and stark.

"Fuck, Daniel!" Bel's guts churned. "What the fuck!"

"It's okay," Daniel said, reaching for him. "Fuck me, Bel, please."

Bel stepped away, running his hands through his hair. "No. You fucking tell me what you've done!"

Daniel sat up, wincing. "It's nothing. I just wanted it to hurt, that's all. I just used a plug."

"You're *bleeding*."

"It's okay," Daniel said, breathless. "You've got a condom. It's safe."

"Fuck," Bel managed. "It ain't about that! You want me to fuck you when you're bleeding? When you're hurting? You want me to feel like a fucking *rapist*?"

"No." Daniel pulled the sheet over himself with shaking hands. "No, Bel . . ."

"That's some sick shit, Daniel." Bel ripped the condom off. "You want to get raped, you go talk to that asshole you picked up online. I ain't doing that for you."

"Please," Daniel said. "I'm sorry."

"You ain't sorry!" Bel began pulling his clothes on. "And you ain't fuckin' sleepin' this time. You know, Daniel, I looked up a whole lot of stuff on the internet for you, to be what you needed, but you don't even fucking know what you need. If you got off on it, maybe I could wrap my head around it. But you don't get off on it, do you? That's why you couldn't stick it out with your boyfriend from the city. You're a fucking head case, and that's got nothing to do with sleepwalking. That's just *you*. I don't know what the fuck you need, but until you can figure out the difference between fucking and fucking yourself up, we ain't doing this."

"Yes, Bel," Daniel whispered.

"I ain't . . ." Bel scowled, his anger dying in the face of Daniel's defeated tone. "I ain't saying we're done, I'm saying we ain't doing *this*. You hear the difference?"

Daniel stared at his lap. "Yes."

"Tell me," Bel said, feeling like a bully but needing to know that Daniel understood. "Tell me the difference."

Daniel opened his mouth. Hesitated. "I'm not sure, Bel."

Bel took a deep breath. Normal people didn't need this. Normal people didn't need to be told why it wasn't okay to stick a nail file in your hand or put a plug up your ass so big it tore you. This was the sort of shit crazy people did.

Bel sat on the bed next to Daniel. Daniel flinched. "Uh-uh," Bel said softly. "You don't have to look like that. It's me."

He wanted to touch Daniel. Wanted to take his hand or something, but his body was still crawling with the memory of Daniel's blood on the condom. He felt as sick as he had when Daniel'd come on to him asleep. Like he was a rapist. Like he was taking advantage of Daniel. He kept his hands on his thighs.

"I'd leave," Bel said. "Right now, I'd walk out that door. That's how angry I am. Except I don't think I can trust you alone."

"Well, I'm angry too."

Bel glanced at him.

"It's my body. My fuckin' body, and I'll do whatever I want with it." Daniel's voice was hard.

"So you're gonna fuck yourself up just because you can, is that it?"

"Better'n someone like Kenny Cooper doing it for me!"

"No," Bel said. "You listen. I ain't playin' down what happened to you. But that's over now. Why would you wanna do the same shit to yourself those guys did to you? Huh?"

"It ain't just that! You don't know fuckin' anything. In prison doctors do whatever the fuck they want. They don't care if the pills they give you make you crazy. If you ain't normal, everyone else gets to decide what to do to you. Well fuck that!"

"Calm down."

Daniel jerked away. "I don't want to. You like this shit well enough to beat my ass in the orchard. So it's only okay if you're the one hurting me? But if I do it, suddenly I'm a psycho?"

Bel stood, anger seizing him. He pointed at Daniel. "That was a *game*. That was a game we were playin', and don't you dare twist it into something else. I liked it because I thought you liked it."

"I *do* like it. And I like it to hurt when I fuck, and I like to bleed."

"No you don't! You do it because you . . ."

"Because I what? 'Cause I'm crazy?"

"I don't know. I ain't John goddamn Frommer. But I figure you don't feel good about yourself so you're doing it as punishment. There is a difference. You got off on what we did in the orchard. You wanna tell me sticking that plug up there was hot?"

Daniel flopped on the bed and rolled over, facing the wall. "I don't want to talk anymore. Leave me, then. I don't care."

"I ain't gonna do that. You're stuck with me, Whitlock. So listen to what I'm saying. This part of what we're doing stops now. The part where you kneel for me, where I tell you what to do. That all stops until you get your head around what you want. What you *want*, you hear? Not what you think you deserve."

"Then I guess we ain't gonna be doing much of anything," Daniel snapped.

Bel ran his hands down his face. He was tired. Fucking exhausted, and this was not how loving someone was supposed to go.

Says who?

He thought about his parents. The savage fights he'd hear coming from their bedroom when he was a kid, and then they'd come out a few minutes later right as rain and laughing.

Bet they never fought about shit like this.

"You're gonna keep working with John," Bel said. "And you're gonna keep getting better. And someday you're gonna stop feeling this—this need to hurt yourself. And then we can play whatever games you want. It's too tangled up now, Daniel. You see that?"

Daniel took a shuddering breath.

"We start at the beginning. We do things that don't hurt. You like some of those things. I know you do."

"Don't hurt me to kneel."

Bel swallowed. "I know that's a game. And I know it doesn't hurt anyone. But just for now, I don't want us to think like that. That one of us is in charge and the other one's got to listen."

Daniel turned slightly. "All you've done the last five minutes is order me to listen to you! And you're the one deciding we're not doing this anymore. I don't even get a say."

"You think you're the only one with limits?" Bel demanded. "I wouldn't ask you to do something you didn't want to do, so show me the same respect, all right?"

Daniel was silent.

"I wanna go back, and I want to learn you. I wanna add the games later, when we're both ready. When we both know what we're doing." Bel paused. "Can you be patient with me?"

No answer. But he thought he saw Daniel nod against the pillow. "I don't know when I'm gonna have anything figured out."

"That's fine." Bel was still standing awkwardly by the bed. He wondered if he ought to insist on cleaning Daniel up. He didn't even know what you did for injuries like Daniel's. Daniel didn't have a bathtub, or Bel might have had him soak.

You don't get to insist on anything anymore, remember?

Shit. Maybe this was gonna be harder than Bel thought.

"You need any help cleaning up?" Bel asked.

Daniel shook his head vehemently. "I got it." He didn't move. Just stayed huddled with the sheet around him, his back to Bel.

"Okay. I'm gonna sleep in the chair tonight. Give us both a little breathing room. But I'm here if you need me."

No answer.

Fine. If that's how he wanted it, that's how it was going to be.

Bel sat in the chair and looked at his watch. Hell, it wasn't even 6 p.m. yet. So much for his night off with Daniel.

He shifted, trying to get comfortable. On the bed, Daniel shifted too.

Bel could sit this out. All goddamn night if he had to.

CHAPTER TWENTY

Daniel didn't sleep. Dozed maybe, but didn't sleep. Didn't slip far enough under that his unconscious was in control. He lay there instead, wrapped in the sheet with his back to Bel, and wondered what would happen if he did sleep. Wondered if he'd beg Bel to fuck him. Wondered if he'd try to hurt Bel. Or maybe he'd do something even crazier. Paint the cabin, make a sculpture out of cans, take the stuffing out of his pillows bit by bit and leave it all over the place. No fucking telling.

Bel didn't understand that. He didn't understand that there was a thing inside Daniel that was completely unpredictable. Random. It wasn't just a push and pull between his ego and his id, or whatever the hell those facets of his mind were called. There was no method to it. No fucking equal and opposite reaction.

Kenny Cooper bashed him and threatened to kill him, so he'd burned down Kenny's house with Kenny inside. Cause and effect. That was all Bel saw, and probably all most people saw. But once, when Daniel was eleven, his dad had run over their cat Smokey. That night Daniel had taken all the cutlery out of the kitchen drawers and laid it end-to-end all the way up the stairs. On his thirteenth birthday, Daniel had gotten the remote control helicopter he'd begged his parents for months to buy. He'd been ecstatic. And that night he'd taken a pair of scissors and cut the living room curtains into shreds.

So fucking explain that.

Daniel didn't want pain because he thought he deserved it, or not just because of that. He wanted pain because it *exhausted* him. He wasn't a masochist, but he needed it. Pain was more reliable than locks and chains—history had shown he could get out of most of those—and better than drugs that fucked with his head.

"But you don't get off on it, do you? That's why you couldn't stick it out with your boyfriend in the city. You're a fucking head case . . ."

It was something Daniel should have been accustomed to by now—the feeling of being misunderstood. Other people had always tried to tell him who or what he was, and it always stung a little, even once he was used to it. But it hurt to have Bel in on it. Bel, the only person who'd refused to buy into other people's ideas of Daniel. Who'd seen what Daniel imagined was the closest thing to his real self that existed.

Daniel heard Bel get up at one point—Daniel checked his cell; it was only a little after eleven—and bang around in the kitchen. Something started sizzling on the stove, and whatever it was, it didn't smell too bad. He tried to resent Bel for using his kitchen, eating his food, but he couldn't. They'd been welcome to each other's stuff for a while now. He listened to Bel eat, heard Bel put his dish in the sink when he was done. Heard him come back to the chair.

Daniel dozed, his stomach tight and empty.

When he opened his eyes again, there was gray light coming through the window. He'd hurt all night, still sore from the plug, and it had kept him awake. He liked it. Pain was *good*. Would have been better if Bel had fucked him hard and hurt him some more, worn him down until he slept. Maybe if they'd fucked, he wouldn't be lying in bed alone. Maybe Bel would have wrapped his arms around him and he would have felt something else as well. Loved. He could pretend that, couldn't he? At least he wouldn't have felt so alone.

You don't get that. You're not normal. The man you love just spent a night sitting in a chair watching you instead of lying beside you, because . . . because . . .

"*You're a fucking head case.*"

It shouldn't have hurt to hear it. Everyone got there in the end, didn't they? Pushed him away, couldn't deal with him. Bel had been more patient than anyone, but it wouldn't have lasted forever.

"Hey," Bel said quietly. "You awake?"

"Yeah." Daniel still didn't roll over. Didn't want to face him yet. Didn't want to face the end.

The mattress dipped. "How you feeling?"

Tired, Bel. So fucking tired of everything. Always so close to slipping under.

Shit. Where was the anger he'd felt yesterday? The anger he'd need later to face Clayton?

"Okay."

Bel stretched out next to him. They lay in silence for a moment. "I gotta get to work. Left you some eggs in the fridge."

Daniel nodded.

"What you got planned for today?"

Daniel hated hearing Bel sound so forced. "Might go down the road and help with the garden. Needs weeding."

Bel wrapped his arms around Daniel.

Fuck, no.

But Daniel rolled over and leaned into the embrace before he could help himself. Returned it.

He couldn't afford to need this, couldn't be weak now, not with what he had to do today. But being in Bel's arms made everything in him relax, except his throat, which clenched tight. Even knowing what Bel thought of him couldn't stop Daniel from loving him. Bel smoothed a hand down his back, stopping just above his ass. "You still hurting?"

"No, Bel," Daniel murmured. "I don't hurt anymore."

Bel gave him a last squeeze and let go.

"If I see you tonight—" Daniel tried to smile. "—we ought to go walking."

"You'll see me tonight," Bel said. "Don't let what I said . . . I'm sorry I got pissed. I meant it when I said we ain't done."

That was almost enough to break Daniel. Bel would be here tonight.

I *might not be.*

Some part of Daniel knew, had known the moment Clayton suggested the fight, that it wouldn't be a fair one. Wouldn't be as simple as Clayton said. If Daniel lost, he just had to stay out of Logan? Bullshit. If Clayton got Daniel on the ground, he wouldn't stop until Daniel was dead.

So he ain't gonna get me on the ground.

"What's wrong?" Bel asked.

"Nothin.'"

Wish I could tell you. Wish you could stop me from going.

Except Bel didn't have any authority over Daniel anymore. And Daniel didn't want anyone to stop him. He *needed* to finish this.

Something wasn't right. Even though Bel was next to him, there was something cold and broken between them.

Bel rolled over and slid out of bed. Went to put on his shoes. "I'll take you somewhere. If you don't think you should be alone, I got people you can stay with."

"No," Daniel snapped, stung. "Christ, Bel. I can control myself."

"Ain't no shame in it if you can't," Bel said quietly.

What the fuck did he know about it?

Daniel turned away. "See you later then."

"Yeah," Bel said. "You have a good day."

Bel finished tying his shoes and left.

When he was gone, Daniel got up and used the bathroom. His ass still hurt too much for him to shit. He took a quick shower to get the dried blood off his thighs. Fuck, he was a mess. No wonder Bel had freaked out.

He shaved, taking his time. Stared at himself in the mirror for a while, telling himself to remember his face the way it looked right now. Might look different later.

He walked out of the bathroom. There was a piece of paper on the table beside the chair. One of Daniel's drawings—a new one. So he had slept after all.

It was just of Bel's shoes, nothing else. No way of telling whether Bel had been awake when Daniel drew it. Daniel felt his throat tighten. Maybe Bel had been awake. Maybe they'd talked. He wished he knew.

Maybe he was stupid for wanting to imagine they'd apologized, that Bel had joked with him, that he'd called Daniel's work beautiful. Maybe Bel had just sat there, asleep, and Daniel had drawn him.

He couldn't afford to think bullshit like that. Not today. Today he had one goal: to beat Clayton.

Daniel went into the kitchen. Looked at the scrambled egg film on the pan in the sink.

He opened the fridge. Bel had put the leftovers in a plastic container with a note that said, FOR YOU.

Daniel removed the note, took the container out, and stuck it in the microwave. Microwaved it a little too long and then had to eat the too-hot, dried-out eggs. He washed the dishes and set them in the rack. Went into the bathroom, where he brushed his teeth. He looked in the trash for the bloody condom but didn't see it. Bel must've buried it.

He should have known better.

Burying stuff didn't help. It would always come back to haunt you anyhow.

Bel was climbing out of the shower when he heard the knock at the door. He wrapped his towel around his waist and went to answer it. Hoped it was Daniel. Hoped he was here, ready to talk even though Bel didn't have the time for that. He'd make the time.

Instead he found Jim waiting in the doorway.

"Hey." Bel unlatched the screen. He wandered into the living room, knowing Jim was behind him, and began to dig through his ironing basket. Pulled on a pair of sweatpants under the towel. "What's up?"

Jim didn't say anything.

Bel turned to face him. "Is Dad okay?"

Belman family code for *How much money has he gambled this time? How much does Mama need?*

"Not here about that," Jim said uneasily.

Here it comes.

"Oh yeah?" Bel rubbed the towel over his hair.

"About Whitlock," Jim said. "You, ah, you and him . . . You the same as him, Little Joe?"

"You asking if I'm gay, Jim?"

Jim shifted from foot to foot. "Yeah."

Bel dumped the towel on the couch. "Yeah, I am."

Jim got the same look on his face that Stump got when he was yelled at for stealing buns. He looked . . . *wounded*. Well, fuck him. Bel had finally got to the point where he could say it out loud. He sure as hell wasn't gonna follow it up with an apology.

"That all you come to ask?" he growled.

"How come . . . how come you never said nothing?"

"What?"

Jim scratched his cheek. "Something big like that, Joey. You think you couldn't trust us? Makes me feel like maybe we let you down."

Bel's anger drained away. "Wasn't keeping secrets, not really. Just it was no one's business but mine."

"Dav told me," Jim said. "I mean, I asked her and she told me. She knew."

"She's got eyes in her head," Bel said. "Same as everyone, except Dav don't only see what she wants to see."

Strange. He'd thought she'd been blind about Daniel. Making him a martyr when he was just a crazy killer, because maybe in her job she needed to believe she had at least one offender like that. Someone redeemable. Bel had thought she was fooling herself, but it turned out Dav was just about the only person in Logan with twenty-twenty vision.

"Whitlock," Jim said. "Is he your *boyfriend*?"

He said the word like it tasted strange.

"Yeah."

"Dav says things about him too." Jim's gaze kept sliding away from Bel's. "Says he ain't just some crazy meth head. That true?"

"Wouldn't be with him if he was."

"Maybe you're just with him because there ain't nobody else in town," Jim said quietly.

Bel snorted. "More men in town with a taste for cock than you think."

Jim stepped back. "Fuck, Joe! Don't say shit like that!"

"Why not? It's true."

Jim ran a hand through his scruffy hair. "You gotta stop seeing Whitlock. People are talking. I was down at the Shack last night, and they're saying you been around town with him. He's bad news, Joe. You know that."

"What I know, Jim, and what this fucking town knows, are two different things. You want to hear what I know?"

Jim just stared.

Well, too bad. He'd started it.

"I know I ain't met anyone like Daniel before," Bel said, seeing how Jim flinched when he said his name. "I know he sleepwalks, and

I know he does shit then that he doesn't even remember doing. I know he has a real medical condition, and I know it's not bullshit. I know what this town thinks of him, and I know he's better than that. I know that he just wants to be left alone, and I know the sort of crap that he still puts up with over something he couldn't help."

"He killed a man," Jim said. "You know that too."

"Yeah." Bel folded his arms across his chest. "I know that too."

"He gonna do that to you one day?" Jim asked. "Maybe you piss him off, do the wrong thing. He gonna burn you in his sleep?"

"That won't happen."

Wouldn't it? Now that Bel had said it, he didn't know if it was true. He remembered the night that Daniel had gone for his gun. If Bel had been slower, caught off guard, what would have happened then? But they were different now, weren't they? Knew one another now. Bel could get through to Daniel when he was sleeping. Talk him down, touch him, guide him gently back to bed.

"He's seeing a shrink," Bel said. "A good one. He's getting better."

"Yeah, I know about that too. You gonna tell him who's really paying for that? 'Cause I know the taxpayers ain't. Or, I guess they are, aren't they? Just it's coming through your salary first."

"Dav tell you that too?" Fucking Dav and her big mouth.

"Yeah." Jim shook his head. "Was gonna hit you up for a loan to buy into the auto shop with Mikey. Asked Dav about it, and she said you might be light on cash. You putting him before your own family now?"

"Fuck you," Bel growled, heading for the kitchen. "You want a loan, I'll go to the bank with you and sign for a fucking loan, but what I do with my money is my business."

"I didn't mean it like that, Joe." Jim followed. "Shit, I'm not saying anything right, am I? I'm worried for you, is all. Whitlock's dangerous. You know that. We all know that. You think I want my kid hanging around his uncle if Whitlock's gonna be there as well?"

Bel stopped. *No. Fuck, Jim, don't say that.*

Taking sides between Daniel and the town? Well, he'd made his choice. Taking sides between Daniel and his own family? Some dumb part of him had never even considered it. Thought they'd understand.

Thought they'd listen about Daniel. Because Bel had, so why wouldn't they?

"You mean that?" he asked woodenly. "Because you ask me to make that choice, it might not go the way you expect."

Jim opened his mouth, then closed it. He had the same look on his face as that time they were kids and their dad had been shouting at Mama something awful, and Billy punched him so hard in the guts that he went straight down. Jim and Bel had just stood there, not believing what they were seeing, before they'd both hightailed it down to Uncle Joe's place. When they came back a few hours later, it was like nothing had happened. Dad and Billy were working on the truck together, and after that, things weren't ever so bad again.

"I'm glad Billy's the oldest," Jim had whispered to Bel that night. *"Glad I didn't have to do it."*

"Me too," Bel had whispered back, and they'd both worshipped Billy a little more from that moment.

Bel almost wished Billy was here now, to tell them what to do, how to sort this out. Knock their heads together if that's what it took. This must be how Daniel felt most times, needing someone to tell him. Needing to know someone could make it right.

Bel needed that right now. Someone who could give him advice. And not just about Jim, but about Daniel too. Last night still made him feel sick. The blood. The way Daniel had thought he wouldn't notice, or maybe that he'd just keep going anyway. Mostly the way Daniel couldn't tell the difference between needing pain and needing to feel safe, and getting them mixed up somehow in his head.

Probably wasn't anyone on the planet Bel could talk to about that.

He wants to hurt, really hurt, and he wanted to make me the one who did it.

He wondered if Daniel's ex from the city, Marcus, had felt sick like this.

"He matters to me," Bel ground out, watching Jim's face fall. "And that's all I can tell you."

"It don't make sense, Joe," Jim said, a note of pleading in his voice.

Bel shrugged. "Makes sense to me."

Without another word, Jim turned and left.

Bel heard the screen door slam a few times behind him before the latch caught.

He sat down heavily on the couch.

Wondered if this was another bridge burned.

If eventually he'd be left standing in a pile of ashes with no place left to go.

Daniel opened his sketchbook and tore out a piece of paper. Sat on the bed and tapped his pen against his thigh. He'd wanted to make a list before he went, to ground or center himself or whatever John was always going on about. But every idea he came up with seemed stupid, inadequate.

How I'm Feeling.

I've fucking been better.

Things I Wish I Could Say to Bel.

I could say anything to him. I just don't.

Stuff I Wish I Could Change.

Goddamn pathetic. Not going down that road.

He settled on What I Got to Do Today.

- Check on garden

- Hydrate

- See Mom and Dad

- Text Bel

- Go fight Clayton

He paused, then added:

- Go walking with Bel

He stuck the list back in the sketch pad, grabbed his keys, and left the house. Headed up the road a bit.

Stopped at Mr. Roan's house, but decided not to knock and bother him. He looked at the garden. It really did need weeding. He stepped over the chicken wire and pulled the worst of the mess out. It was a cool day, but not too bad. Tonight the moon was supposed to be one of those big yellow ones. He was dumb to think he'd get to go walking with Bel. Even if Daniel won the fight, if Bel found out . . .

Everyone'll find out. It's Logan.

Daniel was terrified to jeopardize what he had with Bel, especially when he'd already done so much damage last night. Bel had put so much effort into understanding Daniel, forgiving him. And now Daniel had to ask Bel to forgive him once more. To understand that Daniel couldn't be free until he fought his demons himself. Not in therapy. Not by leaving Logan and trying to forget what had happened here. But by confronting them head-on.

He thought about the bug spray, the magazine, the fire, the pig's head, the paint on his car. The fear he lived in because of Clayton McAllister. The way part of his mind had believed, until now, that he had to sit quietly and take it, because it was what he deserved for Kenny Cooper.

And then Bel had come along and made him believe he deserved better.

I deserve to hurt.

Bel didn't buy that. He didn't *let* Daniel hurt.

Daniel wiped his forehead. Cast a look through the windows of Mr. Roan's house. Saw the old man pottering around inside. Then he stepped out of the garden and walked back to his car.

He ate lunch at the diner in town. Sue-Ellen didn't bat an eye, just brought him coffee like he was any other customer. Whatever progress he'd made in Logan over the last few weeks—and it wasn't much, but it was something—he'd kill it all if he kicked Clayton's ass. He'd be everyone's enemy again. But that was okay, because when he kicked Clayton's ass, he'd be free.

Fuckin' *free.*

He finished lunch and asked for a slice of pie. Left Sue-Ellen a big tip.

Then he drove to his parents' house. His mother answered the door.

"Daniel," she said in that formal way she said his name now. "Come in."

It was so dark in the house compared to outside. Depressed Daniel to go in. The living room smelled like the same potpourri his mother had been buying since Daniel's childhood.

They sat at the kitchen table. She brought him a glass of water. He drained it and immediately got up to fill it again.

Daniel heard his father creaking down the stairs. His stomach tightened. A second later, his father came into the kitchen. "Dan," he said. He stuck out his hand, and Daniel shook it. Daniel couldn't speak for a minute. Hadn't heard his father call him Dan in years.

"How's your— How's work?" Daniel asked, glancing back and forth between both of them. He'd promised he wasn't going to waste time with small talk, but he still had a while before he had to start driving to Bolton Farm, and any plan for what he'd wanted to say had vanished as soon as his father had come into the room.

"Oh." Daniel's mother looked at his father, then back at Daniel. "It's fine. We hired a new director last week. So that's taken some getting used to."

Daniel nodded.

"The plant's good," Daniel's father said, hiking up his pants and taking a seat at the table. "What about the library?"

"Fine," Daniel said, reminding himself not to look down. To keep looking at them. "Same as always."

"So what brings you here?" His mother's gaze kept flitting to the window, as though she expected to see half the neighborhood peering in.

"I been thinkin' about what you said. About maybe goin' off somewhere and gettin' help." He paused. He could hear his father breathing. His mother had her arms wrapped around her like she was cold. There was a fly on the apple in the fruit basket, and Daniel watched it rub its front legs together. "I just want you to know I'm getting out of here. This—this mess I'm in. I'm gonna fix it."

His mother dropped her arms to her sides and tried to smile. "Well. That's great, Daniel. Really. Are you . . . are you going to a hospital?"

Daniel shook his head. "No. But, uh, I wanted to say thanks for the money. I ain't taking it, but thanks. And I'm sorry for . . ." *Shit.* He wasn't gonna choke now. "Sorry for everything. Sorry I'm not— Sorry."

"We know it's not your fault," his father said, but he said it in a wary sort of a way, as though he expected to be struck down at any second for letting a lie like that pass his lips. He looked to Daniel's mother, something helpless in his gaze. *What am I supposed to say next?*

She looked away.

"You, um, you used to call me Dan all the time, Dad, you remember?" Daniel asked.

"I did?" A small frown creased his dad's forehead, deepening the wrinkles there.

Daniel nodded. He didn't trust himself to speak. Stared at the tablecloth instead.

Only called me Daniel when I was in trouble, when you were telling me off. Then it stuck. Then I was Daniel for good, even when you weren't mad. Even when you forgot what you were angry about, it stuck.

His dad cleared his throat. "Your parole is almost up. You leaving after that?"

"Yeah." Probably straight back to jail, though they didn't need to know that. To jail, and meds that messed up his head, but Clayton would *know* then, wouldn't he? Clayton would know what it was like to feel scared, to feel hurt. To feel what it was like to choke on his own fucking teeth.

He thought of his list.

- Go walking with Bel

That wasn't going to happen, was it? That had been a stupid thing to write down, because however this thing with Clayton ended, he wouldn't be walking with Bel again. Daniel knew better than that.

Just like he should have known better than to come back into this house, wanting something that wasn't there anymore. Hadn't been for a long time.

"I should go," he said.

They didn't stop him. Didn't say anything.

"I should go," he repeated, and rose to his feet. Felt like crying, or screaming, or something. Just ran his fingers along the tablecloth as he stood, then turned and headed for the front door.

Outside, he leaned against his car and sucked in some deep breaths that hurt his aching chest. He checked his watch. Two twenty-five. Time to head out and meet Clayton.

Time to text Bel.

He took his phone out of his pocket. His hand shook, and he squinted to see the screen in the sunlight. Began to type out his message.

Hi, Bel. It's Daniel.
The minutes ticked by as he thought about what to say next.

CHAPTER
TWENTY-ONE

Goddamn traffic duty. Bel liked it, usually, the freedom to drive around on the highway for a while, counting down the hours in his shift as the scenery flew past the window. One ear on the radio, and the other on the commercial channels. Singing along when something he liked came on. Today he was out of sorts, over Jim, but especially over Daniel. And there was nothing on the radio that wasn't shit.

US 601 felt like something out of a video game, like he could just drive back and forth on it without ever really getting anywhere. He was nearing the town limits, and he wondered what would happen if he didn't stop. If he just kept driving, out of Logan, out of Orangeburg County, right out of goddamn South Carolina. Everyone had moments like that, didn't they? Moments you felt big enough, free enough, crazy enough that you could drive forever. But really it was about running away.

Wasn't that what Bel would be doing if he left Logan—running?

Uncle Joe had said Bel had no future here with Daniel.

And Bel knew Daniel mattered more than Logan.

But if they left, weren't they caving? Running because they were afraid of what people would think, what people would say?

At what point were they supposed to give up fighting? They couldn't change an entire town's mind. Why make Daniel stay here, miserable and alone, just to prove they weren't intimidated by gossip, by cold stares, by a fucking pig's head on the front porch?

Never see Dav, or the baby, if I left. Wouldn't be around if Mama needed help. Maybe it's selfish to think about leaving.

Bel wasn't even sure Daniel wanted to leave. Yeah, he'd been looking at pharmacy schools and talking to John and Dav about his prospects after parole. But whenever Daniel brought up leaving—which was rarely, around Bel—he always seemed cowed by the idea of leaving his family. Of trying to find a job elsewhere.

"No school's gonna take a murderer," he'd told Bel the other day. *"You want a fucking arsonist counting out your pills?"*

Bel slapped the wheel halfheartedly. They'd figure it out. They'd figure out this whole dominant/submissive thing too. Once they'd learned to be in a relationship where they were both in charge, where Daniel didn't need to hurt—then they could layer on the kinky shit. Daniel might be upset now, but he'd understand. He trusted Bel.

Made Bel proud to think about those moments Daniel gave his trust openly and let Bel take care of him. When he leaned against Bel, or curled in his arms at night, or calmed when he was in the middle of a nightmare and Bel said his name. Bel didn't know how the fuck to reconcile the Daniel who stuck a nail file in his hand or tore his own ass with the guy who nuzzled Bel's throat when they were both half-asleep and he was seeking a last kiss good-night.

Bel pulled over awhile and sat, thinking about what he'd say to Daniel tonight. Last night he'd been caught off guard. He hadn't meant to call Daniel a head case. *Jesus.* And he'd left Daniel alone after a night like that. Had left Daniel alone just because Daniel had snapped at him and said he didn't need help. Like fuck he didn't.

Bel still got his two-thirty text from Daniel. Technically Daniel didn't have to follow the rules anymore, and technically it was two forty, but Bel was glad to hear from him.

The text read: *Hi, Bel. It's Daniel. I feel like the bravest motherfucker in Logan today. I want to say I'm sorry and thanks for everything.*

Bel frowned at the screen, uneasy. There was nothing overtly wrong with the text, just . . .

Thanks for everything.

That was what you said when you were leaving.

I feel like the bravest motherfucker in Logan today.

Why today?

I'm sorry.

There was a dark thought in the back of Bel's brain, but he didn't want to look at it too closely.

No way. Fuck no.

Daniel had hurt himself yesterday. He was in a bad place, and if he'd figured Bel was rejecting him . . .

He wouldn't. Wouldn't fucking kill himself. He's smarter than that.

Bel looked at the screen again.

Thanks for everything.

He dialed Daniel's number and put the phone to his ear. Closed his eyes and prayed as it rang—actually *prayed* for the first time in years. No answer.

Bel texted: *I'm coming to get you right now. Wait for me.*

He turned the car around and sped toward town. He was eight miles from Kamchee, and he'd have to cross Logan to get there. *Fuck.* Another shitty pop song came on the radio, and Bel slammed the Off button.

He slowed when he saw a guy walking through the ditch on the left side of the road. Thought for a wild moment it was Daniel. *Hoped* it was, because, fuck, Bel would take him in his arms right now if he could, would apologize, would promise Daniel anything. He'd tell Daniel to get in the car and they'd drive out of here right now, together. They'd go wherever Daniel needed to go to heal, and Bel would be patient. Wouldn't leave him, no matter what.

Just please don't let him have done anything.

The guy walking through the ditch wasn't Daniel, it was Jake fucking Kebbler from Greenducks. Motherfucker. Bel ought to ignore him. Wasn't illegal to walk through a ditch. But Jake was miles from town, and he was staggering. He was waving his arms too, and shouting. Bel pulled over, got out of the car, and crossed the road.

"Kebbler!"

Jake was hobbling like he'd hurt his ankle. When he saw Bel, he fell over. Like one of those fucking fainting goats, just hit the ground. Bel rolled his eyes and hurried over. Jake scrambled to his feet, red eyes wide. "Oh man, thanks for stopping. Can I hitch a ride?" Then his face fell. "Aw, shit, man. Officer, I mean. Didn't know it was a cop car. Ain't you supposed to identify yourself or somethin'?"

High as a goddamn kite.

"The lights on top didn't give it away?" Bel asked.

"I'm not saying nothing 'less you got a warrant," Jake announced, swaying.

"You flagged me down, you idiot. I don't have time for this shit right now. What're you doing out here?"

Jake glanced at his hands, which were filthy. His shoulders jerked.

"What're you on, Kebbler?" As if Bel didn't know.

Jake started to hobble away again. "Gonna watch the fight," he said.

"The fight," Bel repeated. "That don't sound like a good reason to be out here. Why don't you get in the car?"

"Mm-hmm. My money's on Whitlock."

Bel froze. "What're you talking about?"

Jake stopped walking. His shoulders jerked again. He put a finger in his mouth and gnawed on the side of it. Grinned quickly, then the smile faded. "I don't think you're invited, Officer."

"Listen, you don't tell me what you're on about right now, I'll take you to the station. What's gonna happen if you piss in a cup, Kebbler? Huh?"

Jake flinched and put a hand over his face. Peered at Bel through his fingers. "I, uh . . . I gotta go."

Bel put a hand on his shoulder, stopping him before he could move. "Go where?"

"Whitlock, he might need some help. Ain't gonna be a fa . . . ain't gonna be a fair fight. Might need someone on his side, and I know Whitlock. I like him okay. Want that McAllister kid wiped out. My money's on Whitlock."

Bel shook him lightly. "What's happening? Is something happening with Whitlock and McAllister?"

Jake's glassy eyes searched Bel's. "McAllister. I heard him. Him 'n' R.J. 'n' Brock. They was talkin' about what they'd do to Whitlock. Whitlock thinks he's just fighting Clayton, but they're all gonna be there. Gonna gang up on 'im. Least if I'm there, it's two on three. Odds are better."

"Where are they fighting?" Bel demanded. He had a sudden image of Daniel standing over Clayton, bloody fists clenched and a snarl on his face. Except that was crazy. Daniel wasn't gonna win. Even if he didn't get beaten . . . well, there was no way for Daniel to win.

"Bolton Farm."

Bel pulled Jake out of the ditch. "Come on. We're going to my car. You gotta tell me everything you know, okay?"

As they drove toward Bolton, Jake said, "They didn't know I was there!" He spoke belligerently, as though Bel had tried to argue to the contrary. "Heard 'em say . . ." Jake moaned and knocked his head against the window.

"Heard 'em say what?"

"Hey, where we goin'?"

"To Bolton Farm, Kebbler. I'm gonna throw my coffee on you in a minute here. What'd they say?"

"They was gonna fix Whitlock good. They figured he was just expectin' Clayton. And Clayton's a fuck face, Officer." Jake pounded on the divide. "He's an animal."

"When did you hear all this?"

"Last night. At the Shack."

"What'd'you want with the Shack?"

Jake laughed. "You'd be surprised how many straight guys'll give you pills for head."

Bel glanced at Jake in the mirror. "That ain't something you should be telling me."

"You asked." Jake leaned back. "I think it's a freak show thing, though. A fag's a trained animal." He lolled against the seat back. "Lemme off, okay? Lemme off. I don't feel good."

"Focus, Kebbler. If you heard them planning to do something to Daniel, why the hell didn't you call the cops?"

Jake rolled his head to meet Bel's gaze in the mirror. "Whitlock'll be okay. He's fuckin' killed someone before. Jus' the numbers—the numbers ain't fair. He can't take all three at once."

"So your tweaked ass was gonna help him fight. Is that it?" Bel couldn't quite process what he was hearing. Why the hell would Daniel agree to a fight with Clayton? "And Whitlock said he'd fight Clayton? At Bolton Farm?"

Jake's eyes were closed.

"Tell me!"

Jake snapped up. "What?"

"Did Whitlock say he'd fight Clayton?"

"Well, I ain't talked to Whitlock! But Clayton said today at three. Three, three, thuh-ree," he muttered.

Bel checked the clock. 2:57. "Well you weren't gonna make it there anywhere near three staggering through the ditch. They might've killed Whitlock before you got there."

They might still.

Jake nodded. "We ain't all got wings."

"You're gonna sit tight. When we get there, you're gonna sit tight, okay, and I'm gonna handle this."

I want to say I'm sorry and thanks for everything.

Fuck. Bel had been an idiot. A complete fucking idiot to leave Daniel alone. And not to ask—not to even think to ask what had happened yesterday that had made Daniel want to hurt himself so bad.

I feel like the bravest motherfucker in Logan today.

Bel gripped the wheel. *Well you ain't, Daniel Whitlock. You're about the stupidest. Only one guy in Logan stupider than you right now, and that's me.*

The sun was dipping lower, casting a gentle golden glow on Bolton Farm, making the weathered old barn look like the centerpiece of one of those paintings in the gallery downtown. The ones by local artists that made Logan look idyllic—open and free and yet at the same time quaint and tamed.

Daniel's mother had liked to walk here when Daniel and Casey were younger. She'd taken them up to the fence of the cattle pasture and let them touch the cows' noses.

There were worse places to have to fight for your life, Daniel thought. It wasn't cold, and it wasn't dark. Daniel felt good. Loose but alert. Grounded.

Clayton was already there, sitting on a rock beside the barn. So there'd be no waiting. No chance to get nervous. Daniel had felt his phone buzz a while back, but he hadn't looked at it. Couldn't deal with a reply from Bel. And who else would be texting him?

Clayton spat when Daniel approached, but his expression didn't change. That hollowness again. Clayton was seeking a kind of peace too. Daniel didn't let himself pity Clayton. But it helped to know he wasn't facing a monster. Wasn't up against something so purely evil it was indestructible. The hollowness made Clayton more dangerous, but it also made him more human.

Daniel nodded. Clayton got up. Daniel wasn't sure what you said to the guy whose ass you were about to kick, so he didn't say anything. Clayton was skinny. Strong, probably, but he looked manageable. Kenny had just been so fucking big, and Daniel hadn't been ready for him. He'd tried to fight, but that first blow with the gun had left him stunned.

No sense remembering that right now. He was fighting partly out of anger, sure, and partly out of fear. But partly for love, too. So the world could see how strong loving Bel had made Daniel.

"Around back," Clayton said, starting toward the back of the barn.

The ground was still soft from a recent rain. Clayton stopped when the barn hid them from the road. He spat again as he turned to face Daniel. "I'm doin' this for Kenny," he said.

For just a second, Daniel was afraid. There was a raw power in Clayton. Clayton didn't assume a stance or do anything to ready himself to fight—he was always ready, violence coiled in his wiry muscles. He had an easy confidence, so far from the coldness, the open cruelty Daniel had seen yesterday. His hatred was quiet but consuming. He seemed resigned to what he was about to do rather than excited.

"I'm doin' this because of Kenny," Daniel said. "And I'm doin' it for me. For me and Bel."

One side of Clayton's mouth twisted up. Disbelieving more than mocking. "You and Bel? Belman the cop?"

Daniel jerked his head in a nod.

Clayton spat once more. "Shit, I figured even Belman had more sense than to stick it in you, but I guess I was wrong about that. Or maybe you stick it in him, huh? Make the piggy squeal."

Daniel clamped his jaw shut, his tongue finding that gap where his two back molars used to be. Maybe Clayton was trying to goad him, make him lose his temper. That wasn't going to happen.

Clayton looked at his watch, and for a moment Daniel wondered what the hell they were both doing. Wondered if they could step back from this precipice they were standing on.

"Hey, Clayton, I'm sorry I killed your friend."

"That's okay, Whitlock. I'm sorry I helped him beat the living shit out of you."

Daniel almost smiled at the thought.

The sound of an engine, of tires crunching in dirt, caught his attention. Clayton's old red pickup swung around the barn, with R.J. at the wheel and Brock leaning out the passenger window. Brock whooped as he saw Daniel. "He came," he shouted. "Yeah, you did, you dumb faggot!"

The truck rumbled to a stop, and R.J. and Brock got out, Brock dragging a bag.

If Clayton had been unexcited a minute ago, now his face changed. "What?" he asked Daniel. "You think you gave Kenny a fighting chance?"

"Jus' wanted to end this," Daniel said in a low voice, hoping he'd understand.

"It's gonna end." Clayton's expression was hard. "I promise you that."

Adrenaline flooded Daniel. *Run, just fucking run.*

"Hey, Whitlock!" R.J. called, reaching into the back of the truck and drawing out a hunting rifle. "Don't you move until we're done talking to you."

Talking? Wouldn't be just talking.

"Ask 'em what's in the bag, Whitlock," Clayton said with a grin. "Ask what they found out at your cabin."

"What?" Daniel asked, dry-mouthed.

Brock whooped again and dumped the bag on the ground. "Oh man, you're a sick motherfucker, ain't you, Whitlock?" He ripped the zipper open and upended the contents in the dirt.

His cuffs and chains. His locks. The aluminum paddle. And—*fuck no*—the plug from the night before.

Brock kicked at the plug. "That really fit up you, Whitlock? You must be looser'n a pair of old boots!"

"My stuff," Daniel managed. "It's my stuff."

The realization should have been followed by rage, but in that moment he was just too stunned to truly believe it.

"You like to be chained up, Whitlock?" Brock asked. "You like to have things shoved up you? Sick freak."

Daniel stared at his stuff lying in the dirt. Stared at Brock, then past him to R.J. with the hunting rifle. Turned his head to look at Clayton. "Came out here for a fair fight."

"Didn't give Kenny a fair fight, did you?" Clayton asked.

"No," Daniel agreed. A day didn't go by without thinking about it. Kenny, sleeping in bed, as the place burned. Except he hadn't been found in his bed, it came out at the trial. He'd been found near the back door. Must've woken up, the place thick with smoke, and tried to get out. Must've been terrified.

Daniel raised a hand to his throat and rubbed the skin there. BRAVEST MOTHERFUCKER IN LOGAN. He could still be that. Could still hold on to that.

Brock picked up a pair of cuffs and swung them on his finger. "You gonna put these on, Whitlock?"

Daniel shook his head. "I ain't doing that."

Brock grinned and looked to R.J.

Fuck. The rifle. They *wouldn't* ...

"Do it," Clayton said.

Brock tossed the cuffs over, and Daniel caught them reflexively.

"No," he said, and wished he could follow it up with a brave retort. *You're gonna have to shoot me before I do that*, or something. But he didn't, because there was suddenly no doubt in his mind that they'd do it. They'd shoot him. But the cuffs? Hell no. He couldn't.

The guys were watching him, grinning a little.

"No," Daniel repeated.

R.J. raised the rifle.

Fuck. No. Jesus. Daniel fumbled with the cuffs, dropped them in the dirt, and went down onto his knees after them. Heard their laughter like this was all a game. Just like last time.

I can't, he would have said to Bel, or to Marcus when they wanted him to do something that scared him. *You can*, they would have said, and, just like that, it would be true. Because he trusted them. But he couldn't do *this*. He didn't feel like the bravest motherfucker in Logan now.

I ain't gonna put 'em on. They'll kill me anyway. Rather die fighting.

He lifted the cuffs and opened one.

"That's right, Whitlock." Clayton took a step closer. "Show us how good you look in 'em."

That hit Daniel straight in the gut. Because Bel had said Daniel looked good tied up, and he'd meant it. Clayton didn't get to mock that.

He lunged suddenly, swinging the cuffs by one end. The chain struck Clayton's knee, wrapping around for a second. It must have hit a good spot, though, because Clayton's leg jerked, and he doubled over. While Clayton was recovering, Daniel leaped at him and knocked him to the ground. Daniel straddled him, pulled back his arm and swung, nailing Clayton in the jaw. Clayton's head snapped back, and he grunted. Part of Daniel was waiting for a rifle blast that never came, but most of him didn't care. He just kept hitting Clayton. He heard R.J. and Brock pounding toward him. Felt their blows, their efforts to pull him off. But they couldn't budge him.

He struck Clayton one more time, and blood gushed from Clayton's nose. He became aware he was yelling something, but he wasn't exactly sure what. The butt of the rifle caught him across the shoulder blades, and he fell forward. Felt Clayton's blood soak his shirt, felt Clayton gasping for breath. Then thick, sunburned arms pulled Daniel off Clayton. Daniel started fighting again, hitting and kicking anything he could reach. He was screaming too, and now he recognized his own words: "You animals, you fuckers, fucking *animals . . ."*

He bit one of the arms that held him, drawing blood. Brock—or maybe R.J.—yelled in pain. A fist connected with Daniel's temple, stunned him so he couldn't scream.

And then he was on the ground, his arms twisted painfully, his wrists pinned. R.J. had the barrel of the hunting rifle inches from Daniel's groin.

"You move again, I'll blow your dick off!" R.J. shouted.

Daniel stilled.

Animals. Fuckers. You're the freaks, not me.

Clayton walked over, his nose pressed to the crook of his arm. When he took his arm away, his face was smeared with blood. He crouched and picked up the cuffs. Daniel kept his gaze locked with Clayton's, breathing hard, trying to put all the hate he felt into his expression. "Give me your hands," Clayton said quietly.

No. Fuck no. Bel said, *"Give me your hands."* Said it softly, and Daniel obeyed, put out his hands so Bel could cuff him. Clayton wasn't allowed to say it.

Clayton nodded at Brock, and Brock wrenched Daniel onto his side, pulling Daniel's arms behind his back. Daniel's crotch pressed against the end of R.J.'s rifle. Daniel gave a furious cry and spat, the glob of saliva hitting the barrel of the gun. He felt the cuffs lock around his wrists. The click of the padlock. Brock shook him.

"Shut the fuck up, Whitlock."

He was rolled onto his back again, his arms underneath him. He stared up at Clayton.

"You play your cards right, you might live through this," Clayton told him.

Daniel didn't believe him, but he wasn't about to fight with that gun pointing at his dick.

Clayton took out a pocketknife. Daniel closed his eyes, but Clayton only pulled his shirt up and cut through the damp, bloodstained fabric. He handed the shirt to Brock. "Tie his ankles."

Brock moved down to bind Daniel's feet. Clayton rested the knife blade on the skin between two of Daniel's ribs. Daniel didn't breathe. Clayton met Daniel's gaze, just holding the blade there. His eyes were blank. His thin mouth quirked, and then he slipped the knife back in his pocket. Leaned over and picked something else up. The aluminum paddle.

"What the fuck is this?" he asked Daniel, his voice still quiet. When Daniel didn't answer, Clayton raised the paddle and struck Daniel hard on the chest with the edge of it. Daniel couldn't get enough air to make a sound.

"That hurts," Clayton said. It wasn't a question. He tapped the flat of the paddle against Daniel's nose, then raised it and swung down. Daniel closed his eyes as it descended.

But nothing happened. Daniel opened his eyes to see that Clayton was twirling the paddle in the sunlight. No expression on his face.

Daniel panted, trying to dig his fingers into the earth. Trying to anchor himself. Why wouldn't they kill him already?

Clayton tossed the paddle aside and stood. "Get him to the river," he told Brock and R.J.

Brock grabbed Daniel by the hair. With his other hand, he gripped the chain between Daniel's wrists and hauled him away from the barn. R.J. followed with the rifle. Clayton walked beside Daniel but didn't look at him. Daniel wasn't sure what hurt worse, his arms or his scalp. His chest was still throbbing where Clayton had hit him. He had to gather his strength. Had to get ready to fight again. Couldn't be afraid of that fucking gun.

"You play your cards right, you might live through this."

How?

Daniel thought about Bel.

I wanna go walking with you tonight, Bel. I want this to be a dream.

Bravest motherfucker in Logan. How did Bel figure that?

He thought about Bel's hands on him. Bel holding him, touching him. Bel's hand on his hair when Daniel knelt for him.

He had to keep fighting.

They dragged Daniel to the river. The water was stagnant here, swampy. There was shade now, and Daniel was glad. He was sweating something awful. He ought to be scared, but he felt not quite here. He blinked several times when Brock dropped him. He didn't hurt anymore.

Love you, Bel. That's what he should have said in his text. That's what Bel ought to know.

Clayton held something over Daniel's face. The keys to the cuffs. "Here's how this is gonna work," Clayton said. "Look here." Daniel watched as Clayton threw the keys into the center of the river. They disappeared with a little *plop*. "They'll be in there with you. You find 'em; you get yourself out—we'll let you go." His smile seemed hollow.

Daniel blinked again. Stared at the surface of the water. He couldn't remember where the keys had landed. Not that it would have helped.

They were gonna drown him. Water. Not fire.

Brock and R.J. laughed.

Clayton nudged Daniel with his toe. Said, so quietly it almost seemed tender, "You think about Kenny, all right? You think about Kenny when you can't fucking breathe. You think about him as you die."

Clayton and Brock lifted Daniel. Waded out until the water was at their waists, until Daniel could feel it cool against his back. Farther, until the water was to their chests and Daniel was half-submerged. He didn't fight yet. He'd need his strength to stay afloat. He just let them hold him. Felt the water lapping his skin.

They let him go suddenly. Didn't say anything else to him, just shoved him away. Kept shoving him, kicking at him underwater, forcing him to the center of the river, where the water was deep.

He tried to use his bound legs like a tail to propel himself toward the opposite bank. But with his hands chained behind his back, he couldn't get his upper body above the surface. He had a glimpse of Brock and Clayton heading back to shore. He didn't try to shout. Didn't struggle. He worked on getting his head up. Each time he slipped under, he felt for rocks or weeds or anything he might be able to pull himself across to the opposite bank. When that didn't work, he tried to kick the shirt off his ankles. If he could free his legs, he had a chance.

He was running out of air. He had to get a breath, a full breath. He pumped his hips, but the cuffs were making his body corkscrew, keeping him from treading water.

So I'm stupid, Bel. And I'm sorry. If I got to know you for a little while, that's maybe enough, yeah? 'Cause with you, I was awake, and with you, I was alive, and with you, I'm brave.

He closed his eyes.

There were worse things than dying. The hard part was over. Now he just had to give up.

That meant saying good-bye to Bel.

He imagined Bel's hands lingering on his wrists after he'd put the cuffs on. Bel gave him a light squeeze, then let him go.

"Good night, Whitlock," he whispered.

'Night, Bel.

Daniel let himself go under.

Bel pulled up the drive to Bolton farm. Daniel's car was parked to one side of the old barn. A truck was parked nearby. Clayton's truck. Bel jerked his key out of the ignition. "Stay here," he said to Jake. "Don't fucking move." Bel threw the door open and got out. Slammed it behind him and ran for the barn. "Daniel," he shouted. "Daniel?"

No answer.

"Daniel, where the fuck are you?" he shouted, as loudly as he could.

In back of the barn was a roughed-up patch of ground—flattened grass, an indent in the soft earth. And something glinting.

The aluminum paddle. And beside it, a plug.

What the *fuck*?

He heard a car door close and ran back to the front of the barn. It was just Jake. "Kebbler! What'd I tell you?"

Jake was freaking out, red-faced, hands waving. "The river! They're down by the river!"

Bel ran, one hand on his gun and one on his radio.

He saw three figures on the bank. One of them was holding a fucking rifle. Holding, not pointing, but that could change in a heartbeat. Bel yelled into his radio for backup, but didn't stop running. Not when he couldn't see Daniel. Not when he needed to know he was okay.

The three guys—Clayton, R.J., and Brock—bolted. Could have picked one to chase, could have caught one, but Bel's gaze was fixed on the river now. On something in the water that was thrashing one second, then not.

Years ago and not too many miles away, he'd walked up to Daniel Whitlock on the riverbank.

"Hey."

"Hey."

So fucking nervous of Casey's big brother, because he was weird, because he was smart, because he was older, and because he was cute.

"You coming in? It's real nice."

He could hear Jake shouting behind him, but couldn't make out the words. Just fixed his gaze on the point in the muddy water he'd last seen movement, hoped to fuck he wouldn't break his neck, and dived in.

Daniel must have been sleeping, because sunlight hit his face, and Bel was there. Arms around him, the pair of them soaking wet just like when they'd skinny-dipped in the river when Bel was supposed to be working. Laughing and wrestling. Kissing.

He must have been sleeping, because he didn't know what was going on.

Bel was holding him.

Had to be a dream.

CHAPTER
TWENTY-TWO

"**N**ow I know that your firearm is mostly plastic and all," Uncle Joe said at the hospital, "but that doesn't mean it likes to go swimming." He clapped Bel on the shoulder and tightened his grip. "You good, Little Joe?"

Bel managed a nod. "I'm good."

"How's your—ah, how's Whitlock?"

"They're checking him over now," Bel said. "Okay, I reckon. Swallowed a lot of water, but he's okay."

Has to be okay. If he's okay, then maybe we're okay as well.

"We got R.J. down at the station," Uncle Joe said. "Reckon the others will turn up sooner or later."

Bel nodded dully. Where the hell could they run?

"This is a real mess." Uncle Joe rubbed the heel of his hand against his forehead. "R.J.'s not saying shit about what happened. Don't suppose you know what Whitlock was doing out there?"

Bel thought of the text that Daniel had sent. *I want to say I'm sorry and thanks for everything.* He'd known he was putting himself in danger. Maybe he hadn't known how much danger, but he'd thought to send Bel a good-bye text. And why? Hadn't Bel given Daniel enough of a reason to want to stay safe? "There was a fight," he said. "Jake Kebbler said Whitlock and Clayton arranged to have it out. But I . . . I don't think Whitlock figured on it going like this."

Or did he?

Could Bel have talked him out of meeting Clayton, if he'd asked *why* Daniel had hurt himself last night, instead of getting pissed about it?

Uncle Joe squeezed his shoulder again. "Well, I guess you got some things to talk about."

"Guess we do." Bel's chest ached with the knowledge that he hadn't been enough to keep Daniel from slipping.

"I brought you some dry clothes from your locker," Uncle Joe said. "Figured you'd want to wait here awhile."

"Thanks."

"You remember what I said, Little Joe?" Uncle Joe asked. "About there being no future for you in this town?"

Bel nodded again.

"World's a big place," Uncle Joe told him. He patted Bel on the shoulder. "Come by the station when you're done, and we'll talk some more."

"You firing me, Sheriff?" Bel asked stiffly.

"Maybe I'm transferring you. If that's what you want."

"Maybe." Bel paused. Couldn't deal with this now. "I don't know."

"You think on it some. No rush."

Bel watched as he walked away, then went and changed his clothes in the hospital bathroom. He shoved his wet uniform into a plastic bag a nurse found for him, then headed down the corridor to Daniel's room.

Daniel was lying on his side in bed, his back to the door. His hair was still damp.

Bel dumped his bag on the floor, and went and sat on the mattress. "You awake?"

"Yeah, Bel," Daniel murmured, but didn't turn.

Bel rubbed his back gently, waiting for that moment that always came when Daniel relaxed under his touch. But Daniel continued to hold himself rigid. "You gonna talk to me?"

"Sorry, Bel."

"I'm sorry too."

Daniel twisted his head around. "What are you sorry for?"

A moment ago, Bel wouldn't have known what to say. But now the words came easily. "Hurting you."

Daniel turned away again. Hunched his shoulders and pulled the sheet tight around his body. "You didn't."

"Reckon I did. Didn't do a very good job bein' what you needed. Or you wouldn't have—"

"It was for *you*," Daniel interrupted. "'Cause you *are* what I need, and I had to—I had to get free so I could be better for you. I got—all these good feelings now, but they crash up against all the shit I'm still scared of." He paused. "It doesn't make sense. I know that. I'm sorry."

Bel closed his eyes as relief washed over him. It made a little sense. So he held back the *What the hell were you thinking?* and *How was getting yourself killed supposed to help?* "Hey. Look at me."

Daniel rolled over.

"Daniel." Bel kept his voice soft. Wasn't sure what to say now. Didn't want to tell Daniel how scared he'd been when he'd gotten that text. When he'd thought he might have lost the one thing that made the world seem like the big place Uncle Joe had talked about. When he'd thought it was his fault.

Daniel made Logan seem smaller than it had ever been to Bel before. They both needed to get free. But where did they go from here? *My uncle says he can transfer me. So pack your shit and we'll go try to make this work somewhere else.*

In the end, all Bel could say was, "Clayton ain't worth it."

"I wasn't gonna kill him," Daniel said. "Just fuck him up so bad he'd know what it felt like. So bad he'd leave me alone."

"And what if he'd killed you? He came pretty damn close, didn't he?"

"He played dirty." Bel could hear the anger in Daniel's voice. "He said if I won, he'd never bother me again. But it was never gonna be a fair fight." Daniel tilted his head back and gazing at the ceiling. "I figure I knew that."

"And you went anyway." Bel held out his hand. "What am I gonna do with you?"

Daniel didn't move. "Dump me, I reckon."

Bel reached under the sheet and found Daniel's hand. Drew it out and twined his fingers with Daniel's. "You don't listen very good. Remember I said we ain't done?"

Daniel swallowed a couple of times. "Why not? I'm never gonna make you happy. I'm just gonna keep screwing up."

"Already make me happy. And I'm plannin' to keep screwing up too. So if you want company, you've got it."

Daniel shook his head. "I'm starting to think I'm not the crazy one."

Bel grinned. "I'd run crazy circles around you any day of the week." He squeezed Daniel's hand and his smile faded. "You've had it rough, ain't you?"

"Dunno, Bel."

"You have. But it ain't your fault, okay?"

Daniel stared at him. His jaw trembled.

"None of it. Not the sleepwalking. Not getting bashed."

"I told Kenny Cooper I wanted to suck his dick."

"Don't matter if you got on your knees and undid his fly. What he did ain't your fault."

"What about what I did?" Daniel asked softly.

"You did your time. You paid, Daniel. Time to let it go."

"What if I can't?"

"You're gonna try for me. Yeah?"

"I don't know. I don't even know why you're still hangin' around me."

"Because I love you."

Daniel didn't answer for a long moment, long enough for Bel to get plenty nervous. But he wasn't sorry he'd said it. Daniel needed to know.

"Well that ain't fair to spring on a guy." Daniel's voice was hoarse.

"Is it really news, Whitlock?" Maybe it was. Shit, the way Bel had bailed on him. What he'd said: *"You're a head case . . ."*

Daniel gripped Bel's hand so hard it hurt. His eyes watered. "Do I have to go to jail?"

"No, you don't. R.J.'s at the station. We're lookin' for Clayton and Brock."

"I hit him. Clayton. The other guys had to pull me off."

"We're gonna sort it out," Bel promised.

"I woulda beat the shit out of Clayton if it was just me and him." Daniel blinked several times, rapidly. "Ms. Davenport's not gonna think much of me."

"Dav's glad you're all right." Bel hadn't talked to Dav yet. But he knew she'd be glad.

Daniel shifted. Took a breath. "Are we still . . . You're not gonna ditch me, then?"

"I'm gonna take you home in a few minutes here. And we're gonna have a good long talk."

Daniel picked at the sheet with his free hand. "'Kay."

"What is it?"

Daniel looked at him. "You're right, what you said, 'bout me not knowing the difference between fucking and fucking myself up." He dropped his gaze, and when he lifted it again, his eyes were shining with tears. "Don't hurt me, Bel. I don't wanna play those games for a while. Maybe never."

"We're gonna take it slow." Bel rubbed his thumb over Daniel's swollen knuckles.

"I just—" Daniel faltered. "I just want to see what it's like when I don't hurt."

"You trust me?"

Daniel nodded.

Bel gently removed his hand from Daniel's and stroked Daniel's cheek. Ran his fingertips down Daniel's throat, then up the side of his neck and through his hair. Daniel leaned into the touch, closing his eyes. "It ain't gonna hurt anymore."

Not until it was something Daniel wanted for itself, if he ever did. They could find out together what worked, start again from the beginning.

Daniel swallowed. "John's gonna be mad too. He thought I was doing better."

"No one's mad." Bel stroked the curls at Daniel's nape. Needed a haircut again. "Just rest a minute while I go see about gettin' you released."

Bel started to get up. Daniel caught his wrist. "Don't—just—sorry. Stay a minute?"

"Of course." Bel sat back down.

"I love you too. I hope that ain't news. I meant to tell you."

Bel leaned forward and kissed his cheek. Daniel turned so their lips touched. Bel closed his eyes. "It's good news."

Daniel pressed his forehead to Bel's. "There's no magic fix for me. Not therapy, not drugs, not even you."

"I know that. I ain't in this to *fix* you. Just to be with you and help you any way you need."

"Yeah." Daniel huffed, sitting back. "You smell bad."

"So do you," Bel grinned. "Muddy and stinky. You want to take a hot shower at my place?"

"You gonna wash my back for me?"

"Gonna wash every goddamn inch of you," Bel said. "You like that idea?"

Daniel smiled. "Yeah, Bel."

"You sit tight, then. I'll be right back."

Bel kissed Daniel again and stood.

"Don't go anywhere," he said over his shoulder.

"I ain't goin' anywhere, Bel. Not without you."

The next few days passed in a blur for Daniel. The police station, Bel's place, out to the cabin to collect some clothes, back to Bel's place, the police station again. Dreaming of fire and water, and waking up with Bel's arms around him. With Bel talking low and gentle in his ear: "I got you, Daniel, I got you."

Daniel had cried the first night and was fucking embarrassed by that. Cried and couldn't stop, while Bel held him and watched and worried. It was only when Daniel was afraid he'd end up in the hospital again that he managed to stop his tears, to tell Bel he was okay. Which probably wasn't the sort of breakthrough John would recommend.

"They say fire's cleansing," he'd told Bel once in the middle of the night, caught between awake and asleep, "but it's dirty. Bel. It's real dirty."

"I know it is," Bel had said sleepily, "but you're clean now."

"Did the river clean me?"

"No." Bel had tightened his grip on Daniel. "You were already clean."

Shit. Was that the sort of stuff he came out with when he was sleeping? When his subconscious took control of his mind? Daniel wondered how much crazy shit he'd spewed out in the middle of the night, how much Bel had to put up with. The next morning, he wished he hadn't remembered saying it. Wished they could both pretend he was normal.

"You okay going out with Jekyll and Hyde?" he joked at breakfast on the third day.

Bel narrowed his eyes over his toast. "You ain't Jekyll and Hyde."

Daniel fumbled with the butter knife. "Just, if you don't know it, I appreciate it. Putting up with the shit that happens when I'm sleeping, I mean. Makes me wonder if the awake stuff is worth it for you." He caught Bel's scowl. "Not trying to put myself down or anything. You're more patient than me, I mean. Feels wrong to ask you to do that when I don't think I could do it for someone."

"Makes us a good fit, is all," Bel said. "It's not something you owe me for."

Daniel nodded.

Bel pushed his plate away. "Do you know what you do, when all the world sleeps?"

I fuck anything. I kill people. I'm crazy.

"You talk a lot. We talk a lot."

"We do?"

"Yeah." Bel's voice was soft. "You draw, and we talk."

"What do we talk about?"

"Nothing much," Bel said. "Sometimes you tell me about what you're drawing. Sometimes you tell me about things you remember from growing up. Once you promised to make me waffles for breakfast, but you never came through on that." Bel smiled.

"I talk about the fire?"

The smile disappeared. "Sometimes."

"Good. Because it ain't all funny, is it? It ain't all waffles and pretty pictures. It's fucking *frightening*, Bel. It's . . ." He sighed. "There's this side of me that does all this stuff, or that talks to you, and I don't even know what happens, or what I say. It's like I'm not even there."

"You are there," Bel said. "It's you, Daniel. It's always you."

"I don't want us to talk when I'm sleeping," Daniel said, his throat aching. "I want to *remember* it."

"I can tell you if you want," Bel said. "Every morning."

"That ain't fair on you."

"I can decide that for myself."

"Nothin' about this is fair on you," Daniel said. "I'm wrecking your job, and don't pretend that's not true. I saw the looks the other cops gave you at the station."

"There're other jobs."

"You really wanna go back to working at Harnee's? Because you know there's nothin' much else in town!"

"There're other towns," Bel said.

"No." Daniel shook his head. "You ain't leaving Logan."

"Why not?"

"'Cause you like it here. Your family's here."

"They'd still be here when I came back to visit."

Daniel's throat ached worse. How the hell was he supposed to make Bel understand how unreasonable this was?

"My job ain't wrecked. I can stay here if you want to stay here, but I don't think you do."

Daniel looked down. It wasn't a secret. He'd been talking to John and Ms. Davenport for a while about moving. About maybe going to school. Just, he'd never let the idea seem real. But after the river . . .

There was nothing he wanted from Logan anymore. He didn't care if it was running away. He'd tried to face his demons, and he'd failed. They'd beaten him. You had to know when to quit, didn't you?

And couldn't it be a kind of winning, to get out of here? To turn his back on a place that would always hate him?

Or was he just trying to justify being a chickenshit?

Bravest motherfucker in Logan.

Maybe he'd be braver somewhere else. This place scared him.

"Daniel?"

He looked back at Bel. "There maybe isn't much here for me."

Bel nodded. "I'd go with you. Wherever you need to go."

"I don't . . . I don't know right now. I can't think about this yet."

"When you're ready." Bel finished his breakfast and took his plate to the sink.

"What if we got somewhere and something happened to us, and then you resented me for dragging you away from here?"

Bel stepped behind Daniel and placed his hands on his shoulders. Rubbed at the knots of muscle until Daniel sagged in his chair. "That what we ought to think about right now? How about we start with figuring out where we want to go and goin' there?" He squeezed Daniel's shoulders, then released. "You worry too much."

Daniel laughed. "I got some pretty good reasons to."

"And just as many reasons to relax and let me love you," Bel said quietly.

Daniel went still. Bel rubbed his thumb in circles at the base of Daniel's neck. "Love you too, Bel. I'll think about it, if you want."

"If *you* want."

Daniel gave another uneasy laugh. "Sometimes I like doing what you want."

Bel leaned down and kissed the edge of his ear. "That so?"

Daniel held his breath. He'd asked Bel not to hurt him, and Bel had said he wasn't going to be in charge anymore. But Daniel hoped he'd understand. He wasn't asking for pain, wasn't asking to be Bel's sub, just . . . "Yeah." He reached behind him and took Bel's hand, drawing it to his mouth. He kissed the pad of Bel's finger, then sucked it into his mouth. He heard Bel's breathing quicken. Released Bel's finger. "Anything you want." He turned and looked up at Bel. "Even . . ." He stopped himself. He'd wanted to offer to suck Bel off, but he still wasn't sure he could do it. And he didn't think Bel would like him offering if it wasn't something he would enjoy. He grinned to show Bel he knew they were playing a game. "Anything you want," he repeated.

Bel tugged lightly on Daniel's hair. "All right. Get back in the bedroom."

Daniel got up. Left his plate on the table and went to the bedroom, Bel close behind.

"I wanna strip you," Bel said when they got in, running his hands underneath Daniel's T-shirt and pushing the fabric up. He kissed and nipped the back of Daniel's neck, then pulled the shirt off. Ran his hands back down Daniel's naked sides and hooked his fingers in the waistband of his pants. Yanked them down roughly. Daniel stepped out of them and turned to face Bel. Their lips collided with bruising force, and Daniel tugged and shoved at Bel's shirt until he got it off.

Bel kneaded Daniel's shoulders and back, then his ass through his underwear. He backed Daniel toward the bed, slid a knee gently between his legs, and nudged him onto the mattress. Daniel was already breathing hard, dizzy with want, desperate to feel Bel's hands on him again. Bel pulled Daniel's underwear off and dug his nails into Daniel's thighs. Daniel arched eagerly.

Bel climbed between his legs, and Daniel scooted back to make room for him. Bel kicked off his shorts and dipped to lick Daniel's cock. His tongue pressed Daniel's erection against his belly, and Daniel could feel his own wetness. It made him squirm more. Bel licked him again, then knelt and leaned over Daniel to grab a condom from the nightstand. "Please, Bel," Daniel whispered. He brought his fists down on the bed and pushed his hips up, begging every way he knew how.

"Impatient," Bel growled. He placed his hands around Daniel's wrists, pinning them. "You can't hold still on your own, I'll have to hold you still."

"Yeah." Daniel moaned as Bel rubbed his cock against Daniel's.

"That what you want?"

"Please."

Bel let go briefly to put the condom on and lube himself, then he took Daniel's wrists and guided his arms above his head. Held them against the pillow. He sucked and bit at Daniel's throat, his cock sliding in the cleft of Daniel's ass. Daniel whimpered, pushing against Bel's hands. Bel held fast.

"Show me how much you want it," Bel whispered against Daniel's jaw.

Daniel wrapped his legs around Bel, and Bel shifted until the tip of his cock nudged Daniel's hole. He pushed in slowly. It still hurt a little from when Daniel had torn himself up with the plug, but Daniel didn't mind. That slight pain anchored him in this moment. He used his legs to urge Bel in quicker, and then to hold him there. He grunted as Bel entered all the way. His instinct was to use his hands, brace himself against Bel's shoulders, but he couldn't. He twisted and rocked his hips. Bel fucked him slowly, ignoring Daniel's breathy pleas to go faster, speeding up only at the end. Daniel kept up an unsteady, frantic rhythm with his hips, rubbing his cock against Bel's body so that when Bel came, Daniel came too.

Bel collapsed onto him, but didn't release Daniel's wrists. He kissed Daniel all over, licked the cum from his belly, then finally rested his chin on Daniel's chest with a lazy smile. "Might never let you go," he teased.

Daniel tried halfheartedly to pull free, then grinned too. "All right by me."

Bel rolled him onto his side and then shifted so his chest was against Daniel's back. Reached around and took Daniel's wrists again. "I'm wore out. Got the whole day off. So I don't have to let you go anytime soon."

Daniel slowed his breathing. Bel's grip was gentle but firm. So much better than the fucking cuffs. Daniel felt safe, held. Free. "Good," he whispered. "I don't want you to."

Bel ran his thumbs over Daniel's wristbones. His breath was warm on the back of Daniel's neck. His body familiar, perfect.

Didn't matter that Clayton and his friends had fucking cuffed him and put him in the water to die. Didn't matter all the times Daniel had cuffed himself and had lain in bed afraid, alone, and in pain. This was something different. Something good. This meant he was Bel's, and also his own, because he chose this. He loved this.

He loved Bel.

CHAPTER TWENTY-THREE

"Look at those clouds," Daniel said. "It's gonna rain, and we're gonna be sorry we didn't stay home."

"Would you quit?" Bel pulled onto Dav and Jim's street. "It's a nice day. That cloud'll pass in another minute."

"Forty percent chance of rain."

"You're not getting out of this," Bel told him. Daniel had been getting worked up all afternoon. In the end, Bel had blown him in the living room, just to take the edge off. Which had been no hardship at all. The look on Daniel's face when he came was nothing short of beautiful.

"I'm not tryin' to. I'm just saying reasonable people don't have barbecues when it's about to rain."

"Dav and Jim do have a house, you know. With a roof and everything." Bel parked across the road from Dav and Jim's. "See? There it is."

"Great," Daniel muttered, unbuckling his seat belt. "All right. Let's go."

Bel put a hand on his shoulder before Daniel could open the door. Daniel turned to him.

"What?"

"There ain't nothin' to worry about," Bel said.

"Yeah. I heard you the first fourteen times. And I ain't—I'm *not* worried."

Bel grinned. "You too good to say 'ain't' now that you're going back to school?"

"Shut up."

"Uh-huh," Bel said. "You think you're fooling me? You're nervous as hell."

"Can we just get this over with?"

"I'm on your side," Bel said quietly. "And they're on my side. You get it?"

Daniel slouched back in his seat. "Yeah, Bel," he said finally. "I get it."

"Jim gives you any trouble, you let me know. And you'll like Stumpy."

"Yeah, maybe." Daniel was frowning again. "They know, right? This ain't—*isn't*—gonna be like coming out and meeting me all at the same time, is it? Because, shit, that's too much. You're not just gay, but hooking up with a crazy."

"They know," Bel said. "They've known for years, I guess, but I talked to my mama last night just to make sure. And you ain't crazy, Daniel."

"Yeah. I'm walking into your brother's house to meet your whole family like I'm just a normal guy, and I ain't crazy? Feels pretty goddamn crazy to me."

"Come on," Bel said. "You do this with me, and on the way home we'll stop at the diner and I'll buy you a sundae as big as your head."

Daniel snorted. "You will?"

"Sure." Bel squeezed his shoulder. "Or maybe just take you home and ravish you."

"Well, that sounds more my speed."

Bel laughed and opened his door. "Come on then, let's go."

Daniel got out of the car, walked around it to join Bel, and they crossed the road together.

Daniel hadn't spoken to Billy Belman since high school, when they'd both shared classes with Kenny, Clayton, Brock, and R.J. He knew from a few things Bel had said in passing that he idolized his oldest brother, so out of all of them Daniel guessed meeting Billy would be the worst. His high school past colliding with his crazy-killer past, colliding with his now, and his future.

He stuck out his hand when Billy opened the front door to them, and waited for Billy to ignore it.

Killed a boy we sat in class with, and now your little brother's fucking me.

Billy shook his hand and met his eyes as well. "Hey, Whitlock. Daniel, I mean. How's it going?"

"Um," said Daniel. "Okay, Billy, thanks."

"Jim and Dad are out back cooking the steaks," Billy told Bel. "Dav's got me putting together some sort of fucking torture device for babies, and the instructions are mostly in Chinese. You wanna lend a hand?"

"It's a motion bed!" Ms. Davenport yelled from somewhere inside the house, at the same time another woman called, "Billy! Language!"

"Yeah," Bel said. "We'll go say hello first."

He reached out for Daniel's hand and drew him further into the house.

"Hey, Mama." Bel led him through to the kitchen. "Hey, Dav."

Mrs. Belman wiped her hands on her apron, her smile slipping slightly as her gaze traveled from Bel to Daniel and down to their clasped hands. Daniel resisted the urge to pull away from Bel, to put some distance between them.

"Mama, meet Daniel."

Mrs. Belman extended her hand. "It's nice to meet you, Daniel."

Daniel took it, afraid his voice would crack. "Nice to meet you too, Mrs. Belman."

That's what this afternoon would be, he guessed. A series of uncomfortable introductions where everybody said the same polite things, while wondering when he was going to crack and set fire to something. Or someone.

Ms. Davenport walked to the fridge, her belly leading the way. She pulled out two beers and handed them over. "Glad you could make it, Daniel."

"Thanks, Ms. Davenport," he said.

"Dav," she told him. "We're not at work now."

Daniel nodded but wondered if he'd ever be able to see her as anyone apart from the woman who'd asked him the same questions, week after week, about work, and who he was associating with, and whether he was keeping out of trouble.

"So?" she said.

Daniel glanced at her nervously. Was he supposed to tell her something? "Um. What?"

"So how the hell are things? School—you excited? Dreading it? What?"

"Uh, well. I'm pretty excited, I guess. My sister, she's in Charleston, and she says she's gonna help us settle in. But I mean, it's gonna be weird, moving. For Bel especially." He looked at Bel and tried to grin. "He's never been to the city before."

"I've been," Bel said.

"Goose Creek's not a city. Not like Charleston."

Bel nudged him. "What? You think you're a big shot now?"

Daniel laughed. "Not really."

"Charleston'll eat you alive," Dav said to Bel. "You can't spit in the street there, you know."

"What, there a law against it? And I don't spit, anyway."

"Now and then you do," Daniel said.

"More than now and then," Mrs. Belman said from across the room.

"Yeah, when I'm around people I know don't mind," Bel protested.

Daniel surprised himself by mouthing to Dav, *I mind.*

Dav laughed and swigged her Coke.

A big, black dog careened into the kitchen and made straight for Bel.

"Oh, hey Stumpy," Bel said, crouching to pet the dog.

Dav wrinkled her nose. "Who let you in, stinker?"

Daniel extended a tentative hand toward the dog, which was whacking him in the leg with its thick tail.

"He's all right," Bel said. "Just dumb."

"I don't know much about dogs," Daniel admitted. Stumpy licked his hand.

Bel pointed. "Head. Tail. Pets go here." He pointed to the dog's head again. "Farts come out here." He pointed to the dog's back end. "That's all you need to know about Stump."

Daniel leaned down and ran his hands over Stump's soft coat. "He does stink."

"No kidding," Dav said. "So you guys gonna help Billy with the motion bed or what?"

Daniel didn't know what that was, and from the look of it, neither did Bel.

"Sure," Bel said. "Three guys, some beer, and a baby bed. What could go wrong?"

He led Daniel out of the kitchen and down the hall to the nursery. Billy was in there trying to attach what looked like a giant wad of netting to a stand. "Thank God," Billy said when they came in. "See if you can make hide'r hair of this."

"What *is* it?" Bel asked.

"It's, uh . . . I dunno. It's in that magazine over there. Some kind of baby hammock. See? You put the baby in this, and it hangs from this hook thingy and then it—see, it kind of rocks it, so the baby falls asleep." Billy kicked the instructions on the floor. "It's more complicated than you'd think."

It didn't look like a baby torture device, Daniel thought. In fact, it seemed really nice. Something that would hold you securely, but still let you move. Marcus used to say they ought to go to a dungeon sometime so Daniel could try out a sling. He'd thought Daniel would really like it.

Daniel was embarrassed to be thinking about shit like that in the baby's nursery. He leaned down and picked up the instructions. "We'll figure it out."

"Maybe you guys can take a swing at it while I go grab another beer," Billy said.

"You bet." Bel clapped him on the back as he left the room. He reached over and took the instructions from Daniel. "Lemme see those. It's a baby hammock, how tough can it be?"

"Bossy," Daniel said. He stepped over to the windowsill and picked up the catalog Billy had indicated. He started leafing through it. It was full of fancy baby stuff. Wheeled dinner plates shaped like fire trucks and bulldozers, circular cribs, and even a toddler urinal. "Seems like a bad idea to put a baby's plate on wheels."

"What the hell?" Bel said. His arms were tangled in the net. "How do you even . . . couldn't they label it 'this side up' or something?"

Stump had nudged his way into the room and was sniffing around Daniel's pants. "Want help?" Daniel asked.

"Just give me a minute. I'll figure it out."

Daniel shook his head and continued to stare at the catalog. "Oookay."

Daniel turned the page. Stopped.

"Hey, Bel," he said after a minute.

"Yeah." Bel had gotten the hammock mostly onto the hook. "Look at that. That looks good, right?"

"Looks nice." Daniel stepped toward Bel with the catalog. Checked the door to make sure no one was coming in. Lowered his voice. "What do you think of this?" He showed Bel the page.

Bel scratched his head and stared where Daniel was pointing. "That an alarm?"

"Yeah," Daniel said. "Stops your toddler from escaping in the night."

"Or your boyfriend," Bel said.

"Yeah." Daniel wrinkled his nose, too—*what?* Nervous—to feel hopeful. Like he was asking Bel for some kind of commitment, even though it was just a cheap plastic device, and Bel had already given him more than he'd ever had from anyone. "Would wake you up, I guess."

"We oughta get a few," Bel said. "Bedroom and main doors." He smiled. "It's a good idea. You never tried them before?"

"Never had anyone who stayed before," Daniel said.

Bel wrapped an arm around him and pulled him close. "You got me now," he said, and kissed him.

Daniel closed his eyes.

"Hey, um," Billy said from the doorway. "You'd better be celebrating finishing the baby hammock."

Daniel tried to pull away, but Bel only laughed and held on to him. "Shut up, asshole. You never been in love?"

Daniel's face flooded with warmth and not just from embarrassment.

"Nope," Billy said, bending down to pick up the discarded instructions. "You know me. I got ninety-nine problems, but . . ." He grinned.

Bel snorted and shook his head.

Jim appeared in the doorway behind Billy. "Hey, you guys made it. You hungry? Food's up."

"Yeah, we've been working up an appetite doing your job for you," Billy said, gesturing at the instructions.

Jim made a face. "You ain't done yet?"

Bel toed the hammock. "Yeah, seems like this should be a job for Daddy."

Jim widened his eyes. "No way. I mean, I painted the goddamn room already. Twice, 'cause Dav didn't like the color the first time. Trust me, this is a job for the *uncles*."

Daniel smiled politely as Jim's gaze flicked to him.

"How's that gonna work?" Billy asked, poking Bel in the ribs. "This family's already got an Uncle Joe. You gonna be Uncle Bel, maybe?"

"I guess so," Bel said.

"Yeah," Jim said. "We'll figure something out." He shrugged. "Anyhow, you all coming out back to grab something to eat? Before Dav eats the whole damn cow." Then he groaned. "Don't tell her I said that, okay?"

Bel and Daniel sat together on foldout chairs in Jim and Dav's backyard, Stump at their feet. It was nice, listening to the crickets as the sun went down, and listening to the family rehash all their oldest, dumbest stories. Bel would miss this in Charleston. They'd get back on some weekends, he guessed, and the family could come and visit. Wasn't like it was the other side of the world.

Moving away from the only place he'd ever lived, starting a new job in a department where he didn't know anyone; a few months ago, the thought of it would have made Bel nervous. Hell, okay, he was still nervous, but he and Daniel needed this. A fresh start where not every set of eyes in the street would be hostile. Where not everyone would look at Daniel and wish Clayton, Brock, and R.J. had done the job right. There was gonna be some fallout when they went to trial, Uncle Joe had said. None of them could claim a condition where they hadn't been in charge of their own selves. They might get more time than Daniel had over Kenny's death, since they'd lured him there and planned it, and that was something most people in Logan wouldn't understand at all. Wouldn't even *try* to understand.

Daniel was supposed to have attended a hearing to determine if he'd violated his parole in going to fight Clayton. But the hearing had been abruptly canceled, and no matter how Bel pressed Dav, she wouldn't give details. Daniel would catch plenty of flak for that too.

So they needed Charleston. They weren't running, Bel had decided, they were starting fresh. They'd both earned that.

Dav eased herself down into a chair on the other side of Daniel. "You all packed up?" she asked around a mouthful of burger.

"Almost," Bel said. "Just a couple of things to sort out still. Uncle Joe says I can borrow his trailer to shift stuff, so that's good."

"Where is he anyway?"

"Someone's gotta look after this town now I'm going," Bel told her with a straight face.

She laughed and reached over Daniel to punch him in the shoulder. Jim looked over toward them from the barbecue, almost smiled, then turned away again.

The family would come around. He didn't know what his mama struggled with most: that he was gay, that he was with Daniel Whitlock, or that he was moving away from Logan. His dad hadn't said much about anything at all. And Bel figured that sooner or later Jim would fall in behind Billy and accept it. Dav would have his balls if he didn't.

Bel grinned at the thought of that, and leaned forward to scratch Stump between the ears.

This awkwardness wouldn't last. The days and months would chip away at it, and in time, they'd see past what Daniel had done, and see instead what he meant to Bel. Maybe they'd even see what sort of man he really was.

"Okay," Dav said. "I'm going back for more. Help me up." She braced her hands on the sagging arms of the foldout chair. "Seriously, I feel like a beach ball trying to escape a sock here. Help me up."

Daniel passed his plate to Bel and stood. He held Dav's hands and pulled her out of the chair.

"At least one of you is a gentleman," Dav said, and headed back toward the food. Stump looked after her, then back to Daniel's plate, calculated his chances and stayed where he was. Daniel sat down again, and Bel handed him his plate back.

"Had a crazy dream last night," Bel said in a low voice, watching Jim embrace Dav over by the barbecue.

"All dreams are crazy," Daniel murmured, balancing his plate on his knees.

"Yeah, I reckon they are. Make sense when you're in 'em though."

"Yeah."

Bel reached out and caught his hand, twining their fingers together. "Anyhow, this crazy dream. Jus' you and me in it, with nobody else around."

Daniel turned his face toward Bel's, smiling slightly. "What's so crazy about that?"

"Well, jus' you and me, all alone, and we weren't fucking."

Daniel snorted, and Stump jumped in alarm.

"We was just sitting there, watching the sun go down," Bel said, "and falling asleep together."

"You dreamed about falling asleep?" Daniel asked him.

"Falling asleep *together*." Bel smiled. "And it was weird. You know what I said to you?"

"What'd you say?"

"I said, 'Don't go too far without me.'"

Daniel squeezed his hand. "And did I?"

Bel shrugged. "Don't know. I woke up."

"Well," Daniel said quietly, leaning back in his chair. "I'll try not to, just so you know."

"Reckon I'd follow you about anywhere."

"Don't know why."

"Yeah you do."

"'Cause I need looking after?"

"'Cause you used to come into Harnee's, and I knew you were somethin' different."

"I was asleep."

Bel nodded. Looked at him. Hoped he could say what he needed to say without sounding too foolish. "Still you, though."

Pain flashed in Daniel's eyes. "Still me when I burned Kenny Cooper, then."

Fuck. Bel had meant to give Daniel a compliment. "Maybe so. But there's beautiful things about you, awake or asleep. You're the bravest guy I ever met." Bel looked down. "Sorry. I was tryin' to be romantic, and I got you feeling shitty instead."

"I don't feel shitty." Daniel offered him a smile. "I feel happy. And I can worry about whether or not I deserve it later."

"You deserve it," Bel said. "Trust me." He wasn't sure what else to say and was relieved to hear Uncle Joe's voice in the front yard. "Uncle Joe's here. I'm gonna go say hi. You can stay here if you want."

"Are you kidding? I can follow you as well as you follow me, Harnee's kid."

Bel laughed and offered Daniel a hand up. Pulled him close, pressed his lip to Daniel's cheekbone, and then nipped the edge of his ear. "Prove it," he whispered.

He set off, Daniel right beside him, both of them smiling.

Both of them together, just like they were supposed to be.

Dear Reader,

Thank you for reading Lisa Henry and J.A. Rock's *When All the World Sleeps*!

We know your time is precious and you have many, many entertainment options, so it means a lot that you've chosen to spend your time reading. We really hope you enjoyed it.

We'd be honored if you'd consider posting a review—good or bad—on sites like **Amazon, Barnes & Noble, Kobo, Goodreads, Twitter, Facebook, Tumblr,** and your blog or website. We'd also be honored if you told your friends and family about this book. Word of mouth is a book's lifeblood!

For more information on upcoming releases, author interviews, blog tours, contests, giveaways, and more, please sign up for our weekly, spam-free newsletter and visit us around the web:

Newsletter: tinyurl.com/RiptideSignup
Twitter: twitter.com/RiptideBooks
Facebook: facebook.com/RiptidePublishing
Goodreads: tinyurl.com/RiptideOnGoodreads
Tumblr: riptidepublishing.tumblr.com

Thank you so much for Reading the Rainbow!

RiptidePublishing.com

ALSO BY LISA HENRY

Sweetwater
He Is Worthy
The Island
Dark Space
Tribute
One Perfect Night
Fallout, with M. Caspian

With Heidi Belleau
Tin Man
Bliss
King of Dublin
The Harder They Fall

ALSO BY J.A. ROCK

Minotaur

The Subs Club series
The Subs Club
Pain Slut
Manties in a Twist
24/7

Coming Soon
The Silvers

Wacky Wednesday series
Wacky Wednesday
The Brat-tastic Jayk Parker

By His Rules
Calling the Show
Take the Long Way Home
The Grand Ballast

ALSO BY LISA HENRY & J.A. ROCK

Playing the Fool series
The Two Gentlemen of Altona
The Merchant of Death
Tempest

The Boy series
The Good Boy
The Naughty Boy
The Boy Who Belonged

Prescott College series
Mark Cooper Versus America
Brandon Mills Versus the V-Card

ABOUT THE AUTHORS

LISA HENRY likes to tell stories, mostly with hot guys and happily ever afters.

Lisa lives in tropical North Queensland, Australia. She doesn't know why, because she hates the heat, but she suspects she's too lazy to move. She spends half her time slaving away as a government minion, and the other half plotting her escape.

She attended university at sixteen, not because she was a child prodigy or anything, but because of a mix-up between international school systems early in life. She studied History and English, neither of them very thoroughly.

She shares her house a log-suffering partner, too many cats, a dog, a green tree frog that swims in the toilet, and as many possums as can break in every night. This is not how she imagined life as a grown-up.

Blog: lisahenryonline.blogspot.com.au
Twitter: twitter.com/LisaHenryOnline
Goodreads: goodreads.com/LisaHenry

J.A. ROCK is the author of queer romance and suspense novels, including *By His Rules, Take the Long Way Home*, and, with Lisa Henry, *The Good Boy* and *When All the World Sleeps*. She holds an MFA in creative writing from the University of Alabama and a BA in theater from Case Western Reserve University. J.A. also writes queer fiction and essays under the name Jill Smith. Raised in Ohio and West Virginia, she now lives in Chicago with her dog, Professor Anne Studebaker.

Website: www.jarockauthor.com
Blog: jarockauthor.blogspot.com
Twitter: twitter.com/jarockauthor
Facebook: www.facebook.com/ja.rock.39

Enjoy more stories like
When All the World Sleeps
at RiptidePublishing.com!

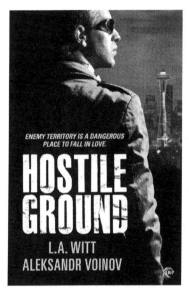

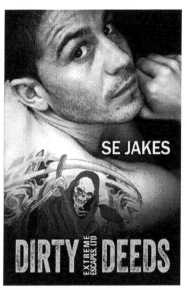

Hostile Ground
ISBN: 978-1-62649-124-3

Dirty Deeds
ISBN: 978-1-62649-093-2

Earn Bonus Bucks!

Earn 1 Bonus Buck for each dollar you spend. Find out how at RiptidePublishing.com/news/bonus-bucks.

Win Free Ebooks for a Year!

Pre-order coming soon titles directly through our site and you'll receive one entry into a drawing to win free books for a year! Get the details at RiptidePublishing.com/contests.

67635849R00215

Made in the USA
Lexington, KY
17 September 2017